THE
DROWNING
GIRLS

BOOKS BY LISA REGAN

DETECTIVE JOSIE QUINN SERIES

Vanishing Girls

The Girl With No Name

Her Mother's Grave

Her Final Confession

The Bones She Buried

Her Silent Cry

Cold Heart Creek

Find Her Alive

Save Her Soul

Breathe Your Last

Hush Little Girl

Her Deadly Touch

THE
DROWNING
GIRLS

LISA REGAN

bookouture

Published by Bookouture in 2021

An imprint of Storyfire Ltd.
Carmelite House
50 Victoria Embankment
London EC4Y 0DZ

www.bookouture.com

ISBN: 978-1-80019-635-3
eBook ISBN: 978-1-80019-634-6

For Christine Brock, for being the glue that held us together when our whole world shattered.

ONE

Cold air stings her cheeks like a thousand tiny needles pricking at her skin. Dried leaves and twigs crunch under her feet. Several times, her feet slip in patches of snow that still linger on the ground. A heavy hand presses down on her shoulder, steering her through the darkness. The barrel of a gun knocks against the base of her skull and her scalp still burns from where he grabbed her hair, pulling until it started to tear from the roots. The rest of her body is numb with the cold. She wishes she had her coat.

"I'm freezing," she says, wishing her voice didn't sound so much like a whimper.

"Shut up," he says. His fingers dig into the flesh just below her collarbone. The cold metal of the gun bites into her skin.

"Please," she says. "I need a coat or something."

"Don't need a coat where you're going," he says brusquely.

Where is she going? A shallow grave in the woods? The thought—no, the stark reality—that she is on her final march to death sends a juddering breath through her. Her teeth begin to chatter, from the cold or the panic building inside her with every step, she doesn't know. How can he even tell where they are going? Everything around them is inky black. The moon is a smudge behind translucent clouds.

"You don't have to do this," she says, and this time she makes no attempt to hide the pleading in her tone.

"You made your choice," he growls.

"P-p-please," she stammers.

"Shut up."

He pushes her violently and her legs go out from under her. Blackness rushes at her face, and her hands shoot out to break her fall. The sharp edge of a rock slices into the palm of her left hand. Before she can react, his hand tangles in her hair again, lifting her. The gun is at her temple now, digging into her skin.

"Now," comes the gravelly voice. "You're going to give me what I want."

TWO

The smell of burnt popcorn invaded Josie's nostrils. Muted popping could still be heard from the microwave, but black smoke pressed against the inside of the door's glass pane. It didn't take a culinary genius to know that that wasn't a good sign. Josie took a step toward the entrance to the kitchen, straining to hear if her family and friends in the living room had noticed the smoke. Nothing.

Yet.

Her Boston Terrier, Trout, yipped and ran circles around her. His soulful brown eyes stared up at her, worried. She muttered a curse under her breath and pulled the microwave door open, unleashing the dark, eye-stinging cloud. This time, a long string of profanities issued from her mouth as she waved her hands in the air, trying to disperse the billows before her smoke alarm went crazy. The charred remains of the popcorn bag sat in a sad heap inside the now-grimy hull of her microwave. Behind her, she heard her friend Misty Derossi's voice a second before her smoke alarm began bleating overhead.

"What is burning in here?" said Misty.

Josie winced and coughed, looking around, realizing now

that there was a lot more smoke than she first realized. The shrieks of the alarm hurt her ears. Trout barked in time with the alarm, positioning himself in front of Josie, as if to protect her from a threat. Misty stood in the doorway, hands on her hips, eyes squinted and already watering. Josie couldn't hear her words over the alarm, but she could read Misty's lips. "Popcorn? *Really*, Josie?"

Shaking her head, Misty crossed the room in three strides, slid open one of Josie's kitchen drawers, and pulled out two large potholders. She threw one to Josie who waved it in the air. Misty held onto the other, flapping it in front of her face as she threw open the back door and then dragged a chair into the corner of the room, beneath the smoke alarm. Josie moved to the door, ushering the smoky air out into the wintry December night with her potholder. Trout ran back and forth between Josie and the door, still barking, confused as to what he was supposed to do: remain by Josie's side and defend her against the smoke alarm, or go out back and relieve himself on the crepe myrtle tree in the corner of the yard. Misty climbed on top of the chair. Expertly, she popped the face of the smoke alarm off and snapped the battery out of it.

Silence never sounded so good.

Josie kept waving the smoke out into the darkness. Trout froze and watched her. In the kitchen doorway stood Misty's six-year-old son, Harris. He took in the tableau before him and slowly shook his head.

"It wasn't my faul—" Josie started to say, but his little feet were already tapping against the hardwood floors in the hall as he ran back to the living room. Josie could hear him yelling, "Aunt Shannon! Aunt Trinity! Uncle Christian! Uncle Pat! Miss Brenna! Aunt JoJo burned down the kitchen again!"

Josie frowned. "Could you explain to him that this doesn't constitute burning down the kitchen?"

Misty chuckled. "No. No, I cannot. Well, I could, but I don't really want to."

Josie threw the potholder at Misty's face, but her friend caught it in the air, nearly doubling over in laughter this time.

Pushing the back door closed, Josie mumbled, "House full of people and you asked me to make the popcorn? I don't know what any of you were thinking."

"That's a fair point," Misty agreed, straightening up. She used both potholders to rescue the remains of the popcorn bag and dispose of it. "Go," she told Josie. "I'll handle this."

Relieved, Josie started toward the living room, Trout padding along beside her. At the doorway, she stopped and turned back to Misty. "I really did follow the instructions on the bag."

Misty winked at her and said, "I know," but didn't offer anything else. What could she say? Josie was hopelessly, notoriously incompetent in the kitchen. Give her the simplest task and she'd find a way to screw it up—even when she followed the instructions. As a detective for the small Central Pennsylvania city of Denton, Josie had faced down and outwitted some of the most savage and cunning killers on the planet. But she couldn't make popcorn.

With a shrug, Josie turned away and went to the next room. She pulled up short in the foyer, staring into the living room. Multicolored lights from the small Christmas tree she and Noah had put up—mostly for the sake of Harris—sparkled, casting a festive glow over the room. Her family was crowded on and around her couch across from the large television. Her biological family: mother and father, Shannon and Christian Payne; brother, Patrick Payne and his girlfriend, Brenna; Josie's twin sister, Trinity Payne. Josie felt a swell inside her—part pain, part gratitude. When she and Trinity were only three weeks old, a vile human being had set their family home on fire and kidnapped Josie. For thirty years, the Paynes believed that Josie perished in the fire. During that time, Josie's kidnapper had abused her and then eventually discarded her, leaving her in the care of a woman named Lisette Matson. Both Josie and Lisette had had every reason to believe that Lisette was Josie's grandmother—until she and Lisette learned about the Paynes and Josie's true identity was revealed. Still, Lisette had raised Josie, had been everything to Josie. Her anchor and north star. Her one and only source of unconditional love and stability in a life that had sought to crush her at every turn.

Now, Lisette was missing from this family gathering. Gone forever. Murdered eight months earlier before Josie's eyes. A tickle scratched at the back of Josie's throat, the precursor to tears. Now was not the time. She wished her husband, Noah, was home but he, too, worked for the Denton Police Department as a lieutenant, and their schedules often conflicted.

Harris was nestled between Shannon and Trinity in the center of the couch, watching the television expectantly. A trailer for a piece that was set to appear on the next morning's national news show played. Harris pointed to the older man on screen talking about how he turned his life around through his faith. "Look," he said. "It's the God guy."

Trinity laughed. "The God guy?"

Shannon said, "That's Thatcher Toland. He's got that megachurch they're building just outside of Denton."

Christian added, "He bought that old hockey stadium— used to belong to the Philadelphia Flyers' farm team until they moved. It was sitting abandoned for years. Apparently, he's rehabbing it and turning it into a church."

"It's made traffic in East Denton an absolute nightmare," said Patrick. "They're constantly bringing in construction equipment and supplies. They claim it will open on Christmas Eve. I hope it does, 'cause when I come back for next semester I don't want to have to deal with that mess."

Shannon said, "He just wrote a book. I haven't heard the

end of it from my next-door neighbor. I think she expects us to join the church when the new place is done."

"The God guy is on TV *all the time*," said Harris, dragging out the words "all the time" and rolling his eyes.

"I know who he is, Mom," said Trinity, laughing at Harris's antics. "If I was still a morning news anchor, I'd be the one doing that interview."

"Is it almost time for *your* show?" Harris asked.

Trinity checked her phone. "Five more minutes. But Harris, this is a grown-up show. Did your mom give you permission to watch it?"

"But you're in it," he said. "And I know you."

Trinity laughed. "Yes, I'm in it. But it has very grown-up themes—things—in it."

"But it's your show, so can't you say whether I watch it or not?"

"No," Trinity said patiently. "Only your mom can make that decision."

He jumped up. "I'm gonna ask her!" Running toward the kitchen, he suddenly stopped where Josie stood in the doorway. Trout's little bottom wiggled, his tongue lolling as he watched Harris. "Aunt JoJo," Harris said. "Since Gramma Lisette is in heaven, shouldn't we put her vase on the table so she can see Aunt Trinity's show, too?"

Josie's entire body went still. The conversations in the living room ceased. All she could hear was Misty moving around in the kitchen. The whir of the microwave. The low hum of the television. Trout whined.

Shannon jumped up from the couch. "Harris, I think that's a great idea. I'm sure Aunt JoJo would be fine with that. Right? JoJo?"

Josie knew her mother's eyes were boring into her but all she could see was the gleam of Lisette's silver urn on a bookshelf across the room. She sensed Trinity at her side, felt her sister's hand on her forearm. "Josie," she whispered. "You okay?"

Josie tore her gaze from the urn and looked at Harris's hopeful little face. As always, she was rendered speechless by the way Harris saw the world. One of the worst parts about grieving for Lisette was Josie's fear that one day she would be nothing more than a collection of memories. Something old, dusty, and irrelevant that you kept under your bed and never spoke about. Harris, in his innocent way, was keeping her alive, keeping her present before Josie's eyes. In her mind, Josie saw Lisette's mischievous smile, heard her giggle; heard her voice as sure as if she were standing next to her. *"I'd like to see the show, too, you know."*

Josie's feet carried her across the room. She picked up the urn, struck by the fact that this was all that was left of her vibrant, vivacious grandmother—a shiny vessel of ashes. She'd lost many hours to these thoughts. The last eight months had been the hardest of Josie's life. Turning back, she managed a smile for Harris. "Gramma Lisette would have loved this," she told him.

Christian and Patrick made room in the center of the coffee table and Josie set the urn there. The flickering lights of the television bounced off its gleaming surface as did the ones from the tree. Misty appeared in the foyer with a bowl of perfectly popped popcorn in each hand. "It's almost time," said Shannon.

Harris said, "Mommy, can I watch the show with the grown-ups?"

"Sure, sweetheart," Misty said. Lowering her voice, she looked at Josie and said, "Only because he'll be asleep in ten minutes."

Everyone crowded into the room. Josie sat beside Trinity on the couch, Harris in her lap. He leaned his head back against her chest, and she felt his little body relax against hers. Misty was right; he'd be asleep in no time. On either side of them were

Shannon and Christian. Patrick and his girlfriend took up the love-seat and Misty sat on the floor, Trout at attention beside her, watching as each morsel of popcorn went from the bowl to her mouth. Misty glanced back toward the couch and said, "Trinity, shouldn't you be watching this at some big premiere in New York City? With Drake on your arm? Being photographed in some stunning evening gown?"

Trinity laughed. "Drake had to work, of course. Some big case. It's always a big case with the FBI. Anyway, the network doesn't do those premiere sorts of things for shows like mine. Besides, this is just a sneak peek. They're playing this episode now to try to drum up interest, and then the show will premiere with two full episodes after the Super Bowl."

Shannon clapped her hands together. Her face was flushed with anticipation. "This is so exciting!"

The room went completely silent as the first few notes of the theme song began to play. The words *Unsolved Crimes with Trinity Payne*" flashed across the screen with a fast-moving slide show of generic stock crime-scene photos behind it. Then Trinity appeared beside a large television screen, dressed smartly in a form-fitting red skirt suit that accentuated her full red lips and long, silky black hair. She gave off an air of solemnity, standing straight and tall, her hands positioned in front of her in the classic television-anchor pose—one hand clasping the fingertips of the other.

"Good evening," on-screen Trinity said. "And welcome to *Unsolved Crimes*. I'm your host, Trinity Payne. On today's episode we're going to present to you the case of the Rose Glen Three..."

For an hour, the room was largely silent, riveted by the unsolved cold case that Trinity and her team of producers and writers had carefully laid out for the audience, including the prevailing theories among law enforcement and those closest to the victims as to who was responsible. As the credits rolled, everyone congratulated Trinity. Josie shifted Harris's sleeping form on her body. "That's amazing, Trin."

Patrick said, "Will you follow up if any leads come from this?"

Trinity started to answer but a knock sounded from the front door. Misty jumped up. "I'll get it."

A moment later, she reappeared and lifted Harris from Josie's lap. "It's Mettner," she said. "He wants to talk to you."

Josie stood and pulled her T-shirt away from her body. It was moist with sweat from where Harris had lain against her. "Did you tell him to come in?"

Misty settled Harris back onto the couch by himself, covering him with a blanket while the adults talked about the show. Trout immediately jumped up and curled himself next to Harris. "He didn't want to."

Josie walked out to the foyer. Her front door was ajar. On her front stoop stood Detective Finn Mettner. This was his night off, too, Josie knew, so he was dressed casually in jeans and an old Phillies sweatshirt. His brown hair was in disarray and as Josie got closer, she saw that his brown eyes were wide and haunted.

Something was wrong.

"Josie," he said, the name puffing out in a visible cloud in the cold air. "I need your help."

THREE

Detective Finn Mettner had come up through the ranks of Denton Police Department after Josie and Noah. He'd started on patrol and been promoted to detective. He had the least experience of anyone on their team, but it had never stopped him from helping them to solve some of the most confounding cases. "Mett," Josie said. "Come on in."

He jammed his hands in his pockets. "I can't. I just—I need your help. I was hoping you could come with me."

A nagging feeling of unease unfurled itself in her stomach. Josie stepped out onto the stoop, hugging herself. "What's going on, Mett?"

He took a step back from her. "It's Amber," he said.

Amber Watts was the Denton PD's press liaison. She and Mett had been dating for over a year now although beyond that, Josie knew nothing about their relationship.

The unease began to wriggle inside her. She looked him up and down, searching for signs that he had been in a struggle or was under duress. At once, she felt guilty for making these assessments. Although she didn't know Mettner well personally, he had never struck her as the kind of person who would become violent or get caught up in a criminal situation. Still, something felt off to her. "Mett," she said. "Where is Amber? Is she hurt?"

"I don't know. That's just it. I don't know where she is and there was something weird—there was—I went to her house and —listen, do you think you could just come with me?"

Ignoring his request, Josie said, "You went to her house and what, Mett?"

He looked back toward the street. Josie followed his gaze but all she saw beneath the dull glow of the streetlights were the vehicles of her family crowded into her driveway and parked along the street. Everything else was quiet and still. "She wasn't there," he said. "I don't know where she is and something was weird. There were some strange things at her place."

For a moment, she wondered if he was in shock. "Weird in what way? Mett, I need you to tell me right now if you think Amber is hurt or in some kind of trouble."

"I don't know," he replied. "Can you just come see?"

Josie looked back inside the house. Everyone was fully engaged in a conversation about Trinity's show. Josie's family was staying with Josie and Noah for the week to celebrate the holidays, so she would see them when she came home. "Sure. Okay, but I'm going to call Gretchen and Noah. They're both on shift tonight. If something is really wrong, then they'll need to come out and—"

"No," said Mettner, cutting her off. "Please. Not yet. I don't even know that a crime has been committed. I just need someone else to come out and tell me if I should be worried or not."

"I don't like this," Josie told him. "When is the last time you saw or spoke to Amber?"

"Two days ago," he said.

"Did you try calling her?"

"Her phone is at her house. So is her car. Her purse. ID, everything. Even her coat. Most of the lights were on in the house. I know you're going to ask me all these police questions, but I've already asked them myself. Everything is there except for her."

"You sure she didn't go out for a walk or a run or something?" Josie asked.

"I checked her phone. There are missed calls and texts from me going back the last two days but that's it. Yesterday was her day off—"

"And today she didn't show up for work," Josie filled in. "Noah mentioned it earlier. He called me after he got on shift. The Chief was pissed that she hadn't called or emailed to say she wouldn't be in. Mett, I think we should just call him. Or Gretchen."

"Not yet," he said. "What if I'm being stupid? I don't want to turn this into a case if it's not. I don't want Amber to think I'm crazy, you know? Like, a stalker. I just want to see what you think of the scene first."

The scene. Josie sighed. "All right. Wait here then. I'll be right out."

Back inside, Josie made apologies, told everyone she had to help Mett with a work thing, went upstairs to get changed, and left the impromptu watch party. "You drive," she told Mettner. "My car is blocked in."

Once inside his Jeep Grand Cherokee, he cranked up the heat. Josie rubbed her gloved hands together and put them against the vents as they pulled away. Christmas was only days away and holiday lights blazed from the homes of most Denton residents. On any other night she might enjoy the festive decorations. But tonight Mettner was giving off a nervous energy that Josie didn't like at all.

He weaved his way through the streets of Denton, out of Josie's neighborhood, across the center of town and into Northeast Denton. The city took up roughly 25 square miles in the mountains of Central Pennsylvania. The main business district was located in the center of a valley along a branch of the Susquehanna River. The rest of the city sprawled outward like the legs of a spider, reaching deep into the surrounding mountains.

"This is her street," Mettner said as he turned down a wide street with detached single-level homes lining either side of it. Each one sat on what Josie estimated was a half-acre of land. Most of the houses were red brick. She knew this area of Denton was older than most of the other neighborhoods. The crime rate here was low to moderate, Josie knew from her work on the police force. Many of the homes were rentals, occupied by young professionals without children who wanted more elbow room and privacy than they might find in an apartment complex. Josie counted only two houses with holiday lights up as Mettner rolled down the block. He pulled over behind a light blue sedan which Josie recognized as Amber's Toyota. It sat in front of a small house. The windows glowed brightly. The front lawn was bisected by a concrete walkway. Mettner got out of his car and stepped onto the sidewalk. A flashlight appeared in his hand. Josie followed behind him as the beam of light bobbed up and down, side to side. A single step led to the front stoop. Over it was a small red awning. A light was affixed to the left side of the doorway, but it wasn't on. Mettner shone the flashlight onto a small security camera to the right of the door. Josie recognized it as one of the more inexpensive kinds that operated from batteries rather than being hardwired into your home and worked wirelessly via an app on your phone. No lights came on to indicate it had picked up their presence.

"The batteries are gone," Mett said.

Josie leaned in and took a closer look at the rectangular camera. It was seated perfectly in its mount. The discomfort she had felt earlier at her house returned. "How do you know that, Mett?"

"I checked," he said. "Plus, there's an app on her phone that shows any activity the camera picks up. Amber left my house on Friday afternoon and there's footage of her getting home. Then Sunday night—last night—it looks like someone came up from the side, out of range of the camera, and took it out of its seat. Then the screen goes blank, and the app shows that the battery is out. But there are no batteries in it, so someone took them."

"Could Amber have reached out and removed the batteries without her person being picked up on camera?" Josie asked.

"Well, yeah, I guess. But why would she take the batteries out of her own surveillance camera? Just come on."

He pulled open the storm door and put his free hand on the heavy knob of the front door. "Mettner," Josie said. "Do you have permission to enter Amber's house?"

He froze. "I, uh, yeah, she leaves the door unlocked for me sometimes."

"But you said she wasn't home. Was the door unlocked?"

He said nothing.

Josie sighed. "Mettner, how did you get into her house?"

His hand slipped from the doorknob. Turning back to her, she could see his dark eyes flash with fear as the flashlight beam bobbed between them. "I thought she was in trouble."

Josie put a hand on her hip. "How did you get in?"

He pointed the flashlight at his feet. "I got in through the back door."

"You broke in."

"No," he said. "I didn't. I just—"

"Jesus, Mett. You're a police officer. Is this why you brought me here? Because you think I'm going to cover for you for breaking and entering?"

"I only broke one pane of glass so I could reach in and unlock the door, and I cleaned it up and put cardboard in the window," he insisted. "I thought she was in trouble. I thought maybe she was laying in there injured or dead. For Chrissake, it's Monday night now and no one has heard from her!"

"You mean *you* haven't heard from her—"

"She didn't show up for work and didn't call. It was reasonable to think she might be inside injured or dead."

"But she's not, which means you can't just go traipsing into her private residence, and you can't bring me here either unless you think a crime has been committed, and if you think a crime has been committed, then you should have called Noah and Gretchen who are on shift right now. What the hell is going on here, Mett?"

She snatched the flashlight from his hand and directed it straight upward so they could see one another's faces. His jaw was set. When he didn't answer her, she turned away and said, "Let's go back to the car."

She heard his heavy footsteps behind her as she returned to his Jeep. Under the dull glow of the streetlight, she snapped the flashlight off and looked at him expectantly.

"We had a fight, okay?" he said. "On Friday. She walked out of my place. I tried calling and texting her and got no response. Then she didn't show up for work. I was worried."

"Mettner," Josie said.

He held up both palms. "I didn't want to call Noah or Gretchen because I know how it looks. We get into a fight. She vanishes. I break into her house."

"Yeah," Josie agreed. "It looks pretty damn bad."

"I swear to you I didn't do anything to her. I don't know where she is or what happened to her, and I'm worried."

"If you're worried, you call the police, Mett. You ask for a welfare check. Like a normal person."

"What I did was a welfare check!"

"It was until you broke in! What's really going on here?

Think carefully about how you answer because you're already in deep shit. I need to know everything."

He pushed a hand through his hair. "I thought I'd let things cool off for a day. On Sunday I tried texting her, but she didn't respond. Then today I called and texted her but again, I got no response. I called the station, but she wasn't there either. I came here. Knocked on the door, rang the doorbell. Nothing. I could see through the window in the back that her phone, purse, and keys were on the kitchen table and her coat was hanging on the back of one of the chairs. Her car was right here. The lights inside the house were on. I knocked on the back door. Tried to peek in the windows around the front and side of the house. Couldn't see much. One of the blinds in the bedroom window wasn't entirely closed so I could see that the room was empty, and her bed wasn't made, but that was it. I couldn't see anything else. Then I came back out here and that's when I saw her windshield."

"Her windshield? Why wouldn't you lead with that?" Before he could answer, Josie stalked off, letting the flashlight lead the way to the front of Amber's sedan. Josie expected to see shattered glass but instead was greeted with a frost-covered windshield. It took her a moment to realize something had been traced into the frost. Ghostly letters, most likely made by a fingertip, stared back at her as she moved the flashlight beam across the glass.

Russell Haven 5A

"I don't understand," Josie said.

"Me either," Mettner said. "She never mentioned anyone by that name. I looked it up in the TLO database but didn't find anything. Not here in Pennsylvania, anyway. I thought maybe the 5A was like an apartment number or something. Why would someone write this on her windshield? It's weird, right? I couldn't tell how long it had been there. I knocked again, front and back. Nothing. I know I shouldn't have but I was really worried, so I went in."

"You know damn well that's not the point," Josie said. "You entered the premises without her permission. Nothing you saw from the outside would lead you to believe that a crime had been committed or that she was in immediate danger. Amber is a grown woman. If she wants to drop off the face of the planet, she's allowed to do it."

"But Josie, she wouldn't. She wouldn't just leave everything behind and walk away from her life."

"You don't actually know that," Josie pointed out. "How well do you really know her? You've dated for little more than a year!"

"Something's wrong. She's not there. Her bedroom is a mess, which is unlike her but other than that, it's like she just got up and left without her phone, purse, coat, ID, or car, which she would not do. We were planning a future together!"

She stared at him. She wanted to tell him the one thing he hadn't learned on the job yet: sometimes even the people you loved and trusted most lied and let you down; sometimes the people you loved and trusted most were not at all who they claimed to be. Josie had no idea what kind of person Amber was—she only knew her to be good and efficient at her job and loyal to the investigative team. Mettner knew her better, but that didn't mean much in Josie's opinion. She had known her first husband, Ray, since they were nine years old and, as it turned out, she didn't know him at all. But Josie didn't have time to explain all this to Mettner. Besides, it was a lesson he'd have to learn on his own one day—whether it was via Amber or someone else. She glanced back at the words on the windshield, mentally reconstructing Mettner's actions in the last two days.

"You think Russell Haven is a person," said Josie. "You

didn't want to be embarrassed if she'd simply gone off to meet another guy."

Sheepishly, his gaze dropped to his feet.

Josie sighed. "Jesus, Mett."

"If she's seeing someone else, I'm going to look like a real jackass," he conceded. "And a stalker, probably, too."

"But if she's in trouble, you're going to look involved. Dammit, Mett. I'm calling Noah and Gretchen. Also, Russell Haven isn't a person."

He looked up, the whites of his eyes aglow in the night. "He's not? It's not?"

Josie handed him the flashlight and took out her phone. She pulled her gloves off. Her fingers flew across the screen as she tapped out a message to Noah and Gretchen. "I thought you grew up here," she muttered.

"I did."

"Russell Haven used to be a development, Mett, and I mean that in the loosest sense of the word. It was a cluster of about a dozen houses on the river at the edge of South Denton. About fifty years ago it got washed away in a flood. It was horrible. Tragic. Most of the families died. The ones who survived lost everything. The city built a dam there after that."

"What? How the hell do you know all this?"

Josie pocketed her phone and looked at him again. "Well, for one thing, I live here, and for another, I pay attention to the local news. Construction to convert the old dam into a new hydroelectric power station was completed at the Russell Haven site about three years ago."

"Shit. Why would someone write the name of a dam on Amber's windshield?"

"No idea," Josie said. "But I am pretty sure that 5A isn't an apartment number. It's a time. Five a.m."

Mettner shone the flashlight back onto the glass, the beam focused in on the five and the letter A. "Someone wanted her to meet them at the old Russell Haven site at five," he mumbled, almost to himself. "Shit."

"Today or yesterday, yeah," Josie said. "That would be my guess. Mett, there's a cryptic message written in the frost on her windshield; the batteries in her home security camera are missing; all of her things are still here; and her lights were still on. I think the next logical move is to head over to the Russell Haven site and see if we find anything there. Any indication that she was there in the last forty-eight hours. I'll tell Noah and Gretchen to meet us there."

"How would she get there?" he asked.

"I don't know," said Josie. "First, let's see if there is any indication that she was at the dam, and we'll go from there."

"What about the house?"

"We can't go into the house," Josie told him. Her fingertips were already freezing. She pulled her gloves back on. "You know that. Even if it's a rental—which I assume it is—Amber has an expectation of privacy which means the landlord can't give us permission to enter."

"We could get a warrant," he said.

"No. We can't. No judge will grant one. There's no evidence that a crime has been committed here, except for you breaking and entering. Since Amber's not here to press charges —and I hope when we do find her, she decides not to—you should be okay on that front for now, but I've got to tell the Chief about this."

"Josie," Mettner pleaded.

"Did you come to me because you wanted me to cover for you? Did you think I would?"

"No, I—I wanted you to... I don't know. Look, I just want to find Amber and know that she's okay. That's it. I thought you would know what to do."

Josie's tone softened. "It's different when it's someone we care about, isn't it?"

He nodded.

She held out her hand. "I can't tell you what to do, but I can tell you what I'm going to do, which is meet Noah and Gretchen at the Russell Haven site. You have to stay out of the way, though. Give me your keys. I'm driving."

FOUR

The streets of Denton grew darker as they moved out of the heart of the city and to its southernmost point where the tall mountains yielded to rolling hills and farmland. The sparkling holiday displays faded as Josie pulled onto a single-lane rural road that led to Russell Haven Dam's private service road. Josie knew that either Noah or Gretchen would have tried to get in touch with either the dam manager or the duty operator in order to get access to the areas that were kept off-limits to the public. It was late in the evening though, so she wasn't sure how much luck they'd have.

Spindly branches of trees reached out from the darkness, closing in on the SUV from both sides as Josie drove. The tires slipped on black ice a few times. From her periphery, she saw Mettner grab onto his door handle, posture stiffening. It had been an exceptionally warm and wet fall. Only now, in late December, had the weather grown frosty. They'd had some minor snowfall the last few days that melted in the daylight and froze again during the frigid nights. Only patches of snow remained here and there, but the icy roads were still a threat.

"You want me to drive?" asked Mettner.

Josie shot him a hard look. "Do you know where the Russell Haven Dam site is?"

"No," he mumbled.

Josie turned her gaze back to the inky road ahead, knuckles white from gripping the steering wheel so hard. Ahead on the left, the headlights illuminated a white sign with black letters: RUSSELL HAVEN DAM. Josie knew that you could access the dam on either side of the Susquehanna River. This entrance would take them to the bank that held the large hydroelectric power station, a tall gray building that extended out into the river to where the spillway began. As they drew nearer to the power station, the foliage on either side of the access road receded until there was nothing but blackness all around them. The golden glow of the power station's exterior lights led them forward to a black metal gate. A stop sign was affixed to the center of it. Below that were signs announcing: AUTHORIZED VEHICLES ONLY BEYOND THIS POINT. A red pickup truck sat on the other side of the gate.

"Do you come out here a lot?" Mettner asked.

"No," said Josie. "But I've been out here on cases. We lost a couple of kayakers here. On the other bank. I got called in on both of those cases, but they were open and shut. Accidental."

Josie nosed Mettner's SUV within inches of the gate.

"Kayakers?" Mettner said. "You mean they went over the dam? Over the top of the spillway?"

"No," Josie said. "They came in traveling upriver, toward the face of the spillway. There's a lot of rocky outcroppings and small islands that are accessible when the water is low. When they release water from the dam, it gets a little wild, especially up close to the bottom of the water release chute and spillway. Some of them like to do a version of whitewater rafting in their kayaks. Dangerous, especially with the water release. They're not supposed to be there, but there are always a few who do it anyway. Only two have died."

A set of headlights appeared in the rearview mirror. A moment later, a car stopped behind them. Josie watched in the side mirror as Noah hopped out of the driver's seat and jogged up to Mettner's vehicle. His breath came out in clouds. "We tried calling the main number, but the calls are being routed to a voicemail telling us to call back during business hours. The Chief is back at the station trying to find the cell or home numbers of either the plant manager or duty operator—anyone who can get us inside."

A car door slammed and then Gretchen appeared beside Noah. She wore a thick purple winter coat and matching knit hat over her short, spiked brown-gray hair. In her late forties, she was the oldest and most experienced on the investigative team. Her résumé had included fifteen years on the Philadelphia PD, most of that time spent in homicide. Josie had hired her during her short tenure as interim Chief of Police. Gretchen waved her phone in the air. "Chief says he can't get anyone, but he'll let us know when he does."

"I thought that would be an issue," said Josie. "Until we can get in touch with someone, why don't we go over to the other side of the dam? That's not fenced off in any way. It's accessible to the public. We can take a look around."

"What's over there?" Mettner asked.

Josie said, "From what I remember, there's a control house and then the water release chute. It's an old fish ladder that was converted to a water release chute when they built the hydroelectric plant. They put in a mechanical fish lift on this side to replace the ladder."

"Wait," said Gretchen. "Fish ladders and lifts? What are you talking about?"

They all stared at her. She shrugged. "What? I spent fifteen years on the Philadelphia PD before I came here. I don't know these things!"

Noah said, "The American Shad—that's a fish, by the way—

migrates upriver every year in May in order to spawn. There has to be something in place along the dam that allows them to actually get upriver. Thus, the fish ladder."

Josie remembered the emergency crews pulling the kayakers from the river just below the fish ladder. "It's a structure, kind of like a wide set of steps, that lets fish go upriver around a dam. The one here is made of concrete. It's like a long concrete chute. There's a wall that separates it from the spillway."

"That's different from a lift?" Gretchen asked.

Noah said, "Yeah, a lift is a mechanical device. The fish collect inside a chamber and then that chamber is lifted up and over the dam and the fish are released from it."

"Whatever," said Mettner. "Let's just go over there and check out the ladder or chute or whatever the hell is there."

Josie touched his arm to quiet him.

"What about the control house?" Noah asked. "Does anyone man it?"

Josie shook her head. "The last couple of times I worked cases here, no one manned it although it does have an exterior camera. The control functions are duplicated, and the camera accessed from the main control room of the dam." She pointed to the closed gate ahead of them and the huge building beyond it. "In there."

Gretchen sighed. "It's worth a look. Maybe by the time we're finished the Chief will have gotten in touch with the plant manager or the duty operator."

FIVE

They drove their vehicles to the other side of the river, which took nearly twenty minutes since they had to drive back out to Denton's South Bridge, cross, and return to the dam. Josie led the way with Noah and Gretchen in tow. Mettner tapped one hand against his thigh the entire ride. Neither of them spoke. Josie knew he was wondering the same things as she: what would they find on the other side of the dam? Would they find Amber? What would she be doing out here at this time of the night, in this cold? How would she have even gotten there without her car? Had someone brought her?

Was she still alive?

Josie felt an involuntary shiver work its way up her spine. She turned onto the service road that would lead them to the old fish ladder, now the water release chute on the other side of Russell Haven Dam. Here, the woods were much thicker, revealing nothing of their surroundings but what the headlights illuminated.

She thought about the message on Amber's windshield. Who had left it? Why leave it there? Why not slip a note under her front door? So she would be sure to see it when she left the house? Even if she had missed it while walking to the car, once she sat in the driver's seat, it would surely have been visible—assuming she got into her car in the morning which was when it would be most visible, scratched into the frost. The question then became, when did she see it? If she saw it at all…

Along the access road, they passed one of what Josie knew were many signs that led to this side of the Russell Haven Dam. DANGER, it read. WATER LEVEL RISES SUDDENLY WITH EXTREME TURBULENCE.

"What time does Amber usually leave for work?" Josie asked.

Startled from his thoughts, Mettner's head whipped toward her. "What?"

"In the morning, what time does Amber usually leave her house for work? Do you know?"

"Seven, I think," Mettner said. "Why?"

Josie said, "What time did you go to her house?"

"This evening. Like, six, I guess."

"But the camera batteries were removed last night," Josie clarified.

"Yes."

"It would have been dark at six, Mett. It's been cold but I'm not sure that the frost would have formed by six p.m. It forms during the night. How did you see the writing?"

"What are you getting at?" Mettner asked.

"Just answer my questions, Mett," Josie said. "How did you see the words on the windshield if there wasn't frost on the window?"

"How the hell should I know?" he shouted.

Josie shot him a stern warning look and he held up a hand. "I'm sorry, I'm sorry," he said. "I don't know. I… was looking at everything really closely. I checked the house and when I didn't find her there, I went out to her car to see if the hood was warm. If it had been, then I'd know that she had just come home from somewhere before she disappeared. It wasn't warm, by the way. I was standing there with my flashlight and I saw the streaks on the glass. Whoever did it must have used their fingertip—no gloves—because without the frost, the message was still there. The oils from their skin, I guess. It was really hard to see but eventually I was able to make it out."

Although it was entirely possible, Josie still felt unease in the pit of her stomach.

"You said her bed was messed up." Amber definitely struck Josie as someone who would make their bed each morning— although even people who were meticulous about doing it might have a late morning now and then during which they didn't have time to do it. "That's unusual?"

A quick glance at him showed the whites of his eyes as he stared at her. "Yeah. She even makes my bed when she sleeps over. Drives me nuts. Why are you asking me about her habits?"

"Something isn't adding up," Josie pointed out. "If she did make it out here somehow, she would have had to see the message on her car. But if she always left the house at seven, then how would she have seen the message before the meeting time? Assuming that the message means what we think it means —to meet someone here."

"You're saying that the message would have had to been written on her car some time on Sunday night—last night?"

"I'm saying I'm not sure she even saw it," Josie said. "Even if she had, why would she leave it there and how would she get out here?"

"Someone brought her here?" Mettner suggested.

"Right. If someone brought her here, they didn't give her a chance to even put her coat on, let alone gather her phone and purse. Also, her doors were locked, but you said the keys were inside, right?"

Another sign came into view. DANGER. FOR YOUR SAFETY, SOUNDING SIRENS AND FLASHING

LIGHTS INDICATE YOU MUST LEAVE RIVER IMMEDIATELY.

"Yes," said Mettner. "Front and back doors were locked, and the keys were in her purse. But if someone was going to take her, why bother leaving the message? You're right. None of this is making any sense."

Before Josie could respond, the wail of sirens reached them, two intermittent bursts of noise at varying pitches. *Weee-wooo. Weee-wooo. Weee-wooo.*

Josie turned the vehicle into the small parking area that the power company had allotted for people who came to the dam for recreational purposes. Theirs and Noah's cars were the only ones there. Noah pulled up right beside her. They left their headlights on, shining down a broken-down flight of stone steps that led to the riverbank and the old fish ladder chute.

Weee-wooo. Weee-wooo.

As they emerged from the car, wind whipped Josie's long black hair across her face. Pushing it away, she saw Noah and Gretchen starting toward the stairs, each with heavy flashlights in hand. Beside her, Mettner shouted, "What is that?"

Weee-wooo. Weee-wooo.

"The alarm that goes off before they release water through the dam," she hollered back. "Let's get the flashlights from the car."

A minute later they were following Gretchen and Noah down the steps, which cut a wide path down the embankment. On either side, barren tree branches swayed in the wind. Josie saw flashing lights before they reached the bottom. Straight ahead were more trees and what looked like rushing water, light bouncing off it, white froth rising as it whirled and crashed on the rocks jutting up from the riverbank. To their left was the control house, a tiny one-story structure with tan siding and no windows, only a single entry door. A bubble camera hung from one corner of the peaked

roof. Beside that was a flashing orange light, strobing in time
with the sirens.

Weee-wooo. Weee-wooo.

She gauged their distance from the camera. As long as they
kept to the far right of the staircase, they'd avoid the camera
altogether. She made a mental note to get the footage from the
camera for the last forty-eight hours once they got in touch with
someone from the dam. A path to their right led away from the
control house, zigzagging downward to where the riverbank
opened up beside the chute.

Ahead of them, Noah asked Gretchen, "See anything?"

She shook her head.

Weee-wooo. Wee-wooo.

The zigzagging dirt path ended at a long, flat expanse of
mud, dirt, and dead, trampled greenery. Beyond that was the
water release chute. On the riverbank side, there was only a
slim, crumbling half-wall separating the chute from the shore. It
tapered off at the bottom of the chute where they now stood.
Large stones rose up to meet them. The water snaked through
them, the line where the riverbank ended and the river began
blurred and indistinct. Josie felt her boots sink into mud. Even
in the freezing cold she could smell the fetid aroma of soil and
water mixing with storm water runoff and waste from the
wildlife. The wind lashed at them with greater ferocity as it
came off the river.

The flashing orange light was weaker here on the bank, so
they used their torches to pan the long, concrete chute. It was
exactly as she remembered it from the cases with the kayakers—
topped by a large metal gate and with a much higher wall on the
side opposite the bank, the curved concrete barrier separating it
from the spillway. Josie estimated that the chute was twenty to
twenty-five feet across. Although it was no longer used as a fish
ladder but for water release, its condition was poor. Most of its
steps were cracked and broken. Rocks were strewn everywhere

and in several places, large boulders had rolled down from the incline along the riverbank and come to rest in the chute.

Weee-wooo. Weee-wooo.

She felt Mettner's hand clamp down on her forearm a second before Gretchen cried out, "There!"

Josie's eyes searched the chute, but Gretchen and Noah's flashlight beams were jumping erratically as they ran up toward the metal gate, keeping to the riverbank. More sounds joined the shrieks of the siren. A metallic creak and then the thunderous roar of water. The water release had begun.

"What is it?" Josie shouted, trying to pick her way after Noah and Gretchen, even as Mettner held onto her arm. With a steely grip, he turned her flashlight beam so that it lined up with his, shining up and toward the other side of the chute. Several boulders had collected there, leaving what looked like a crease between them and the chute wall.

"It's her!" Mettner cried.

Then he was gone. Josie steadied the flashlight, again searching for the crease, the beam of her light weaker the further out it reached.

Weee-wooo. Weee-wooo.

The rush of water was getting louder now, closer.

Her torch found the spot once more. This time, she saw what everyone else had seen: a mess of dark auburn curls, like a tumbleweed with nowhere to go. A vise tightened around her chest. Even over the water and the sirens, she could hear Noah, Gretchen, and Mettner shouting from several feet away. They were higher up, closer to the gate. The water had already reached them. It crashed against the opposite wall, the base of the fish ladder, and the stones scattered all about with deadly force.

"...won't make it..." Noah was shouting as he held Mettner back from trying to cross the chute, to get to Amber.

The water hadn't yet reached her.

Everything was happening so quickly—heartbeats, it seemed—and yet, in Josie's mind, each and every second seemed to be slowed down. Between the strobing orange lights and the flashlight beams, she was able to see the wall of water smashing and battering its way down the chute, whitewater rising several feet in the air. She watched her colleagues arguing, trying to stop Mettner from killing himself by attempting to rescue Amber. She saw the distance from the water, to herself, to Amber—a triangle. Noted the rocks standing between her and Amber—footholds if she was swift enough. Several large gouges in the wall across from her, which separated the chute from the spillway, would hug her fingers and toes if she vaulted herself up swiftly enough. She could straddle the wall, avoid the water, pull Amber up, maybe keep her out of the water long enough for the gates to close.

The calculations took place in her mind at lightning speed.

Weeee-wooo. Weee-wooo.

Even in the best-case scenario, she could still get killed. Swept away, crushed against the rocks. Then both of them would be dead—if Amber wasn't dead already. Surely, she was already dead.

The beam of Josie's flashlight bobbed toward Amber's hair once more. Time was running out.

Weee-wooo. Weee-wooo.

"...Stop! Mett! You're not going out there! You'll die. She's already gone, man!"

A pale hand emerged from the mess of hair, from the cleft in the boulders, waving weakly.

Josie's stomach dropped to her feet. "Shit," she mumbled.

Then she tossed her flashlight aside and leaped directly into the path of the raging water.

SIX

Somehow, over the sirens and the pounding of the oncoming water, she heard the cries of her team, Noah's most loudly. "Josie, no!" She didn't have time to register the prick of guilt in her heart. Her body was on autopilot now, launching from the half-wall on the riverbank and into the chute, feet barely touching each stone as she cut a path straight toward the opposite wall above Amber. It was just like when she'd been a kid and her grandmother, Lisette, had taught her to play The Floor Is Lava—jumping from one of piece of furniture to another to avoid falling into it. Light feet, soft touch. In seconds, she was flying over Amber's head, the toe of her boot catching one of the gouges expertly. Outstretched hands strained to reach the top of the wall, the concrete tearing at her gloves as she just caught the edge of it.

She felt the spray of water on her face like icy needles hitting her. The water slammed past the space she'd just covered, smacking her left side up to her thigh just as she pulled herself entirely onto the wall. Straddling it like she was riding a horse, she ignored the pain and cold seeping through her jeans.

Weee-wooo. Weee-wooo.

She lowered her chest onto the wall and reached down, searching through the onslaught of water for Amber's hand. In all the mental calculations she'd made in the space of a few heartbeats, she hadn't factored in the height of this wall. Her coat wasn't helping, its puffiness taking up inches she desperately needed to reach Amber. Taking a deep breath, she sat up, pulled her coat off and with it, her gloves, and tossed them away. Then she swung both legs around, letting them dangle over the spillway side—a fall that she knew without looking would surely kill her.

Josie folded her upper body over the chute side of the wall, a human seesaw, and reached both hands down into the churning current. The water was so cold, within seconds she could no longer feel her fingers. Still, she searched until her hand hit something soft. Her body rocked as she grasped it with both hands, knowing immediately it was a hand. She tightened her abdomen and pushed the tops of her knees into the other side of the wall, bracing her body to give herself enough leverage to pull Amber up. If she could just get her head above water, she might have a chance.

Weee-wooo. Weee-wooo.

Another wave of putrid, freezing river water sluiced against the wall, splashing up to Josie's shoulders and into her mouth.

"Puh," she spit out the water but held onto Amber's hand, continuing to pull on it as the water dislodged some of her weight. Amber's body surged upward, nearly knocking Josie back off the wall. She tried to reposition herself to get a better grip on Amber but her body teetered, off balance. Her fingers crept down Amber's hand to her forearm, nails digging into Amber's skin. The sound of Amber's skull knocking against the wall as her body jostled upward in the current made Josie's stomach turn.

Josie hooked one knee back over the chute side of the wall, spinning her body ninety degrees, keeping her pelvis pressed to the top of the wall and dragging Amber up so that her head was above water, the rest of her body still submerged and being batted about by the frothy current.

"Amber!" she shouted over the sirens.

Her arm shook in Josie's grip as her body spasmed with coughs. Josie was close enough to hear the sound of her retching. More water splashed over Amber's head and into Josie's face, stinging her eyes, pummeling her skin with cold.

How long did a water release take? It felt like she'd been trying to drag Amber up out of the water for an eternity. Between the cold numbing her fingers and the water making her skin slick, Josie's grip on Amber began to slip away. She pressed her thighs into the wall, straining to keep herself in place so she could try to gain better purchase. But each time Amber coughed, Josie's clutch weakened, until she was only holding onto Amber's thin wrist, her hands like two blocks of ice.

"Josie!" came shouts from the riverbank. Noah, Mettner, and Gretchen had moved back down so that they were directly across from her, her view of them obstructed every few seconds by another swell of water, whitewater rapids separating them.

The alarms raged on. *Weee-wooo. Weee-wooo.*

Finally, she heard what sounded like the screech of the metal gate above trying to shut down the water release. She sent up a prayer to anyone who would listen that this would be over soon.

Josie tried to readjust her grip on Amber's wrist but more water came sloshing down in their direction, its trajectory changed by the closing gates. It shot toward them, punishing, and for a split second, Josie imagined it as a living thing filled with wrath, bearing down on their tenuous connection.

The water slapped Amber right out of Josie's grasp. Josie felt her fingers clutch at Josie's wrist as she was swept away, pulling Josie off the wall and into the chute with her. She didn't

even have time to cry out. Her lower body plunged into the
seething water, one knee and her other shin knocking against
the boulders below. As she half slid, half fell into the crease
she'd just dislodged Amber from, her fingers caught on another
gouge in the wall. With both hands digging into it and one of
her knees pressing down into the opening of the cleft below, she
stayed in place just long enough for the gate to scream shut and
the water to slow to a lazy swirl.

She bobbed, feet paddling to keep her head above water.
She let go of the gouge in the wall and looked around, adrenaline pushing all physical sensation from her consciousness.
Her eyes searched the darkness, the shafts of light cast by three
flashlight beams wobbling in her direction. Noah howled as he
threw himself into the water, half paddling, half rock-climbing
over toward her. His arms circled her waist and she let him pull
her from the wall.

"My God, Josie. What were you thinking?"

Her body fell into sync with his, moving without thought
toward the riverbank where Gretchen and Mettner waited. Still
she looked downriver, hoping for some sliver of hope, a lock of
auburn hair somehow visible in the darkness.

But Amber was gone.

When they were firmly on the bank, Noah dipped down
and slid his arm under her knees, scooping her up, and began
carrying her toward the path. Josie didn't protest. Both her body
and her mind had gone numb. The only thing she could feel
was the phantom touch of Amber's hand just before she was
sucked into the watery night.

Over Noah's shoulder, Josie saw Mettner standing alone,
arms slack at his sides, flashlight dangling. He looked up. Josie
saw the whites of his eyes from the light of the torch.

"I'm sorry, Mett," she said, throat raw, voice scratchy. "I'm
sorry."

SEVEN

It didn't take long for the parking lot to fill with emergency vehicles: a marked police unit, two ambulances, and the marine unit truck with its rescue boat on a tow behind it. Josie even recognized Chief Chitwood's black Dodge Charger. Flashing lights drove out the night. Gretchen had made her and Noah sit in the front of Noah's vehicle with the heat blasting on them. Noah reached into the back seat and grabbed the blanket he used for when their dog, Trout, got extra muddy on an adventure and wrapped it around Josie.

She opened her mouth to offer at least half the blanket to him or to say something about their combined body heat being useful but her teeth chattered so hard, she couldn't get the words out. From the window, she watched Gretchen talk to the other responders while Mettner leaned against the side of his vehicle, head hanging. Josie felt an ache in her chest, familiar and uncomfortable. She looked away, not wanting to think about those first agonizing steps on the journey of unfathomable loss that Mettner now faced. Noah wouldn't look at her. She could tell by the set of his jaw that he was angry.

He didn't get angry often.

"I'm sorry," she croaked, pulling the blanket tighter around her shoulders. The smell of wet dog was welcome after her plunge into the river.

"Are you?" he asked quietly.

"Noah."

"I know I promised I would always run toward the danger with you, Josie, but there's danger, and then there's certain death."

Guilt pricked at her again. "I knew I could make it," she tried.

"Knew? You could not have known. You could have died out there. You almost did."

"I had to try," Josie responded. "She was alive, Noah. She was still alive when I jumped across the chute. She was still alive when she got swept away. Maybe she still is—"

"I'm not sure anyone could have survived that," he interjected. "All those boulders, the current... but Josie, this isn't about Amber—"

She readied herself to launch into a spiel about the dangers of their job, about all the near-death experiences they'd already had and survived, about how this was what she did; this was who she was; that he had always known that about her; how he had never had a problem with it before, or at least he'd never verbalized that; but her energy was sapped. Again, she felt Amber's fingers press into her wrist and then slip away.

A few moments ticked by with only the rush of hot air from the vents filling the silence between them.

"I just want to grow old with you, Josie," said Noah.

She shook her head, feeling tears now sting the backs of her eyes. Although she'd grown better at crying—as if it were a skill to be honed—in the months since her grandmother's murder, she still hated doing it. She certainly didn't want to do it at an active investigation scene.

"Just consider the risk next time, would you?"

"Okay," she said. But she wondered what would feel worse —having tried to rescue Amber and failed, or having never tried at all? Either way the outcome was the same. Or maybe it wasn't. Was she deluding herself, thinking there was even the slimmest possibility that Amber had survived? Avoided the rocks? Pulled herself to shore?

A rap on the window made them both jump. Noah pressed the button on his side, lowering it. Gretchen poked her head into the car. "I want both of you in the nearest ambulance. Fraley, I'm sure you're fine but the boss got a lot wetter for a lot longer. She definitely needs to be checked out."

"What about Amber?" Josie asked.

Gretchen looked away for a moment, turning her face upward to the wintry night sky. She wiped at her eyes before looking back at Josie, but still her voice cracked when she spoke. "The marine unit is going to be out tonight searching. For now, they're calling it a rescue mission. But if they don't find her on one of the islands or along the bank before the morning, then it becomes a recovery mission. In that case, once daylight arrives, we'll see if we can get more resources on it."

Beside her, Josie felt Noah's hand slip into hers. Amber wasn't a police officer, but she was one of them. They'd worked with her on a daily basis for over a year. She'd become part of their team, and she'd been a good fit in spite of how much resistance they'd shown her when she first started.

"Mett?" Noah said.

Gretchen sucked in another breath, trying to compose herself. "Chief's going to handle him." She tugged the door open. "Let's go. Ambulance. Now."

Josie's legs were stiff and achy as she moved toward the open doors of one of the ambulances. Noah walked behind her, his hand warm on her lower back. "Shit," he said when they reached the cab.

Josie looked inside and saw Sawyer Hayes, dressed in his Denton City EMT uniform and readying his supplies.

Noah said, "We can go to the other ambulance."

"No," she said. "This is ridiculous. He's the one who isn't speaking to me. You go get our emergency bag out of your trunk. There should be a change of clothes for each of us."

He made a noise in his throat but then she felt him disappear and heard his footsteps over the gravel heading back to the car. She climbed into the cabin and stood on the other side of the gurney from Sawyer. If he was surprised or disappointed to see her, he didn't show it. He patted the gurney, indicating for her to sit down. Without looking at her, he said, "The Great Josie Quinn," but his voice was soft and without malice. Still, it made her wince. The last time he'd called her that, his tone had been dripping with bitterness and rage. Before she could respond, he said, "You'll need to get out of those clothes."

"What? I—"

"Josie, you'll freeze in those. I promise, I won't look. At least down to your undergarments. I've got blankets."

He turned away from her, rummaging in one of the many compartments along the wall until he came up with a gray fleece blanket. Keeping his back to her, he held it out. She took it and began stripping down to her bra and panties.

"Just drop your clothes and shoes on the floor," he said. "I'll put them in a bag."

Once she was mostly naked, she laid on the gurney and covered her body with the blanket. "Can I have another one for over my shoulders?" she asked him.

He found another blanket and turned toward her, wrapping it carefully around her shoulders, making sure no skin was exposed except her neck and face. Josie studied him. His penetrating blue eyes. The shock of black hair falling across his forehead. He looked so much like Eli Matson, it never failed to throw her. The woman who kidnapped Josie as an infant had brought her to Denton and passed her off as Eli Matson's daughter. Eli had been a wonderful, caring, devoted father. Then he died, leaving Josie in the hands of a woman whose cruelty knew no end. Eli's mother, Lisette, had fought hard to get custody of Josie, eventually winning and transforming Josie's hellish life into something wonderful.

"Did you get the photo album?" Josie asked him.

"I did," he said softly, still not meeting her eyes. He found a thermometer and tucked it beneath her tongue, waiting until it beeped.

What none of them knew was that before Josie came into Eli's life, he'd had a brief relationship with Sawyer's mother, who then got pregnant with Sawyer. However, she kept his father's identity from him his entire life, only telling him when she was on her deathbed. She had never even told Eli.

"You're welcome," Josie bristled.

Sawyer chuckled. "I'm happy to have it. It's a connection to Lisette."

Once his mother died, Sawyer discovered that his only living relative on his biological father's side was Lisette, his grandmother. He had gone to her, asked her to take a DNA test, which she readily agreed to do. They'd grown close in a short span, making up for lost time. Then Lisette had been murdered, and Sawyer blamed Josie.

He asked for an arm next, taking her blood pressure and then checking her pulse and oxygen saturation.

"Why am I not at all surprised that you jumped in the river?" he muttered.

"I didn't, actually," Josie said. "I mean, not technically. I was on the wall, trying to pull Amber out of the water. She—"

"She got swept away," Sawyer filled in. "Gretchen briefed everyone. For what it's worth, I'm sorry."

Josie pulled her arm back inside the warmth of the blankets. Sawyer turned away again, tapping at his onboard computer and then looking for something else among the equipment. He came back with a pile of hot packs. One by one, he shook them to activate the heat.

"Did you know her?" Josie asked. "Amber?"

"I didn't know her well. I knew her to say hello. Saw her around. Why was she in the river in the first place?"

"I don't know," Josie said. "Mett hadn't heard from her for a couple of days. He got concerned, went to her house. Something we found there led us to believe she might be here."

Sawyer stopped, brow kinked, a frown on his face. "You think she tried to hurt herself?"

"No," Josie said. "I think she was meeting someone here or someone brought her here against her will."

Sawyer started placing the hot packs in her armpits, managing to do so without ever exposing her. Handing her two, he said, "These go in your groin. I assume you'd rather place them yourself."

Face aflame, Josie took them and tucked them in the creases of her inner thighs. In spite of how awkward she felt wearing nothing but a blanket and some flimsy undergarments in front of him, she was so grateful for the warmth, she could think of little else. He placed two more hot packs under her knees and then one behind her neck, pursing his lips as he worked. Josie didn't know him well—they'd always seemed to rub each other the wrong way—but she knew that was something he did when he was hiding something. It took her a moment to realize how she knew that. Her father—or the man she'd grown up believing was her father—Eli had done it too.

"What is it?" she asked.

"I'm not sure it matters," he said.

"Tell me and I'll tell you if it matters or not."

He didn't respond. Instead, he began picking up her discarded clothes and boots and stuffing them into a bag labeled: "Patient Belongings."

"Is it about Amber? I thought you said you didn't really know her."

"I don't—I didn't," he said. "But I knew who she was, knew she was dating Mettner. He brought her as his date to your wedding."

"Sawyer, what's going on?"

"It's just that I saw her a couple of weeks ago with another guy."

"You mean a guy who is not Mett?" Josie said.

"Right."

"Were they kissing? Did they look intimate?"

He shook his head. "No, no. It's not that. They looked like they were arguing. He grabbed her arm, she snatched it away. Then he reached for her again and she pushed him."

"When was this?"

"Maybe two weeks ago?" he said.

"Where did you see them?"

"Outside of that bookstore in the central shopping district—a few blocks over from the police station. McAllister Street. But I don't know the context. I was just driving by. I have no idea what they were saying to one another. It just seemed tense, especially when the shoving started."

Josie raised a brow. "You didn't stop?"

Sawyer matched her raised brow expression. "Why would I stop?"

"To make sure Amber was okay."

He studied her for a long moment, brow now furrowed. "Josie Quinn doesn't strike me as the type who believes in damsels in distress."

She rolled her eyes. "That has nothing to do with this. I didn't say Amber was some kind of damsel in distress. If I saw two people shoving one another on the sidewalk, I would stop to make sure everyone was okay—that it didn't escalate, that no one got hurt."

"Of course you would," he muttered, turning away. Before she could make a caustic remark that she'd regret later, he added, "No. I didn't stop. I looked in my rearview mirror and Amber was alone. The guy was walking away from her. I assumed that whatever had gone on between them was done."

The doors to the ambulance opened and Noah appeared. He had already changed into his backup clothes—jeans, a heather-gray T-shirt, and a pair of sneakers. He held out a bag to her. "These are yours."

Shooting Sawyer a dirty look, Noah climbed inside and sat down on one of the vinyl benches lining the wall. Sawyer gave him a wide berth. They didn't like one another either. In fact, one of the last times they'd seen one another, they'd come to blows.

"Thanks," she said. "Sawyer, tell Noah what you just told me."

With a sigh, Sawyer crossed his arms. He recounted the story for Noah's benefit.

Noah asked, "What did this guy look like?"

"White guy. Tall. Taller than you. Dark hair. Average build. He was wearing a long black coat, jeans, and black sneakers. Hard to estimate his age because I was far away and driving. That's all I can tell you."

Noah handed Josie the bag of clothes. "Why don't you get changed into these and we'll go talk to Mett?"

EIGHT

Sawyer and Noah vacated the back of the ambulance so Josie could get changed. The dry clothes felt heavenly against her skin. The only issue now was that she had no coat or gloves. Her phone had been in the back pocket of her jeans. Miraculously, it had not fallen out. It wasn't the first time it had gotten wet, and she was confident it would recover from her dip in the river. She took the patient belongings bag that Sawyer had put her things in and stowed it in the trunk of Noah's car.

"Where's Mett?" she asked Noah.

"He's still on scene. In his car," Noah answered.

They walked over to Mettner's SUV. His hands were folded in front of him, forehead resting atop them. His eyes were tightly closed, and Josie could see his lips moving. He was praying. In spite of the cold, he hadn't turned the engine on. Josie rapped on the window. When he saw them both, he stepped out.

"I'm suspended," he said. "Chief told me. He let me stay here, though. Said I could. Until they find… something, I guess. He's down on the riverbank with Gretchen."

Josie knew that the Chief was keeping him there for the

same reasons she had brought him along in the first place. If there was any question about Mettner's involvement in any type of crime, they'd at least be able to account for all of the hours that he'd been with them. When neither of them responded, Mettner said, "You guys okay?"

"We're fine," said Josie.

Mettner looked toward the steps leading to the riverbank. The marine unit had a large spotlight on one of their vessels. Every now and then, its blinding white light cut through the trees, reaching all the way to the parking lot. "Maybe you can get a warrant for her place now," Mettner said. "Now that she's—"

He didn't finish the sentence. A sob rocked his body and he tried to push it down, sucking in several deep breaths. Noah gripped his shoulder, squeezing. Josie met his eyes as Mettner tried to regain control of his emotions. Her own sense of help-lessness was reflected back to her. Both Josie and Noah knew from experience that there were no words of comfort that either one of them could offer. There was no comfort, no easing of the kind of pain that Mettner had now been saddled with—there was only living with it. Badly and uncomfortably until one day it became your new normal.

Turning back to them, Mett said, "A warrant. You can get one now for her house. Maybe there's something I overlooked. Maybe you guys could go there tonight and see."

"We can't do that, Mett," said Josie gently.

"What?"

"We can't get a warrant," Noah said, giving him some space. "Unless we positively identify her and there is evidence of foul play."

Mettner's eyes flashed. "You don't think there is?"

"Of course I think there is, Mett," Noah shot back. "But we still have to work within the rules. You know that. Or at least, I thought you did."

"Screw these rules—" Mettner began, but Josie cut him off, wanting to focus on what had now become a case.

"Mett, you're closer to Amber than any of us. What can you tell us about her family and friends?"

"She doesn't keep in touch with her family. She said they were 'toxic' and she hasn't spoken to any of them since she left for college ten years ago."

"Did she say anything about them, though?" Josie asked. "Are both parents still alive? Does she have siblings?"

"Her parents are divorced, she said. I guess they're still alive. I'm pretty sure she has one brother and one sister but I'm not a hundred percent certain."

"Who did she celebrate holidays with?" Josie asked.

"A friend from college," Mettner said. "Before we met. Her name is Grace Power. I met her once. I could find her contact information for you. She lives in Lewisburg."

"What about other friends?" Noah asked. "Local friends?"

Mettner crossed his arms over his chest. "She's got a couple of friends she went to college with that she goes out for drinks with now and then—oh, and a secretary who works at city hall—but that's it."

"Ex-boyfriends?" Josie asked.

"She didn't talk about that."

Josie and Noah looked at one another. Ex-partners were usually a topic of conversation between people who were committed to one another, especially if they were planning a future, as Mettner had said.

Noah asked, "Did you tell her about your ex-girlfriends?"

"Well, yeah, not that there's much to tell."

"You never asked her why she wouldn't talk about hers?" Josie said.

"I didn't want to know," Mettner said.

"You ever have a serious relationship before?" Noah asked him.

Mettner shrugged. "No. I mean, I never even felt like I was in love before I met Amber. I dated, sure, but nothing ever felt like... this."

In the flashing lights of the emergency vehicles, Josie saw fresh tears glisten in his eyes. Amber had been hired by the mayor's office as the press liaison for the police department. It would be easy enough for Josie's team to contact human resources and find out who she had listed as her emergency contact. She didn't want to bring it up in front of Mettner, not here and now, but there was a good chance they'd have to contact Amber's next of kin in order to identify her body.

Noah said, "Assuming that Amber came here to meet someone or that someone brought her here—the person who left the message on her windshield—do you have any idea who that person could be?"

Slowly, Mettner shook his head. "No, none. If I did, I would have gone right to that person to see if they knew where she was."

"You didn't find anything on her phone?" Noah asked.

"Noah," Josie admonished. "We can't use anything he found on her phone. He broke into her house to access it!"

"You're really not going to ask him?" Noah said.

"If we follow a lead as a result of something that Mettner found after illegally entering Amber's home, it will become a nightmare in court. Either it will be inadmissible or it will cause issues during trial or on appeal." She threw up her hands, making a noise of exasperation in her throat. "What is going on with all of you today? You know the rules just as well as I do! If someone lured Amber here or brought her here, hurt her, and left her in those rocks to die, then I want to catch that person and make sure he goes away for as long as possible. That means we have to do things by the book."

"That's rich," said Mettner. "Coming from someone who was suspended twice for *not* doing things by the book."

"Hey," Noah said. "Watch it."

Josie put a hand up. "It's fine. That's fair. But Mett—I'm trying to learn from those instances. I want to get this right."

"There was nothing on the phone," he said.

Before Josie could say another word, they were interrupted by the sounds of more vehicles pulling into the gravel lot. Two vans from the local television news station, WYEP, pulled up beside the ambulances. Out hopped cameramen, a couple of producers, and two reporters.

"Shit," Josie said.

"Yeah," said Noah. "We don't need this. Mett, get back in your car. Don't get out again."

A young male reporter, barely out of college, ran toward them, his phone held out like an offering, but Josie knew he was merely recording any conversation they might have. "Detective Quinn, it's you! Detective Quinn! Is it true that a woman drowned in the river?"

Josie put her hands up and motioned for them to step back. "I need you guys behind the ambulances, please."

"But we heard on the police scanner that the marine unit was called out. Was there some issue with the dam? A dam employee? Who would be out in the river this late at night?"

"Please," Noah chimed in, walking toward the reporter and his crew, backing them up a few steps at a time. "We need to keep this area clear. Emergency personnel are responding to a situation."

The reporter scoffed. "A situation? Really? That's all you're going to give me? I got more from the scanner. Fine. Don't give me anything, but I'll just be calling your press liaison. I have her cell phone number. I'm sure she'll love being woken in the middle of the night."

Josie had some choice words for the kid but she held back. Noah jogged over to a marked unit and asked one of the uniformed officers to keep the reporters behind the ambulances.

"At least tell me if it's a rescue mission or a recovery mission," the reporter went on.

Josie heard rustling behind her, then footsteps. "Quinn! Fraley!" barked Chief Chitwood.

Josie and Noah turned to see the Chief standing at the top of the steps leading to the riverbank. Although he towered over them, he was so thin that his large brown jacket seemed to swallow him up. A dark knit hat covered his balding scalp. He waved a gloved hand, beckoning them over. Mettner stepped out of his SUV but the Chief snapped, "Don't even think about it." Turning back in the direction of Josie and Noah, he said, "Come on, you two. I don't have all night."

They were halfway down the steps, trailing behind him, following the beam of his flashlight when Noah asked, "What did you find?"

"A dead woman," Chitwood said over his shoulder, his tone solemn.

Josie had known logically that this news was forthcoming, but still, it felt like an uppercut to her stomach. "Oh, Amber," she said.

Chitwood pulled up short and shone the light into both of their faces momentarily. "Not Amber," he said.

"What are you talking about?" Josie asked.

"The woman we just pulled from the river is not Amber," Chitwood told them.

"But we saw her," Noah said. "Her hair..." He looked at Josie. "Did you see her face?"

"No," Josie admitted. "I didn't. I just assumed it was her."

"Well, it's not," said Chitwood. He turned and trudged onward.

"If that's not Amber, where the hell is she?" said Noah.

NINE

Amber's feet scrabble against the rock-strewn ground, trying to gain purchase, trying to keep her scalp from being torn. Fear seizes her, her body stiff and paralyzed in its clutches. She blinks rapidly, trying to bring anything but darkness into focus. How can he see a thing? Then it occurs to her that he doesn't need to see their surroundings. He is so familiar with them, he can navigate in the dark.

"Please don't do this," she croaks.

He yanks her head to the side and her body goes flying. The trunk of a tree slams into her back, and the breath whooshes out of her. As her body crumples to the ground, she tries to draw in oxygen but can't.

Over the roar of panic consuming her brain, she hears his feet crunching over stones, twigs, and long-dead leaves. He paces before her. The moon emerges from behind the clouds for a moment, its silver light slicing through the barren trees. She sees the gleam of his gun.

"I am doing what needs to be done," he says.

She opens her mouth to respond. Only a gasp comes out. She clutches at her throat and chest. Something hot and wet spreads across her skin. Blood, she realizes, from when she cut her palm.

"Tell me what I want to know," he snarls. "You can end this right now if you just tell me."

Finally, words slip from her throat. "End this? How does this end? How many people are you going to kill to cover up what happened?"

His frenetic movements stop. "You think this is about covering something up? About hiding? This is about protecting the truth!"

She pulls her shirtsleeve down, balling the fabric up in her torn hand. Her body is too cold to register the pain. "Protecting the truth?" she spits. "Do you hear yourself? Do you even know what you're doing? You've gone insane! No one benefits if I tell you. No one. I can't tell you."

She feels him loom over her. His breath cascades down the back of her neck. "You have to tell me. If you don't, you'll die."

TEN

The woman was definitely not Amber. They reached the shore, where members of the marine unit and Gretchen waited, flashlights hanging from their hands, standing around a body bag. A portion of it had been left unzipped, enough so that Josie and Noah could see the face of the woman inside it. The same auburn curls they'd seen in the rocks earlier framed her pale cheeks, but her features were not as delicate as Amber's; her jaw was squarer, her nose flatter and wider, eyes narrower. Still, she was young, in her mid- to late twenties, and whoever she was, now she was dead. A familiar sadness rose up in Josie's chest. She loved her job. Loved putting terrible people behind bars, loved trying to right wrongs whenever possible. But she never got used to this—life snuffed out tragically and senselessly. Josie shivered and hugged herself, feeling the full onslaught of cold without her coat for the first time since she had emerged from the ambulance.

"Any ID on her body?" Noah asked. He, too, had no coat on although if he was as cold as Josie, he didn't show it.

"Nothing," Gretchen answered. "There is a strong resemblance though. Does Amber have a sister?"

Noah said, "According to Mett, yeah, but she hasn't talked to her family in a decade."

Josie noted a split in her bottom lip, bruising on one of her cheeks and around one of her eyes as well as a large purple lump near her left temple. "Was she...?"

"She was dead when they pulled her from the water," Gretchen said. "There was nothing anyone could do."

"Someone's gotta tell Mett," said Noah.

"Someone's gotta keep Mett from going back over to Amber's place and busting in there, looking for answers," Chitwood said.

"He can stay with me," Gretchen offered. "It's just me, my grown daughter, and a tyrant of a cat. Plenty of room."

Chitwood snapped off his flashlight. One of the marine unit officers squatted down and zipped the bag closed.

Gretchen continued, "I already called Dr. Feist. She'll be waiting at the hospital. Since this woman was pulled from the river, she didn't feel a need to have a look at the scene. She said to stop by around nine thirty or ten in the morning and she should have something."

"Noah and I can go," Josie offered.

Chitwood said, "You all knew each other before I took over this department. I brought Mett up through the ranks and promoted him to detective because he was a great investigator. He deserved it. Stellar record. Checked all the boxes. No nonsense with him. But you tell me, is he involved in whatever the hell is going on here? I need to know right now if any of you have any suspicions."

Josie looked at Noah and then at Gretchen. The marine unit officers hefted the body bag onto a litter. No one spoke.

"Quinn?" Chitwood said.

"I don't know, Chief. I mean, we all know Mett from work, but we don't see him very often socially. Do I think he did something to Amber? Based on what I do know about him, I'd say no."

"But people do crazy shit when they're in love," Noah interjected. He rolled his right shoulder. It was an unconscious movement. Only Josie noticed that he did it sometimes. She had shot him once in his right shoulder. She hadn't wanted to do it. At the time, she thought she had no choice. She did it to protect someone vulnerable, someone in trouble. Josie never forgave herself for it, but Noah insisted he forgave her. He had stood by her since that day, first as a friend, then as a lover, and now as her husband.

She shot him and he married her anyway. She tried to imagine herself in Mettner's shoes, back before she and Noah were married, when they lived apart. What if Noah had just up and disappeared? Josie hung her head thinking about exactly which window she would have breached to break into his house just to make sure he was alive. And what if he wasn't there? What if everything he owned was there but not him?

"What about you, Palmer?" Chitwood asked. "You have an opinion?"

"Sorry, sir," Gretchen said. "My instinct is to say Mett is completely innocent, but in this job, who the hell knows?"

"It's always the boyfriend," Chitwood muttered, almost to himself.

"What's that?" Josie said.

Chitwood turned his gaze back to her. "We want to believe Mettner just went lovesick crazy here breaking into Amber's house with only good intentions because he's one of us, but what if they got into a fight and he did something to her, and all this is just a smokescreen? Him covering his tracks as best he can?"

Noah said, "That doesn't really explain who this other woman is or why she was here—or the message left on Amber's windshield."

"True." Chitwood gave an exasperated sigh. "Fine. Here's how we'll play it. Mett's on suspension for breaking into that house. Since Amber's not here to decide whether or not to press charges against him, that's not a concern right now. But I do not want him near this case. I do not want him near her house. I want to know everything he knows but I want him out of this. You need to find out if he knows how to get in touch with her family so we can find out if this is her sister. Like Palmer said, there is a resemblance."

"Not a problem, sir," said Josie.

"I also want eyes on him," Chitwood said. "So he doesn't muck things up while we're trying to figure out what the hell is going on here."

"I'm on it, sir," Gretchen said.

Chitwood held up his cell phone, the screen aglow. "I heard from the plant manager. When we're finished here, at least one of you will have to go back to the other side of the dam and talk to the duty operator. We need to see what's on their surveillance cameras. He'll open the gate when you arrive."

"Josie and I can do it," Noah volunteered.

Chitwood signaled to the marine unit to wait. Josie and Noah ran ahead to tell Mettner the news before he saw the body bag being carried out of the woods. He got out of his car as soon as he saw them. "You found her," he said, voice high-pitched. "She's—she's dead, isn't she?" He strode toward the stairs. "I have to see her. I have to see."

Noah put his body between Mettner and the stairs. "It's not her, Mett."

"I have to see."

Josie walked up beside him and touched his shoulder. "Mett, it's not Amber."

Still he struggled to get past Noah. In the light of the bobbing torches, Josie could see that he looked like a frightened animal. She had to shout at him to get his attention. He stopped trying to get around Noah and looked at her, seeing her but not understanding anything she said.

"The marine unit found a body," Josie said, clearly and loudly. "It's not Amber."

Mettner looked to Noah, as if he wanted an explanation for Josie's words. He wasn't comprehending. Noah nodded at him. "It's true. It's not her. It's not Amber."

Mettner pushed against Noah's chest with both hands. "You don't know that. Get out of my way. I need to see."

Josie joined Noah in blocking Mettner from the stairs, both of them standing firm each time Mettner pressed against them or tried to shoulder past. "We know what Amber looks like," she told him. "It's not her."

"People look different when they die. You know that! It could be her. You don't know her like I do. I'll know. I'll know if it's her. I need to see."

Noah grabbed Mettner's upper arms, holding him in place. "You cannot see her," he shouted.

Noah hardly ever raised his voice. In fact, Josie was hard-pressed to think of a time when he had. Mettner was just as startled as her. Tears leaked from his eyes. After a long moment, he said, "She's got a scar on her back. A burn scar. From when she was a kid. They were camping and she fell backward into the fire. It's big. You'll be able to see it."

Josie and Noah looked at one another. She said, "I'll go and look, okay, Mett? But you have to stay here with Noah."

He said nothing. Josie turned and jogged back down the stairs and then along the twisting path, the beam of her flashlight jerking with her movements. At the bottom, the two marine unit officers stood sentry over the body, one at the head and one at the feet. They watched her, faces hard. They were probably freezing, just like her, and ready to get off the riverbank. Chitwood said, "Well?"

Josie explained Mettner's request. Chitwood sighed heavily

and shook his head but gestured toward the body bag. "Go ahead," he said.

Gingerly, the two marine officers squatted down and unzipped the bag, handling the woman's body with care as they turned her onto her side and lifted the back of her shirt as high as it would go. Josie, Chitwood, and Gretchen all shone their torches onto the body. Her skin was pristine. Chitwood said, "Thank you."

The officers secured her back inside the bag. Josie ran back up the path and then the stairs to where Mettner waited, still blocked by Noah, but craning his neck over Noah's shoulder, his eyes wide and afraid. As soon as she locked eyes with him, she said, "No scar. It's not her."

Mettner dropped to his knees and wept. It was relief, Josie knew. There was still a chance that Amber was alive, still a chance that Mettner could be reunited with her, if only they could find her.

ELEVEN

They couldn't stop the press from getting video of the woman's body being loaded into one of the ambulances. The reporter lobbed questions at each of them as they got into their vehicles and drove away. Josie watched him punching fingers frantically against his phone screen as they left. He was probably trying to contact Amber. The knot in her stomach grew larger. While there was a palpable sense of relief among the team that the dead woman was not Amber, the fear that she would turn up dead next infected them all. Gretchen drove Mettner back to the police station while Josie and Noah returned to the hydro-electric plant to speak with the duty operator.

As they pulled up to the entrance, the gate slid open, barely making a sound other than a low whir. Noah parked next to the red pickup. As they got out, a door opened and closed at the front of the hydroelectric station building and a man emerged from the slice of light. He was tall and slender with shaggy, sandy hair and eyes that gleamed from beneath his ballcap. "You them cops?"

Noah fumbled inside his jeans pocket for his wallet and

produced his credentials, flashing them at the man. He pointed to Josie. "This is Detective Josie Quinn, my colleague."

"Still need her ID," said the man. "I gotta know who's coming in and out of here. We're not regulated by the federal government or anything so it's not like there's big, secret, classified stuff in this place, but I got supervisors at the power company I gotta answer to. Anything goes wrong, I'm gonna need to give 'em the names of everyone who came through."

He was covering his ass, Josie realized. Luckily, since this was her night off, she'd left her credentials in the car and they were unscathed by her plunge into the river. She pulled her identification and badge out of the back pocket of her jeans and handed it to him. The man studied it and then sighed. "Fine, then. Come on. My name's Will Wilson, by the way. My plant manager talked to your chief on the phone."

Wilson turned away from them, leading them to the door he'd emerged from. He held it open, and they entered a vast room with ceilings higher than Josie and Noah's two-story home. It seemed as though it was made entirely of steel beams and glass windows. Steel walkways led from one giant round generator to another. Josie counted three of the behemoths in total, which took up the majority of the space in the building. Each one was round with its own set of walkways leading to and around the top of it. From beneath them came the whir of the turbines and the hum of electricity which vibrated beneath their feet. Josie smelled a combination of different industrial lubricants and a faint hint of ozone.

It wasn't much warmer than outside, but it was an improvement, seeing as neither Josie nor Noah had their coats on. They followed Wilson down a set of gray steel steps to a concrete floor that she knew was below ground level. At the end of the building closest to the river was a door marked "Counting Room." Along the left-hand wall Josie saw more doors marked

"Restroom" and "Break Room." Lining the wall to their right was a number of tables which held a bank of computers.

"I'm the duty operator for the night shift here," Wilson said. "After your Chief called and talked to the plant manager, I went back and checked the tapes. I got a lot of video of all of you out by the control house tonight but nothing other than that. No one's tried to come to the station in the last few days. Only regular workers. Though there's never much activity in this area this time of year. Usually, everything's froze up, including the river, but even with the winter drawdown, all this rain has been a problem."

He sat down in his chair, the back of it creaking under his weight. He touched the mouse of the computer nearest his seat, bringing its screen to life. It showed several small gray boxes—video feed from various spots in and around the dam, including the gate they'd just driven through. Most of the cameras were surrounding the building—ensuring that no unauthorized personnel breached the perimeter of the hydroelectric station. A few cameras were positioned in the small parking area where they had come in. "I've been over these for the last two days, like your Chief asked, and like I said, there's nothing unusual—not over here by the power station."

Josie said, "Was there anything unusual out by the control house?"

Wilson clicked a few more times. The squares on the screen rearranged themselves and then one popped to the center of the screen, enlarged. Josie saw dirt, trees, and in the periphery, a chain-link fence, and she knew it was the one that surrounded the control house. The rest of the view was of the start of the path that cut through the trees on either side, mud flattened by foot traffic. Wilson clicked back to the early-morning hours. Monday. The daylight was just a hint of gray on the screen. The timestamp on the video read 4:49 a.m. Something flew into view, collapsing onto the path, and remaining there while the seconds ticked by. One, two, three, four.

"That's her," said Noah.

It was definitely a woman, dressed in dark clothes, with long wavy hair, but her face was turned away from them, in the direction of the river. She was on her knees, her head lolling and barely visible.

"Can you rewind that?" Josie asked.

Wilson clicked until the footage played again. The early light of morning crept onto the portion of the path that the control house camera did manage to capture. Then the woman flew into the frame, stumbling, and falling to her knees. She didn't move.

More seconds ticked by. Then a gloved hand reached into the camera's view and gripped her upper arm, dragging her out of the camera's eye. Still, the camera offered no view of her front.

"Don't know if that helps you," Wilson said. "Even in December we get hikers, dog walkers—all kinds of people—out walking around. I've been saying we should try to fence that side in, but no one will hear of it. This one is kinda strange though. This lady here who fell don't look like she's in great shape."

Josie said nothing.

"Is this all you've got?" asked Noah. "From that side of the dam?"

Wilson nodded, leaning back. His chair squeaked again. "Yep. Don't tell you much, does it? That camera don't show the full path but it's really only there to see if people are messing with the control house, so that's why they never move it. You get what you need?"

Noah said, "That's the only camera on that side? There aren't any along the stairs, the path, the bank, or the parking lot?"

Josie knew what he was getting at: whether or not there was footage of the other person, perhaps returning from the riverbank. Or footage of that person's vehicle.

Wilson kinked a brow at him. "Son, did you not just hear what I said? This is all I got."

Josie said, "Can we get a copy of that to take with us?"

"Sure thing," said Wilson. "Give me a minute."

While he queued up the footage and copied it to a flash drive, Josie asked, "Don't any of these cameras alert you if someone shows up on them?"

Wilson shook his head. "On that side of the dam? Only if someone breaches the control house. Other than that, it's not that kind of system. Like I said, that side of the river? There'd be alerts going off all damn day. We don't have time for that. Same over here. We only get alerts if any of the entry points to the power station are tampered with."

Noah said, "How long does your system keep the footage?"

"A week," Wilson said, handing Josie the flash drive.

Josie said, "Thank you. Does someone monitor these cameras on a regular basis?"

Wilson's chair squealed as he spun it around, gesturing to the space around him. "Does it look like we've got the staff to have someone on these cameras twenty-four hours a day?"

"What about the day shift?" Noah asked. "Business hours."

Wilson shook his head. "I'm here till seven and no one's monitoring while I'm here. Don't think day shift does either, but look here, even if someone was monitoring and saw what you got there in your hands—that's not an emergency by any stretch. You know how many hikers and kayakers and dog walkers fall down in the woods? Wouldn't nobody in this plant go running for something as silly as that."

Josie felt a quick flash of anger, thinking of the woman trapped in the rocks and then getting swept away by the raging river. But Wilson had no idea what Josie had witnessed in the water release chute. Plus, he was right. There was nothing particularly alarming about the video except that the woman seemed dazed. Even the gloved hand was not a red flag. It was December. In fact, Josie wished she hadn't thrown her own gloves into the river.

"Tell you what," Wilson conceded. "I'll ask the daytime duty operator about it, okay? How's that?"

"That's great," Josie said. "If you could also make us a list of all of the employees who worked in the last seventy-two hours, we'd appreciate it."

He let out a heavy sigh and shook his head, as if she was taking things a step too far, but then he reached behind his computer and came up with a notepad and pen and began scribbling names.

TWELVE

Josie and Noah kept the heater on full blast as they drove to Denton's police headquarters. The large three-story stone building loomed over them as they pulled into the municipal parking lot in the rear. In the dark of night, it was an intimidating edifice, but Josie loved the old building. It had been converted from the town hall into the police station almost seventy years ago. With its bell tower and ornate double-casement arched windows, it closely resembled a medieval castle. The inside could stand to be modernized, but since it was on the city's historical register, and the department would have to go through a lot of bureaucratic red tape to do so, Josie knew it would remain the same probably until she retired.

They trudged in through the back door together, taking the stairs up to the second floor which housed the Chief's office as well as the great room—a large open area filled with desks and filing cabinets where the investigative team convened and patrol officers came to do the endless, unglamorous paperwork that went with policing. Gretchen and Mettner were already there. Of the police officers, only Josie, Noah, Gretchen, and Mettner had permanent desks in the great room. The four desks were pushed together to form a large rectangle. Josie checked the time on her phone as she plopped down in her chair. It was after three a.m. In a few hours her own shift would start. She should be in bed with Trout's warm, snuggly little body pressed against her side, awaiting Noah's return. At least there were plenty of people for Trout to cuddle with at their house, and she was sure either Shannon or Trinity would take him out when they woke.

The only other person with a permanent desk was Amber. Hers was in the corner of the room, meticulously organized and brightly decorated, everything from her stapler to her paper tray in a matching white and teal striped pattern. She even had fancy, multicolored thumb tacks in the corkboard she'd had Mettner hang on the wall next to her desk. Josie walked over and studied the documents attached to the board, each one lined up perfectly in a neat row. Interdepartmental memos. A calendar of public outreach events the city council had issued. A police department directory with names, phone numbers, and email addresses. A flyer printed on bright green paper announcing the date and time of the holiday party. The only remotely personal item was a black letter board roughly the size of a sheet of paper with a thick wooden frame around it. The letters spelled out: "Create A Present Your Future Self Will Love."

Across the room, Mettner slouched in his chair, hands jammed into his jacket pockets. Chitwood had disappeared into his office, but Josie could hear him taking phone calls and by the sounds of the conversations, they were from the press. Gretchen went down to the first-floor break room to put coffee on.

"Why am I here if I'm suspended?" Mettner asked.

Noah took a seat and began booting up his computer. Josie knew there would be reports to write. "We need to know what you know."

"I told you guys everything I know. You don't need me now."

Josie scanned the surface of Amber's desk, but it was more of the same. A blotter in calendar form without a single note on it. Josie knew from working with Amber that she used an app on her tablet and phone to keep track of her schedule. Josie said, "If we tell you to go home, are you really going to go home?"

His head swiveled in Josie's direction, but he didn't answer. One of his eyelids twitched.

"Thought so," Josie said. "By the way, you're staying with Gretchen for at least the next forty-eight hours."

"You can't make me stay with Gretchen!" Mettner exclaimed.

Josie started opening the drawers of Amber's desk. The side drawers held nothing but office supplies. Pens, tape, printer paper, index cards, highlighters, a pair of earbuds. Josie had seen her wearing the earbuds from time to time while using her tablet. Amber was never without her tablet. Josie opened the center drawer to find it sealed inside a soft case that matched the rest of her office supplies. She took it out of the drawer, unzipped the case, and slid the tablet out.

"No," said Noah. "We can't make you stay with Gretchen. But we can strongly recommend it. You know you're in hot water here, Mett, right?"

"I don't care," Mettner said, voice almost rising to a shout. "I don't care about being in hot water or deep shit or whatever. I don't care what I did. I don't care about my job. I care about finding Amber. I need to know she's okay, don't you get that? Someone left a weird message on her car about Russell Haven. We go there and find some other woman who looks like her? And now she's dead? Amber's in trouble. I know it."

Josie held up the tablet. "Why is this here? I thought Amber always took it home with her."

Mettner glanced over. "She forgot it when she left work on

Friday. She said she was going to come back in on Saturday morning and get it but then we had our fight, and I didn't hear from her and . . . well, here we are. Obviously, she never made it in to get it. Anyway, who cares about her stupid tablet? I told you, she's in trouble. I have to do something. I need to help her."

Josie tried to power up the tablet, but it wouldn't come on. She found a charger inside the case and plugged it in. "You'll help her by answering our questions, that's how you'll help her. You'll help by not leaving here and going to her house and adding another count of breaking and entering to the list of shitty decisions you've made in the last twenty-four hours."

"Don't police-talk me," Mettner said, face screwing up in agitation. "I know how this works."

"All right, then," Noah interjected. "Let's get to work. We need you to fill in some blanks for us."

Josie's fingers felt the slim edge of something in the back of the middle drawer. Pinching it with her fingernails, she drew it out. It was a greeting card. A birthday card.

Mettner shifted in his chair, hands still deep in his jacket pockets. "Like what?"

Josie opened the card. The canned message was fairly generic, but the words Mettner had written at the bottom made her feel like some kind of voyeur. *I want to celebrate every birthday with you,* he had written. *I'll never stop loving you.*

Josie discreetly tucked it back into the drawer and closed it. She said, "Let's start with you and Amber. How long have you been dating?"

"Come on. You know this. You were all here."

"We know you two were dating, yeah," Noah said. "But we don't know anything more than that. How long?"

"A year. We just celebrated a year. But listen, what does this have to do with anything? This is not going to help you find her. We need to find her."

Josie checked the other drawers, then under the desk itself, including the contents of Amber's trash bin, but found nothing of interest. She checked the tablet, but it still didn't have enough charge to boot up. She made sure the plug was properly plugged into the wall, which it was, and as she stood back up and turned, her elbow caught the edge of the letter board, knocking it on its face.

"Be careful," Mettner said. "Those are her things."

"I'm sorry," said Josie. She picked up the frame. It was heavy in her hands. Unusually heavy. Josie set it back in place but then picked it up again and shook it. A muted knocking sound came from inside.

"What are you doing?" Mettner said.

Maybe Amber kept the other letters in the back of the frame and that's why it was so thick? Josie hadn't ever seen her change the message on the letter board but then again, she hadn't really paid that much attention to what Amber did at her desk. She placed it on its face again and flipped the small latches on the back of it, lifting the black backer board off. As she suspected, in a small baggie, there were several white letters. Under the baggie was something else. A bright yellow Post-it note in Amber's compulsively neat handwriting read: "Josie Q." It adhered to what looked like a young girl's diary. It was a small book with a plain, pink vinyl cover and a broken strap dangling from its side. A heart-shaped lock was still affixed to the front of it, no match for whatever had simply torn through the strap itself.

"What's that?" asked Noah.

"I don't know," said Josie. She ran her fingers over the Post-it. How many Josie Qs were there in the world? In Amber's world? Noah and Mettner stood beside her suddenly, staring down at it in her hands.

"Is that yours?" asked Mettner.

"No," said Josie. "It was in the back of this frame."

"Open it," Noah said.

Mettner put one hand on Josie's forearm. "Don't. What if it's private? She hid it for a reason, right?"

Josie looked into his eyes. "Mett," she said softly. "Right now nothing is private if it helps us find her."

Josie felt his hesitation in the heaviness of his palm. He eased it from her arm, his face a picture of conflict. With a sigh, he said, "Okay, open it then."

THIRTEEN

Josie opened the cover of the diary. On the first page was an ornately drawn box. Inside it, in faded pencil, was Amber's name. As Josie turned another page, the book nearly fell apart in her hands. Several pages fluttered to the floor and both Noah and Mettner scrambled to pick them up. They laid them out on Amber's desk, turning them onto one side and then the other, but all of them were blank. Josie put the book onto the desk's surface and carefully paged through what little remained inside the diary. Jagged edges of paper poked from the spine. One of the pages bore the ghostly imprint of words that had been written on the page right before it, which had obviously been torn out. Josie tried to make out the letters but couldn't. On one of the last pages, Amber had made a list of numbers. Josie counted the rows. There were eleven in all.

625800049595
112786009
900017623343
07b-32-004-01-111
334689006

99-16-03
175821451
99-23-46
04c-00-321-32-009
09a-66-127-19-131
900016528173

These, too, were in pencil and they were faded and smudged. "This is old," said Josie. "It has to be from when she was a kid or a teenager." She pointed to the list of numbers. "These mean anything to you, Mett?"

He stared at them for a long moment. "No."

Again, Noah picked up each page they had spread across her desk and looked at each side. "These are all blank."

"Every page is blank," Josie agreed. "Looks like the ones that she wrote on were torn out. Except the one with the numbers."

Noah fingered the open letter board frame. "Why would she hide this, though?"

Mettner reached across Josie and turned the cover over so the Post-it note was visible. "And why is your name on this?"

Josie said, "I have no idea."

Noah said, "What do those numbers mean? Do you recognize them, Josie?"

"No," said Josie. "They're not phone numbers or zip codes or social security numbers."

"Maybe bank account numbers?" Noah asked.

"I suppose they could be," Josie said. "Although some of them have letters in them. Do some banks put letters in their account numbers?"

"I'm not sure," Noah admitted.

"Maybe they're from different banks?" she suggested. "Or they could be something else entirely. We don't even know if this is relevant to her disappearance."

Mettner said, "Why would she want you to have this diary?"

Mystified, Josie continued to stare at the numbers. "I have no idea."

She and Amber had not been close. They had a solid professional relationship, but they didn't even see one another outside of work unless it was in a larger social setting like a wedding or the holiday party.

"But Amber didn't give it to Josie," Noah pointed out. "She kept it hidden here."

Josie muttered, "Why keep it at work, though? If it was something you wanted to hide, why not keep it at home? Amber lives alone. Mett, have you seen her with this before?"

He shook his head. "Not that I remember."

Noah asked, "Do you stay at her place a lot?"

"Sometimes," said Mettner. "But most of the time we're at my place."

"Why is that?" asked Josie.

Mettner glared at her. "How is this relevant?"

Josie put a hand on her hip. "If she always insisted on staying at your house because she was hiding something and that something led to her disappearance, then it's relevant to this investigation."

Noah said, "Mett, we're just trying to get a picture of her life, especially in the weeks leading up to yesterday. You two have a fight; she goes missing; someone who looks a hell of a lot like her turns up dead; there's some weird message on her car; and you've broken into her house. Now we find this strange blank kid's diary hidden on her desk at work, but you've never seen her with it. There's a Post-it with Josie's name, not yours. We have a lot of questions, Mett, and no answers. No good ones, anyway. We're just trying to figure out what the hell's going on here."

At his sides, Mettner's fists clenched. "You mean you're

trying to figure out if I killed her and buried her body somewhere and am now pretending that she disappeared?"

"Mettner," Josie said, gathering up the pages of the diary and tucking them back inside. "No one is saying that."

"But you're thinking it. You're all thinking it. I didn't do anything to Amber!" His voice rose to a shout. One of his fists slammed down on Amber's desk.

Josie closed the diary and tucked it under one arm. Unflinching, she met his glower. "No one said you did, Mett. We just want to talk."

He pointed a finger at her. "You think I don't see what you're doing? I know how you operate. I've seen you in the interrogation room dozens of times. You're manipulating me."

"I'm asking questions," Josie said.

"Calm down, Mett," Noah said, his voice low but tinged with a warning. He took a step, angling his body so that he was between Mettner and Josie. "After the shit you pulled today, you're lucky you're not in an interrogation room, but we can do it that way if you want. Is that what you want?"

A long, tense moment crept past. Josie heard the tick, tick, tick of the wall clock over the stairwell door. Finally, Mettner's posture relaxed. He turned away from them and stalked back to his chair, plopping down into it. He stuffed his hands into his pockets. Josie took the diary to her desk and sat down. With her phone, she took photos of the diary and the list of numbers while Mettner stared over her head.

She said, "You said you two were planning a future. What do you mean by that?"

Another moment of silence. Josie wasn't sure he was even going to answer. The second hand of the clock ticked onward. Mettner met her eyes long enough to purse his lips and flash her a nasty look. This was another of her techniques. Saying nothing. She stayed relaxed, like she had all the time in the world.

Easy silence. Most people scrambled to fill it. Mettner knew that. He also knew that Josie would wait as long as it took.

"Fine," he said. "I had asked her to move in with me. She said yes. This was last month. But we had to wait because she rents her house, and she couldn't get out of the lease early. But we were starting to go through my things, throw out some stuff, make room for when she came. Not that she had much."

"You were going to move in together, but you don't have a key to her house?" Noah asked. "Did she have a key to your place?"

"Yeah, she did—she does. I don't have one to her place 'cause like I said, it's a rental, and she said the landlord won't allow it."

Josie knew there wasn't anything stopping Amber from making Mettner a key anyway, but she didn't mention that. "Was she excited to move in?"

A hint of a smile flickered across Mettner's face. "Yeah, we both were. We are."

"But you said you'd gotten into a fight. A fight so bad that she stopped taking your calls," Josie said. "What happened?"

His face closed up. That was the only way she could describe it. He shut down completely. "What happened is that we had an argument. Like all couples do."

"About what?" asked Noah.

Mettner didn't look at him. "Private stuff."

"Mett," Josie said.

"It's not relevant," he argued. "Trust me. It's not. It has nothing to do with this investigation."

"You don't know that," Noah said.

Mettner's hands came back out, gripping the edge of his desk now until his knuckles turned white. "Yes. I do. I do this job too, remember? Why are you treating me like an idiot? Why can't you just trust me? Nothing that we argued about has anything to do with Amber disappearing or the woman in the river."

The stairwell door slammed. They looked up to see Gretchen carrying a tray with four mugs of steaming coffee on it. She pulled up short next to the desks, looking at each of them with one brow raised. Josie knew she could sense the tension. "What's going on?" she asked, putting the tray on Josie's desk. No one spoke.

"Okay," Gretchen said. She turned to Josie. "You ask him about the sister?"

"We're getting there," Noah said.

"What are you talking about?" Mettner said.

Josie took a coffee mug from the tray Gretchen held and handed it to Mettner. After having worked together for so long, Josie could tell by the precise hue of the coffee which mug belonged to whom. Gretchen distributed the other mugs.

Josie replied, "The woman in the river. We think it might be Amber's sister."

"Because of her hair?" Mettner asked.

Gretchen sat at her desk and sipped her coffee. "There's a resemblance, Mett. What can you tell us about her sister?"

"Nothing," he said. "Amber never talked about her family. I don't even know her sister's name."

Josie put her coffee onto her desk and nudged her computer mouse, bringing the screen to life. "Never talked about them, or refused to talk about them?" she asked.

Mettner took a moment to consider this and then said, "She refused."

Josie pulled up one of their databases and typed in Amber's name and her address. Josie found results immediately but no known associates. "She never told you any names," Josie asked. "Parents? Siblings? Anyone?"

Mettner shook his head. "No."

The database showed a woman who had entered the world

at age eighteen completely alone. There was a driver's license, several addresses, most of them in the town in which she had gone to college. Utilities in her name, a car, a couple of former employers. That was it. "Was she in foster care?" Josie asked.

"I don't think so," said Mettner.

Josie looked up Amber's surname, Watts, in the database. There were far too many people with that last name in the Commonwealth of Pennsylvania for their department to track down, and that was assuming Amber had grown up there.

Noah said, "Did she ever tell you any stories about her childhood?"

"No. She hated talking about that stuff. She only said she moved around a lot."

"Do you know where she was born? Was it here in Pennsylvania?"

"I don't know," Mettner said.

With a sigh, Josie closed out the database. "I need you to get in touch with her friend. What did you say her name was?"

"Grace Power."

"Yes," Josie said. "Go home with Gretchen. Grab a few hours of sleep and in the morning, Gretchen can track Grace down and talk with her while Noah and I meet with Dr. Feist. It can't be a coincidence that we found a message leading us to Russell Haven on Amber's car and then we find a woman who looks almost identical to her. If this is Amber's sister, then someone from their family is going to have to identify the body and claim it."

FOURTEEN

Josie and Noah finished up their reports and went home to try to catch a few hours of sleep, much to Trout's delight. They took a hot shower together and Noah fell instantly to sleep the moment his head hit the pillow. Every time Josie started to drift off, she felt the woman's fingers on her wrist. That final touch. When she finally fell asleep, she dreamt of her grandmother. She'd had nightmares nearly every night since Lisette's murder. They were always the same: a dream-memory of the night she died, Josie unable to save her. This time, Lisette was trapped between the boulders at the Russell Haven Dam. Josie tried to save her before the water descended on them, but there was no chance. She woke gasping for breath, Trout licking her face and whimpering worriedly.

Knowing she wouldn't be able to sleep restfully, she went downstairs and booted up her computer. She pulled up the photos of the numbers that Amber had written in her diary. Trout snoozed at her feet, opting to keep her company rather than stay in bed with Noah. He must have sensed her agitation. He usually did. Josie started by entering each number into Google but got nothing. She counted up the digits in each number, making lists and charts to try to find some pattern. She made a list of possible formats the numbers could correspond with. Bank accounts were at the top of that list, but it would be impossible to ask each bank in the country to search their records for each number. Even if she wanted to do that, Josie would need a warrant and there wasn't enough connecting the mysterious numbers to either Jane Doe's death or Amber's disappearance to get one.

By the time Noah appeared in the kitchen, freshly showered, sunlight streamed through the windows. "Hey," he said. "Did you get any sleep at all?"

"A couple of hours," Josie sighed. She checked the time. They were due to meet Dr. Feist at the city morgue in less than an hour.

Thirty minutes later, Josie and Noah were back in his car headed to Denton Memorial Hospital. The large brick building sat atop a rock-strewn hill overlooking the city. As they turned up the long road to the parking lot, Noah changed the radio station again and again, but they were all playing the morning news, and it was all about the unidentified woman who had been pulled from the river near Russell Haven in the middle of the night. "Police are describing her as a Caucasian female in her mid-twenties, about five foot four, one hundred thirty pounds, long auburn hair and blue eyes. If anyone has any information, please contact Denton Police Department."

Noah turned the radio off. "Guess the Chief gave them the description. Maybe we'll get some leads."

They parked and made their way inside. The morgue was located in the windowless basement of Denton Memorial Hospital. The hallway leading to the suite of rooms presided over by Dr. Feist was dreary. Its walls were grimy with age and dirt, and its once-white tile floors were now a sickly jaundiced yellow. As always, the entire floor was eerily silent. Dr. Feist stood at the stainless-steel counter that lined one of the exam room walls, tapping away at her laptop. She wore blue scrubs. Her silver-blonde hair was tucked into a skullcap. Josie's stomach churned at the smell of chemicals and decomposition. She'd been in this room countless times, but the smell never failed to jar her. Dr. Feist looked up as they walked in, offering a thin smile. Dark circles smudged the pale skin under her eyes.

Noah walked over and handed her a coffee which turned her smile much wider. "We know you've been up all night."

"Thank you," she replied. "I was already here on another case for the county sheriff. Figured I'd just make a night of it."

Josie looked over to the exam tables. Only one of them held a body, covered in a white sheet. She could see auburn curls peeking out from under it.

"That's your Jane Doe," Dr. Feist said. She took a swig of coffee and set the cup down next to her laptop, walking over to the exam table. "You have any idea who she is?"

"No," Josie said. "We think she could be Amber's sister but without next of kin to identify her, we can't say for sure."

"No word on Amber?" asked Dr. Feist.

"Nothing yet," Noah said.

Dr. Feist sighed and folded the sheet down to Jane Doe's shoulders. Here, in the stark and unforgiving light of the autopsy room, the woman looked much paler, her skin waxy now, the large lump on her temple a starker purple than the last time Josie saw it.

"Your Jane Doe was brought in wearing a pair of jeans, bra, panties, and a long-sleeved cotton T-shirt with no markings on it. Plain, white cotton socks. One sneaker. She likely lost the other one in the river. No coat, gloves or winter hat. I had Officer Hummel from your Evidence Response Team come over and take her clothes into evidence, but we didn't find anything that would help us identify her. She appears to be a very healthy twenty-something. No underlying conditions that are evident on exam or autopsy. No scars, no birthmarks, no tattoos. No signs of sexual assault. Cause of death is drowning. Typically, a diagnosis of drowning can be given once every other possibility has been excluded. Since this woman was pulled from the water, and since I was told that one of you confirmed that she was alive before she was swept away, it was a pretty sure bet that she drowned. Nevertheless, I did a full exam and autopsy. As I would expect, I did find froth in her upper and lower airways; fluid in her sphenoid sinus as well as emphysema aquosum."

Noah said, "What's that?"

Josie put in, "It means that her lungs were overinflated and waterlogged."

"Basically, yes," Dr. Feist confirmed. "As is also typical in certain drowning cases, there were indentations of her ribs on her lungs as well as Paltauf's spots, which are subpleural hemorrhages, on the surface and margins of her lungs. I did a test to see if she had diatoms in the fluid found in her lungs, but the results of that will take a couple of days."

Noah said, "You mean you're testing to see if she took in algae from the river?"

"That's a gross oversimplification but for our purposes, yes. Diatoms are a group of algae. Single-celled organisms. They can usually be found in the tissue or organs of victims who have aspirated diatom-rich water. It's a very effective tool for determining drowning as a cause of death. I took tissue samples from her brain, liver, and kidneys to forward to the lab as well. If she was still alive when she aspirated, we would expect to see diatoms in the tissue samples because they would have circulated through her body. If she was already dead when the water entered her lungs, then diatoms will not be present in the tissue samples, only in the lung fluid. I also sent out samples for toxicology but as you are aware, those results take weeks."

"We're confident in your assessment that this woman

drowned," Josie said. "Did you find anything else we should know about?"

"Actually, there are some other significant findings. First of all, it looks as though she was beaten recently. She's got healing bruises on her arms, legs, and torso. As you may know, bruising takes place as a result of force. Small blood vessels burst and the blood pools beneath the skin. In the first day or two, the bruise would be red. After one to two days, that blood begins to lose oxygen, causing the skin to change color to black, blue or purple. Beyond that, as the body produces biliverdin and bilirubin to break down hemoglobin, the bruise turns a green or yellow. That stage takes place about five to ten days after the initial injury. At ten to fourteen days after that first bruising, you would see a yellowish-brown or light brown. She's got bruises ranging from purple to yellow-brown all over her body."

"If they're in various stages of healing," Josie said. "Then she was beaten more than once in the last two weeks."

"I believe so," Dr. Feist said. "The pattern of abuse here is consistent with her having been beaten more than once in recent days or weeks."

"But you can't say for certain?" Noah asked.

Dr. Feist frowned. "I can't tell you with certainty how old these injuries are because bruising, as well as any injury, really, depends on a lot of factors."

"Like what?" Noah prodded.

"This woman's clotting factor, health factors, whether or not she was anemic. Any number of things."

"You can't tell those things from the autopsy?" said Noah.

"I'm afraid not. Think of it this way." She pointed to the corner of the autopsy table. "My assistant, Ramon, and I both occasionally bump our hips into this corner. I bruise but he does not. It's the same variation as you would see among people who fall. Children, for example. One child might take a spill off the end of a sliding board, hop up, and be just fine. Another child might have the same exact fall but sustain serious injuries. Every person is different. As you know, if I ever had to testify in court to my findings on this autopsy, I would not be able to testify with certainty as to the timing of any of these bruises."

Noah made a noise of frustration in his throat. "But you just gave us that whole rundown of the stages of bruising."

Dr. Feist nodded. "Yes. What I can tell you is that her injuries are consistent with her having sustained these bruises sometime in the last two weeks. Also, she has a broken rib that is only just beginning to heal, and some healing cuts inside her cheeks that are consistent with her being slapped or possibly punched in the face multiple times. Also, this cheekbone," Dr. Feist pointed to the woman's left cheek, "has a fracture that is beginning to heal, which leads me to believe all of the injuries were inflicted antemortem."

"Before death?" Noah asked. "How can you tell how old they are?"

Dr. Feist waved them over to the stainless-steel countertop where her laptop sat. She pulled up a set of x-rays marked "Jane Doe." The first one she enlarged was a rib cage. "Here," she said, pointing to what looked like a thin vertical line cutting through one of the ribs. "See how there it looks like there's almost a cloud around it? That's called callus. When a bone breaks, there is a lot of inflammation and usually a blood clot forms at the site. After about a week, a callus begins to form, bridging the fracture. It's just made up of fibrous tissue and cartilage. Sometimes it's observable on x-rays as early as a week after the break but sometimes not. If it were an older fracture, I would expect to see more calcification. Same with the cheekbone." She closed out the rib x-ray and pulled up one of Jane Doe's face, repeating her findings. "In terms of the cuts inside her cheeks, there is evidence of clotting which would not happen had she been dead. I did find some cuts on her body and a few fractures which appear to have happened postmortem, probably as a result of her body being swept downriver and coming into contact with rocks and other debris."

"The lump on her temple," said Josie. "Can you tell how long ago that occurred?"

Dr. Feist returned to the body and pointed to Jane Doe's head with a gloved finger. Josie was grateful that she had arranged the hair so that they could not see the saw line where the skull had been removed for examination of the brain. "Again, I can't give you an exact time but its appearance is consistent with an injury that occurred sometime within the twenty-four hours before her death. I know it did not happen postmortem because she had to have been alive for the blood to settle here and cause the lump in the first place. Internally, she had an acute subdural hematoma which would have accounted for why she was in a weakened and probably disoriented state when you found her."

Josie asked, "Any idea what caused it?"

"Unfortunately, no. She could have fallen or someone could have hit her with a blunt object. Often when victims are struck with an object, we see patterned injuries, meaning that the object causing the injury is sometimes reproduced on the skin. However, here there are no marks definitive enough to tell me what caused the bruising or the hematoma. That doesn't mean she wasn't hit with a blunt object, just that if she was, we have no way of guessing the object. However..."

Pausing, Dr. Feist stepped toward Jane Doe's waist and carefully uncovered one of her arms. Josie immediately saw one of the significant findings Dr. Feist wanted them to note. Circling Jane Doe's wrist were a number of ugly red and purple abrasions and in some spots, slices where something straight-edged had cut into her flesh. Angry red slashes in a bed of purple bruises. "These are very fresh," said Dr. Feist, "but over-laid onto older ones—and when I say older, I mean only a few days or possibly a week or two."

Noah said, "You mean they're consistent with abrasions caused a few days or possibly a week or two ago."

Dr. Feist smiled. "You're getting the hang of this now."

"She was bound," Noah said. "What would do that? Zip ties?"

Dr. Feist nodded. "I believe so, yes." She moved to the other side of the table and uncovered Jane Doe's other arm which looked equally brutalized. "Clearly, she struggled to get out of them not long before she died. Otherwise, we would not see so much damage to the tissue. Some of these abrasions are quite deep. Also, if you look here—" she lifted Jane Doe's arm so that they could see the outside of her wrist, on the pinky finger side, where long, bright red abrasions went from the zip tie marks almost to her elbow. "It looks like she tried to get them off herself by rubbing them against something. Both arms look like this."

"Could she have tried scraping them against the boulders?" Josie asked. "She was lodged between two large boulders when we found her. If she'd been restrained, that would explain why she didn't simply climb out."

"Yes," Dr. Feist said. "I was able to get some of the dirt and debris that had become embedded in her skin from these injuries. I'm sending the samples to the state police lab for analysis but knowing what I know about the area, I would not be surprised if the results came back as consistent with soil samples which Hummel will take from the river."

Noah moved to the bottom of the table and used his coffee cup to motion toward Jane Doe's feet. "Were her legs restrained as well?"

Dr. Feist nodded and joined him at the foot of the table. With great care, she folded the sheet up to Jane Doe's knees. There were some bruises and abrasions on her shins, but they weren't severe. Her ankles, however, showed several angry red rings where the skin had been rubbed away. Her toenails were painted bright pink. "These don't look as fresh as the ones on her wrists. You can see that they definitely did not cause the types of deep abrasions you see on her wrists. It looks like she scraped or banged her shins sometime in the hours before her death, but I can't say for sure whether or not her feet were bound while she was in the river."

Noah said, "The river is powerful, but would it break zip ties on someone's ankles?"

"I'm not sure if there is any way to know that," Josie said.

Dr. Feist agreed. "I think all we can say with certainty is that within the last days or possibly weeks before her death, this woman was bound both hand and foot with what appears to have been zip ties."

Noah frowned. "She was walking on the path to the riverbank. We have her on video. She fell but there was no indication that her feet were bound. If her legs weren't bound, she should have been able to climb out from the rocks," Noah said. "Don't you think?"

Dr. Feist grimaced. "I haven't seen the rocks you're talking about, so I don't know. What I can tell you is that she was out there for a long time. You didn't notice her fingers, did you?"

Josie and Noah shook their heads. Dr. Feist stepped around to one of Jane Doe's still-exposed hands and lifted it in the air so they could see. As Josie stepped closer, the unnatural pink coloring of the dead woman's fingers came into greater focus. It looked like she had put her fingers into scalding water up to the second knuckle.

"Frostbite," Josie said.

"Yes," agreed Dr. Feist.

"It was only just below freezing yesterday," Noah said. "Is frostbite even possible at twenty-five to thirty degrees?"

"With the wind chill making the 'feels like' temperature outside far lower than that, it's possible. It would depend on the wind speed and how long she was exposed. If she was out in the dam area for several hours trying to break free from her restraints with a high wind speed and a 'feels like' temperature well below freezing then yes, this case of frostbite is certainly possible."

Josie ran through the scenario in her head: this woman arrived at the Russell Haven Dam at almost five a.m., possibly meeting someone but more likely, having been brought there by someone. Then her attacker left her hands restrained and somehow placed her between the boulders? They would have had to force her to walk out to where the boulders were; she wasn't sure it was possible to carry a grown woman, even a slight one, across the chute to those boulders and deposit her there.

Noah said, "The frostbite wouldn't prevent her from getting free."

"No," said Dr. Feist. "But if she was out there all day trying to break free, she would have gotten frostbite."

"She wasn't restrained when we got to her," Josie said. "She raised one hand in the air. That's how I knew she was alive. But even with the water making her buoyant, I had a very difficult time getting her dislodged from the boulders. Is it possible she was trapped there, managed to get the zip ties off but then still couldn't get out from between the stones?"

"Again, I can't theorize without having seen the location where you found her, but I can definitively say that the broken rib would have severely limited her mobility and the head injury would have made her weak and disoriented. She likely lost consciousness at some point. Whether that was before she came to be between the rocks or sometime after that, I can't say for certain. However, her coordination might not have been very good after the head injury, particularly once the subdural hematoma began to grow, putting pressure on her brain."

Josie asked, "Would the head injury have killed her? If she hadn't drowned?"

Dr. Feist touched the top of Jane Doe's hand, staring down

at her face. "It's difficult to say. Again, it depends on her individual factors."

Josie thought of how dazed she had seemed in the security camera footage when she fell on the path, how the hand had reached in from off-camera and dragged her off as though she were a ragdoll. Had she been too out of it to put up a proper fight? Had her attacker been able to march her out to the boulders with little resistance?

Noah said, "What about her manner of death?"

Dr. Feist looked back up at them. "Most of the time with a drowning death, unless we have very solid evidence to suggest that another person caused the victim to drown, we have to list the manner of death as accidental."

"Not homicide?" Josie said. "Someone put her into that water release chute, between those boulders, with the intention of her being stuck there when the water was released."

"It's sadistic," Noah added. "You can't possibly believe that she wandered out to those rocks on her own with that goose egg on her head, a cracked rib, and all the bruises and abrasions she sustained. We know someone was with her. We have video of someone helping her up from a fall on the path to the riverbank."

"It's not about what we believe," Josie muttered. "It's about what we can prove. We can't prove that someone put her between those rocks."

Dr. Feist held up both hands to silence them. "Let me finish. You're right. It is about what we can prove and what I think will withstand the cross-examination of a defense attorney in court, should you find the person who did this and bring them to trial. In this particular case, given my belief that she was not physically able to extricate herself from the chute due to her antemortem injuries, I will rule this as a homicide."

Josie couldn't help but think of the fear that must have seized Jane Doe, knowing that at any moment the water would crash down on her but that she was unable to escape. "Thank you," she whispered.

Dr. Feist tucked Jane Doe's arm back under the sheet. "Now, why don't the two of you work on your end of this investigation and find the person who tortured and killed this woman."

"Gladly," Noah said. "Doc, is there anything else you can tell us that might help us figure out who this woman is or who tried to kill her?"

"I wish there was. Hummel took her fingerprints while he was here. He called to tell me he had run them through AFIS but didn't get any hits. Until you figure out who she is and get her next of kin to claim her body, she'll stay here with me."

"We'll be working on that today," Josie promised.

FIFTEEN

Josie and Noah parked in the municipal lot behind police head-quarters. Josie left Noah there and walked to Komorrah's Koffee which was only a block away. She would never make it through this day without copious amounts of caffeine. Noah had given her one of his old winter coats to wear until she bought a new one for herself. It was large on her, and the freezing December air flew up beneath it, chilling her torso. The warm air pressing in from all sides inside the café was a relief, as was the realiza-tion that the line wasn't very long—only two people ahead of her. The scents of coffee and pastries filled her nose. Her stomach gave an enthusiastic growl. The man in front of her turned and offered her a bemused smile from beneath his base-ball cap. Josie felt a jolt of familiarity but she wasn't sure why. She didn't know him. He was older, probably in his sixties, with salt-and-pepper stubble lining his sharp jaw and white hair curling from under his green Philadelphia Eagles hat.

"Rough morning," Josie mumbled.

She looked up at the television playing in the corner of the room. On WYEP, the reporter they had seen last night stood in the Russell Haven Dam parking lot, giving a report on the body recovered from the river. The news cut back to its national morning show. Thatcher Toland's face filled the screen. He sat in a chair across from one of the network's morning show co-hosts. Wearing a navy sweater over a collared shirt, tan slacks, and brown dress shoes, he looked relaxed, at home in front of the camera. Thick, wavy gray hair covered his head. Blue eyes sparkled as he talked. Josie knew from the extensive press he had been getting that he was in his early sixties, but the lines around his mouth and eyes only served to make him look more handsome.

"Your ministry has exploded in the last year," said the news anchor. "What do you think it is about your message that has resonated with so many people?"

Toland smiled. "It's God! I owe all of this worldly success to God. I'm just the vessel he uses to convey his message. To answer your question, that message is very simple: faith is there for all of us. It's waiting for us to open our eyes to it."

The anchor gave a practiced smile. "You've often said that a person can change their lives by 'waking up' to faith in God. What do you mean by that?"

Toland's expression grew earnest. He scooted to the edge of his chair a little, resting his elbows on his knees and staring at the anchor intensely. "When you embrace faith in God, you surrender to him. It takes a great burden from you. Opening your eyes to what God offers means relieving yourself of the burden of our earthly existence. When you wake up to your faith, you begin to see the damage you've done to others throughout your life."

"Yes," agreed the anchor. "I've heard you say often that the most important thing a person can do is make up for the wrongs they've committed."

"I believe that wholeheartedly. When you begin to take responsibility, to hold yourself accountable for the sins you've committed, God will set you on the path of atonement. You need only follow. Even the worst of us can be reformed in God's eyes if we do this."

"Next!" called the barista.

Josie's eyes jerked away from the television. The man in front of her stepped up and gave his order. The barista tapped away on the tablet that served as a register as he spoke. Then she asked for his name, and he hesitated. "Uh, um, it's..." His uncertainty made her look up at him. She stared at him, then looked at the television screen, and back to him.

"Oh my God," she said. "You're that famous preacher, aren't you?"

He waved both hands in the air. "No, no."

"You are! That's you on TV!" She pointed to the screen where Toland was now talking about how to use faith to reform your life. "My mom read your book!"

From behind him, Josie could see his posture stiffen beneath his tan utility coat. "No," he said. "I'm sorry. You're mistaken. My name is John. Just put John on there, would you?"

Josie looked down at his feet and saw brand-new boots over the top of pressed jeans. This was a guy trying to blend in as an average Joe in Central Pennsylvania. Given his attire, he could be a hunter, some kind of laborer, a skilled tradesman, or even a truck driver. He was dressed for warmth, comfort, and to protect his feet from getting wet or injured. Except the look was not natural for him. He looked like he was wearing someone else's clothes.

"You can tell me," said the barista in a conspiratorial tone.

Josie stepped up beside him. "You're talking about Thatcher Toland, aren't you?"

"That's it!" exclaimed the woman.

Josie looked up into the man's now-pink face. Giving him a wink, she turned back to the barista. "This isn't him."

The woman raised a brow. "What? Are you sure?"

"I'm sure. What would Thatcher Toland be doing here? He's on the television being interviewed."

Lines appeared on the woman's forehead. "It could be prerecorded, you know. They do that on TV."

Josie smiled tightly. "Well, my sister told me he had an interview with her network's morning show this morning in New York City, and there he is on television, so I'm pretty sure this is live."

Distracted by the mention of her sister and the network, the woman asked, "You're Josie Quinn, aren't you?"

"You're new," replied Josie.

She gave a weak smile. "Sorry. But they left me a note about what you guys usually get. Anyway, I'm sorry, Mr., uh, John. Your order will be right up."

She left the counter to make his drink. In a barely audible whisper, Thatcher Toland leaned over and said, "Thank you, Miss Quinn."

"Detective Quinn," she responded.

He gave a half-smile. "Detective? Impressive."

Josie shrugged. "Is there a reason you don't want to be recognized?"

The barista returned with his drink. He handed her a fifty-dollar bill. "This is for mine as well as whatever the detective would like. You keep the change."

She stared at the bill for a beat and then looked back at him. "Are you sure?"

"My pleasure," he replied.

She looked to Josie for approval. Josie didn't really want Thatcher Toland paying for her coffee—she didn't even know him, and she was naturally suspicious of random acts of kindness given what she saw on the job each day—but she didn't want to cause a scene. "Sure," she told the barista.

"I'll be right back."

With that, the woman snagged a piece of notepaper from

the other side of the register and went off to make more drinks.

"It's silly," said Thatcher. He studied her. "The reason I prefer not to be recognized. Your sister. She's Trinity Payne, isn't she?"

"Yes," said Josie.

"Then you must know what she deals with. The price of fame."

Before she could stop it, a laugh erupted from her throat. "Trinity is a reporter. A journalist. It's not quite the same level of fame. I've seen your face a half-dozen times in the last twenty-four hours and not by choice. Not including right now."

His gentle smile didn't waver. "I just wanted a blond vanilla latte. My wife, bless her, likes to coordinate and orchestrate every public appearance, no matter how small. She would be horrified if I was recognized getting my own latte."

"That sounds restrictive."

He sipped his latte, letting out a low moan of pleasure. "Vivian has almost single-handedly turned me from a pastor of a church with a congregation of only forty into a famed public figure with thousands of congregants. The more people who join me on my journey to God, the more good I can do in this world. When she talks, I listen."

Josie thought of the multimillion deal the Tolands had closed on the old hockey arena nearby. She suppressed an eye-roll.

He said, "You think it's only about the money."

"I didn't say that."

"But you're thinking it."

"John," said Josie, using his fake name. "Unless you've killed, kidnapped, assaulted, or robbed a citizen of my city, it's really none of my business what you do or why."

He gave a full-throated laugh, and in spite of herself, Josie liked the sound of it. His delight was genuine. "I can assure you I've done none of those things," he told her. "You seem..."

He trailed off and the moment stretched between them.

"Impatient?" Josie suggested. "Bitter? Jaded? Brash? Abrupt?"

Again, he laughed. "No illusions, huh? I like that, Detective. However, what I was going to say is that you seem as though you're carrying a great burden."

Here it comes, she thought. This guy is going to try to get me to join his giant church. "Isn't everyone?" she said.

"I suppose, but some burdens are greater than others. Yours is made of guilt, though."

Immediately, Josie thought of her grandmother. Months of therapy had not disabused her of the notion that Lisette's murder was her fault. He was right, and she could see by his warm and easy manner how it would be effortless to talk to him. She could see how people might reveal their innermost secrets to him, but Josie's deepest, darkest thoughts were more carefully guarded than the nation's nuclear codes, and the last time she'd met a person as intuitive and charismatic as Thatcher Toland, that person had turned out to be a murderous cult leader with a gaggle of murderous followers.

Thatcher said, "My ministry is based around unburdening, you know. Guilt is the heaviest thing we can bear. Even heavier than grief, I believe. But when we wake up to our faith, we're able to give all of our burdens to God and in doing so, we're set free. Don't you want to be set free?"

"I want coffee, John. I just want coffee."

"Here you go," said the barista brightly. She pushed a cupholder with four paper cups in it toward Josie, along with a brown bag of pastries. Four cups. For Josie, Noah, Gretchen, and Mettner. Except Mettner wasn't on this case because he was suspected of involvement in his girlfriend's disappearance.

With a sigh, Josie scooped up the cupholder and gave Thatcher Toland one last look. "If you pray today, ask God to help us find the killer we're looking for, would you?"

SIXTEEN

Back at the station, Gretchen was hunched over her desk, typing at her keyboard. Noah was at his desk, riffling through a stack of paperwork. Josie set the coffees and pastries from Komorrah's on her desk and started handing out cups. Gretchen's reading glasses teetered on the end of her nose, and when she took her cup, Josie noted the large bags under her eyes.

"Did you sleep at all?" Josie asked.

"What do you think?" Gretchen said flatly.

"Where's Mett?" Josie asked.

"At my place. Passed out, finally. Paula's home, so she'll keep an eye on him, let me know if he leaves. Wouldn't tell me shit, by the way."

"You mean about the fight he had with Amber?" Josie said.

"Yeah. Makes me nervous wondering what he's hiding."

Josie said, "Did Noah tell you about the autopsy?"

"Yeah," Gretchen said. She took a sip of her coffee and then resumed typing. "The Chief released a description of our Jane Doe to the press. He's hoping that someone will come forward."

"We heard on the radio," Josie said. "And I just saw the

report on television. He doesn't want to go public with the fact that Amber is missing yet?"

Gretchen shook her head. "And invite all the unwanted press that comes with the police liaison vanishing? No. Not at this point. Especially since we cannot connect the murder of Jane Doe to the fact that Amber is missing. All we have right now are theories, no hard evidence. None that we can present to the press, anyway. The Chief wants the Russell Haven windshield message and Jane Doe's resemblance to Amber withheld from the press. He doesn't want to have reporters asking questions about whether or not the two are connected until we know more. He said to keep the Amber thing quiet for now, and focus on finding out what we can about our Jane Doe. I've also got two uniformed officers tracking down all the power station employees to check them out. They'll let me know if they find any red flags. Noah tells me you were up half the night trying to figure out the numbers in Amber's diary. You get anywhere?"

Josie plopped into her desk chair. "None. I can't figure out what they're for or what they mean or why they'd be in some diary that Amber had when she was a kid. The best I can come up with is that they're possibly bank account numbers."

"But even to access Amber's bank account numbers, we'd need a warrant, which we can't get right now," Gretchen said. "Unless we can connect those numbers to her disappearance or Jane Doe's murder in some way."

Noah said, "We don't even know if they're relevant at all to either case. They were hidden, which is strange, but I'm not sure how we make a connection between the numbers—or even her childhood diary—to the two cases at hand."

"I'll keep trying to figure them out," said Josie. "How about it, Gretchen? Any luck with Amber's friend? Grace Power?"

Gretchen stopped typing. "As a matter of fact, yes. I spoke with Grace about an hour ago. She should be here soon. Driving from Lewisburg. Also, I checked with HR to find out who

Amber listed as her emergency contact, and they're going to help one of us get into her work tablet later today. They couldn't give me her password because she set it herself, but someone from over there will call later and walk one of us through resetting it so we can access it."

"That's great," said Noah. "Who is the emergency contact?"

"Grace?" Josie asked.

"It used to be," Gretchen said. "A month ago, Amber changed her emergency contact from Grace Power to Finn Mettner."

"Things were getting as serious as Mett said," Noah noted.

"But she didn't give him a key to her place," Josie put in.

"You don't buy the landlord thing?" Gretchen asked.

"What? That her landlord forbade her from giving anyone else a key?" Josie scoffed. "Even if the landlord did, there is nothing stopping her from making an extra key and giving it to someone. It's not like the landlord would be able to police that in any way."

"Right," said Noah. "Before I bought my house I lived in an apartment in South Denton. Same thing—I wasn't supposed to give anyone else keys, but my mom and my ex each had one."

"What was she hiding?" Gretchen said. "What was she keeping from Mett that she was planning a future with him but wouldn't give him a key?"

But the question wasn't meant to be answered. They didn't know. Everything at this point in the investigation was speculation. Josie looked at her desk, where the mysterious diary sat with its shiny gold heart clasp, its broken strap, missing pages, and list of unusual numbers. Noah added a few more questions for them to consider. "If that's Amber's sister and she went to Russell Haven at five a.m. yesterday as per the message on Amber's vehicle—"

"She didn't go there," Josie cut in. "Someone took her there against her will."

Noah nodded. "If someone took her there, then where is Amber and why was the message left on her car? How did she disappear from her home without her car or any personal belongings or anyone even seeing anything?"

"The batteries in her front door surveillance camera were missing," Josie said. "That's what Mett told me. Plus, we don't know that no one saw anything. We haven't canvassed her street."

"Because she's a grown woman and grown women are allowed to disappear if they choose to do so. Plus, there's no sign of foul play at her house," said Gretchen. "At least, from what we can see from the outside and what Mett told us. So we're not really looking at a potential crime."

Noah shook his head. "We got a body out of the river last night that looked an awful lot like Amber. We may not be able to get into her house to look around, but there's no reason why we can't canvass. Especially considering the Russell Haven message was there, and that's where we found our Jane Doe. We can probably pull prints from Amber's car, too."

Gretchen picked up her cell phone. "I'll have a patrol unit canvass, and get Hummel to pull prints from the car."

A moment later, her desk phone rang. She answered, listened, and hung up. "Grace Power is here. Lamay put her into the first-floor conference room."

"Let's go," said Josie.

They filed down the stairwell and found Grace Power sitting at the long, glossy wooden conference table. She was small and slight with olive skin and dark hair that framed her face in a chic bob. A large, puffy coat sat on the back of her chair. She wore jeans and a sweater with a patterned scarf around her neck. She offered them a weak smile as they introduced themselves and thanked her for coming on short notice. Josie offered her coffee or water but she declined, clasping her hands together and resting them on the surface of the table. She said, "Have you heard anything?"

"I'm sorry, but we haven't," said Josie.

Grace unlaced her fingers and reached over into her purse, which sat open on the chair beside her. From it, she pulled a tissue which she used to dab at the tears leaking from her eyes. "She's my best friend. I can't believe this is happening. You really have no idea where she went? Do you think someone took her?"

Noah said, "That's what we're trying to figure out. Ms. Power, did you have a key to Amber's house by any chance?"

Grace fisted the tissue and shook her head. "No. I live so far away, it didn't make sense. In any case, she rents, so her landlord can get into the house if she ever has any trouble. When I say trouble, I mean locking herself out. I never thought..."

Josie said, "When is the last time you spoke with her or heard from her in any way?"

"Two weeks ago," Grace said. She reached into her purse and pulled out a cell phone. After some swiping, she turned it toward them and slid it across the table. They all leaned over to read the text exchange, but it was just Amber apologizing for not coming for Thanksgiving and saying she had had a wonderful time with Finn's family. They went back and forth about their holiday and then agreed that they'd meet for lunch or dinner before Christmas. There was nothing remotely ominous or alarming in any of the texts. Josie pushed the phone back to Grace, who returned it to her purse.

Noah asked, "How long have you two known one another?"

"Almost ten years. We went to college together. We were roommates in junior and senior year. Both communications majors. I went right into the non-profit world out of college. I'm now communications director for The Women's Law Center of Pennsylvania. Amber went from job to job, but wasn't really happy until she came here. She spoke so highly of all of you and of course, Finn..." Grace's eyes glistened with tears. "You really don't know where she is?"

"I'm sorry, Grace," Gretchen said. "But we don't. That's why we asked you here. Mett—I mean, Finn—told us that she always spent holidays with you and your family. Is that right?"

A smile curved Grace's lips. "Yes. Since college, when I realized she was staying on campus for every holiday. She came up until this past year when she moved here and met Finn. We missed her, but I was happy that she seemed to have found her... family."

Josie said, "Speaking of family, what did she tell you about hers? Surely you discussed it."

Grace nodded. "Of course we did. We had a lot of long, drunken nights in college. That was the only time she would really talk about her family—when she was drunk."

"What did she tell you?" Josie asked.

"Let's see. She said her parents were divorced and that she hadn't spoken with any of her family since she left for college at eighteen. She said they were toxic. Oh, and dysfunctional."

The same word that she had used when talking to Mettner about her family, Josie realized. Toxic.

Grace went on, "She said she was better off without them. I asked her if it ever made her sad, being alone, and she said no, that she was happier on her own and she never regretted walking away from them."

"Did she ever indicate whether they were abusive?" asked Noah.

A tear slipped from the corner of Grace's eye. "I think they were. Well, maybe. I don't know."

"What makes you think they were?" Gretchen coaxed.

Grace wiped the rogue tear from her cheek. "I just—well, she's got this scar on her back."

"We're aware," Josie said. "Finn said it was from an accident she had while camping with her family."

Sadly, Grace shook her head. "Oh, no. Is that what she told him? I don't know why she is so embarrassed or... ashamed... or why she never wants to discuss it. It wasn't her fault."

The scar that ran from Josie's ear down her jawline to the center of her chin burned like it was on fire. She remembered the searing pain of the knife slicing her skin the night her abductor gave her the scar. Josie's own upbringing had been a special sort of hell. Ripped from her biological family, she was passed off as Eli Matson's child. Eli hadn't known any better and he had loved her so fiercely that it got him killed, leaving Josie alone with a monster. The years after Eli's death were filled with one terror after another until Lisette finally got custody of her. In adulthood, Josie never spoke of her abuser unless she absolutely had to. "What did Amber tell you about the scar?" she managed to choke out.

"It wasn't an accident," said Grace. "Someone did that to her. One of them. I mean, when we first met, she gave me that camping accident story. We were roommates. I saw her once or twice without a shirt on and worked up the nerve to ask her about it. She said she was a kid and went camping with her family and fell backward into the fire. But then a couple of years later, we had come home from a night of drinking, and we got to talking. She got really sad and started crying and that's when she told me. Someone in her family pushed her into that fire. They made her lie about it when they took her to the hospital."

Josie tried her best to suppress the shudder that worked its way through her body, remembering her abuser's grip on her in the hospital, insisting that she lie about what had caused the cut on her face. Beneath the table, Noah placed a warm palm on Josie's knee. To Grace, he said, "She didn't say who had done it? Mom, dad? Siblings?"

Grace shook her head. "She wouldn't say, except that I got the impression that they were all there. They all knew what really happened. Which is really messed up."

Gretchen said, "Did she ever tell you their names? Her family members?"

Grace shook her head. "No. She just said my dad, my mom, sister, brother. Oh, and there was some aunt on her dad's side who was always around. She was a real bitch, apparently."

As much comfort as Noah's touch brought, Josie couldn't stop the anxiety swelling within her. For over a year she had worked with Amber. She'd had no idea that Amber had endured something so similar to her own traumatic past. She hadn't tried to know. Josie was always wrapped up in her work. Even her husband, bless him, had to compete with her obsession with her job. It helped that he did the same work.

"Do you think her aunt gave her the scar?" asked Noah.

Josie stood abruptly, knocking her chair back against the wall. Everyone stared at her. A flush crept up her neck. "I'm sorry," she said. "I just—I have to—can you excuse me just a moment? I'll be right back."

Noah and Gretchen continued to stare. Only Grace offered a smile and the words, "Of course."

Josie tried not to sprint out of the room. She heard Grace's next sentence trail her out the door. "I don't know who gave her the scar... she never..."

In the stairwell, Josie stopped and took several deep breaths. Leaning against the wall, she did the breathing and meditation exercise that her therapist had taught her. It had seemed so stupid to her at first. It still did. Trying to breathe while her anxiety was at full capacity felt like trying to wrestle an alligator into a teacup. Impossible. The feelings were too big; the task too difficult. But she tried it anyway because the alternative was a nervous breakdown at work, in a stairwell, while one of her colleagues was missing and another was under suspicion. She used to be able to compartmentalize like a champion, but since her grandmother's murder, since she'd started feeling all her feelings in therapy, it was harder.

"Stupid feelings," she muttered to herself, doing her breathing exercise through gritted teeth. In her mind, she could hear Dr. Rosetti patiently coaching her: "Relax your jaw, Josie. Relax your facial muscles."

The only way she could bring herself back from the brink was imagining Dr. Rosetti's voice. It never worked with her own internal voice. That woman was too busy screaming her head off.

Once her heart rate returned to an acceptable range, she took the stairs to the second floor two at a time and snatched Amber's diary from her desk. When she burst back into the conference room, only Grace looked up, smiling at her.

"Did she say where she grew up?" Noah was asking.

"She said they moved a couple of times a year, sometimes more. I got the sense from her that it was all very unstable. I think that's why she was so happy here, especially after she started dating Finn. She had stability for once. She seemed happier than she'd ever been, which was really quite lovely."

"What about ex-boyfriends?" Gretchen asked, and Josie knew she was thinking of the man that Sawyer had seen Amber struggling with on the street.

Grace waved a hand in the air. "Oh, there weren't many. The most serious relationship she had before Finn only lasted six months and it all seemed very... passionless."

Josie held the diary against her stomach and sat back in her chair.

"There was no one who was really hung up on her?" Noah asked. "No old boyfriends who became obsessed with her, maybe? Stalked her?"

Grace shook her head. "Oh no. Not that I'm aware of."

Josie cleared her throat, drawing everyone's attention. "I have something of Amber's I was hoping you could look at."

She put the diary on the table and slid it over to Grace.

Sighing, Grace ran an index finger across its cover. "This old thing. My God. She's still got it."

"It's blank," Josie said.

"No. Not blank. It was full. Her aunt tore all the pages out of it when she was a teenager," Grace explained.

Noah asked, "Did Amber say why?"

"'Because she was a bitch.' That's what Amber said."

"Why did she keep it all this time?" asked Gretchen.

Grace touched the golden, heart-shaped clasp. "I don't know. Spite, maybe? Or to remind herself of what they were really like so she would never be tempted to go back?"

Josie flipped the cover open and paged to the back of the diary to the list of numbers. "Do you know what these numbers mean?"

Grace pulled it closer and studied the list. Confusion blanketed her face. "No. This is Amber's writing, but I don't know what they're for or what they mean."

"Had you seen the inside of the book before?" asked Gretchen. "Seen these numbers?"

"No. The only time Amber ever showed it to me, she flipped through pretty quickly. All I saw were blank pages and these," she touched the jagged flaps of paper where pages had been torn out.

Noah said, "Why would her aunt rip pages out of this rather than just destroying the entire thing? Did Amber ever speculate?"

Grace sighed. "I'm not sure."

Josie knew why. The same way she knew why Amber had held onto the diary all these years even with its remaining blank pages and broken strap. A diary—especially that of a teenage girl—was intimate, private, and even though there was probably nothing written inside it that the same teenage girl would care about as an adult, it was still a precious thing, a place to keep her innermost thoughts and secrets. Tearing pages from the diary was an act of cruelty in and of itself, but otherwise leaving it largely intact and in Amber's possession was just plain spiteful. Every time Amber looked at the diary after that she would be reminded of that cruelty, of the way her inner world had been violated and desecrated.

Josie thought of all the times her own abuser had let her think she had control or let her keep something she loved but then ruined it completely. Josie was willing to bet that keeping the diary was Amber's way of tangibly holding onto shreds of her own identity, although that didn't explain the list of numbers. This time, Josie was able to suppress a shudder. Amber had grown up with cruelty, but did that have anything to do with her disappearance? Josie asked, "Do you know her aunt's name? Or if she's even still alive?"

Grace shook her head. "I don't know. Amber never said her name. I assume she is still alive. It seems like Amber would have mentioned it if she'd died. I think she would have been relieved."

Josie closed the diary. "You said that Amber talked about having a sister. Did you ever meet her?"

"Oh, no. I never met any of her family. She wasn't kidding when she said they had no contact."

Gretchen said, "Does Russell Haven Dam mean anything to you? Have any significance?"

Looking puzzled, Grace slowly shook her head. "No. Why? Should it?"

Noah said, "Did Amber ever mention it?"

"No, not that I recall."

"Besides her family, had Amber ever had trouble with anyone in the past?" Josie asked. "Maybe a neighbor or co-worker or something like that? Is there anyone you can think of who might have wanted to harm her?"

Grace gave another slow shake of her head. "No. Definitely not. I don't recall her ever having trouble with anyone. Quite the opposite. Amber always struck me as very lonely. She would never say it, but she was alone all the time, you know? That had to get depressing sometimes."

Gretchen slid a business card across the table to Grace. "If you think of anything else—anything at all—please contact us immediately, and thank you for meeting with us today."

Grace took the card and tucked it into her purse. "Please let me know as soon as you hear anything," she implored. "I'm really worried about Amber. I don't want anything bad to happen to her."

They agreed to do so, but all Josie could think was that something bad had probably already happened to Amber.

In her pocket, her cell phone trilled, buzzing against her hip. She took it out, swiping answer when she saw Dr. Feist's name on the screen.

"Josie? I think you guys might want to get over here to the morgue. I've got a woman here who claims that Jane Doe is her daughter."

SEVENTEEN

Josie expected to see someone in the dingy hallway outside the morgue doors, but the area was empty. Noah had gone to check on Mettner while Josie and Gretchen went to the morgue to meet the woman claiming to be Jane Doe's mother. Except there was only Ramon, Dr. Feist's assistant, in the exam room, cleaning instruments and straightening up. He glanced up when they walked in, nodding a greeting. "The doc is in her office with our guest," he told them. "Just a minute."

He left them standing in the middle of the room. This time, Jane Doe was not on an exam table but inside a body bag on a gurney that had been wheeled into the room. The door that led from the exam room into the doctor's private office swung open. Dr. Feist stepped through, followed by a small, slight woman whose brown shoulder-length curls were threaded through with gray. She wore a thick double-breasted tan skirt suit that made her look like the austere headmistress of a private school. Only her brown ankle-length Gucci boots softened the look. Even wearing those, she was shorter than Josie. Over her shoulder hung a brown leather crocodile-skin Hermès bag. She carried herself with gravitas, entering the room as though she was a foreign dignitary making a visit. Her fingers were laden with large diamond rings, and she wore a diamond pendant around her neck. Diamond studs sparkled from her earlobes. Josie studied her face as she stood perfectly still before them, waiting for someone to speak. There was a passing resemblance to Amber and to Jane Doe, but it wasn't striking.

"Detectives," said Dr. Feist. "This is Lydia Norris."

Lydia did not offer a hand. Instead, she said, "It was Watts at one time."

Gretchen asked, "Are you Amber Watts' mother?"

A strained smile crossed her face. "Yes, I am." She gestured toward the body. "I came because I heard on the news that police had recovered a body from the river that matched the description of my daughter."

"Amber?" Josie clarified.

"Yes, Amber."

"Mrs. Norris," said Gretchen. "It wasn't Amber who was recovered from the river last night."

Worry formed a vertical line between Lydia's eyebrows. "How well do you know Amber? Well enough to identify her? I gave birth to her."

Josie looked at Gretchen and then back to Lydia. "We worked with Amber every day for the past year or so. Our colleague, he and Amber, well—we know this isn't Amber, but we have been told that Amber had a sister."

Lydia's still façade faltered for a moment. Confusion creased her forehead. "I don't—what would—my other daughter wouldn't be here. Amber was here. She was living here, working here. It had to be her. I'm sure of it."

Josie met Dr. Feist's gaze and gave a small nod. Lydia followed the doctor as she went to the body bag and carefully unzipped it, parting it so that only Jane Doe's face was visible. Lydia's hand flew to her mouth. "Oh," she gasped. A tremor ran the length of her body. "This is... this is my... my Eden."

"Eden?" said Gretchen. "That's the name of your other daughter?"

She reached forward, as though she was going to touch Eden, but then stopped. Her fingers trembled in mid-air before she snatched them back, pressing them to her chest. "Yes," she whispered. "Eden Watts. This is my daughter. She... I don't understand. What happened?"

"We were hoping you could help us figure that out," said Josie. "Amber has been missing for three days now. We found a message outside of her home indicating that she should meet someone at the Russell Haven Dam. But when we found Eden, she was stuck in the rocks near the water release chute. She had been tortured and restrained in the days leading up to that. She was badly injured but still alive. We tried to save her but she drowned."

Gretchen added, "Someone wedged her between two rocks. Whoever did it meant for her to drown."

Lydia formed a fist with her right hand and pressed it into her mouth. Her eyes closed. Dr. Feist zippered the bag back up and put a hand on Lydia's elbow, turning her away from Eden's body.

"Would you like to sit down, Mrs. Norris?" Josie asked.

She shook her head but kept her eyes closed a moment longer, composing herself. When she opened them again, Gretchen asked, "When is the last time you saw or spoke to Amber?"

"It's been years," said Lydia. "I divorced her father when the kids were teenagers. The kids didn't take it well, wanted nothing to do with me after that. I tried to keep tabs on them—that's how I knew that Amber was here in Denton—but we didn't talk often."

"You're saying you haven't spoken to or had any contact with Amber in years?" Josie said.

Lydia gave her head a quick shake. "Yes. No. I mean, I'm

sure I talked to her sometime in the last... I don't know. Maybe it was when she moved here? I really can't recall. Like I said, she wasn't happy with me or her father. None of them were."

"None of them," said Gretchen. "You mean Amber, Eden, and your son?"

"Gabriel, yes. I haven't seen or spoken with him in almost six years. Ever since he joined that church. You know the one? Thatcher something? He's on television all the time."

"Thatcher Toland?" asked Josie. "He's building a megachurch nearby."

Lydia snapped her fingers. "Yes, the Rectify Church. Odd name, don't you think? But I guess if you start your own nonde-nominational church, you get to call it whatever you want. Anyway, once Gabriel joined Rectify, he stopped speaking to me altogether."

Josie said, "Does Gabriel have something he needs to rectify? Is that why he joined?"

Lydia gave a tittering laugh. Her eyes looked everywhere but at Josie. "No, no," she said. "I don't think so. Unless there was something after I left."

"What about Eden?" asked Josie. "When is the last time you were in contact with her?"

Lydia glanced over her shoulder to where Eden's body rested. Her tone was sad, wistful, even. "I usually talk with her on the phone a couple of times a year. She won't see me. I haven't seen her in person for almost ten years, but still, she was the most forgiving of all my children. I hadn't spoken with her since the summer, though. She was my July baby. How did Eden...? I don't understand what's happened. She lives in Phil-adelphia. Why would she be here?"

"To see Amber?" Gretchen suggested.

Lydia shook her head. "No, no. Amber wanted nothing to do with any of us. This makes no sense."

Gretchen and Josie looked at one another, silent communication flooding between them. Finally, Gretchen said, "Mrs. Norris, this is a very delicate matter, and I know this is a terrible time for you, but it's been brought to our attention that Amber had a large burn scar on her back."

Lydia nodded. "She did."

Josie picked up the questioning. "A friend of hers told us that although she usually claims that she got it by accident, in fact, someone gave her the scar. On purpose. Do you know anything about this?"

Tears glistened in Lydia's eyes. Again, her head shook slowly from side to side. "The truth?"

Josie and Gretchen nodded.

"I think my sister-in-law did that to her, but I could never prove it."

"Your sister-in-law," said Josie. "Amber's aunt?"

"Yes. Nadine. My ex-husband Hugo's parents died when he was a child. There was only Nadine. She was twelve years older than him, and their dynamic was much more of a parent–child type of thing than a sister–brother. Nadine had to have absolute control over everything. Every aspect of our lives. As you can imagine, that didn't sit well with me, especially where it concerned my children. There were a few times that I left Hugo before things fell apart once and for all, and he would usually leave the kids at Nadine's house rather than parent them himself." Frustration shook her voice. Her lower lip trembled and one of her hands squeezed into a fist. "God forbid he act like a father. Anyway, one of those times that we were separated, the children were there at Nadine's, and the next thing I know I'm getting a call from Towanda Hospital saying that Amber's been in an accident."

"Towanda," said Josie. "That's north, near the state line."

"Yes, just south of New York State. Nadine has quite a large house in Sullivan County. The closest hospital was Towanda. That's where they took Amber. I went to see her—to collect all the children—and she was in terrible shape. She said they were having a campfire and she fell backward into it. I never believed her, but I couldn't get her to tell me the truth. She was too afraid of Nadine. We all were."

Gretchen said, "Why? You were a grown woman. Their mother. Why would you be afraid of Nadine?"

Lydia shuddered. "She would find ways to make our lives a living hell. Insidious, maddening ways. There was no getting away from her. Hugo felt a certain loyalty to her that he never extended to me or our children. That was ultimately one of the main reasons I left. He refused to distance us from her."

Josie said, "Amber had a diary that she kept as a teenager. She told her best friend that Nadine tore most of the pages out. Did you know about that?"

Lydia's brow knit together. "No, I didn't. But it doesn't surprise me. It sounds like something Nadine would do."

Josie took out her phone and pulled up the photo of the diary page with the list of numbers. She showed it to Lydia. "Do you know what these numbers mean? Amber wrote them in her diary."

Lydia took the phone from Josie, studying them for a long moment. "I have no idea," she said. "What are they? Bank account numbers?"

"That's what we're trying to figure out," said Gretchen. "You have no idea what they could be from or what they mean?"

She handed the phone back to Josie, sadness lining her face. "No. I wish I did. Do you think they have something to do with what happened to Eden or where Amber went?"

"We're not sure at this point," said Josie. "When is the last time you saw Nadine?"

"Probably fifteen years ago. Once I left Hugo—for the final time—I didn't look back."

"Your children didn't want to come with you?" asked Gretchen.

Lydia's thumbs rubbed against the bands of her rings on the insides of her palms. The rings moved slightly on her fingers, casting a thousand tiny sparkles across the ceiling. "Gabriel was grown by that time. The girls were both nearly out of high school. We had moved a lot when they were growing up. I think they just didn't want to be upended with only one or two years of school left. Besides, they blamed me for all of it."

"All of what?" said Josie.

Lydia shrugged. "All of life, I guess. Every bad thing that happened in their childhoods, and now... God, this is just awful."

Sensing Lydia was about to lose her composure, Josie asked, "Where do you live, Mrs. Norris?"

"Oh, about an hour from here. Look, I can show you my identification." She patted her jacket pockets and then came up with a thin wallet from which she pulled a driver's license. Josie studied it, noting that she lived in Danville.

Dr. Feist said, "With all due respect, ma'am, if you haven't physically seen your daughter Eden in several years, how do you know this is her?"

"I know," Lydia said, voice husky. "A mother knows."

Josie knew that Dr. Feist was going to need more than this logic to release Eden's body to this woman. "Perhaps I can take down some more information from you," said Dr. Feist. "Have you fill out some forms. I'll do some work on my end to confirm Eden's identity. If you know where she lived, perhaps we can track down her dentist and confirm via dental records. Then I can release her to you."

"Of course, of course," said Lydia. "I suppose I have to make funeral arrangements now, don't I?"

"You have time," Gretchen said gently. "I'm sure Dr. Feist

can give you a day or two. In the meantime, Detective Quinn and I can take you anywhere you'd like to go. A hotel, maybe?"

"Oh, I drove here," said Lydia. "I think I'll just stay at Amber's for now."

Josie said, "As we told you, Amber hasn't been at her house in at least two days, maybe three, Mrs. Norris. She's missing."

Lydia smiled, the motion forced, so that it looked more like she was baring her teeth. "But I've got a key. She said I could stay anytime even if she wasn't home."

Josie could practically hear Gretchen's thoughts and see all the imaginary red flags go up in her mind. "When did she give you a key?" she asked Lydia.

Lydia touched her temple. "Oh, I don't know. When she moved in, I suppose. Anyway, I'll just fill out those forms now, then I'll head over there."

Dr. Feist disappeared into her office to gather the paperwork.

Gretchen asked, "Do you know where Amber went? Where she might be right now?"

Lydia shook her head. "Oh, no. I don't. I thought she was the one—I thought she had died. I saw it on the news and worried. That's why I came. I knew no one would claim her body. But I was wrong. It wasn't Amber. I'm sure she will turn up in a day or two. Until then, I'll just wait at her place and make arrangements for Eden to be laid to rest."

"Mrs. Norris," Josie said. "We're not so sure that Amber is going to return. We have reason to believe that she could be in danger. Since she gave you a key to her place, would you allow us to have a look around?"

Josie watched her face carefully for any signs of surprise or hesitation, but there was nothing. Only a polite smile. "Of course," she said. "Of course."

EIGHTEEN

Amber remembers nothing from after he pistol-whipped her in the dark woods. Now she wakes to more darkness, except she is inside. The floor beneath her is unyielding, cold concrete. A dank, mildew smell permeates the air around her. Still, it is better than the icy wind battering her. Mentally, she inventories the aches and pains in her body, flexing each limb slowly as she moves to a seated position. The gash in her palm aches, and her head throbs so badly she has difficulty staying upright. There are other places on her body that are sore, but she pushes past the hurt and gets onto her hands and knees. With infinite slowness, she crawls from one end of the chamber to the other, feeling her way along the floor and walls, trying to figure out where he's taken her.

There is no furniture. In fact, there seems to be nothing in the room except for her. In one corner, a series of pipes comes from the floor and reaches upward. They are cold to the touch and silent. He's brought her to a basement of some kind, it seems. Exhausted, she collapses against one of the walls, letting her head loll onto her chest. Sleep comes for her quickly. She has no idea how much time passes but when she opens her eyes again, a bright light flares across the room. Metal clangs against metal and there he stands, alone, gun in hand, just as he was when he came to her house to take her.

"Have you come to your senses?" he asks.

Amber scrambles to her feet and looks around at the empty room. It is just as she suspected. A concrete chamber all painted slate blue. The pipes she felt come up from the floor and go through the ceiling. There is nothing else except her and cobwebs.

"Where are we?" she asks.

"We're in the place you're going to stay until you tell me what I need to know."

"Or you'll kill me?"

He looks away from her. "I'll do what I have to do."

Her mind makes some quick calculations. "If you were going to kill me, you would have done it already. You can't do it. If you kill me, the secret dies with me."

He taps the barrel of the gun against his thigh. "No. If I kill you, it will just make it a lot harder to find the truth."

"It will make it impossible," Amber says.

He takes a step closer. A vein in his temple throbs in the low overhead light. "Shut up."

The gun rises slowly upward, the eye of its barrel staring her square in the face. Trembling, she steps forward and presses her forehead against the cold steel of the barrel. Then she closes her eyes. The calm in her voice surprises even her. Then again, she knows she is doing the right thing. She can die at peace. She always tried to do the right thing. "I'm not telling you," she says softly. "If you're going to kill me, just get it over with."

The seconds tick by. One, two, three, four.

"Wait," she cries. "Please. Finn—"

She opens her eyes just in time to see his finger pull the trigger.

NINETEEN

Josie and Gretchen waited in the parking lot while Lydia Norris filled out the paperwork required by Dr. Feist. Gretchen sat at the wheel of the car while Josie used the Mobile Data Terminal to look up Eden Watts' personal information. Eden was twenty-six and had lived in a number of apartments in Southeastern Pennsylvania, most of them in Philadelphia. Just as Lydia said, her current driver's license listed her as a resident there which meant that she was two hours from home when she turned up at Russell Haven Dam at five in the morning. She had one vehicle registered in her name: a red 2016 Mini Cooper. That hadn't been found anywhere near the dam, but then that was to be expected if she had been held against her will and then taken to the dam. Was the vehicle in Philadelphia? Or had Eden driven to Denton and then been taken? They'd need to get in touch with the Philadelphia Police Department to get many of their questions answered. Until then, Josie snapped a photo of Eden's license and texted it to Noah, instructing him to show it at local hotels to see if she had checked in anywhere in Denton recently.

Josie kept searching. Unlike Amber, Eden had known

associates listed in the TLO database which included Gabriel and Hugo Watts. Both lived in Pennsylvania—Hugo in the Williamsport area of the state and Gabriel in a small town only a half hour from Denton called Woodling Grove. Josie pulled up both of their driver's licenses and saw that Eden and Amber had gotten their thick auburn locks and striking looks from their father. Gabriel, with his dark brown hair and broader face, resembled Lydia. Josie snapped photos of father and son and texted them to Sawyer, asking if either of them was the man he'd seen shoving Amber in the street a few weeks earlier.

His text came back seconds later. *The younger guy, maybe. Can't say for sure. They were too far away.*

Josie tapped out a thank you and showed Gretchen the text exchange.

"Great," Gretchen sighed. "Her brother may or may not have been here in Denton in the last couple of weeks and had contact with her."

"We could track him down," Josie suggested. "Ask him ourselves."

"We should," Gretchen agreed. "Does Woodling Grove have its own police department?"

"No," said Josie. "The county sheriff handles minor matters, and the state police handle major crimes. For now, I can ask someone in the county sheriff's office to drive over there and see if they can get him to go with them to their station in the county seat. We could head over there at that point. At least until we're finished here."

"Do that," said Gretchen. She leaned over and snapped a photo of Eden Watts' driver's license. "In the meantime, I'm going to send this to my old partner in the Philly PD and see if he can turn anything up on Eden while we're working the case here."

"Good idea," Josie said as Gretchen's fingers flew across the screen of her phone. "Make sure he looks for her car. If it's not there, I'll put out a BOLO."

"You got it," said Gretchen.

Josie called her contact at the Alcott County Sheriff's office, Judy Tiercar, and explained the situation. Judy promised to call back if and when she made contact with Gabriel Watts. After hanging up, Josie used her phone to search for Eden Watts' social media accounts. She didn't have Facebook, but she had Twitter and Instagram accounts. Her posts were mostly about different types of coffee and various places around Philadelphia —clubs, a yoga studio, a pottery place. A couple of posts from the summer showed her feet, toes painted blue, on the sand in front of the ocean. The hashtags read #jerseyshore, #getaway, and #oceanvibes. Other than that, there was nothing personal. With a sigh, Josie closed the apps on her phone.

Gretchen watched the doors to the hospital lobby, waiting for Lydia Norris to emerge. "What is it about this entire scenario that stinks to high heaven?" she muttered.

Josie tapped Lydia's name into the TLO database next. "Everything," she said. "All of it. Amber told Grace Power, her oldest friend, that her family was toxic and dysfunctional, and she hadn't spoken with any of them since high school—the same thing she told Mett—but her mother has a key to her house?"

The results for Lydia Norris were almost as thin as the ones Josie had found on Amber. There had been a single address in Danville for her for the past twelve years, but that was it. She kept her driver's license up to date and paid her utilities on time.

Gretchen said, "Do you think she really has a key or is she bluffing?"

Josie thought about the look on Lydia's face when she'd asked if they could look around Amber's home. "She didn't seem as though she was lying, but why would she tell us to come over there with her if she really didn't have a key?"

"You think Amber didn't give Mett a key because she had given one to Lydia and didn't want the two of them ever running into one another by accident?" Gretchen asked.

"I don't know." Josie tapped in the name "Nadine Watts" but got nothing. It was likely that the woman was or had been married. Josie made a mental note to ask Lydia about Nadine's last name.

Gretchen said, "She seemed very surprised to see her other daughter in that body bag."

"I think anyone would be shocked to find their child in a body bag," Josie mumbled.

"You know what I mean," Gretchen groused. "Also, did you see her rings? I think one of them was a Harry Winston and one was Blue Nile. Expensive. I'm talking tens of thousands of dollars per ring, maybe more."

Josie looked over at her. "I didn't peg you for a diamond expert."

Gretchen shrugged. "I had a big home invasion murder case in Philly before I came here. Wealthy couple. Mansion. The wife had a pretty large collection of extremely expensive jewelry. I got a crash course."

"You're saying Lydia is wealthy."

"I'm saying one of us could retire on just what she's wearing on her fingers. Here she is!"

Josie looked up to see Lydia Norris striding out of the hospital entrance, adjusting the straps of her purse on her shoulder. Gretchen gave her a beep and she waved to them. She had agreed that they would follow her back to Amber's house so they could have a cursory look around. She got into a black Mercedes-Benz and pulled away. Josie logged back into the MDT to see that she did, in fact, have a black Mercedes-Benz S-class sedan registered to her at the same rural address on her driver's license. "You were right about her being wealthy," said

Josie. "She's driving a car that costs over a hundred thousand dollars."

Gretchen followed Lydia as she weaved through Denton's streets, occasionally having to turn around and switch directions.

"She doesn't know where it is," Josie said. "She doesn't even know where Amber lives!"

But after twenty minutes, Lydia turned down Amber's street. She pulled up behind Amber's car and parked. Gretchen came to a stop right behind her. As they all got out, Lydia circled to the front of Amber's car. She stared at the windshield.

Gretchen and Josie walked over.

Lydia leaned closer to the glass. "Are those streaks, or does that spell something?"

Gretchen answered, "Russell Haven, five a.m. But it wasn't Amber who was there at five a.m., it was Eden."

Josie asked, "Does Russell Haven mean anything to you?"

Lydia shook her head.

"It doesn't have any significance to Amber or Eden or anyone in your family?" Gretchen prodded.

"No, not at all," Lydia said. She drew in a shaky breath and gave them a pained smile. "Shall we?"

They followed her up the walk. In the daylight, Josie noticed a black wrought-iron shepherd's hook to the left of the walkway, next to the house. No plant dangled from it. Instead, Amber had fashioned a spray of holiday red and silver bows and fixed that to the end of the hook. As Lydia climbed the single step to the front stoop, keys jangled in her hands. She reached for the front door. Josie counted five keys in addition to her car key. One by one, she fitted them into the lock and tried to turn. None of them worked.

Gretchen said, "Mrs. Norris, you don't have a key, do you?"

Lydia didn't turn back toward them but shook her head. "Of course I have a key. I just brought the wrong key ring with me."

She slouched and sighed. "I'll have to drive back to Danville to get it." Turning, her gaze landed on the shepherd's hook. "Or I can just use the spare key that Amber keeps out here in case of an emergency."

"What spare key is that?" Josie asked.

Without answering, Lydia dropped the keys into her purse and set it down next to the front door, walked into the grass, and clutched the shepherd's hook with both hands.

"Mrs. Norris?" Gretchen said.

She pushed the hook back and forth, back and forth, pulling and pushing until she pried the base of it from the frozen ground. Her face was flushed by the time it came loose. As she lifted it out of the dirt, Josie saw a plastic bag dangling from the spike, tied to it with twine. Lydia snatched the bag, breaking the twine with one swift movement. She placed the shepherd's hook back in the ground, now canted to the right. One of the ribbons fell to the ground. A key slid from inside the bag into her palm.

"When my kids were young, I did this with keys. For when I couldn't get home before them. Some people use those fake rocks with secret compartments or put the key under a mat or something like that. Too obvious. I devised this—some kind of garden decoration with the key buried. No one guesses it." Smiling, she brushed off her skirt and went back to the door. The key slid easily into the lock. Lydia turned it and the door clicked open. She gathered her purse.

"Did Amber tell you this is where her spare key was?"

"Of course," Lydia answered as she crossed the threshold into the house. Josie and Gretchen looked at one another. Josie knew that Gretchen was thinking the same thing she was— Lydia Norris had just completely bluffed her way inside Amber's house. Still, they followed her inside.

TWENTY

The front door opened directly into a living room that contained only a few items of furniture: a sofa, one chair, a coffee table, and one end table. Josie followed Lydia and Gretchen through the rest of the house. It was small, sparsely furnished and meticulously kept, with only one floor. Each room was color-coordinated. It looked like it had been staged for photos, like the kind that real estate agents took when they listed your house for sale. Amber was neat and orderly, but something about the house felt off to Josie. In spite of the color coordination, none of it reflected her personality—or any personality at all. As Mettner had told them, nothing looked disturbed. They followed Lydia as she wandered through the living room, dining room, and kitchen. Again, Josie wondered if this was her first time here.

In the kitchen, Lydia stopped and put her hands on her hips, looking around. Over her shoulder, Josie studied the room. White cabinets and drawers with black knobs and handles. A toaster and coffeemaker on the black faux-marble countertop. A fridge with no magnets on it at all. Josie thought of hers and Noah's fridge. Barely an inch of its surface was visible beneath all the drawings from Harris and from Noah's niece as well as photos of them together, them with family and friends, and invitations to parties and other events. She thought of what Grace had said about Amber living a lonely existence. The white kitchen table was small and functional, with two black chairs tucked beneath it. On its surface was a cell phone, purse, and a set of keys, all lined up side by side. On the back of one of the chairs hung Amber's winter coat.

Beyond the table was the back door with a pane of glass missing and patched with cardboard. This was where Mettner must have broken in—smashing the glass and then reaching through to unlock the door. He'd cleaned up his mess and patched the window, just like he'd told her. If Lydia noticed this one tiny thing out of place, she didn't say anything. She was busy studying the kitchen, eyes panning the rows of cabinets and drawers. She walked over to the countertop and opened a drawer directly beneath it. As Lydia riffled through the dish towels and potholders inside, she said, "I'd offer you coffee, but I'd have to have a look around. I can't remember where Amber keeps everything."

"That's not necessary," Gretchen told her.

She continued to look in the kitchen drawers and cabinets in spite of Gretchen's words. "Well," she said when she finished, turning to them with an awkward smile. "There doesn't appear to be any coffee here anyway."

"It's fine," Gretchen said. "Really."

Josie walked over and stared down at Amber's phone. Now that Jane Doe was confirmed to be Amber's sister, they could likely get a warrant to search Amber's house as well as warrants for her phone and financial records. However, those things would take time—time Amber might not have. Lydia could give them permission to look at the contents of the phone immediately. They'd still need a warrant to get the actual records, which would include anything Amber or anyone else might have deleted from the phone, but for now they could confirm Mettner's assertion that there was nothing on it. Josie pointed to it. "Do you mind if I have a look at Amber's phone?"

No hesitation. "Not at all," said Lydia. "If you think it might help locate her. If you truly think she's in grave danger, no resource should be spared to find her."

Josie dug a pair of latex gloves from one of her pockets and snapped them on before picking up the cell phone. The lock screen showed a selfie of Amber and Mettner, faces pressed cheek to cheek, grinning at the camera. Amber wore a knit hat, and both their faces were flushed red. In the background, Josie saw the yellow and orange of fall foliage. The photo had likely been taken in September or October when the leaves of Denton's trees changed colors. Josie swiped and the phone requested a passcode. Mettner had told her he'd gone through Amber's phone, which meant that although he didn't have a key to her house, he knew her passcode. "Mrs. Norris, do you know Amber's passcode, by any chance?"

"Oh no, I'm sorry. I don't. I thought the police had some special program to get into people's phones."

Ignoring that comment, Josie said, "Would you mind if we took this with us to examine and brought it back later?"

"Certainly."

Josie pocketed the phone. "How about the contents of her purse? We'd like to prepare a warrant to review her financial records to see if any of her accounts are being used."

"Sure," said Lydia.

Gretchen added, "We'd like to have a look at the bedrooms, if you don't mind."

"Of course," Lydia said. She followed them down the hallway that led to the bathroom and bedrooms. In the bathroom, a crumpled towel lay in the bottom of a hamper. A few toiletries were lined up on the counter, but Josie saw nothing out of place or even unusual. One of the bedrooms held only a treadmill. The other bedroom was furnished with a queen-sized bed, a nightstand, and a matching dresser. As Mettner had told her, Amber's bedclothes were rumpled. Other than that, the room didn't look any more lived-in than the rest of the house. On the nightstand was only a lamp, alarm clock, and phone charger.

Josie scanned the room. There were no visible personal touches whatsoever. She opened Amber's closet, oddly relieved to see some evidence that Amber had really lived here. Several items of clothing hung from the rack and along the floor were several pairs of shoes. The shelf above the clothing rack held folded blankets and bath towels. Josie saw nothing alarming or useful in terms of figuring out what happened to Amber. Gretchen pulled open the drawers of the dresser one by one and Josie could tell from the heavy sigh that issued from her lips when she was finished that she, too, had found nothing.

Josie opened the drawer of the nightstand, but it only held one item: a book. *Wake Up To Faith* by Thatcher Toland. Josie picked it up and looked at the cover. Toland's weathered but handsome face stared back at her, a cautious smile directed at the camera. In the photo, his blue eyes looked much older than his sixty-some years. When she'd seen him that morning, out of his element, he'd seemed more youthful. The subtitle read: *My Journey from Self-Destruction to Hope and New Life*. Josie shook her head as she paged through it. Amber had never struck Josie as a particularly religious person, but Toland's star had been on the rise nationally for months and everywhere Josie went, she saw people reading his book. He was also on just about every talk show imaginable promoting it, and now with the opening of the megachurch nearby, he was sure to continue to be on television for many weeks to come.

Lydia drifted into the room after them, walking slowly, as if she were afraid of waking someone. As she drew closer to Josie

128   LISA REGAN

and noticed the book, she said, "That was here? In Amber's home?"

Josie used one hand to point to the open drawer in which she'd found it. "Right there."

Lydia shook her head. "That's very unlike Amber. She never... went in for this kind of thing."

"Religion?" asked Gretchen from the other side of the bed. She was on her knees, looking under it.

"No," said Lydia. "Televangelists and such. She always thought they were fake."

Now, given what Lydia had told them about Gabriel Watts joining Rectify Church, Josie wondered if it was possible that Gabriel had given the book to Amber. If he was the person Sawyer had witnessed accosting her on the street a couple of weeks earlier, perhaps he thought that Amber had something to rectify.

As Josie turned more pages, something fell from the book and fluttered to the floor. Lydia bent to pick it up and stared at it. A small gasp escaped her lips. Her free hand clamped over her mouth. Josie craned her neck to see what it was but couldn't get a clear view. It looked like some sort of news story printed on copy paper.

Josie said, "Mrs. Norris? Is something wrong?"

She shook her head, moving her hand away from her mouth. Josie couldn't keep track of the emotions flashing across her face: surprise, shock, fear, then relief. Lydia handed the paper to Josie. The headline read: *Sullivan County Woman Murdered in Apparent Drowning.* It was a small article, but someone had written something over the text in thick black Magic Marker: *DING DONG! THE WITCH IS DEAD!*

Josie tried to read the story beneath the marker, but all she could come up with from the disjointed typescript was that Nadine Fiore, formerly Nadine Watts, had been murdered at her home. There was no date and no indication as to what newspaper it was from.

Lydia rested her hands on her chest, as if she were trying to keep her heart from bursting out of her body.

Josie held the article up. "Did you know about this?"

Lydia shook her head.

"Do you have any idea who would have given this to Amber, or sent it?"

"No. None."

"Your son, maybe?" asked Gretchen as she came over and took the article from Josie's hand to study it.

"I don't know. I doubt it. He and Amber never got along. Maybe Eden? Nadine was cruelest to my girls."

"Was Eden a member of Thatcher Toland's church?"

"Oh, no. Absolutely not. She hated—" Lydia broke off.

From across the bed, Gretchen stood up. They both stared at Lydia, who seemed to be floundering for the rest of her sentence.

"Hated Thatcher Toland?" said Josie. "Church?"

"Organized religion," Lydia blurted finally. "She would never read something like this. Ever."

"Do you think Gabriel gave Amber this book with the clipping? What was his relationship with Nadine like?"

Lydia pressed her lips into a thin line. Then she said, "It wasn't great. I don't think Nadine ever did anything to him—physically—but she hated him just the same. But that message: 'The Witch Is Dead,' that sounds more like Eden than Gabriel."

Of course it was possible that Amber had bought the book herself, and that someone had sent her the clipping and she'd tucked it into the pages of the book. Or she had gotten the book from Gabriel and the news article from Eden. There was no way to know for certain—not at this juncture.

Josie said, "Can we keep this?"

"Certainly, yes," Lydia agreed instantly.

Josie tucked the clipping back inside the cover of the book. "Is there a phone number where we can reach you if we have more questions?"

"My cell phone," said Lydia. As she rattled it off, Josie typed it into her phone and saved it.

Gretchen said, "Mrs. Norris, we'll leave you for now. Let me give you my card in case you need to get in touch. Just one last thing. Would you mind if we took Amber's surveillance camera from the front door? We'll return it with the phone and other items as soon as we've finished with it."

Lydia gave them a watery smile. "Sure," she said. "Whatever you want."

TWENTY-ONE

Gretchen used gloves to remove the outdoor camera from its seating and deposited it into an evidence bag. "I'm going to have Hummel come get this to take prints from it," she told Josie. She wrote Mrs. Norris evidence receipts for Amber's phone, purse, camera, news article, and Thatcher Toland book, and then she and Josie headed back to police headquarters. Once they turned off Amber's street, Gretchen gave a low whistle. "I can't tell what the hell is going on here."

"Me either," Josie said, watching the streets of Denton flash past. "What I can tell is that no crime was committed in that house, though. Other than Mett breaking in. If Amber was taken from there, she did not put up a struggle, which tells me she either knew and trusted the person or she was taken at gunpoint. I'm guessing gunpoint since she left everything behind."

"I agree," said Gretchen. "But none of this makes any sense. It's like having pieces to two different puzzles and trying to force them together."

"Meaning what?"

"We've got two cases here: Eden's murder and Amber's

disappearance, and the only thing connecting them is the dam and the fact that they're sisters except that Amber wasn't in contact with her sister, according to everyone we've talked with so far. If they haven't spoken in a decade, then how did they both get caught up in something that got one of them killed and the other..."

"Abducted?" said Josie. "We're missing a bigger connection here. By all accounts, even by her own mother's, Amber wasn't in touch with anyone from her toxic family, except possibly her brother."

"Which we have not confirmed," Gretchen reminded her. "But if he was the man Sawyer saw her with, that means he had a physical altercation with Amber before she went missing."

"I'll text my contact at the sheriff's office and see if she's tracked him down yet," said Josie, firing off a text to Deputy Judy Tiercar. "But I think this is coming together. We've got two, possibly three members of the family—the children—all involved in this somehow."

"Do we?" said Gretchen.

"What do you mean?"

"I mean, we only know for certain that Nadine Fiore and Eden Watts were murdered in two different jurisdictions and that Amber is missing. We don't actually know who she had a run-in with the day Sawyer saw her. I don't want to look too closely at the family and miss something else. Lots of people have shit families. Most of them aren't murdered or kidnapped by shit family members."

Josie's phone buzzed with a text. Glancing at it, she sighed. "That's Deputy Tiercar. Gabriel Watts is not home. She's going to stop back in a couple of hours and see if she can catch him. Anyway, what are we not examining that you think bears more scrutiny?"

"Mett," said Gretchen. "They were going to move in

together, and she never even told him that she'd run into her brother. Why not?"

"Because she didn't want to answer all the questions that would come from that conversation," Josie said. "Come on, Gretchen. She had a crappy upbringing. You and I both know what that's like. She didn't want to talk about it."

"It doesn't sit right," Gretchen said. "She never told him. Sawyer saw her on the street with some guy. What if Mettner saw her with him too, and thought she was cheating on him? What if she *was* cheating on him?"

Josie opened her mouth to immediately shoot down Gretchen's theory, but then she thought about how Mettner had immediately assumed Russell Haven was a person. He'd worried about it. "There was nothing on her phone to indicate she was cheating on Mett—well, that was according to Mett, though. Besides, wouldn't he just confront her? Wouldn't he just go to her and flat-out ask if she was cheating?"

"Would he?" Gretchen replied. "He's pretty smitten with her. I'd say it borders on obsession. How well do we really know him? Can we really say with any degree of certainty that we know what he's like behind closed doors?"

Josie thought about the birthday card she'd found in Amber's desk. Mettner's handwritten note flashed through her mind: *I'll never stop loving you.* That one sentiment could be either delightfully sweet or darkly menacing depending on the context.

Gretchen continued, "To that end, we really can't say for certain that Amber wasn't cheating. Like you said, as of right now, we only know there was nothing of any significance on her phone from Mett. We have to consider the source. He could have erased all evidence of her infidelity from her phone. He would have a pretty good idea of how to do it, given that he is law enforcement."

"There are ways to find those things even if they're delet-ed," Josie pointed out. "Ways even Mett couldn't get past."

Gretchen shook her head. "Not by anyone on Denton PD. That's forensic work we're not equipped for."

"So? We'd send it out to a department that has that capabili-ty," Josie argued. "And Mett knows that as well. What are we really talking about, Gretchen? You think Mettner did some-thing to Amber? But what about Eden?"

"Maybe he did something to her, too. Maybe she showed up at the wrong place, wrong time, he had to kill her, too, and then figure out a way to set things up to make it look like something else was going on."

"No," said Josie.

"It's not entirely out of the realm of possibility," said Gretchen. "Mett's one of us. He'd know what to do to confuse us and throw us off."

Josie thought about his reaction in the dam parking lot when they thought it was Amber who had drowned and then when they told him it wasn't her—how desperate he had been to see the body for himself.

"I don't know," said Josie. "He seems sincere."

"He broke into her house, boss," Gretchen reminded her.

Josie sighed and turned her gaze to the window where the streets of Denton flew past in a blur. The sun was out but there was no warmth to be had. Even with its rays streaming down on the city, everything felt cold and gray. Oppressive. Josie didn't want to think the worst of Mettner, but she knew the price of letting corrupt police officers get away with murder. A chill drilled down through her spine. "I hate this," she said. "But we have to look at this objectively. As if it wasn't Mettner."

"That's what I'm saying," said Gretchen. "Let's look at it. Boyfriend has fight with girlfriend. Two days later, boyfriend says he hasn't heard from her. He breaks into her house. Nothing in the house is missing or destroyed—"

"Except all of her things have been left behind, her lights are on, and the surveillance camera appears as though it was tampered with," Josie interjected.

"Yes."

Gretchen said, "Someone wrote 'Russell Haven 5 a.m.' on the windshield of her car in frost which is not really a reliable way to leave anyone a message."

"We only know about that message because the boyfriend brought it to our attention," Josie said.

"He brought it to the attention of a friend. You weren't in your official capacity as a detective, Josie. He came to your house. Off duty. It was your idea to go to Russell Haven," Gretchen reminded her.

"True," Josie agreed. "The message leads us there where the girlfriend's sister has been assaulted, restrained, and dumped among the rocks to drown. The girlfriend is still nowhere to be found."

"A search of the girlfriend's work desk turns up a hidden diary from her childhood with a cryptic list of numbers inside it."

"The girlfriend's best friend confirms that the diary was from childhood though," said Josie. "I'm not sure that's relevant."

"It's relevant that she hid it from the boyfriend," said Gretchen. "It's relevant that she put your name on a Post-it note attached to it, especially when her boyfriend is a detective for the police."

"That's strange, but again, I'm not sure it relates to Eden's murder and Amber's disappearance. Also, their mother shows up and basically confirms everything that both Mettner and Grace Power told us already, which is that Amber grew up in a 'toxic' environment."

"The mother knew where the spare key was," Gretchen pointed out. "Mettner did not."

"I think you're trying too hard to put this on Mett," Josie argued.

Gretchen's jaw was set. "To our knowledge, Mettner was the last person to see her alive. He was the last person in her home, the last person to touch her phone. He could have hidden anything incriminating from us. We let him direct us from the beginning of this investigation. Think about that."

Josie knew what Gretchen wasn't saying, which was that in their last big case, the killer had pointed the investigation to themself right off and in doing so, they'd been able to control the direction of the investigation almost the entire time. It had been a massive oversight on Josie's part—and that of the team.

"Shit," said Josie. "He wouldn't tell us what their fight was about, either."

"That doesn't look good," Gretchen agreed. "I think we need to put a little more pressure on him. We should be looking at him just like we would anyone else in her life—like her boyfriend, not our colleague. At the very least, we need to eliminate him so we can use our resources elsewhere."

The Denton police headquarters came into view. Josie's stomach tightened. "Did I mention that I hate this?"

TWENTY-TWO

Noah was at his desk, phone pressed to his ear. Amber's work tablet sat in front of him, its screen aglow, asking him for a password. From the phone conversation, Josie could tell he was speaking with tech support, trying to get into the tablet. Covering the receiver with one palm, he told them, "All the hydroelectric plant station employees checked out. The reports are on your desk. Mett's down in the conference room if you want to talk with him. I went to see him at Gretchen's and had him follow me here."

Gretchen carried the evidence bags containing the camera, the purse, and the Thatcher Toland book, complete with newspaper article, and followed Josie down the steps to the first floor. Mettner rested in the same chair Grace Power had occupied a few hours earlier, but his arms were on the table, his face buried. When Josie and Gretchen walked in, he looked up. Half of his brown hair stuck straight up in the air. A pink splotch marred his cheek where it had rested against his shirtsleeve.

"Have you heard anything?" he asked.

Josie pulled out the chair next to him. She took off her coat, arranged it on the back of the chair and then and sat down. "You want coffee?"

He stared at her for a long moment, the fog receding from his sleepy eyes. "No. I don't want coffee. I want to know what's going on."

Josie tugged at the arm of his chair until he turned to face her. Amber's phone appeared in her hand. "She told you her passcode?"

A flush crept into Mettner's cheeks, enough to match the sleep spot on his face.

From the other side of the table, Gretchen said, "Jesus Christ, Mett."

He kept his eyes on Josie. "I saw her put it in a few times."

"You didn't have permission to look at her phone?"

"She wasn't there! She's gone. I was worried. I am worried. Why are you asking me about her phone?"

Gretchen reached across the table and snatched it up. "I can probably get a warrant to get into this."

She took the evidence bags with her and left the room. Josie said, "Amber's mother showed up at the morgue today to claim Amber's body because she saw the news story. We told her it wasn't Amber. She didn't believe us. When we showed her Jane Doe, she told us she was Amber's sister, Eden."

"What? How did this woman know to come? Are you sure it's really Amber's mother?"

"Mett, why else would someone show up to a morgue to claim a body? It costs thousands of dollars to lay someone to rest. Why would anyone impersonate Amber and Eden's mother?"

He said nothing.

"Mrs. Norris knew where Amber kept her spare key."

He gave a slow blink. "What? No. She doesn't have a spare key."

"She does. Mrs. Norris knew where it was, and she let us look around Amber's house. Mett, nothing was amiss."

"You're wrong," he said. "The key—that's a mistake. Something's off. She wouldn't keep that from me. Why would she?"

"I don't know," said Josie. "Why would she keep things from you?"

A beat of silence passed between them. Then he pointed at her. "Don't do this. Don't even go there. You think I was... you think she was keeping things from me because she was afraid of me?" His voice dipped low on the word "afraid" as if it was too horrific a thought to even voice.

Josie wanted to get up and leave the room. Every fiber of her being railed against doing this. Mett was a colleague and a friend. But this was her job. "Was she afraid of you, Mett?" she managed.

He shook his head, leaning back in the chair and folding his arms across his broad chest. "Of course not. Don't be absurd. No, she was not afraid of me. There would never be any reason for her to be afraid of me. Everything I've told you is the truth. We fought. I didn't see her or hear from her for a couple of days. I got worried. I went to check on her. Yes, I broke into the house and yes, I accessed her phone also without permission, but that is it. You're wrong that nothing was amiss in that house. I'm telling you. She's very rigid with how she does things. She has a routine. The bed was unmade! The lights were on! All her stuff is there, but she's not!"

"Where were you on Monday morning at five a.m.?"

The color drained from his face. "Are you kidding me right now? You think I did something to Amber's sister? I didn't even know Russell Haven was a place!"

Josie could hear Gretchen's voice in the back of her head playing devil's advocate. Did he really not know about Russell Haven Dam, or was that all an act? Was he involved in Eden's murder and Amber's disappearance? If so, how deeply? Again, she felt the ache of discomfort all over her body. This felt unnatural, and yet, Josie knew it was necessary. She plunged ahead.

"We need to search your house. We'll get a warrant to do it if you don't agree, but I think it would be best for everyone concerned if you just gave us permission to do it."

Mettner's jaw clenched. Through gritted teeth, he said, "Search it, then. Search all of it." He pulled his keys and phone from his pants pocket and tossed them into her lap. "You know where I live. I'll stay with Gretchen until you're finished. I don't want my family to know I'm under suspicion for making the woman I love disappear—or for murder. Jesus. Process my truck. It's in the lot. The key is there. Impound it if you want. Look through my phone, too. That will be next. The passcode is 5231. You can check everything from there—my email and social media platforms. None of this is going to help you find Amber. Josie, I need to know what happened to her."

"What did you fight about?" Josie asked.

"I already told you. It's private and completely irrelevant. It's not going to help you locate Amber."

"You don't need to be embarrassed if it's something—"

Mettner slapped the table. "It's nothing embarrassing. It's just private, and I want to keep it that way. Now go, do whatever you have to do to eliminate me as a suspect so that you can focus on finding Amber—and whoever killed her sister."

Josie took his phone and keys and went back upstairs to the great room. Noah was still on the phone, tapping one unsuccessful password after another into Amber's work tablet. Gretchen pecked away at her keyboard, working on the warrant for Amber's phone.

Hummel, the head of their Evidence Response Team, was there, writing out a chain of custody vouchers for the surveillance camera, printed news article, and Thatcher Toland book before he took them with him. "You just want prints, right?" he said.

"Yeah," Gretchen said. "I mean, see if you can pull anything off the camera first, but I'm not sure the data is stored on it. I think it goes right to the cloud."

Hummel opened one of the brown paper evidence bags and peered inside. "Yeah, I'm not getting anything off this. It goes with an app. But if you get into her phone, the app should be on there. You should be able to see whatever videos it captured that she hasn't erased. By the way, I pulled prints from the outside of her car. I found her prints, Mettner's prints, and a half dozen prints we can't match to anyone in the system."

"A dead end," Gretchen sighed.

Josie pulled a key from Mettner's keychain and handed it to Hummel. "This is to Mettner's truck. It's parked outside. Can you have a look at it?"

Hummel stared at her as if she'd just sprouted another head.

"Please?" Josie said.

"Sure," he mumbled before leaving.

Gretchen looked up at the clock hanging on the wall. "I'm going to run this warrant over to get it signed by the judge. I also need food," she announced. "You guys?"

Noah gave her a thumbs-up.

"Would love it," Josie said.

Once she was gone, Josie made a half-hearted effort to straighten up her desk. She took another look at the diary and the numbers inside. She stared at them for several minutes, again racking her brain for what they could possibly mean. Sighing in frustration, she put them aside once more and pulled up a photo on her phone that she'd taken of the clipping she'd found in Amber's Thatcher Toland book. A nudge of her mouse brought her computer screen to life. It took her less than five minutes to find the online version of the article in the *Sullivan County Review*. It was dated two weeks ago.

On Thursday morning, the body of real estate mogul, Nadine Fiore, was found in the pond located on her 760-acre estate in Eagles Mere. Local handyman, Christopher Wills, arrived for an appointment with Fiore that morning. When she didn't answer her door or her phone, he took a walk around the property. "I was supposed to hang some pictures for her. I thought maybe she was in one of the other buildings. Then I saw her in the pond. I jumped in and pulled her out, but it was too late. I called 911 but they couldn't do anything either. It's real sad."

When it became clear to first responders that foul play had led to Fiore's death, they called in the state police. State Police Detective Heather Loughlin indicated that Fiore had defensive wounds on her body and that the coroner would likely rule the manner of death as homicide. "Unfortunately, Ms. Fiore lived alone and did not have surveillance cameras in this section of her property. In the coming days, we'll be processing the scene as well as Ms. Fiore's residence for additional evidence."

Anyone with information is being asked to contact state police.

Josie printed the article out. She and her team had worked with Detective Heather Loughlin on several cases in the past. Loughlin was a skilled investigator and a team player. Picking up her phone again, Josie dialed Loughlin's cell number. After five rings, Loughlin answered. "Josie Quinn. What can I do for you?"

One of the things Josie loved about Heather was that she got right to the point. Josie said, "What can you tell me about Nadine Fiore?"

"Seventy years old. Married once. Widowed. Lived alone in a two-million-dollar home right on the edge of World's End State Park. I'm talking a huge estate."

"Huge enough to have people coming in and out to maintain it? Landscapers? House cleaners? Snow removal? Repairmen?"

"I know what you're getting at. The answer is yes, it took a lot of people to maintain a property that large. Even so, she kept the list of people coming on and off the premises small. Keep in mind this is Sullivan County, though. One traffic light in the entire county. It's not teeming with people waiting to work for this lady. The locals hated her, and she hated them right back, even after maintaining a home there for over twenty years. Anyway, all the people working for her checked out, including Christopher Wills."

"The man who found her?"

"Right," Heather confirmed.

"Tell me about the body," Josie said. "The paper said she had defensive wounds."

"Bruising around her wrists, skin under her fingernails. Some bruising on her forearms. Fingerprint bruises around her throat," Heather listed. "Someone held her under the water. We'll have a DNA profile from the skin under her nails, but you know how it goes."

"It'll take weeks, if not months, to get it back and match it to someone," Josie filled in. "And it will only match if the perpetrator is already in the system for an arrest or conviction."

Heather sighed. "You are correct."

"Was she restrained?" Josie asked, thinking about the abrasions around Eden's wrists and ankles.

"No. It looks like someone grabbed her wrists, struggled with her, pushed her into the water and held her there until she drowned. Autopsy confirmed."

"Any cameras catch anything?" Josie asked.

"She's only got cameras around the house itself, and they only showed her walking off her back porch around one the afternoon before Chris Wills found her," Heather answered. As if anticipating Josie's next several questions, she continued,

"Not much in the way of electronics, which isn't surprising since the internet and phone service up there is still shit. We couldn't find any evidence of anyone stalking her or of her feuding with anyone. She was just an eccentric old lady living out in the middle of nowhere enjoying her piles of cash. Evidently, she's got quite the real estate investment portfolio. Next of kin is her brother, Hugo Watts. Lives in Williamsport. He was notified the day after she was found. He's got an alibi."

Josie sighed. Sullivan County was extremely rural and remote. Getting there, especially in the winter, could be challenging. Many of the more isolated houses could be difficult to find. Whoever killed Nadine Fiore had targeted her.

"She drowned in her pond," Josie said. "It wasn't frozen?"

"No," said Heather. "It's been unseasonably warm. We only just got snow last week. It's probably frozen now. It's cold as hell out there."

"Right," Josie said. Denton had had the same weather.

"You got something for me?" Heather said.

"I don't know," replied Josie. She recapped their cases.

Heather gave a low whistle. "Maybe this is some unfinished family business."

"Starting to look like it," Josie said. "We're in the process of tracking down the remaining Wattses—Gabriel and Hugo."

"You'll keep me posted? Gabriel Watts isn't on my radar but if he turns out to be involved in your cases, you let me know."

"Sure thing," said Josie. "Hey, Heather. You said the locals hated Nadine Fiore. What makes you say that?"

"Well," Heather said. "Every local person I talked to said the same thing about Nadine Fiore, and I quote: 'She was a bitch.'"

TWENTY-THREE

Gretchen returned with an early dinner and coffee for everyone. Noah still didn't have access to Amber's work tablet, but he was waiting for a return call from tech support. Josie texted Alcott County Sheriff's Deputy, Judy Tiercar, who replied that she'd stopped once more at Gabriel Watts' home in Woodling Grove, but he still wasn't there. She took another look at the numbers in the diary, trying to find a pattern, anything that would help her figure out what they meant. Still nothing came to her except frustration. They scarfed down their food while Josie and Gretchen brought Noah up to speed on everything they'd learned from Lydia Norris and what they'd found in Amber's house; and then Josie told them both about Nadine Fiore's murder. Josie used their database to find mobile phone numbers for both Hugo and Gabriel Watts. Neither answered. She left them both voicemails. Gretchen's cell phone rang.

"It's my old partner in Philly," she said before swiping answer. She listened for a long moment, nodding even though he couldn't see her, and then said, "Yeah, yeah. I'll meet you there."

Hanging up, she looked at Josie and Noah. "He's got information about Eden Watts. I'm going to meet him halfway between here and Philadelphia. He's got her Mini Cooper on video getting onto the turnpike ten days ago."

Noah said, "Eden Watts left Philadelphia ten days ago in her own vehicle and somehow ended up in the rocks of Russell Haven Dam? Where's the car?"

Josie said, "Let's get a statewide BOLO out for it right now."

Gretchen pulled her coat on. "That would help. When I get back, if your contact in the sheriff's department hasn't found him, we'll pay Gabriel Watts a visit ourselves."

Josie used the Pennsylvania Crime Information Center database to issue a BOLO – "Be On the Lookout" – for Eden Watts' Mini Cooper. The alert would go out statewide so that law enforcement in other districts would know that the Denton Police Department were trying to locate it. When she finished with that, she moved on to the National Crime Information Center database to flag the Mini Cooper's tag so that any law enforcement officer who came into contact with the vehicle would know to stop it and hold it for processing. Researching navigation systems, she found that Mini Coopers had their own app called Mini Connected. However, it was only available for models from 2019 onward which meant that Eden Watts' vehicle wouldn't have it. Still, Josie put in some calls to various navigation systems companies to see if anyone had a record of Eden Watts or her Mini Cooper. Some gave her the information over the phone—they had no record of either Eden or her Mini Cooper. Others required warrants, which Josie prepared. She braved the cold again to have them signed by a judge; and when she returned, emailed them to the respective navigation systems companies. If they could locate Eden's car, it might tell them a lot more about where she'd been and perhaps even who she had been with between leaving her home in Philadelphia and dying in the Susquehanna River in Denton ten days later.

Noah was back on the phone with tech support, Amber's

tablet glowing before him, again demanding a passcode none of them had. While she waited for him to finish, she dozed. They were all running on practically no sleep, and now with a full belly and a comfy seat, Josie could barely keep her eyes open. In her half-asleep state, Josie felt Amber's fingers against her wrist again. *Not Amber*, a voice in the back of her head reminded her. *Eden*. Trying to hold on. Trying to stay alive.

As Josie slipped in and out of the dream, she heard the rush of the water bearing down on them and startled awake. She sat up straight in the chair, hands gripping the arms. Sweat beaded across her forehead. Directly across from her, Noah looked up from where he was tapping away at Amber's tablet. "Nightmares?" he asked.

Josie nodded and took a sip of the coffee Gretchen had left for her.

"Lisette?"

"No. Eden Watts. I keep feeling her slip away."

"It's when you feel helpless that you get them, you know," he said.

"What do you mean?" Josie said, taking another sip of the coffee, the liquid burning the inside of her mouth.

"Your nightmares. They come when you feel most helpless. Lisette, Eden. You were helpless to save them. Powerless. That's your worst fear."

A lump formed in Josie's throat. She tried to swallow over it but ended up coughing. She wasn't fully awake enough for this conversation.

"Your childhood," Noah continued. "It was just you at the mercy of all these adults. Only Eli and Lisette had your best interests at heart and even they failed you in many ways. Not for lack of trying."

He was right, Josie realized. Trying to save her from the woman who had taken her from her real family had cost Eli

Matson his life. Lisette had spent years and tens of thousands of dollars trying to get custody of Josie.

"You've been chasing it ever since," Noah told her, still looking at the tablet screen, swiping and scrolling.

Josie cleared her throat again. "Chasing what?"

"Power," he said matter-of-factly. "Agency. You've had it for a while now, though. Ever since Lisette got custody of you at fourteen. It's just that when you lose someone—" He met her eyes, "—through no fault of your own, you feel guilty because you were powerless to stop it."

"Have you been talking to my therapist?" Josie said, trying to force a smile. Her hand trembled when she brought the coffee cup to her lips again.

Noah smiled. He picked up the tablet and came around to her side of the desks. Kneeling beside her, he put the tablet on her desk. "No, of course not. But you should talk to Dr. Rosetti about this stuff. You can't fix everything, Josie. Some stuff you just have to live with. Uncomfortably. Here. Tech support finally helped me reset her password and access the tablet." He pointed to the glowing screen. Josie leaned forward to see what he had pulled up. It was an email, sent to Amber's work account a week before they found Eden. It was from lydwanor@spurmobile.com. The subject line was blank. The body of the email said: *I received this in the mail today. Do we need to talk?*

"Is there an attachment?" Josie asked.

"There are two." Noah clicked on the first jpeg and a photograph of a postcard on a shiny wooden table popped up on screen. The photograph showed an overhead view of Russell Haven Dam. Noah clicked on the other jpeg and the back of the postcard filled the screen. There was nothing on the back of the postcard except for Lydia Norris's name and address, which had been typed and printed on an adhesive label. The postmark was dated the same day as the email and read: Harrisburg, which wasn't helpful as all the mail in Central Pennsylvania passed through the central postal hub in Harrisburg.

"Russell Haven again," Noah muttered. "What's the connection?"

"I don't know," said Josie. She pointed to the email address. "Lydwanor? Lydia Watts Norris. Lydia sent Amber this email. But why?"

"Lydia Norris didn't mention this when you and Gretchen spoke with her, right?" Noah asked.

"Right," said Josie. "She was very vague about the last time they'd been in touch. Also, she claimed that Russell Haven meant nothing to her."

"She lied."

"Definitely."

"No one knows what the significance of this dam is," Noah said. "Grace Power had no idea. Mett didn't even know it was a dam. But look at this email. What does she mean when she asks, 'Do we need to talk?'"

"We'll have to ask Mrs. Norris," Josie said. "Did Amber respond?"

Noah's face lit up. "She did, and it's even more cryptic than the first email." He clicked a few more times and then the email from Amber to Lydia took up the screen. It had been sent moments after Amber received Lydia's email with the photo attachment. It simply said: *We don't need to talk. Don't talk to anyone at all. No matter what happens, don't say a word. Don't contact me again.*

"No matter what happens," Josie muttered.

"Sounds ominous, right?" Noah said.

Josie squeezed the bridge of her nose between her thumb and forefinger, feeling a headache pulsing at the edges of her consciousness. "If Amber didn't want her to contact her again, why would Lydia insist on going to Amber's house after we left the hospital? What was she hoping to find there?"

"We'll have to ask her the next time we speak with her," Noah said.

"Is there anything else on the tablet?"

His eyes were focused on the tablet screen as his fingers moved across the mouse pad. "I don't see anything that raises any red flags."

"Search history?" Josie asked.

Noah's eyes tracked across the screen. "A lot of work stuff. Also, she perused some real estate listings on a realty website, but none of the properties are located here in Denton. Philadelphia, Coatesville, Harrisburg, Doylestown, Ardmore, Collegeville, Pittsburgh, Villanova, Edgeworth, New Hope, State College, Pocono Springs, Newtown. The list goes on. She visited this real estate site weeks ago."

"Maybe she was thinking about taking off?" Josie suggested.

He shook his head. "Not on her salary. All of these homes are over a million dollars."

"Really?" said Josie. "Were any owned by Nadine Fiore?"

More swiping and clicking on the mouse pad. "Some of these places are located in counties that put their property record listings online. Of those, I don't see any that are currently owned by Nadine Fiore. The rest of them are located in counties that do not make their records searchable online. For those, I'd have to check with the records department of each and every county to find out."

Josie sighed. "Let's hold off on that for now. I'm not sure it's relevant, especially if she visited the site weeks ago."

Noah turned off the tablet and met her eyes.

"What if she's dead, Noah?" Josie whispered. "Whatever she was involved in, she was one of us. Mett's in love with her."

His eyes darkened with concern. He was doing the same thing Josie and Gretchen were doing, which was pushing all of those questions and all of their own emotions away so they could solve the case and find Amber. But for Josie, the reality kept creeping back in.

"What if we can't figure this out?" she said quietly, her fingers brushing against the pink diary on her desk.

Noah leaned over and cupped the back of her head with one hand. He planted a kiss on her lips. "We will," he told her. "Because we always do, and whatever happens, we'll deal with it. Come on. We'll go talk to Lydia Norris about those emails and why she decided to go to Amber's house. Then if we have time, we'll take a ride over to Gabriel Watts' house and see if we have better luck than Deputy Tiercar."

Josie looked at Mettner's phone and house key on the corner of her desk. "We still need to check out Mett's place. He gave me the passcode to his phone as well."

"Add it to the list. I'll drive," said Noah. "You can go through his phone in the car. Let's head over to Amber's house."

TWENTY-FOUR

Lydia Norris was not at Amber's house. The place was dark, and Lydia's car was no longer there. Instead, an empty Denton PD patrol car sat in its place. Josie knew this was the officer that Gretchen had assigned to canvass the street. He'd clearly been there the better part of the day since it was early evening now. Josie could just make out the shepherd's hook in Amber's front yard. Its ribbon display had fallen on its side, scattering holiday bows across the lawn. While Noah walked around the house peering into windows, using a flashlight he'd retrieved from their car, Josie tried to call Lydia at the number she had given them, but it went straight to voicemail. The outgoing message was a robotic voice that told her she had reached the number she had just dialed and encouraged her to leave a message, which she did.

She had little hope that Lydia Norris would call back.

Noah came from the alley alongside the house. "I don't see anything," he said. "Not that there's much to see. Most of the blinds in the windows are pulled pretty tight." Noah pointed toward the street. "Look," he said. "That's our patrol unit canvassing."

Josie turned to see a uniformed officer with a notepad in hand emerging from the house directly across from Amber's. Josie and Noah walked back to their car and waved him over. His name tag read: Daugherty.

Josie greeted him and then pointed to his car. "Did you happen to see a black Mercedes-Benz parked anywhere on the street when you pulled up?"

Daugherty shook his head. "No."

"How long have you been out here?" Noah asked.

"A few hours. I actually came back to talk to this neighbor here," he pointed to the house he'd just come from. "Because he had seen a male here at this residence a few times in the last week. I called Detective Palmer to see if she had any photos she wanted me to show him."

"Did she?" Josie asked.

He took out his phone and showed them. "One of Detective Mettner. The guy said it wasn't him. He knew that Mettner was her boyfriend. He said this was a different guy. So I showed him this one." He swiped to the next photo that Gretchen had texted him. Josie recognized the driver's license photo of Amber's brother, Gabriel Watts. "He says this could be the guy but he can't be certain."

"How many times did he see this guy?" Noah asked.

Daugherty put his phone away and looked back at his notes. "Three times. The first time was about two weeks ago and then twice in the last week. Lurking. That's why he noticed him. He kept standing out on the pavement like he was waiting for Amber to come out or something."

"Did she?"

"Nah. Not while the guy was there. Not that this neighbor saw, anyway."

"What about his clothes?" Josie asked.

Daugherty referenced his notes again. "Long black coat and sneakers. That's all he could give me."

It sounded like the same man Amber had gotten into a physical altercation with on McAllister Street the day Sawyer had seen her.

"What about the last three days?" Josie asked. "Did he see anyone else?"

Daugherty shook his head. "No. He said he's only seen Mettner over there and then you and Detective Palmer with some lady today. That's it. Oh, wait. He said that after you and Detective Palmer left, another guy showed up and knocked on the door. The lady came out, they talked for a while and then he left. A couple hours later, she came out, got into her car and drove off."

"But that was not the same guy he had seen lurking?" Josie asked.

"No. He said this guy was older and he was wearing..." Daugherty flipped another page in his notebook. "A Carhartt jacket, jeans, work boots and a green cap."

"Are you sure?" Josie said.

Daugherty looked up. "Yeah. That's what he said."

Noah raised a brow. "What is it?"

"Thatcher Toland," Josie said. "The preacher. He was here. At Amber's house."

TWENTY-FIVE

"How do you know it was Thatcher Toland in Komorrah's?" asked Noah once they were back in the car.

Josie turned the heater to full blast and raised her voice to be heard over its roar. "It was him. Trust me. I'm sure."

"What was he doing in Denton?" asked Noah as he pulled away from Amber's house.

"He never did answer that question," said Josie. "I assumed he was checking in on the hockey arena."

Noah shook his head. "Right, but why was he at Amber's house?"

"I'm going to find out," she said. Josie was already on the Mobile Data Terminal trying to get his phone number. There were a dozen numbers for him and for his wife, Vivian. While Noah drove toward Mettner's house, she called each one. A few were disconnected. The rest went to voicemail. Josie left messages.

"You'll never get in touch with him," said Noah. "He's a celebrity now. There's probably an army of people between him and the public."

"I'm not the public," Josie said.

"We're better off trying to figure out where he'll be and showing up there."

Josie sighed. "You're probably right. Let's drive over to the hockey arena now."

There was a beat of silence. "It's almost six at night. Are you sure anyone, let alone Thatcher Toland, would be over there right now?"

"They're in a mad rush to get that place opened by Christmas Eve, which is only a few days away. Someone will be there, believe me. Even if it's not Thatcher, having the police show up to their work site is going to rattle some cages."

Noah pulled to the side of the road and did a U-turn, heading back to East Denton and Thatcher Toland's new megachurch. As they drew closer, roadblocks appeared. The construction taking place both inside the old hockey arena and outside to its parking lot and the surrounding property was so extensive that several local roads had to be closed off so that heavy equipment and large trucks could be moved in and out. Noah skirted the area until he found a construction entrance, then he turned in, following a large box truck down a long road. Ahead, the huge circular building rose up with newly pointed brick walls, shiny new glass panels along the second level of the building—one of its concourses, from what Josie remembered—and large neon signs pronouncing: RECTIFY CHURCH: ALL ARE WELCOME and THATCHER TOLAND MINISTRIES.

The truck in front of them turned off and wove its way around toward the back of the building. Several smaller trucks and vehicles sat directly in front of the entrance. The exterior lights blazed, blotting out the December night. Noah found an empty space to park and they both got out. Several sets of glass doors lined the entrance of the building. They walked over to one that had been propped open with a shiny chrome trash bin. As she and Noah stepped inside, heat rushed at Josie's face, a welcome balm to the biting night air. What used to be a concrete floor dotted with food and beer stains was now a plush, wine-red carpet. Another set of doors greeted them. Josie was relieved when she pulled the handle and it opened easily.

The lobby was awash in the soothing glow of soft golden light pouring out of evenly placed sconces along the walls. Josie's feet seemed to sink even deeper into the dark red carpet – or maybe it was just that the lushness of the room gave that impression. What used to be the ground-floor concourse still curved around the inner sanctum of the building, but it was no longer filled with food and beverage counters or hockey merchandise booths. Its concrete walls had been covered with textured wallpaper showing golden vines snaking up and down a paler yellow background. Tufted benches, the same color as the carpet, sat at regular intervals. Between them were small teak tables which held brochures. Josie stopped at one and eyed them. Thatcher Toland's face beamed from each one, although he was dressed differently in every photo depending on what the brochure called for: a youth program; a community outreach program; summer camp; various support groups; and even offerings to hold weddings and other "important life events" at the Rectify Church. As they walked around the lobby area, Josie noted the expected array of crosses and photos of Toland lining the walls. There were also glass display cases with framed photos, news articles, and awards celebrating Toland's journey and success as a minister.

"Can I help you?" said a male voice.

Josie and Noah turned to see a man dressed in pressed black slacks and a maroon polo shirt with the words "Toland Ministries" embroidered in gold letters over his left breast. He was in his mid-thirties, Josie guessed, with blond hair brushed back from his wide face. One of his hands held a clipboard and the other a cell phone which he wielded as though it were a weapon. Josie could see the glow of the screen, his thumb hovering over something—likely the send button. She wondered if he had 911 queued up in case they were there to cause trouble.

Noah stepped toward him, giving that charming smile that almost always put people at ease. He held out his police credentials. "Lieutenant Noah Fraley. This is my colleague, Detective Josie Quinn." Josie stepped over and flashed her credentials as well. Noah went on, "We're from the Denton Police Department. We'd like to speak with Mr. Toland."

The man didn't move, although when his phone screen went dark he made no move to power it up again. Warily, he said, "Is there a problem?"

"Not at all," said Josie. "We just have a few questions for him."

"About what?"

"We're not at liberty to say," Josie replied.

The man tucked the clipboard under his arm and cupped his phone in both hands. His fingers brought the screen to life once more. "I'm sorry. Mr. Toland isn't here right now, but I can take your numbers if you'll just tell me what this is about."

Nice try, thought Josie.

Noah said, "We've already left him some messages. We thought we might catch him."

"Well, like I said, he's not here. I can ask him to call you if you would just tell me—"

A woman's voice interrupted him. "Paul? Where are you? I've been calling for you. There are still some chairs that need to be replaced—" As she drew up behind him, she saw Josie and Noah and stopped speaking. Josie immediately recognized her as Vivian Toland. Although she preferred to let her husband have the spotlight, she had done some press alongside him. In her late fifties, she was tall, slender, and imposing with short, sandy hair that was usually teased, curled, and hair-sprayed a couple of inches off her head. Now it fell in short waves, held back from her face by a black headband. Instead of her usual matronly skirt suit she wore jeans, boots, a long-sleeved black shirt and a down vest over it. In person, wearing less formal clothing, she looked much younger than her age.

Extending a hand to Josie first, she smiled. "Vivian Toland. You look familiar. Have we met?"

Josie shook her hand. "No, we haven't. I'm on the news a lot. Detective Josie Quinn of Denton Police. Also, my twin sister is Trinity Payne. She's a journalist."

A look of surprise and delight lit up her features. "Oh my! I am such a fan of Miss Payne's! I saw the preview of her new show the other night on television. What a great pleasure to meet you." Turning to Noah, she repeated, "Vivian Toland."

He shook her hand as well. Both Noah and Josie showed Vivian their credentials while Paul stood behind her, shifting his weight from foot to foot and scowling at them. When the introductions were over, he said, "They won't tell me why they're here."

Vivian looked back toward him. "Maybe you're not the person they have business with, Paul. I'll handle this. Could you go inside and look at the first row of chairs in section 209? They need to be replaced, I think."

His scowl loosened only slightly. For a long moment he simply stared at her. Then he spun on his heel and stalked off. Turning back to them, Vivian rolled her eyes. "I'm so sorry! That's our Paul. He's worked with us since we were just a tiny congregation in Collegeville. He's such an asset to the ministry, but sometimes he can be very suspicious of newcomers." She laughed. "Imagine that. We're a church! I've asked him time and again to be more welcoming. Anyway, I apologize. What can I do for you two?"

Josie said, "We need to speak to Mr. Toland."

Vivian's genial smile didn't waver. "I would love to make that happen for you, but Thatcher is speaking at a Christmas children's charity event in Philadelphia this evening. He'll be back late tonight. I can have him call you first thing in the morning. Unless of course there's some way I can be of assistance."

Noah said, "Earlier today, a witness saw Mr. Toland knocking on the door of the home of a woman named Amber Watts. Do you know her?"

Vivian shook her head. "Amber Watts, you said? Isn't that your press liaison? I've seen her on TV. She does a fabulous job. I'd love to have someone like that working on PR for us. You said Thatcher went to talk to her? That could be why."

"At her home?" Josie asked.

Vivian shrugged. "Who knows? Thatcher does what Thatcher wants to do."

"Really?" Josie said. "Because I ran into him at a coffee shop this morning and he was in disguise. He said you'd be very upset if you found out he'd made an unscheduled appearance in public."

At this Vivian clapped her hands together and laughed. "Oh my!" she said. "He's so dramatic. I do manage his schedule, and yes, I can be quite strict when he's got events coming up, but that's only because he gets easily distracted. People wait a long time to see him, and I want to make sure he's on time. He thinks I'm nagging him, but really I'm just trying to get him places on time. He thinks I'm such a harsh taskmaster but that's just him being melodramatic. He does love making mountains out of molehills. Let me guess: he was wearing a pair of work boots that never touched dirt and a Carhartt jacket that looks like it should still have the tags on it."

Josie raised a brow. "You were aware that he'd gone out?"

Vivian waved a hand in the air. "Not specifically, no, but I'm aware of his little 'disguise.' He uses it a lot. Sometimes he just likes to go out without being recognized or having to sign autographs or be 'on.' I guess to him it sounds better to say I'm the one keeping him from being in public rather than admit that a man needs a break now and then."

Clanging sounded from the center of what used to be the game area. Vivian cocked her head in the direction of the noise. Then she waved her hand, beckoning them forward. "Come on in and see the place while we talk."

They followed her to a set of double doors which she threw open. On the other side was a short hallway that had been padded with golden silk brocade. It led to the lower level of the church. Row upon row of cushioned maroon seats surrounded a large stage where center ice used to be. Josie and Noah looked around the cavernous space. There were three levels of seating plus the floor seats that surrounded the stage. Several men dressed similarly to Paul worked on the stage, dragging wires here and there, toying with the lighting, and testing microphones. In front of the stage was a rectangular stone wall. As they drew closer, past the lower level and onto the floor of the church, Josie saw that it was filled with water, almost like an inground pool. From its center rose a large, circular stone basin spilling water back into the pool.

Vivian's eyes glowed with excitement. "It's our baptismal font. Isn't it gorgeous? It's my favorite part of the new place here. Come closer."

The smell of chlorine stung Josie's nostrils as they approached the font.

"This place is just amazing," Vivian went on. "Thatcher thought I was crazy—wanting to buy up and renovate a hockey arena—but he couldn't see my vision."

Josie said, "When I spoke with him, he said when you talk, he listens."

Vivian circled the pool and they followed. Laughing, she said, "As if it were that easy! Thatcher has a mind of his own, and he's very stubborn, but he did listen to me on this one. I started out in real estate, you know, before I became the wife of a televangelist."

Josie tried to remember if she'd heard that in the many interviews she'd seen on television in the past several months, but she had never paid that much attention to them. "Real estate?" she said. "Did you know Nadine Fiore, by any chance?"

Vivian stopped walking and perched on the edge of the wall. She pressed a finger to her chin. "I don't believe so, no."

Josie said, "She used to be Nadine Watts."

"Oh," said. "Oh dear. Was she related to your press liaison? Amber?"

"Her aunt," said Josie.

Vivian slowly shook her head. "I'm sorry, but it doesn't ring a bell at all. Where is her office located?"

"Sullivan County," said Josie.

Again, Vivian shook her head. "I've been based out of Montgomery County for most of my life, which, as I'm sure you know, is quite far from Sullivan County. I don't recall ever meeting her. I can ask Thatcher? Maybe he knew her?"

"Mrs. Toland," Noah interjected. "Is there any other reason that you can think of as to why your husband would visit the home of Amber Watts besides recruiting her for PR for the church?"

Vivian turned slightly and looked up. High above her, in the 200 section, Paul stood over a chair that he had pulled from the first row. He marked something on his clipboard.

Turning back to them, Vivian said, "I really don't know, officers."

"Detectives," said Josie.

"Detectives," Vivian echoed with a conciliatory smile. "But you can certainly ask him yourself tomorrow. Let me guess, when you saw him in the coffee shop, he tried to convert you? Did he ask you to come to the church? I always tell him not to push it so hard. Let people find their own way to you. They always do. He can't help himself, though. The ministry isn't just a thing he does, it's who he is."

"He was very persuasive," Josie agreed.

Noah said, "Mrs. Toland, Amber Watts has been missing for three days. We have reason to believe that there may be foul play involved. In addition to that, her sister, Eden Watts, was found murdered around the time that she went missing."

Vivian's features fell. "Oh no. I'm so sorry. Here I am, prattling on about my husband and the church and you two are trying to solve an honest-to-goodness crime. I apologize. I can tell you that other than seeing Amber Watts on television, I didn't know her or her sister—what did you say her name was?"

"Eden," said Josie.

Vivian nodded solemnly. She folded her hands under her chin as if in prayer. "Eden," she said softly. "I will pray for her and for Amber tonight."

Noah said, "I'm surprised you hadn't heard of them. Their brother Gabriel is a very loyal member of the Rectify Church."

Vivian's eyes widened. "Is he? How wonderful! I'll have to ask Paul to track him down for us. He'll need Thatcher's counsel for sure after enduring such a tragedy."

"You don't know him personally?" asked Josie.

Vivian's head tilted to the left. She frowned. "I am so sorry, but I do not. Unfortunately, our congregation is so large now that it's impossible for me to know each member personally. I would love to be able to, but as you can see," she waved a hand around their expansive surroundings. "The scope of what we're doing with Rectify means that some of the personalized attention is just not there anymore. We hope to make up for that with our specialty programs and by having our youth and associate pastors take on more duties."

"How about your husband?" asked Noah. "Is it possible he knows Gabriel Watts personally?"

"He's never mentioned it, but I suppose it's possible. If he doesn't, he will. Thatcher will want to offer Mr. Watts any support he needs right now. My goodness. Imagine losing a sister right before the holidays."

Josie held out a business card. "Please have your husband contact us as soon as possible."

Vivian took the card and tucked it into one of her vest pockets. "I will, thank you. Now I know this isn't why you're here, but I do encourage both of you to come to our grand opening. We're having a service on Christmas Eve. All are welcome. Detective Quinn, you're well known in the community and well liked, I'm sure. If people knew you were comfortable attending Rectify Church, they might be more inclined to attend themselves."

Josie gave her a tight smile. "We'll see. For now, just ask your husband to call us."

TWENTY-SIX

By the time they drove away from the Rectify Megachurch, it was nearly seven thirty in the evening. Josie's body ached and her eyes burned from exhaustion. She knew they should go home and get some proper rest, but all she could think about was Amber. What if Amber was alive and being held somewhere like Eden had been? Every moment meant something. Although she knew they'd have to sleep at some point, Josie wasn't ready to call it a day. As Noah navigated around all the street closures, Josie said, "Let's go to Mettner's house."

"You got it," said Noah. "Speaking of Mett, what about his phone? Find anything on there?"

"Hang on," she said, fishing in the pockets of her coat for Mettner's cell phone. She scrolled through it while Noah drove. Mettner's social media platforms were hardly used at all and seemed only to exist so he could like and comment on his brothers' wives' posts and, judging by the number of photos of his nieces and nephews that he liked and commented on, to keep up with their lives. One photo showed two young boys, Josie estimated between seven and ten, out fishing with one of Mettner's brothers over the summer, each one holding up a trout, wide, toothy smiles splitting their faces. Mettner had commented: *They're getting so big! Great catch! Tell them Uncle Finn will take them ice fishing in the winter!* Below that, his brother had replied with a thumbs-up emoji followed by a smile emoji and the words: *They can't wait to see you again. You should take them for the whole winter. LOL.* Then their mother, judging by her name, commented: *This momma bear is keeping her cubs all year round! But they do miss you, Uncle Finn!* She ended it with a heart emoji.

There were only a handful of photos of Mettner and Amber on his page, but he hardly ever posted, so Josie was not surprised. There were, however, hundreds of photos of Amber and the two of them together on his phone. Josie scrolled and scrolled. Amber at Komorrah's Koffee; Amber in the city park; Amber at Mettner's house—in his living room, kitchen, bedroom, even brushing her teeth and wearing a tiny silk pajama set. In the bathroom picture, Mettner stood behind her, bare-chested, both of them caught in the mirror. Amber smiled suggestively at him even as she brushed her teeth. Josie swiped quickly past it, again feeling like a voyeur. There were more photos of things they'd done together: fishing, hiking, attending a Fall Festival, a concert, Josie and Noah's wedding. There were photos of them at Mettner's family Christmas from the year before and this year's Thanksgiving.

"I don't think you've ever had this many photos of me on your phone," Josie mused.

Noah glanced at her, smiling. "I've been obsessed with you since I was fourteen years old, Josie. I've got pictures."

She laughed and swatted his shoulder. "Don't be creepy. But seriously, at what point does this go from love to... obsession?"

"Unhealthy obsession?" Noah asked.

"I don't know," Josie sighed. She kept swiping. "She looks so damn happy in all of these photos."

"Maybe she's got just as many pictures of him on her phone. We haven't been able to look at it yet."

"Or maybe she just smiled for pictures, and she was thinking of leaving him. Maybe that's what they fought about, and he didn't take it well and then something bad happened?"

Noah didn't answer.

Josie closed out the photo gallery app and opened Mettner's email. Most of it was work-related. The only personal emails were from his brothers about buying a joint Christmas gift for their parents. There were weeks of text messages between Amber and Mett, most of them sweet and saccharine. Some were suggestive. Others had to do with whose place they were staying at that night or where they were going to eat. At the end, from Sunday morning through Monday afternoon, were numerous texts from Mettner to Amber with no response from her at all. No red flags. Nothing useful. With another sigh, Josie closed out of the texting app and put the phone back in her pocket. "Nothing," she said.

"You should be happy about that," Noah said. "I don't think any of us wants Mett to be some kind of..."

She knew he couldn't bring himself to say murderer. "Monster," she filled in.

"Right."

Again, she heard Gretchen's voice in the back of her head: *what if he erased anything questionable from his phone before he gave it to you?*

"This is it," said Noah.

They pulled up in front of Mettner's house. They'd both been there before, whether it was to pick Mettner up for a shift or the occasional barbecue or other get-together. He lived on the edge of the city, on a rural road. His sizeable driveway led to a modest three-bedroom house with gray siding and maroon shutters. The spacious porch was filled with rustic wooden furniture. Mettner had a few acres behind the house, part of which was wooded. There was no garage, but Mettner had built a carport under which he kept a four-wheeler and a small boat, covered in tarps for the winter. The headlights of Noah's vehicle flashed across both of them as they parked next to the house.

Josie unlocked the door and let them in, flicking on lights as they went from room to room. She still couldn't shake the feeling that she was invading Mettner's privacy. Even though he'd given them permission, it still felt wrong. But she knew it was all in the service of finding out what had happened to Amber and hopefully, her sister as well, so she pushed her guilt away as they moved through the house, searching for anything amiss.

Mettner's home was the opposite of Amber's. Every room seemed overcrowded with furniture. A crumpled fleece blanket sat in the corner of his puffy brown couch. A pair of men's slippers sat under the coffee table. A pair of women's slippers were tucked neatly in the downstairs closet. Framed photos of Mettner's family adorned every room. In one corner of the kitchen was a mess of fishing rods leaned against the wall. In the living and dining rooms, plain wooden crosses hung from the walls.

Evidence of Amber was everywhere: a travel coffee mug that matched her desk set sat in the draining board. A pink robe lay across one of the recliners in the living room. Two issues of *Cosmopolitan* magazine sat on the coffee table. A sweater that Josie had seen her wear at work on multiple occasions was on the back of one of the dining room chairs. Upstairs, the bathroom counter was cluttered with toiletries that clearly belonged to a woman. There were feminine hygiene products in the bathroom closet next to a basket that contained a hair dryer, hair straightener, and round brush with strands of auburn hair in its teeth.

"It looks like she already moved in here," Noah said.

One of the spare bedrooms was made up as a guest room with a neatly made bed that looked as though it hadn't been touched in months. The other spare bedroom was filled with fishing and hunting stuff, including a gun safe, which was secured. In the master bedroom, the king-sized bed was a mess, blankets balled up at the bottom of the bed, pillows askew. Josie could tell by the end tables which side belonged to Mettner and which belonged to Amber. His nightstand held a framed photo of her next to his alarm clock and lamp. On her nightstand were a pair of hoop earrings, a tin of hand cream, a phone charger and a stack of books. Except these were all romance novels: *Moonlight Over Muddleford Cove* by Kim Nash, *If Only* by Angela Marsons, *The Man I Loved Before* by Anna Mansell, and *Happily Never After* by Emma Robinson. A far cry from the Thatcher Toland book that they had found in Amber's home.

Noah opened the large closet to reveal that half of it had been cleared—for Amber, Josie assumed—but not filled yet. She started opening the dresser drawers. One side of drawers were empty except for the top one which contained ladies' underwear and bras. Josie felt around in the back of the drawer and beneath the undergarments but there was nothing more. She moved to the other side of the dresser. These drawers were filled with Mettner's clothing. The top drawer was also undergarments. As she had with Amber's, Josie felt the back of the drawer and under the clothes. This time, her fingers hit on something that didn't feel like boxer shorts. She pulled out a small gray drawstring bag. Inside it was a black box bearing the logo of a local jewelry store.

"What's that?" Noah asked, looking over her shoulder.

She slid yet another box out of the black box. This one was slightly smaller and navy-blue. It opened like a flower, its sides pulling apart to reveal a bed of velvet. A large, sparkling diamond ring winked at them. "An engagement ring," Josie said. "The biggest one I've ever seen."

Noah leaned in closer and peered at it. "This makes me look bad," he joked.

Josie put the ring box onto the dresser and picked up the drawstring bag, rooting around in it until she came up with a small folded sheaf of papers. Smoothing them out on the dresser, she saw the certification that the diamonds were real, a protection plan, and a receipt evidencing how much Mettner had paid for the ring—and when.

"He bought this after dating her for only three months," said Josie.

Noah leaned over and glanced at the receipt. "So?"

"It seems a little..." She trailed off as she searched for the word.

"Romantic?" Noah suggested.

"Scary."

"He didn't propose to her after three months. He just bought a ring."

"Because he intends to propose to her."

"Josie, they're moving in together. I'm sure Amber expects a proposal eventually."

With a sigh, she repackaged the ring just as she had found it. Digging deeper into the drawer, she found several shiny brochures. Pulling them out, she immediately recognized Thatcher Toland's face. They were exactly the same as the ones she had seen at the megachurch: one for their community outreach program and another inviting congregants to hold their weddings at the church, officiated by Thatcher Toland himself.

Noah said, "That's weird. I didn't think Mettner was into the megachurch thing."

"He had been going to that community church down the street from the stationhouse," Josie said. "I guess Thatcher

Toland's online and media campaign to get more followers worked on him."

She tucked the brochures and the ring back under Mett's boxer shorts. Following Noah back downstairs, she said, "I don't see anything that makes me think that something violent happened here."

"Me neither," Noah said. "But Mettner's one of us. He'd know how to clean up if something bad had happened. Why don't we have Hummel come over and do one run-through with the luminol in some select places to see if there are any bloodstains that we can't see? Even if they were cleaned up, that will show them."

"Sounds good," Josie said. She took out her phone and called Hummel to ask him to bring another member of their ERT to Mettner's house to look for blood.

"I'll be there in twenty minutes," he told her. "By the way, I processed Mettner's truck. We did find traces of blood in the back but it was animal, not human."

"Mett's a hunter," said Josie. "That tracks. We'll see you when you get here."

Josie and Noah waited for Officers Hummel and Chan to arrive. Then they went out to their car while Hummel and Chan worked in the house, looking for evidence they could not see with the naked eye. After a few hours, they'd found nothing of concern and nothing that could be reasonably connected to a crime of any sort. Hummel started packing up their equipment as Josie and Noah pulled away. Josie's phone rang. It was their desk sergeant, Dan Lamay. "What's up?" she asked him after swiping answer.

"Boss," he said. "I know it's after ten at night, but Hugo Watts is here. He just showed up. Should I tell him to come back tomorrow?"

Josie glanced at Noah. "No," she said. "Tell him we'll be there in fifteen minutes."

TWENTY-SEVEN

Back at the stationhouse, Josie entered the conference room first and was immediately jarred by Hugo Watts' smile. It was Amber's smile. In fact, in person, Josie could see the resemblance very strongly, and the same delicate features that made Amber so stunning made her father dashing and handsome. He was much taller than Amber, of course, and his hair was a darker auburn than hers. He wore a black suit with no tie beneath an unzipped gray parka with a faux-fur hood.

Josie made introductions and invited him to sit down. He took off his coat and threw it into one of the empty chairs. He sat down and folded his hands together in front of him, almost as if in prayer. Josie sat next to him, Noah across the table. Worry lines creased Hugo's forehead. "I saw the news this morning—before you called—about a woman being pulled from the river. After you called, I went back and replayed the newscast. The description—"

Josie touched his arm. She kept her tone calm and as soothing as possible. There was no good way to deliver this kind of news. Josie always preferred to do it quickly. "I'm very sorry,

Mr. Watts, but the woman we pulled from the river was your daughter, Eden."

His chin dropped to his chest. One hand swiped over his mouth, dragging down to his chin. "Oh no," he said. "Oh no. No, no, no."

"We're very sorry for your loss," Noah echoed. "I realize this is the worst possible time for it, but we really do need to ask you some questions."

Slowly, Hugo looked up. "H-how?" he stammered.

Josie said, "Someone killed Eden by beating her and then leaving her in the river to drown. At the dam. The water release chute, specifically. We believe that she had been held captive for some time before her death."

Hugo swallowed hard, his Adam's apple bobbing. His voice was barely audible when he said, "What about Amber?"

Noah said, "Amber has been missing for approximately four days now."

Hugo's head dropped to his hands, forehead resting on his laced fingers. "I don't understand what's happening," he said, voice muffled. "None of this makes any sense."

"When is the last time you were in contact with Eden?" asked Noah.

Hugo smiled and then, as if remembering that Eden was gone, tears spilled from his eyes and his smile turned to a wince. His voice cracked when he spoke. "Eden was my sweet girl. She was the only one who forgave and forgot. The kids, they always had this idea that their childhood was so terrible."

"Why would they think it was terrible?" asked Josie.

He shook his head. "I have no idea. Because we got divorced? Moved around a lot? Who knows? The point is that all of them had this warped idea that things were so awful for them. Amber wanted nothing to do with me or Lydia once she turned eighteen. Gabriel stopped speaking to me altogether after he joined that crazy church, but Eden... she had such a great heart. We weren't close but we talked on the phone at least once a month. I tried to see her once or twice a year if she would allow it."

"Did she allow it?" asked Noah.

Josie pushed a box of tissues toward Hugo and he took one, dabbing at his face. "Yes. She did. We would usually meet somewhere between Philadelphia and Williamsport. Have lunch and try to do something for the day. I last saw her in July. The fourth of July."

"What about the last time you spoke?" Josie said.

"Thanksgiving. I called her on Thanksgiving. We talked for a few minutes. If you're going to ask about Amber next, the answer is that I haven't seen or spoken to her in just about ten years."

That meant that Amber had been telling the truth about her relationship with her family.

"How about your ex-wife?"

He shook his head. "I haven't spoken with Lydia in almost twelve years. She left us. Abandoned us. We've had nothing to say to one another since."

Noah said, "Mrs. Norris said that the two of you got divorced and that the kids were angry with her and chose to stay with you."

Hugo laughed bitterly. "We got divorced because she left! The kids had no choice but to stay with me. Their mother disappeared! No warning. She left everything behind, even her own children."

Josie asked, "Is that why Amber told people that she wanted nothing to do with your family?"

He hung his head. "I don't know why. My girls, they were always prone to being overdramatic. I tried my best with them, but it was never enough."

But Amber had never struck Josie as particularly dramatic. She could get stressed out sometimes with the demands of the

job, but that was to be expected. Amber was always professional, even-tempered, and very capable. "Could it have had
something to do with your sister?" Josie asked.

He looked up, scowling. "This again. It's a pity you spoke
with Lydia first. There is only one thing you can always count
on Lydia to do, you know?"

"What's that?" said Josie.

"Lie."

TWENTY-EIGHT

Unmoving, Josie studied Hugo Watts for a long moment. So long that she could hear the ticking of the wall clock. Noah didn't fill the silence. The two of them waited for Hugo to do it. Noah used his index finger to roll a pen back and forth along the table as if bored. To his credit, Hugo went a very long time without fidgeting. Josie started counting the beats of the clock. When she got to one hundred sixty-seven, Hugo unlaced his fingers, rubbed his hands together as though he was cold, and then laced his fingers together once more. At one hundred ninety-three, he cleared his throat. At two hundred five seconds, he said, "What did Lydia tell you about my sister?"

Josie shifted in her chair. "It doesn't really matter, does it? Especially since, as you say, she lied."

Noah let his pen roll away from him and used a palm to slap it in place. Hugo's shoulders jerked in surprise. Noah gave him a genial smile. "Why don't you tell us what really happened?"

Hugo swallowed. "What really happened with what?"

Josie said, "Let's start with what happened to make Amber decide she never wanted to see any of you again."

He brought his folded hands to his forehead and rubbed the

knuckle of his thumb across his eyebrow ridge. Lowering them, he said, "I don't know why, okay? Like I said, both my girls were handfuls. There was no making them happy. When Amber turned eighteen, she said she was finished being a part of the family. She had gotten into college. She said she was leaving and didn't want contact with us any longer. She didn't even want me or Lydia to pay for school. She just wanted a clean break. At first, I thought if we all gave her some space, she'd come back, but year after year passed and she never called or tried to make contact."

"There was no precipitating event for this 'clean break?'" Josie asked.

"No, no. She had been unhappy for a long time, since the divorce, really, and I guess going away to college seemed like a natural time to distance herself."

Something about his explanation didn't sit right with Josie. If Amber's break with her family had been gradual and the result of discord after her parents' divorce, why wouldn't she just tell people that? Why refuse to speak about your family at all, even to your best friend and the man you were moving in with?

"You're saying there were no issues with your sister, Nadine," said Josie.

"My ex-wife left me broke with three kids. I was a young attorney, not yet established. My sister took us in until I got on my feet and found us a place of our own. Unlike their mother, Nadine gave them structure, rules, routine. None of them liked that. They preferred the free-for-all that Lydia always allowed."

Two diametrically opposed stories. Josie wondered if there was any truth to be found in the things either of them said. "Amber sustained a burn on her back when she was a child. What can you tell us about that?"

Hugo laughed but when he realized they were waiting for an answer, annoyance flashed across his face. "How is that relevant to anything we're discussing today? Do you think knowing how Amber got a burn on her back when she was a kid is going to help you locate her? Or figure out who killed Eden?"

Josie said, "Sometimes looking at family dynamics gives us better insight into victims and helps us figure out why certain things happened to them."

"You think that finding out how Amber got a burn on her back as a child is going to help you figure out why she disappeared?"

Instead of answering his question, Josie said, "Let's just talk about your family, then. We've heard Lydia's side of the story. How about yours?"

Hugo heaved a sigh. "What do you want to know?"

Noah shrugged. "Start at the beginning. You and Lydia."

"When Lydia and I were young, we got together. I was seeing someone else. I was a young attorney living alone. With no family to support, I had income to spare. My girlfriend and I decided we would buy a camper. Lydia sold us an RV. My relationship with that girlfriend lasted exactly one camping trip. I returned to Lydia to see if she'd take the RV back, and she sold me a bigger one. We traveled the country in it. Lydia got pregnant with Gabe. Then Amber. We got married at that point. Then came Eden. But after that, Lydia became..."

He drifted off.

"Lydia became what?" Noah prompted.

Hugo unfolded his hands and put them in his lap. He leaned against the back of his chair. "I think that the demands of motherhood were too much for her."

"What makes you say that?" asked Josie.

"Why else would she leave?" Hugo answered. "I don't know why she left the first time, when the children were small, but she did. At first, she continued to care for them when she could although they lived with me."

"When couldn't she care for them?" asked Noah.

"When her new husband didn't want children around," Hugo said. "And there were a few who felt that way."

Josie said, "A 'few' husbands? How many times was she married?"

"Besides me?" Hugo said. "Five. We got remarried between husbands four and five, but it only lasted months."

"You said you got divorced because she left," Noah said.

Hugo shook his head. "It's an oversimplification. We'd already been divorced for several years and she had moved on, getting married four more times, but we were together at the end. Before she left. We were patching things up. At least I thought we were."

"How old were your children the first time you got divorced?" Josie asked.

"They were quite young. Eden had just started walking. Amber was a toddler. Gabe had just started school."

"How old were they when you remarried?" asked Noah.

"They were all teenagers by then, but as I said, the second time only lasted months and then Lydia left again, this time to marry husband number five."

"Did her other marriages end in divorce?" Josie asked.

Hugo nodded. "The last one died, I believe. Mr. Norris. I don't know if they're all still alive. It's been years. You could look them up, although I don't see how that is helpful in this situation."

Noah said, "Do you remember any of their names?"

"Last names, yeah. Let's see. There was Kleymann, Vawser, Purdue, and... let me think... Chasko, I believe."

Noah said, "Amber told people that she moved around a lot when she was growing up. Was it because these husbands of Lydia's lived in different places?"

"Yes. I tried to keep the kids close to her no matter what. Even if she didn't want to see them, I wanted the option there for her and the kids to get together."

Josie said, "Your wife left you, as you say, 'broke with three kids,' and you followed her around the state each time she remarried?"

Hugo nodded, lips pursed. "I know, it sounds crazy, but I thought it was best for my kids at the time. Like I said, the first time Lydia left, we stayed with my sister and they didn't like having rules, so once I got on my feet, I made sure that my kids always had access to their mother. In retrospect, maybe I did more damage than anything, but I wanted the children to have a real relationship with her even if she was married to someone else. If we lived in the same town there was always more of a chance she would make time to come see them. It was probably foolish of me, especially since she ultimately disappeared, but I was a father, and I did my best."

"Mr. Watts," Josie said, changing the subject. "Does Russell Haven Dam have any significance to you or your family?"

"I'm afraid not. I don't know anything about it except that my daughter just died there. Detectives, I've had a long day. I really need some time to process the news, especially about my dear, sweet Eden. I'd like to take care of her arrangements."

Noah said, "That's between you and Lydia and the hospital. If you contact the morgue, I'm sure they'll be happy to help you. Again, we're very sorry for your loss."

"Do you have a number for Lydia?" asked Hugo.

Josie took out her phone and pulled it up. He took a pair of reading glasses from his shirt pocket and studied it before tapping it into his own phone.

"If you get her," said Josie, "tell her we need to speak with her again."

"Will do." Hugo stood and began putting his coat on. "I think I'll check into a hotel here for a few days."

Noah said, "Before you go, I'm sure you understand that we've got to ask where you were on Monday morning around four thirty, five a.m.?"

Sighing, Hugo said, "Of course, of course. You need my alibi, right? Yes, this is a police investigation. Well, I was away in Florida on a golf trip with some friends. I flew down there a week ago and I just flew back in this afternoon. My return flight got canceled and I decided to stay a couple more days."

"Can you provide us with proof of that?" asked Josie.

Hugo retrieved his cell phone from his coat pocket and showed them several emails containing receipts from his hotel, the airline, and the golf club. "I can forward these to you if you'd like."

Noah rattled off his email and Hugo tapped it into his phone. Then he pocketed the phone and zippered up his coat.

Josie said, "Mr. Watts, you don't think it's strange that your sister was murdered two weeks ago and now your daughter, Eden, has also been murdered? At the same time your other daughter has gone missing?"

He met her eyes. "I'm not sure what you want me to say."

Josie went on. "Is there some reason that a killer might target all the women in your family, assuming these crimes are all connected?"

"No, I can't think of any reason," he said.

Noah asked, "When is the last time you spoke with your son?"

"Gabriel? Not for years. I told you, he stopped talking to me ever since he joined that damn church. He's become fanatical. It's like a cult. He kept saying we could have a relationship only if I 'unburdened' myself and tried to 'rectify' my mistakes. No, my 'sins.' That's what he called them."

"The Rectify Church?" Josie said. "Run by Thatcher Toland?"

"Yes!" said Hugo. "Gabriel changed when he joined. He was never the same."

Lydia had said the same thing. It might be the only fact that she and Hugo actually agreed on.

Noah said, "Do you have any reason to believe Gabriel would want to harm your sister and daughters?"

Hugo took a pair of gloves from his other coat pocket and pulled them on, eyes on the table now. "No. I can't think of any reason. It can't be him. He's changed, but I can't see him hurting his own family, even if we are a bunch of sinners to him. Now, really, Detectives. I've had quite the shock today. I'd like to go now."

They watched him walk to the door. Josie said, "If you think of anything that might be relevant to our investigation, please don't hesitate to contact us."

Wordlessly, Hugo gave a final nod and left.

Noah waited until the door closed behind him to ask, "What do you think?"

Josie shook her head. She pulled her phone out to find a text from Gretchen. She was still meeting with her former partner on the Philly PD. Josie knew that in addition to the case, they had a lot to catch up on. Gretchen would likely be out a good part of the night. "I think we need some sleep so we can think more clearly."

Noah walked over to her and held out a hand, which she took. Pulling her up and into his arms, he kissed her. "Let's call it a night."

Exhausted, Josie and Noah drove home. Josie's family was already asleep in the spare rooms. She and Noah took Trout for a late-night walk and then collapsed into bed together, sleep coming so fast and furious that Josie fell into it and mercifully didn't dream of either her grandmother being murdered or Eden Watts slipping away.

She was roused awake hours later by Noah. Gently, he shook her shoulder. She heard him calling her name as if from another room but when she opened her eyes, he was standing over her at the side of the bed, bare-chested and wearing only boxer shorts. His brown hair was mussed, and he held her ringing cell phone in one hand. Its screen glowed with an incoming call. She didn't recognize the number. He squinted against the light of the phone's display. "Your phone's been going crazy, but I don't recognize the number."

The ringing stopped. Josie had another look at the number before the screen went dark. It was local. "I don't recognize it either," she said. "But a call at four in the morning can't be good."

Noah reached over to the nightstand and flicked on the lamp. Beneath the covers, Trout snored on, unaffected. The phone began ringing again. It was the same number.

She swiped answer. "This is Josie Quinn."

A man's voice said, "The detective? One of 'em detectives who was out here the other night?"

"Where's out here, sir?" Josie asked, blinking to get her eyes to adjust.

"Oh, right. Russell Haven Dam. This is Will Wilson. The night duty operator. I didn't want to call 911 on account of I don't really want the press out here crawling all over the place again and neither does my supervisor, but I got a problem."

Noah's eyes sharpened as he overheard the conversation.

"What kind of problem, Mr. Wilson?" Josie asked.

"Well, I'm afraid we've got another body out here."

TWENTY-NINE

Forty-five minutes later, Josie, Noah, Gretchen, and the Chief were standing inside the hydroelectric power station staring at Will Wilson, as he stood before the door on the lower level marked "Counting Room." "Now, this here's real disturbing," he told them. Josie could tell by the pallor of his skin that whatever he was about to show them was indeed disturbing, but all she could think of were the words that her mind had started chanting on a loop the moment she got his call. *Please don't be Amber. Please don't be Amber. Please don't be Amber.*

Chief Chitwood raised a bushy eyebrow at the man. "You got my entire team up in the middle of the night to come out here. You better have something disturbing behind that door."

Wilson lifted the ballcap off his head and put it back on. "I didn't call your entire team, just that one there." He pointed to Josie.

"Never mind," Gretchen said irritably. "Let us see it."

"Now just a minute," said Wilson. "Do you all know what a counting room is?"

Josie could tell by the tortured look on Gretchen's face that she, too, was worried they were about to be shown Amber's body. Gretchen opened her mouth and started to yell. "Mr. Wilson—" but Noah stopped her, putting a hand on her forearm.

She stared at him. Josie read the silent communication from where she stood. Gretchen needed this over with. If the body Wilson had called about was Amber, they all needed this to be over with as soon as possible.

"It's okay," Noah whispered to her. She shook her head and turned away. Josie saw her wipe at her eyes.

Turning back to Wilson, Noah said, "It's the place where you sit and count the number of American Shad that pass through the fish lift in the spring so you can keep track of their migration."

Wilson looked surprised. "Yes, son. That's correct."

Chief Chitwood growled and tried to get past Wilson but the man blocked him. "I'm bein' serious here, Chief. When I let my plant manager in here, he about fainted. I'm tryin' to warn you."

"I've seen plenty in my time," the Chief told him through gritted teeth.

Josie swallowed her trepidation and played along. "How do you count the fish that come through the lift? Does this room overlook the lift?"

"No," Wilson said. "We got a window in this room. When the lift comes up from downriver and over the dam, it's full of water and fish, and there's a big window, kind of like if you were at an aquarium, that looks into the vat. We got a light in there and as the water is released upstream, we can see the fish swimming by."

Josie was glad they hadn't stopped for coffee. She had a pretty good idea where Wilson was going with this, and it made her stomach churn.

Patiently, Noah said, "Mr. Wilson, I appreciate the care you're taking, but the sooner we can see what you brought us here to see, the sooner we can begin our investigation. I can promise you none of us will faint."

Josie knew that was true. They were all seasoned. Yet, if it was Amber behind the door, none of them could be certain that they wouldn't lose their composure.

Wilson shook his head like he didn't believe it but turned toward the door, opening it slowly. The room was small and dimly lit with the station's signature cinderblock walls. An L-shaped desk took up one corner. Above it, affixed to the wall, was a large chrome box with various buttons that Josie guessed controlled some mechanisms of the fish lift. Next to it, just as Wilson had described, was a huge thick window, exactly like the kind one would find in an aquarium. From somewhere on the other side came a faint light, setting the entire window aglow in murky brown and green.

There, floating suspended on the other side of the glass like some kind of life-sized lab specimen, was Lydia Norris.

The four of them stood staring at her. She still wore the schoolmarm outfit she'd been in the day before when Gretchen and Josie met her at the morgue. Her skirt flared in the water. Diamonds sparkled on her fingers and the pendant she wore lifted from her chest, suspended in the water. Even her Gucci boots were still on her feet. Her hair stood on end, gently swaying in the water. Her eyes and mouth were wide open. One of her hands floated down by her side while the other looked as though it was reaching up over her head.

Someone cleared their throat. None of them moved. Finally, Wilson said, "I tried to tell you it was mighty disturbing."

Noah spoke first. "What time did you find her?"

"Maybe an hour before I called your detective, on account of I had to wake up my plant manager first and then he had to come out and take a look-see. Then I called that lady there." He pointed at Josie. "Anyway, one of the plant alarms was tripped. I checked the cameras. There was someone out there."

"Out where?" Josie asked.

"Outside where the fish lift sits." He gave a frustrated sigh and reached over to a nearby penholder, grabbing a handful of pens. From the other side of the keyboard he took a legal pad. "This is the river here," he said, pointing to the pad. "Okay?"

They all nodded. He laid one pen out horizontally on the desk, half of it on top of the legal pad—the river, in his analogy. "This pen is the building you're standing in—the power station. It extends part of the way into the river." He took the cap from one of the other pens and put it on the legal pad beside the pen. "Then you got a steel walkway that goes out and around the fish lift." He positioned another pen perpendicular to the pen cap. "The fish lift goes downriver like so." Finally, he placed a third pen on the other side of the cap, horizontally, reaching the rest of the way across the legal pad. "Then the spillway, which goes all the way across the river." He pointed to the perpendicular pen representing the fish lift. "The fish lift has a top hatch that you can reach from the walkway. Someone was out there."

The Chief said, "Out where? Out by the fish lift?"

Wilson's head bobbed in agreement. His finger tapped the pen representing the fish lift. "Yeah. On the walkway. I've got them on video coming up onto the walkway from the river and throwing this body into the hatch."

Noah said, "I thought the only access to the fish lift was through here, through the station, which is fenced off."

Wilson said, "Yeah, it is, but that's what I'm telling you: this person didn't come through here. They came from the river."

Gretchen finally spoke. "How could they come from the river and still access the fish lift?"

Wilson's voice held a note of impatience as though he was talking to schoolchildren who just weren't getting what he was trying to teach. Now his finger drummed against the yellow legal pad. "Because the fish lift is *in* the river. They came from downriver, not from here. Not from this building or the access walkway."

"How is that possible?" The Chief asked.

"Kayak," said Josie.

They all turned and stared at her. Gretchen said, "I don't think that's possible."

Wilson shrugged. "Actually, she's right. That's probably the only way to get to it from on the river. The lift isn't in operation during the winter. Only in the spring when the Shad migrate. It's just sitting there. Anyone could swim up and access the top hatch."

"Towing a body?" asked Gretchen.

Noah said, "It's possible. If the body wasn't too heavy and you were a skilled kayaker."

"Even with the current taking them downriver?" the Chief asked.

"The power station blocks most of the water between the shore and fish lift," said Wilson. "Makes a loch right there. No current. Also, this is a popular kayaking spot. Always has been. We try to keep 'em on the other side of the river. They like that water release chute over there 'cause it gives them the rapids, but we get them all up and down the dam. Pains in the asses is what they are. Couple of 'em died out there."

"How deep is it out there?" asked Josie. "In the loch?"

"Right now?" said Wilson. "Hell, I don't know."

"Show us the video," said Josie. "Then we'll look outside."

A few minutes later, they crowded behind Wilson as he sat at his desk, clicking away at his keyboard until he found the footage he was looking for, queuing it up for them. He pressed play and blurred gray images of a steel walkway appeared. The camera looked down from high above showing the walkway sandwiched between the power station and the spillway. It extended downriver, forming a long rectangle. Below it, matching its shape, concrete rose from beneath the river, boxing in some of the water. Together they formed a steel and concrete pier of sorts. The area closest to the dam held a metal contraption nearly the size of a small house with various cables, cages, and what looked like a very complicated elevator. Wilson pointed to the spot furthest downriver where the camera's view receded into darkness. "This is where the top hatch is, down here."

"I don't see a hatch," said Noah.

"Right," said Wilson. "It's too dark. But trust me, it's there. Look, you see this line here?" He traced the edge of the concrete wall with one finger.

"Yeah," said Noah.

"This is the wall. On the other side is the river except at this particular spot there's an outcropping."

"What kind of outcropping?" asked Gretchen.

"A shoal. Like a little island that butts right up against the end of the lift," said Wilson.

The Chief said, "So Quinn was right. Someone could kayak from the shore, across the loch, to that little island with a body either on their own kayak or being towed behind them in a second kayak, drag the body up to the wall, and throw it over the top? Right into the hatch?"

"You got it, mister," said Wilson. He pressed play. They waited several moments. Josie's eyes were focused so hard on the line demarcating the wall from the river—or the small outcropping on the other side—that she jumped when a figure popped up like some kind of creature in a horror film. An arm and a leg came over first and then the person—nothing but a black smudged outline of a human—straddled the wall and threw their other leg over. They crouched and a few seconds later, two shadows appeared on either side of them.

"Those are the hatch doors," said Wilson. "Now watch."

The person disappeared to the other side of the wall for

several minutes. Next, they climbed back onto the wall. For several minutes they knelt there, the footage too blurry make out what precisely was happening until a large object appeared along the top of the wall. Not an object, Josie realized, as the figure dragged it toward the hatch doors. Lydia Norris's body. Once they'd dumped her lifeless form into the hatch, they closed the door and disappeared over the wall a final time.

"That's it," said Wilson. "I saw that, ran out there, but by that time, whoever it was had gone. Couldn't see nothing down-river or out on the island. At first, I didn't know what they threw in there. I called my manager, and he came in. We ran the lift and once it got up here to the counting room, well, that's when we saw her."

The Chief sighed. "All right, Detectives. Let's make some phone calls."

THIRTY

Amber loses all track of time. The cold is endless. He keeps the room dark except for when he comes back to play his sick game of Russian roulette. What she hasn't lost track of is how many times he's held the gun to her head and pulled the trigger.

Three.

Three times he made her believe that she was about to die. Three times the gun dry-fired, leaving her limbs weak and her bladder loose. Three times he screamed at her, railing at her to just tell him what he wanted to know and end this. Whatever 'this' was—his psycho game. His quest for information she vowed to take to her grave. So far so good. Except Amber is beginning to think that it will never end. Hours stretch out before her. All she knows now is cold, dark, hunger, thirst, and the rancid smell of her soiled, dirty clothes. She almost wishes he would end it once and for all.

But then he won't get what he wants.

The door scrapes open. Light blinds her. She stays where she is, curled up in a ball next to the pipes in the corner. A couple of times a day they get hot. It is the only warmth she has.

She throws a forearm up over her eyes. She hears his heavy footsteps as he walks slowly across the room.

She jumps when something touches her skin, flailing and screaming until she realizes it is a blanket. Wrapping herself in it, her body trembles with pleasure.

"I need to apologize," he says.

She looks up but he is just a black silhouette against the light flooding in through the doorway. The calm in his voice sends a shiver straight through her, in spite of the blanket.

"I'm sorry for the way I've treated you," he tells her.

Her voice shakes. "You tried to kill me. Three times! You don't get to just apologize for that and act like everything's okay. You're keeping me prisoner."

He kneels in front of her, staring intently. "I am sorry. I want you to know I have no choice."

"What are you talking about?" she says. "Of course you have a choice. You could choose to let me go. We can forget all of this. I won't turn you in. You know I won't. I don't want anyone asking questions about why you took me."

A sigh issues from his throat. "I can't let you go. Not because of that. I know you know how to keep secrets. I can't let you go because I need information you have. I can't let you go until you tell me, but I want you to know that I don't like doing this."

She pulls the blanket more tightly around her shoulders. "But I can't tell you," she says, voice squeaking.

He doesn't speak for a long time. Amber shivers beneath his intense gaze. Finally, he says, "You'd rather die than let go of your secret?"

"I know you can't understand, but yes."

THIRTY-ONE

Josie couldn't feel her fingers or her face or even her jean-clad legs. She stood on the bank of the river several yards away from the power station's security fence. Just as it had the other night, the wind whipped off the river, punishing anyone stupid enough to stay in its path. Ambulance and police lights strobed from the station parking lot. She hadn't been tasked with being part of the team that extricated Lydia Norris's body from the fish lift, and for that she was grateful. Above, the sky dawned a dirty gray. Denton PD's marine unit had been called to transport the ERT members from the bank to the island that abutted the fish lift. It was hardly an island, Josie thought. More like an extremely large and jagged rock slab jutting out from the water. Still, it was big enough to hold several members of the ERT in their Tyvek suits as they studied every nook and cranny of it for evidence.

Noah walked up beside her. "They're taking Lydia Norris over to the morgue now. Dr. Feist will start right away. We haven't found her car yet but now that it's daylight, the Chief sent a few patrol units out to at least cover this area in the event that she met someone nearby since she was seen leaving Amber's house on her own."

Josie nodded and tucked her hands into the large pockets of Noah's coat. She really needed to get a new pair of gloves.

"What do you think?" asked Noah.

"I think that whoever did this is trying to make a statement. It's December. It's freezing. If it hadn't been such a warm fall this loch would probably be frozen. It took a lot of forethought and effort to get Lydia Norris's body out there and dump it into the fish lift. It also took a lot of balls. He probably parked right here on this bank. You can drive right down here from the access road before you even get near the entrance to the power station. It's far enough away from the plant that he wouldn't be seen. No one would be out here during the night. He probably kayaked over, dumped the body, and kayaked back. It would have been dark enough right here for him to do it. It's only Wilson here at night. The shift doesn't change till seven. The biggest challenge, besides towing a body, would be getting back to the car with a kayak—or two kayaks—before Wilson comes out to the fish ladder after the perimeter alarm is tripped. He had to know he'd be caught on camera."

"True," said Noah. "But the camera picks up a shadow, basically. You can't get anything identifying from that footage. He would have to have knowledge of the lift, though, wouldn't he?"

"Yeah, but like you said, all the plant employees checked out. Plus, there are tours of it every spring—not the inside of the plant but the fish lift itself. The tours are open to anyone who wants to take them. They bring high-schoolers out here every spring for a demonstration. I don't think we're going to find this killer that way," said Josie.

"Then how are we going to find him?"

"By figuring out the significance of Russell Haven Dam. Obviously, it means something to the killer. There are plenty of places to dump a body in the middle of December that would be easier than a fish lift. Also, we need to figure out why the Watts family is being targeted because clearly they are on this killer's list."

Noah said, "So far none of the Wattses has been exactly forthcoming, and now we're running out of family members to question. Your contact at the Sheriff's office went to Gabriel's house multiple times yesterday, and he wasn't home."

Josie thought about Amber and again wondered where she was and if she was still alive. "I know. I'll ask her to stop by a few times today until we can get out there ourselves. I'd also like to get a couple of units out here on both sides of the river to keep an eye out in case the killer comes back."

Noah took out his phone and started sending texts. Josie did the same. Gravel crunched behind them, and Josie turned to see Gretchen trudging toward them. The hood of her coat was pulled over her head and tied tight, exposing only a small circle of her face. "Patrol found Lydia Norris's car."

"Where?" asked Josie.

Gretchen pointed to the river. "The other side of the dam. In the parking lot by the steps and trail that lead down to the water release chute."

"Where we were the other night when we found Eden?" asked Noah.

"Yes. Come on, the Chief wants us to follow him over there."

THIRTY-TWO

They drove in a caravan to the other side of the river. The sun crept up the horizon as they pulled into the parking lot. The black Mercedes-Benz had been parked facing the stairs. As they got out of their cars, Noah and Gretchen began walking the perimeter of the parking lot. Josie strode toward the car.

"Quinn," barked the Chief. "Don't touch anything. I don't want anything disturbed until Hummel has a chance to process the scene. He'll need to impound the car."

She gave him a thumbs-up as she reached the car. Careful not to touch anything, she leaned over and looked into the windows. They keys were in the ignition. Lydia's Hermès purse was on the front passenger's side floor. Josie assumed her phone and wallet were inside.

She looked up to see the Chief approach. "She must have met someone here," she said.

The Chief said, "I'll stay here, keep the scene secure until the ERT can come over to this side. Maybe we can get some prints from the car. I'll have them search the path and riverbank just in case. You take Fraley and Palmer back to the station and regroup. This case just keeps getting bigger and bigger, and we're already down a man with Mett out."

Josie didn't have to be asked twice. She called to Gretchen and Noah, and they went back to their vehicles. A half hour later they were behind their desks in the stationhouse great room, steaming cups of Komorrah's coffee in front of each of them. Josie's fingertips still felt numb as she picked up her desk phone and dialed both Hugo and Gabriel Watts' numbers. It was still early, but there was never a good time to deliver the kind of news Josie had to give. Neither answered. She left voice-mails asking each of them to contact her. Leaning back in her chair with her hands wrapped around her coffee cup, she asked Gretchen, "What did you find out about Eden Watts?"

Gretchen still had her coat on. From one of its pockets, she pulled a pair of reading glasses and put them on. Then she flipped open her notebook and began going through her notes. "Eden Watts was a barista at a coffee shop a few blocks away from her apartment. She was friendly with the staff there. In fact, one woman, Karishma Sinha, claimed to be her 'best' friend, although she knew next to nothing about Eden's past or her upbringing, except that Mr. and Mrs. Watts were divorced and they moved around a lot when Eden was a kid."

From his chair, Noah said, "So Eden was keeping things just as vague as Amber but not characterizing them as toxic or dysfunctional?"

"Seems that way," Gretchen agreed. "I will say that Karishma was crushed when she found out what happened to Eden."

"How long did they work together?" asked Josie.

"Two years. Karishma did seem to know a lot about Eden's daily life, although there wasn't much to tell. No boyfriends and no beef with anyone. No unusual contact with anyone in the days and weeks leading up to her leaving Philadelphia. The only thing that stood out to this friend was that a couple of afternoons last month, some old guy came into the coffee shop at the end of Eden's shifts and the two of them went to a corner table and talked for hours. Karishma thought at first it was, and I quote, 'that TV preacher.'"

Josie sat up straighter in her chair. "Thatcher Toland?"

"Right," said Gretchen. "But when Karishma asked who it was, Eden said that she knew him when she was a kid and that they were just catching up. Karishma asked Eden point-blank if the guy was Toland and Eden laughed and said not to be ridiculous. He was just an old neighbor."

"Footage from the coffee shop?" asked Josie.

Gretchen let out a long sigh and flipped a page in her notebook. "Already erased. It's erased once a week. Eden lived in a one-bedroom apartment with a cat that Karishma has now taken custody of; she took pottery classes on weekends; yoga two days a week; and the two of them usually went out for drinks every weekend. Eden seemed very happy, not distraught at all. She had two weeks of vacation coming to her. Apparently, she never took vacation and always worked extra shifts when needed."

"Because she was broke?" asked Noah. "Or because it was something to do?"

"I'm not sure," said Gretchen.

Josie thought of how Amber's best friend had described her existence as lonely until she started working at the Denton PD and met, as Grace Power had described them, "her family." Some family they were, Josie thought darkly. They hadn't even known about her past, and now they might never find out what truly happened to her.

"She took the vacation," said Josie. "That's why she wasn't reported missing? Or did her friend file a report?"

Gretchen flipped another page in her notebook. "There was a report filed by Karishma, although it doesn't look like Philly PD's investigation turned up much. Eden was expected back three days ago. She had given Karishma a key to her apartment so that she could feed the cat. Karishma said Eden stopped answering calls and texts almost as soon as she left."

"Did Eden say where she was going?" asked Noah.

"Just that she was taking a trip to the mountains. That was it."

"In December?" Josie said.

Gretchen shrugged. "That's exactly what Karishma said. 'Why are you driving to the mountains in the middle of December?' Eden was vague about it for some time and then finally, she admitted that there were some people she was going to visit from her past because she needed to atone for mistakes she had made."

Noah said, "What kind of mistakes?"

"She wouldn't say. When Karishma pressed the issue, Eden told her that she'd been watching Thatcher Toland videos online and that the way he talked about how it was never too late to make up for your mistakes really touched her. It made her realize that she could never live a full life until she had atoned for some things she did when she was a teenager. Karishma said it was all very strange. Eden said she'd send her a link to the video, but she never did."

"She was watching his videos," said Josie. "The 'old neighbor' that Eden met with—the one Karishma thought was actually Toland—did she describe him?"

Gretchen looked at her notes. "Jeans, Philadelphia Eagles hat, boots, brown jacket."

"It could have been him," Noah said.

"That's what I'm thinking," Josie agreed. "If that's the case, Eden met with him before she left on her trip. Did your old partner say whether there was a copy of the Toland book in Eden's apartment?"

Gretchen shook her head. "He didn't mention it, no. He did send me photos of the place that he took when Karishma let him in and I didn't see it. He did, however, get Eden's laptop. Karishma knew the password, so we've got access to it."

Gretchen pointed to a paper evidence bag on the corner of her desk.

"Did you look at it?" asked Josie.

"Not yet," said Gretchen. "I'll boot it up for you and you can take a look."

"Okay," said Noah. "We've got Eden possibly meeting with Thatcher Toland, definitely admitting to her best friend that she had watched at least one of his videos, and then going on some kind of trip to atone for her sins. Do we have any idea where she was headed?"

Gretchen handed Eden's open laptop across the desks to Josie and went back to her notebook. "Her Mini Cooper was picked up on camera getting onto the Northeast Extension at Plymouth Meeting, right outside of Philadelphia. She got off on Exit 95."

"She got onto Route 80, then," Noah said.

Josie started by taking a brief look through the photos and documents stored on Eden's laptop but found nothing of interest. She pulled up her internet browser next. A lot of people kept themselves signed in to email and social media accounts on their personal computers, but Eden had not done so. Josie went straight for the browser history.

"We have no idea," said Gretchen. "If she was visiting any of her relatives, she'd likely take Route 80 to get there, but we don't actually know if she ever made it onto Route 80. Philly PD did manage to get her on video stopping at the Wawa gas station and mini-market at that exit, right across from the entrance ramp to Route 80, but that's it. She got coffee and a candy bar."

"But that's it?" asked Noah. "She disappeared after that until we found her at the dam?"

"Looks that way," said Gretchen.

In the weeks before she left Philadelphia, Eden Watts had watched one hundred forty-two Thatcher Toland videos on YouTube. She had visited several online shopping sites, everything from Amazon to a site where you could purchase cat food and have it delivered to your home. She had searched for 'how to make a Long Island iced tea'; 'how to tell if your cat has allergies'; 'what time does the Midnight City Rooftop Lounge open'; 'best mascara that doesn't run'; and a host of other mundane things that Josie would expect of a single, twenty-six-year-old cat owner. She had also browsed some real estate listings. The last item that Josie found in the browser history was the article about Nadine Fiore's death. Eden had visited the link twenty-two times.

Josie turned the laptop around to show Noah and Gretchen. "Look at this. It seems like there is a very strong possibility that Eden was the one who sent Amber the article about their aunt's murder."

Noah and Gretchen leaned over their desks and took a quick glance. Settling back into their chairs, Gretchen said, "From the photos I saw of her apartment, it looks like she did have a printer. Plus, Lydia Norris believed if anyone sent it, it would have been Eden."

Josie turned the laptop back toward her and went back to studying the real estate listings Eden had perused.

Noah asked Gretchen, "What about Eden's phone?"

"I've got to write up a warrant for the records and to see where it last pinged. I'll do that now, get it signed by a judge, and sent out, but we're still looking at a few days to a week before we get anything from the carrier."

One by one, Josie pulled up each listing that Eden had visited until she had over a dozen tabs open.

"We should get Lydia Norris's phone records, too," Noah pointed out. "Now that she's been murdered."

"On it," said Gretchen.

Noah said, "I'll write up a warrant to search her property in Danville, see if that turns anything up. These people were obviously up to something."

"By the way," said Gretchen. "Dr. Feist left a message. She'll call us with the findings from Lydia Norris's autopsy as soon as she has something. How about you two? What did you turn up yesterday?"

Noah recapped the day from Josie's run-in with Thatcher Toland at Komorrah's to what they'd found out from Amber's neighbor about seeing a man fitting Thatcher Toland's description speaking with Lydia Norris, as well as the meeting with Vivian Toland. "Thatcher hasn't called yet, though," he concluded.

Gretchen said, "If this is true—if it was him at Amber's house—that means he was the last person to see Lydia Norris alive."

Josie said, "I need Amber's work tablet."

Noah and Gretchen stared at her.

"Please," she said. "Can you get me into it? Noah?"

"Sure," he said. He fished the tablet from beneath some paperwork on his desk and turned it on. When he handed it to her, she placed it beside Eden's laptop so she could compare the listings.

After a few minutes, she said, "Look at this. They both searched some of the same listings in almost the same time period."

"What are you talking about?" asked Gretchen, standing and coming over so she could see the computer screens. Noah wheeled his chair closer so that he, too, could view the screens.

"Look at this. Amber searched for these properties in various parts of the state, all of them over a million dollars, a couple of weeks before she went missing. Right before that, before Eden took her mystery trip, she, too, searched for several of the same properties."

"How many match up?" asked Noah.

Josie clicked back and forth across devices, trying to match them up. A couple of times, she accidentally closed tabs. Noah placed a hand on her forearm. "Let me do this. I'll print them all out and match them up. You wanted to look into Russell Haven Dam, right?"

"Yes," Josie said, relieved.

"You do that," Noah told her. "I'll take care of this. I already did some searches to see if any of these were connected to Nadine Fiore. I'll make a list of the rest of them, and then I'll start calling county clerk records' offices and getting the actual records associated with them to see if there are any connections that aren't immediately turning up."

Gretchen said, "I've got a ton of reports to finish. Did you get anywhere with the numbers in Amber's old diary?"

Josie shook her head. As Noah relieved her desk of the laptop and tablet, she found the diary and handed it to Gretchen. "I'm totally stumped, but if you want to give it a go, be my guest."

"Paperwork it is, then," said Gretchen, taking the diary. "Until Thatcher Toland calls."

Noah grunted. "Don't hold your breath."

THIRTY-THREE

They settled in for a long, miserable morning of paperwork. Josie wrote up her reports from the morning's gruesome discovery and then she began researching Russell Haven Dam. She started with Google, adding the words "Denton, Pennsylvania" to the search terms. Thousands of results turned up. She scrolled past the hundreds of headlines about the addition of the hydroelectric power station to the existing dam, then several headlines about the possibility of adding a whitewater park to the hydro dam. Then came the stories about the kayakers who had perished in the same chute where Josie had lost her grip on Eden Watts. Those deaths put a stop to talks of installing a whitewater park on the dam.

Several pages back in the results she found a story from the WYEP website from thirteen years earlier. The thumbnail showed a photo of Trinity, microphone in hand, wearing her WYEP polo shirt, standing in front of Russell Haven Dam. Josie fished some earbuds from one of her desk drawers and plugged them into the computer. She clicked on the link and the video began to play. The chyron announced, *Renowned Psychologist Dies By Suicide*. Trinity, looking impossibly young, stood at the site where the huge hydroelectric station building would eventually be built. At that time, it was just a mud lot overlooking a sizeable drop-off. Behind her, the water of the Susquehanna River coursed over the spillway, whitecaps rising from it as it crashed into the river bed.

Josie checked the timestamp. She would have been on patrol then, inexperienced and relegated to traffic stops. She didn't remember this, although there were thousands of accidents, crimes, and other incidents in Denton every year. It would be impossible to remember them all. She turned the volume up so she could hear Trinity's report.

"Earlier this week, authorities recovered the body of renowned psychologist, Jeremy Rafferty, of Harrisburg, from the Susquehanna River. It was here, at Russell Haven Dam, that his body was discovered by kayakers after he had been reported missing by his family. It is believed that Dr. Rafferty died by suicide. His vehicle was located by police a couple of miles upriver. Authorities believe that he jumped into the water there, taking his own life, and that his body washed downriver to the dam. As our viewers will recall, Dr. Rafferty was a guest on our network locally and nationally many times. He specialized in couples' and family therapy. He had a private practice, taught at the prestigious Preston Hill College, had written several books, and was in talks with a cable network to develop his own show. Although some colleagues and patients had noticed that he wasn't quite himself in the last several months, no one expected such a tragedy to unfold. His family has said that although he seemed to be dealing with some low-grade depression, they weren't worried that he would try to harm himself. As to why he chose Denton to take his own life, some of his friends speculate it's because he grew up here before moving away permanently when he entered college."

The screen cut back to the anchors sitting in the WYEP station, both looking appropriately saddened and confounded.

They asked Trinity a few questions. Then a suicide hotline number flashed across the screen before the video ended. Josie started a new search for Dr. Jeremy Rafferty which brought up hundreds of articles about his death and thousands of results for his books and television appearances. He was in his late fifties when he died. Josie did some calculations, realizing that the Watts children would have been teenagers at the time of his death. Amber would have been about fifteen or sixteen years old at that time. Eden would have been thirteen or fourteen.

Was there a connection? Had Amber and her "toxic" family gone to him for counseling? Had they been living in the Harrisburg area at the time of his death? One of the real estate listings on both Amber's work tablet and Eden's laptop was from Harrisburg. Answering those questions would require more research but for now, Josie knew that one of the best sources of information on what WYEP didn't include in their story was her sister. She tugged her earbuds out and snatched up her car keys. Gretchen and Noah had left to get their warrants signed. Then they were going to see Dr. Feist about autopsy results. The Chief hadn't come back from Russell Haven yet.

Ten minutes later, Josie pulled into her driveway. Her parents' vehicle was gone but Trinity's rental was still there. Inside the house, she gave Trout some attention, let him out, and refilled his food bowl. Then she went upstairs, where Trinity was still fast asleep in one of the guest bedrooms. Cell phone in one hand, Trinity was sprawled across the bed in a pair of long flannel pajamas. She'd probably been waiting for Drake to call when she fell asleep. Smiling, Josie nudged her shoulder until she blinked awake. She stared at Josie, unseeing, for a long moment, then at her phone. She groaned when she saw it was almost eleven a.m. "Why would you wake me up? I never get to sleep this late. Ever."

Josie climbed onto the bed and sat next to her. "I'm sorry. I needed to talk to you."

"I haven't seen you in days. I'm a guest in your home, and don't say you had to work. You always have to work."

Josie rolled her eyes. "Like you don't always have to work? Do you really want to go there before you've had your morning coffee?"

Scowling, Trinity sat up and pushed her hair around on her head. It didn't matter what state she was in; somehow she always managed to look glamorous. It defied reason that they were twins. Josie could never get her hair to look that glossy, especially if she'd slept on it for several hours.

"You could have brought coffee," Trinity said.

"I'll make it up to you."

Trinity laughed. "Sure. Okay. 'Cause we both have time for that. Just tell me. What's up?"

"When you worked for WYEP—"

"That's ancient history," Trinity cut in.

"Just listen. You did a story about Dr. Jeremy Rafferty. He died by suicide."

It took a few seconds, but then Trinity's head bobbed as she remembered. "Yes. The famous psychologist. That was horribly tragic. Of all the people you would think would know how to ask for help—a psychologist. Why are you asking me about him?"

"His body was recovered from Russell Haven Dam."

"Oh right, and you're working a case now where a woman was just killed there."

"Two women, as of last night."

Trinity's eyes widened. "What? Really? Murders?"

Josie nodded. "Why didn't you tell me you'd done a story on it after the first victim?"

Trinity elbowed her lightly. "You should really try coming home at a reasonable hour. Like I said, I haven't seen you in days. You have basically been gone since Mett came here the other night. I haven't had time to talk to you about anything, much less that. You think there's a connection between Rafferty's suicide and your two murder victims?"

"That's what I'm trying to figure out," said Josie. "What do you remember from that case? The stuff that didn't make it into your thirty-second TV spot?"

Trinity yawned and put her phone on the nightstand. Her eyes narrowed as she searched her memory. "I just remember how surprised everyone was—everyone who knew him—but then again, everyone who knew him said he'd been depressed. Nobody could pinpoint when it started or why. Just that he didn't seem like himself. It's weird, right? All these people saw him getting more and more depressed each day, but no one thought he'd hurt himself. Maybe because he was a psychologist people just assumed he'd never do that. Anyway, it was only his adult daughter who thought he hadn't killed himself."

"Why was that?"

Trinity shrugged. "I don't remember. It was a long time ago, Josie. I just remember that my producer didn't want to interview her because he didn't want to introduce this alternate theory when the police had the whole case wrapped up pretty tightly."

"Did he leave a note?" Josie asked.

"He left a Microsoft Word document open on his computer with the words typed, 'I'm sorry.' The daughter kept saying anyone could have done that."

"She thought someone murdered him?"

"Or that someone drove him to do it," Trinity said.

"Why would she say that?"

Trinity slouched down on the bed, nestling her head into the pillow, and closed her eyes. "I really don't remember. You could probably ask her, though. I'm sure she still lives in Pennsylvania. She was a college professor, like her dad. Not at the same school or the same subject. She taught kinesiology, which I only remember because it seemed so unusual."

"Kinesiology?" Josie said. "Is that like muscle-testing?"

"The study of how the human body moves. Mechanics and stuff. I don't know. It was all very vague, and that was a long time ago. Anyway, her name was... oh, crap. It begins with a D... Devon— definitely Devon. I remember because it was so close to Denton. Same last name. I don't know if she was married or not. Well, I guess she was married at that time because she said how she was taking fertility treatments after having had all these miscarriages. She miscarried again after her dad's suicide. Stress. It was the saddest thing. One of the saddest stories I ever covered. Her mom had died when she was a kid. All she had was her father. Anyway, she's got a PhD and I think she kept her father's last name. Dr. Rafferty."

"Thanks," said Josie. "Go back to sleep."

Trinity pulled the covers back up to her neck. "Happy to."

Back downstairs, Josie used her laptop to track down Devon Rafferty. To Josie's surprise, she now lived in Denton and taught kinesiology at the university. Josie found her home address easily and punched it into her phone's GPS system. She would try Devon's home first and if she wasn't there, then she would try the university. She really hoped Devon was at home, though as she didn't relish the idea of traipsing all over the huge campus trying to find the right building.

In the car, her eyes burned with exhaustion and yet her mind was on fire with questions. Thatcher Toland had started to look like a front-runner in terms of their persons of interest. But then there was the matter of Gabriel Watts possibly having been seen accosting Amber before her death—and the fact that he'd been unaccounted for the past couple of days. Sheriff's Deputy Tiercar had been checking his home regularly throughout the day and still had not encountered him. Then there was this other tragedy at Russell Haven Dam. It might be completely unrelated, and with the disparate puzzle pieces they already had, it seemed like it would be, but Josie couldn't shake the feeling that the killer had chosen Russell Haven Dam because it was of great significance to him. Although they had a lot of leads to track down, they were really no closer to finding Amber. Josie had to follow any lead she had, no matter how obscure it seemed. She texted Noah and Gretchen to let them know where she was headed, which was either on a wild goose chase or toward a lead that might help her find Amber—and a killer.

THIRTY-FOUR

Devon Rafferty's home was located in the hills above the university campus. It was a beautiful stone building with bright red tin roofing on both the house and the attached three-car garage. It sat about two acres back from the road. Trees crowded around it. Josie imagined they provided ample shade during the spring and summer months. On the far side of the garage was a patio area complete with Adirondack chairs surrounding a fire pit. Against one of the closed garage doors leaned two bikes. Josie pulled down the long driveway. A small tan Toyota sedan was parked behind a silver Land Rover. Josie parked next to the Land Rover and made her way up the stone path to the front door. She rang the doorbell and waited.

A moment later, the heavy door swung open and a young girl, about eleven or twelve years old, stared at Josie. Her hair was cut in a bob. An oversized sweatshirt with the United States Navy logo on its left breast swallowed her small frame. It matched her navy-blue leggings. Brown UGG boots completed the ensemble. She peered at Josie with narrowed eyes. Then she turned slightly and called over her shoulder. "Mom! Dad! That lady cop who's always on TV is here!" Looking back at Josie, she said, "Have you ever shot anyone?"

From somewhere behind the girl, a male voice yelled, "Lilly!" in a warning tone. Then: "Hang on!"

Josie said, "Have you?"

Lilly smiled ever so slightly and folded her arms over her chest. "No. Not yet."

"People go to jail for that kind of thing," Josie told her.

"Not everyone. My dad's shot people. I mean, he says he can't say if he did, but he's a Navy Seal so probably he did and he just can't tell you."

A tall, burly man in jeans and a fleece appeared behind Lilly, carrying a duffel bag. He had a thick head of red hair, a well-trimmed beard, and an infectious smile. A small gold cross hung around his neck. "Lilly!" He dropped the bag on the floor, nudged his daughter aside, and extended a hand to Josie. "I'm so sorry about her. She's a little precocious. I'm Bob. I'm retired—" he looked pointedly at his daughter, "from the Navy. This is my daughter, Lilly. What can we help you with?"

Josie shook his hand. "Detective Josie Quinn."

Lilly looked up at her father. "Maybe she's here to arrest us."

Bob laughed and slung an arm around her shoulder. Looking down at her, he said, "Do they arrest young women for asking strangers inappropriate questions?"

"I only ask because I'm curious," said Lilly. "Mom says I have a curious soul."

He kissed the top of her head. "You get that from your mother. Why don't you go get her? She'll want to talk to this detective."

Lilly ran off, deeper into the house. Bob waved Josie inside. A long, tiled hall led to what looked like a kitchen at the rear of the house. To one side of the foyer was a living room and to the other there appeared to be a home office. The rooms were filled with houseplants, eclectic, brightly colored pieces of furniture, and vibrantly painted abstract canvases. Everywhere Josie looked was color. Life. It was welcoming and cozy. Next to the front door was a collection of shoes. Sneakers, mostly. One set small, one set slightly larger. No men's shoes.

"It's nice to meet you," said Bob. "My ex-wife will be..." he hesitated. His genial smile turned to a grimace. "Happy."

Josie couldn't imagine why anyone would be happy to see her appear on their doorstep in her capacity as a police detective, but she started unpacking his sentence at the beginning. "Ex-wife?"

He kicked lightly at the duffel bag. "We've got an incredible kid, but we couldn't keep the relationship together. I'm dropping Lil off. She had a dentist's appointment this morning. She'll be back with Devon for a week. Then back to me. One week on, one week off. That's how we do it."

"You live here in Denton?"

"Yeah. About ten minutes away."

A woman emerged from the kitchen. Tall, mid-forties, fit, and wearing yoga pants, a sweatshirt, and ankle socks with no shoes. She looked like she had just come from the gym. Her dark hair was pulled back in a high ponytail and Josie saw gray strands starting at her temples. Her brown eyes widened as she approached. "You're here," she said.

Although Josie was used to being recognized in Denton due to her notoriety, the feeling that Devon Rafferty was somehow expecting her was disconcerting. She extended a hand. "Dr. Rafferty. I'm a detective with the Denton—"

"I know who you are," Devon said, shaking her hand. "I've seen you on TV. I know your sister is Trinity Payne. Is that why you're here? I watched her new show a couple of days ago. The *Unsolved* show? She covered my dad's death when she was a reporter here. Did you know that?"

"Yes," said Josie. "I—"

"Dev," said Bob. "I have to run."

"Oh sure," said Devon distractedly. "Lil's in her room getting some extra tablet time."

Bob rolled his eyes. "She'll be out of your hair for at least an hour, then. Nice to meet you, Detective."

He kissed his ex-wife's cheek and left.

The moment the door closed behind him, Devon zeroed in on Josie like a hawk studying prey. "Is Trinity the reason you came? She promised me back then that if she ever came across any information about my dad's death that she thought would help, she would tell me. I was thinking, now that I've seen her show, she could do an episode on him. Kind of a 'what really happened to Dr. Jeremy Rafferty?' With theories. I've got a couple. Come in. My office is right here. I don't have to teach today. Faculty meeting later this afternoon, but that's it."

Josie followed her into the home office. Instead of a desk, there was a long wooden table that had been made from various types of wood, giving it a mismatched, distressed look. More houseplants dotted the room, standing on every surface: table, bookshelves, filing cabinets. The floor was shiny hardwood with a colorful area rug in the center of it. A small round coffee table sat in the middle with two brown wingback chairs on either side of it. In the center of the table sat the Thatcher Toland book. Josie suppressed a sigh. He was literally everywhere she went and yet, getting a meeting with him was proving difficult.

"Sit," said Devon, waving to one of the chairs. She saw Josie staring at the book and smiled. "Have you read it?"

Josie took off her coat and held it in her lap. She perched on the edge of a chair. "No, I haven't."

"Oh, you must!" said Devon. "In fact, you can take that copy with you when you leave."

"I'd really rather—" Josie began, but Devon bent and picked up the book, handing it to Josie. "He's fabulous. Really, and I'm not even into... church. You know about the new place they're building at the old hockey arena?" She didn't wait for an answer. "The grand opening is Christmas Eve. I was going to go. So far I've only seen his videos online, but he'll actually be there in person. You should read this and then come to the Christmas Eve service. Maybe we could—" She broke off, the light in her eyes dimming. Quieting her tone, she said, "I'm sorry. Never mind. You're not here for that. Hang on a second while I find something."

Devon walked over to one of her bookshelves and began searching. "I still want you to have that book, though," she said over her shoulder.

Trying to get things back on track, Josie said, "Trinity mentioned that you had some doubts about whether or not your father really died by suicide."

There was a beat of silence. Then Devon said, "I used to, yes, and to a degree, I still do. I'm not sure. What I do know is that if it was suicide, someone drove him to it." She found a large black binder and pulled it from one of the shelves. Instead of sitting in the chair across from Josie, she sat on the floor, folding her legs beneath her and opening up the binder. "Did you know that in the six months before my dad's death, he withdrew over $50,000 from various bank accounts he owned?"

"No," Josie said. "I didn't—Trinity didn't mention it."

"I didn't know it then," said Devon, finding a green tab and turning to that section of the binder. Then she turned the pages toward Josie, pointing to what looked like a collection of bank statements. "I didn't know it until I went to settle his estate weeks later. My mom died before him, you see, so it was just him. I was already out on my own by then, married to Bob. I didn't need anything from his estate, but still, it was quite shocking."

"Did you speak with anyone at his banks?" asked Josie, studying the first statement where Devon had highlighted three withdrawals. "Surely he wouldn't be able to withdraw large amounts at once without raising some red flags."

"I did. It was three different banks, several small withdrawals over the course of a month. The largest he took out from any single bank was $5,000." She flipped through the statements, showing Josie each withdrawal she had highlighted, along with the dates.

"What did he do with the money?"

"I don't know. That's what I've always wanted to find out. I went to the police, but they said since he died by suicide and it was within his right to take his own money from the bank, there was nothing they could do. I was hoping your sister—with this new show—maybe she could get the public interested in his case."

"I don't know if that's possible," Josie said. "But I can run it by her."

"I'd really appreciate that."

"Dr. Rafferty—"

"Devon, please."

"Devon, is there anything else you found odd about your father's death? Besides the money?"

She flipped back to an earlier section in the binder. "When I went through his files—you know, to return them to the patients, since I had to close his practice—I found one patient file on his desk." From a plastic sleeve she pulled an old manila folder.

"He used paper files?" Josie said.

"Yes, handwritten notes. He was very old-school, and terrified that if he kept them on a computer, they could somehow be hacked into. He took patient privacy very seriously. He was pretty famous, you know. He thought that made him even more vulnerable to anyone who might want to snoop around, get their hands on his files, and threaten to release them. He would have been ruined."

Trying to keep her focused, Josie said, "You said you went through the files. You found something unusual?"

"This." She handed Josie the folder. Josie opened it but there was nothing inside. The tab had a name on it in someone's handwriting: *Ella Purdue.* "That was on his desk, next to the computer which had the note." She said the word "note" with part disgust and part incredulity. "As you can see, it's empty."

Josie felt a small jolt at the sight of the name. Her exhausted mind worked backward through the case. Where had she just heard the last name Purdue?

"Are you sure it wasn't just a new patient who never showed?" Josie asked.

"I thought of that but if that were the case, wouldn't there be some message or note from her somewhere in his office? Anywhere? He used to take down phone messages in a specific notebook he kept on his desk. There was nothing in that. Also I tried to find an Ella Purdue anywhere in the state and couldn't. Did you know there are eighty-seven people with the surname Purdue in the entire state of Pennsylvania? It took me three years, but I got in touch with every single one of them. Not one knew of a woman named Ella or had a relative named Ella."

Josie didn't know whether to admire her tenacity or be saddened by it, but now she understood what Devon's husband had meant by saying she would be happy to see Josie. "What are you saying?"

"I'm saying that maybe someone pretending to be named Ella Purdue swindled $50,000 from him and drove him to kill himself."

Purdue. The name echoed around the chamber of her mind. She thought back to all the interviews they'd done in the last few days. "Swindled him how?" Josie asked.

Devon gave a heavy sigh and took the folder back, tucking it back into the plastic sleeve. "I wish I knew. I really do. I can't think of a way someone could have done that. My father was extremely intelligent. People loved him. He helped a lot of people. He didn't have secrets. That was the next thing I thought—what if someone was blackmailing him? But for what? I can't think of a damn thing. I even had this year of doubt. That's what I call it. My 'Year of Doubt', when I wondered if my own father was really the great man I always believed he was or if he had been harboring some horrible secret that someone used to blackmail him! Can you imagine?"

She stared at Josie earnestly, and Josie felt a surge of sympathy for the woman. She knew what it was to have loss shatter your life completely. She knew what it was to live with a grief so powerful that some days could only be lived on a minute-to-minute basis. She knew what it was like to be consumed by thoughts of your lost loved one and to become obsessed with everything that came before their death, as if an in-depth analysis of those last minutes, last hours, or in some cases, last weeks and months, could somehow help you make sense of the fact that they were dead. When really, no matter how much searching, deconstructing, and analyzing you did, you could never change the outcome. That hurt most of all. Knowing that didn't stop you from doing it. People, Josie included, would do anything to ease the pain of ruptures in their souls that could not be fixed.

"Devon," Josie said, trying to keep her voice steady. "I will talk to my sister about featuring your dad's case on her show. Right now, can you tell me if Russell Haven had any significance to your father?"

"Oh, thank you! Um, no. It didn't. Denton did, because that's where he was born. To be honest, that's why I moved here. If this was the place he came when he felt so low, at the end of his life, this is where I wanted to be."

"I'm very sorry for your loss," Josie said. "I don't know if I said that, but I am."

"Thank you," said Devon solemnly. "I appreciate that.

Thank you for listening to me. Wait, that is why you came, right? Because your sister talked to you about the case?"

"I wish that was the reason, but the truth is that we've recovered two bodies this week from the Russell Haven Dam."

"Oh my God," gasped Devon. She lowered her voice, as if she was afraid someone would overhear. Josie glanced at the doorway, but there was no sign of Lilly. "I heard about one of them on the news, but they just said foul play was suspected. Were they suicides?"

"No," said Josie. "Murders."

Devon's face paled. "Oh my God."

Josie was about to ask Devon about her father's other patient files, when it came to her. Hugo Watts had mentioned the name Purdue when he was listing the names of Lydia Norris's ex-husbands.

"Did her other marriages end in divorce?" Josie asked.

Hugo nodded. "The last one died, I believe. Mr. Norris. I don't know if they're all still alive. It's been years. You could look them up, although I don't see how that is helpful in this situation."

Noah said, "Do you remember any of their names?"

"Last names, yeah. Let's see. There was Kleymann, Vawser, Purdue, and... let me think... Chasko, I believe."

"Detective Quinn? Are you okay?" said Devon.

Josie blinked and smiled at Devon. "Yes. Sorry. I just have a few more questions. In your father's patient files was there any mention of the last name Watts? Patients, family members or friends of patients?"

Devon stood up and went over to her laptop. "I can check. I've got all my father's patient names and addresses in an Excel spreadsheet—except Ella Purdue, since she doesn't seem to actually exist. The list really helped when I had to archive his records and mail copies to patients." She returned to the coffee table, settling back onto the floor. She opened the laptop and clicked away. Finally, she turned the screen toward Josie. "No one by the name of Watts."

Josie leaned forward and studied the names in the spreadsheet. They were organized by last name. She scanned all the last names beginning with W. "Do you mind if I search for a couple of other names? Fiore? Norris?"

"Of course," said Devon. "I can email you a copy of that if you'd like."

"That would be great," Josie replied.

Neither name was in the database. Sighing, Josie turned the computer back in Devon's direction. "Devon, do you know anyone with those last names?"

Devon slowly shook her head. "No. I don't think so. I mean, the last name Watts sounds familiar, but I don't know anyone personally. Don't you have someone in the police department with that last name? She's on TV all the time?"

"Our press liaison," Josie said.

"Yes," said Devon. She touched her ponytail. "Auburn hair, right?"

"That's her," Josie said, giving a tight smile. She took out her phone and scrolled through the list of real estate listings Noah had made for all of them that included properties that both Eden and Amber had viewed. When she found what she was looking for, she turned the phone toward Devon. "Your dad lived in Harrisburg. Was this his home there? Did he ever live here?"

Devon's brows scrunched as she studied the address and photo of the house. "No," she said. "We only ever lived in one house there, and his offices were out back in the carriage house. Here, I can pull it up for you."

She pulled the laptop closer and tapped away at it until she found the listing. Turning the computer back to Josie, she said, "This was our home. Since I was a little girl."

Josie made a mental note of the address, but she already

knew that it wasn't one of the homes that the Watts sisters had researched. "Thank you," said Josie.

Devon closed her laptop and leaned toward Josie, her expression serious. "Do you think that whatever you're working on now has something to do with my father's death? Because if it does, maybe you could reopen his case? All I'm asking—all I've ever asked—is for someone to take another look at his death. Please."

Josie's heart ached at the pleading note in her voice. The Purdue connection was tenuous at best. Maybe this was a dead end after all. "I'll do the best I can," she promised.

Devon continued, "Don't serial killers have that cooling off period or something? What if he kills people and dumps their bodies at the dam? I mean, I know my father's death was a long time ago, but don't serial killers have that cooling-off period, or something?"

Josie smiled tightly.

Face flushing, Devon looked away. "I'm sorry. I watch too much true crime on television. It's just that you don't under-stand what it's like to live with something like this." She touched the binder, caressing it with her fingers as if it was something precious. Josie knew that in a way, it was. It was a connection to her father. It represented the last shred of hope Devon had that he hadn't actually abandoned her.

"My dad never met Lilly," Devon said, almost to herself. "Bob and I were trying to have kids for years before my dad died. I kept having miscarriages. I was actually pregnant when Dad... when it happened."

"Trinity told me," Josie said softly. "I'm so sorry."

Devon kept her eyes on the binder. Her fingers stroked its well-worn cover. "I was further along than I'd ever been. I thought that time would be the one, you know? But the stress of losing my dad like that—so suddenly and in such a horrible way —my body couldn't handle it. The worst part was that he was the person who got me through all the miscarriages before that."

Devon smiled and met Josie's eyes. Tears streaked her face. "He really was a great psychologist."

Josie reached over and laid a palm over Devon's hand, as if taking a solemn vow on the binder itself. "I will take another look at your dad's case file when my current case is concluded, okay? I'll talk to my sister as well."

She let go and Devon quickly wiped her tears. "Thank you. It would mean so much to me."

Josie handed her a business card. "I'll be in touch," she said. She set the Thatcher Toland book back on the small table but Devon picked it up and pressed it into her hands again. Reluctantly, Josie left with it.

The cold air was welcome for once. When she got into her car, she didn't even bother putting the heat on. Instead, she tossed the book onto the passenger's seat and checked her phone, ignoring the tremble in her fingers. She had a myriad of missed text messages from Noah and Gretchen as well as one missed call from Noah.

She scrolled through the messages and updates. All the warrants they had prepared were out, and they were just waiting for records to come in. Noah had made multiple requests to various county clerk records' offices for more information on the properties that both Amber and Eden had searched. No word yet from Thatcher Toland. Noah had stopped by the megachurch again, but neither Thatcher nor Vivian was there, according to Paul. Gretchen hadn't gotten anywhere with the mysterious diary numbers and had left them for the Chief to scrutinize. Although Hummel had pulled a few sets of prints from the Toland book and news article Josie found in Amber's bedroom, none of the prints were in AFIS.

Most interesting of all, Hummel had pulled three sets of prints from Amber's surveillance camera. The first two belonged to Amber and Mettner. Their prints were on file because they both worked for the police department. The third set of prints belonged to Gabriel Watts. His were on file because he'd been convicted of writing bad checks several years earlier.

The last message was from Noah. *We think Gabriel Watts is home. Meet us in Woodling Grove as soon as you're done.*

THIRTY-FIVE

Woodling Grove wasn't much more than a smattering of houses along a winding mountain road northwest of Denton. At the bottom of that road, a single main street featuring a post office, grocery store, hardware store, bar, and three churches sat along a wide creek which had frozen over now that the weather had decided it truly was wintertime. Josie's ears popped as she drove past the main street establishments and up into the mountains to locate Gabriel's house. She toggled the knob for the heater, turning it up higher. Hot air blasted into her face. Proximity to Devon Rafferty and her grief—which Josie recognized and knew all too well—had made the cold seep into her bones.

She saw Gretchen's car pulled onto the shoulder of the road in front of a single-level clapboard house with white siding, now gray with grime. The front yard was overgrown with dead weeds and a sign instructed her to FIND YOUR FAITH. JOIN RECTIFY CHURCH. TEXT WAKE UP TO 33489. Trees closed in all around the tiny house, their bare branches reaching down as though they were going to scoop it up into their spindly arms. A mailbox tilted on the top of a weathered wooden pole. Faded black letters and numbers spelled out "Watts 35."

Josie parked behind Noah's vehicle and got out. Gretchen and Noah joined her, standing at the end of the gravel driveway. At the other end was a decrepit detached garage painted a pale ugly green. Its doors were closed. Josie knew from searching for information about Gabriel Watts that he had an old Ford Bronco registered to him at this address but if he was home, he hadn't left it outside. Josie quickly caught them up on her conversation with Devon Rafferty before they turned their attention to the matter at hand.

"He's home," said Gretchen. "We think. Since we've parked here, the curtains in the windows on either side of his front door have rustled fourteen times."

Josie looked around. There were no neighbors nearby—not within sight. "How many acres does he have?"

Gretchen took out her notebook and flipped some pages. "He's only got one acre. Behind his place and on this side is state game land, and the other side belongs to a neighbor. It's about a half mile to that neighbor's house."

Noah registered Josie's concern. "You think he'd try something?"

"I don't know," said Josie. "We know nothing about this guy."

"We're only here to talk," said Gretchen. "He ought to know that. He's got what? A half-dozen voicemails from you telling him that?"

Josie nodded. Other than his possibly having tampered with Amber's surveillance camera, and possibly having gotten into an altercation with Amber on the street two weeks earlier, there was no reason to think that Gabriel Watts would try to harm them. They had no reason to believe he was armed or danger-ous, and taking on three police officers carrying weapons would be monumentally stupid. Still, she couldn't quell the sense of dread building in her stomach.

"Let's just do this," Josie said.

Gretchen led the way to the front door. A broken slab of concrete made up the crooked stoop. Josie's breath preceded her. She pulled the coat tighter around her shoulders as Noah pounded against the front door.

They waited, their clouds of breath mingling. No sounds came from inside. Noah knocked against the door again. "Gabriel Watts," he called.

From her periphery, Josie saw a movement in the window to their left. The curtains swung. She reached forward and knocked again. "Mr. Watts," she called. "My name is Detective Josie Quinn from the Denton Police Department. I left you several messages. I'm here with my colleagues. We really need to talk with you."

Nothing.

Gretchen knocked on the door and called his name. Still no response. Josie repeated her words from earlier. This time, she added, "It's about your family."

A moment later, a pale face peered through a crack in the door. Dark eyes regarded them warily. "I don't want to talk," said Gabriel Watts.

Noah, Gretchen, and Josie held up their credentials but he didn't glance at them. "Please leave now," he said. "I don't want to talk."

Josie said, "Mr. Watts, this is really important. It's about your family."

"My family is the church."

Gretchen said, "Gabriel, we know you had contact with your sister Amber in the last two weeks. We know that you tampered with the surveillance camera she kept outside her front door."

There was a long silence. His eyes darted to each of them

and then upward, as if he was deciding how much to say. "Yes, I saw her. Now please go."

He started to close the door. Josie raised her voice. "We need to know where she is, Mr. Watts."

The door stopped closing. Only an eye was visible. "I can't help you."

Noah said, "Then tell us what you talked about. Amber told people close to her that she hadn't spoken to anyone in your family in ten years; that she wanted nothing to do with any of you; so why did you go see her? Why did you tamper with her camera?"

Slowly the door swung open, revealing Gabriel in a pair of jeans, long-sleeved black T-shirt, and black sneakers. His wavy brown hair was tousled and flat on one side as though he'd been sleeping.

"Are you awake?" he asked.

Josie stared at him. "What?"

He stepped outside, pulling the door partially closed behind him. His gaze burned with intensity as he addressed her directly. "Are you awake? Are you living in faith? Have you found your faith?"

Gretchen said, "We can talk about faith another time, Gabriel. Right now, we have a very grave situation involving your family."

Noah said, "We're looking for your sister, Amber Watts."

Gabriel turned his dark eyes to Noah. "I told you I can't help you."

Josie said, "What did the two of you talk about?"

His head swiveled back to Josie. "Amber had not found her faith. She wasn't awake. There were things she needed to atone for and I was encouraging her to do that. I wanted her to wake up to her faith, like the great pastor preaches, and do the right thing."

Josie was finding it difficult to reconcile this wild-eyed

disciple with the charming, easy-going Thatcher Toland. Vivian must have been right that Toland didn't know Gabriel personally. Josie wasn't sure he would want to, if he ever met Gabriel.

"What was the right thing?" Noah asked.

"That's between Amber and God."

Gretchen said, "This is very serious. If you know where Amber is then you need to tell us or take us to her."

His piercing gaze stabbed at Gretchen. "I told you already that I can't help you."

"After ten years, you just decided one day that Amber needed to 'wake up?'" Noah said. "Is that how it works?"

"I do what God guides me to do," Gabriel said. "If you want to talk about your faith, we can continue. If not, then I'd like you to leave." He placed a hand on his doorknob.

"When is the last time you saw your sister Eden?" Josie asked quickly.

"I don't know," replied Gabriel.

"How about your mother?" said Gretchen.

He didn't answer.

Noah said, "Where were you Monday morning between four and five?"

For the first time, Gabriel's eerily calm expression faltered, confusion flickering across his face. "I was here," he answered. "Sleeping."

"Alone?" asked Gretchen.

"Yes, alone."

"Can anyone corroborate that?" Noah said.

"No. Why would someone need to corroborate that?"

"Because," Josie said, "that was about the time that your sister, Eden, was being marched to her death at Russell Haven Dam."

A brief series of rapid blinks overtook his eyes. "What does that mean? To her death? What are you saying?"

"You don't know?" said Noah. "Your sister, Eden, is dead. Murdered."

His gaze dropped to his feet. Words poured from his mouth in a tone so low, Josie couldn't make them out at first. Then she realized he was praying. "Mr. Watts," she said. "Please try to remember the last time you spoke with Eden."

"Eden was trying to find her faith," he muttered. "She was trying, but I'm not sure that she or Amber could ever rectify the things they did. Especially Amber. Pastor Toland teaches us to drag our sins into the light and own them and then to do everything in our power to rectify them, but some things can't be fixed. I'm sorry for what's happened to my sisters, but you must understand that there are some sins you cannot atone for."

Josie and Noah exchanged a bewildered glance. Noah said, "What sins? What sins did your sisters commit that they couldn't come back from?"

"That's between them and God. All the rest of us can do is try to guide others in the right direction. We have to help people wake up to their faith."

"Did you help Eden?" Josie asked, wondering if leaving Eden in the dam was some sick sort of baptism.

"I can only help those who want to be helped." The mumbled prayers started again.

"What about your mother?" asked Gretchen. "Did she want to be helped?"

He finished his prayer and answered, "My mother abandoned her sinful ways a long time ago. She has only to rectify. When she is ready, I will help her."

Josie glanced first at Gretchen and then at Noah. Softly, she said, "Mr. Watts, I'm very sorry to tell you, but your mother was murdered last night."

The air was so still that Josie could hear a mourning dove coo somewhere above them. When Gabriel didn't speak, Noah added, "She was killed at Russell Haven Dam. Do you know why your mother and Eden would both be killed there? Does that place have some significance to your family?"

His eyes started blinking rapidly once more. Still, he said nothing.

Josie said, "What about a Dr. Jeremy Rafferty? Does that name mean anything to you?"

He didn't respond, didn't move a muscle.

Gretchen said, "I'm not sure how often you speak with other members of your family but a few weeks ago, your Aunt Nadine was drowned to death in a pond on her estate. Gabriel, we're here because it appears that members of your family are being killed one by one and your sister, Amber, is missing. We know that you approached her before she vanished. We know you disabled her home surveillance unit. I think it would be best for everyone if you came with us and talked with us at the station. It's only a short drive to Denton. We can take you."

He pressed a hand down on top of his head and he blinked several more times. "I, uh, I... let me get my coat."

He disappeared into the house, leaving the door ajar. They heard him moving around inside. Gretchen said, "It can't be this easy."

"It's not," said Josie. She left the stoop and picked her way over the dried, dead brush in the yard and around the side of the house. She had just turned the corner at the back of the house when Gabriel emerged from his back door. He had, in fact, put his coat on. She watched as he carefully and silently closed the back door behind him.

"Mr. Watts," she called. "Going somewhere without us?"

His head jerked in her direction. Josie unsnapped her holster.

Gabriel Watts ran.

THIRTY-SIX

Josie hollered for Gretchen and Noah before sprinting after Gabriel. Dried leaves and twigs crunched under her boots as she weaved around trees. The state game land forest behind his house was dense and thick. She lost sight of him almost immediately. He seemed to know exactly where he was going, and she wondered if he had this planned out. Had he been expecting to need an escape route one day? She was vaguely aware of footsteps behind her, running fast. By the heavy sound of them, they belonged to Noah.

The ground began to drop off, first gradually, and then more sharply. She was chasing a man down the side of a mountain, and she had no idea what was at the bottom. Cold air burned her nostrils and dried her throat. Her cheeks felt numb. She picked up speed as the ground grew steeper, stumbling and grabbing onto tree trunks to keep herself from falling. Ahead, she heard branches snapping. Gabriel was still running. By the time she caught sight of him again, her breathing was labored, and her lungs were on fire. He was below her, running along a ridge, hopping from one large rock to the next. Josie stayed parallel with him, waiting for an opening. A moment later, she seized it. He jumped off a large stone and onto packed mud. She dove from above, onto his back, and tackled him to the ground. Together, they rolled until they hit the base of a large pine tree.

She was crushed between him and the tree trunk, but she kept her arms wrapped around his shoulders. He squirmed to get up but he was disoriented and she was a weight on his back. "Stop," she told him.

"Let go," he said. His hands flew back, trying to hit her but she was too close to him.

"Where is Amber?" she huffed.

"Let go of me."

"Where is she? Tell me. Just tell me where to find her and this will be over."

"Shut up," he said. His upper body lurched forward but she rocked back, keeping him off balance.

"Is she still alive?" Josie tried.

He reached up and grabbed at her arms, trying to peel them away.

"Just tell me," Josie said. "Is she still alive?"

He wrenched her wrist, and the pain shot all the way up to her shoulder, blinding. The next thing she knew, she was on the ground looking up at him. With her good hand, she reached for her gun but before she could touch it, he kicked her in the abdomen. All the air whooshed out of her. Her mouth worked, starving for oxygen, but none would come. He got down onto his knees, his hot breath tickling her ear. She barely heard his words over the sound of her raging heartbeat.

"I did what was necessary."

THIRTY-SEVEN

Noah appeared moments after Gabriel left Josie sucking air in the middle of the woods. She waved him off, indicating that he should keep going and try to find Gabriel while she caught her breath. Noah ran after Gabriel. It took several moments for Josie's wind to return but once it did, she called Gretchen and requested backup. Then she went after Noah. What felt like an eternity later, they both found themselves on the bank of a frozen pond at the bottom of the mountain, exhausted and freezing. Luckily, Gretchen had called in reinforcements. By the time Josie and Noah trudged back to the top of the mountain, the area was teeming with state police and county sheriff's deputies searching for Gabriel. The road was lined with police cruisers, and his house was cordoned off with crime scene tape. Gretchen stood in the yard next to the Rectify Church sign, scrolling furiously on her phone.

"You guys all right?" she asked as they tromped over to her.

Josie's abdomen was sore, but she'd made the long trek back to the house with no issues. She flexed her wrist for the dozenth time since she'd hauled herself off the forest floor. It ached, but she didn't think it was broken. Not that it mattered. She would have let Gabriel Watts break her arm a hundred times if it meant finding Amber. "I've been better," she said. "Did you check the house?"

"She wasn't in there," said Gretchen.

"Shit," muttered Josie.

Noah looked every bit as haggard as Josie. He pushed a hand through his hair. "Can you get a K-9 unit out here?"

"On their way," said Gretchen. "Come on, you two. Get in the car and warm up. We'll talk in there."

Josie and Noah slid into the back seat of Gretchen's car while Gretchen got into the front. She started the ignition and turned the heat onto full blast. Noah pulled Josie close to him, and she let her head rest on his shoulder. No one spoke for several minutes while the frigid air rushing from the vents turned hot. Josie felt like she might melt into Noah as warmth finally found her. As the cold wore off and feeling returned to her body, more aches and pains announced themselves.

Finally, Gretchen turned the heat down so they could talk. She found her notebook on the dashboard and started flipping pages. "The sheriff's office is providing the K-9 unit. The Chief called in every resource to find this guy, especially since he attacked Josie. He's trying to get us a state police helicopter right now, but I'm not sure we'll get one. Hummel and several members of the ERT are inside processing the house. Also, Dr. Feist called. Lydia Norris's cause of death was drowning."

"What?" said Noah. "She was alive when the killer put her into the fish lift?"

"Yes," said Gretchen.

"Let me guess," Josie ventured. "She had a subdural hematoma which made her weak and disoriented, possibly unconscious."

Gretchen turned in her seat so she could look at them. "She actually had one subdural hematoma and a skull fracture. No patterned injury so we don't know what she was struck with but someone hit her pretty hard—twice. No sign of sexual assault. Also, there are some abrasions on her wrists to suggest that she was bound at some point prior to her death."

"Very similar to Eden," Josie noted. "Any phone records yet?"

"Not yet. Oh, and Mettner has been calling me every fifteen minutes."

Josie shifted and fished inside her coat until she came up with her own phone. She checked the notifications. Seven missed calls from Mett. "Shit," she muttered. "One of us should talk to him. No word from Thatcher Toland yet?"

"No," said Gretchen.

Josie looked out the window at Gabriel's sad little house. From the front door, Hummel emerged in his full Tyvek suit with gloves, booties, and a skullcap. Briefly, he spoke to the uniformed officer with the clipboard on the front stoop. Then he jogged over to the car. Noah rolled a window down. "Anything?" he asked.

Hummel rested a forearm against the roof of the car and leaned into the open window. "That place is a dump. It's falling apart, and I don't think this guy has cleaned since he moved in. We did find a gun. A Beretta M9. Loaded."

"Full magazine?" asked Josie.

Hummel shook his head. "Three bullets missing."

For a moment, none of them spoke. Then Gretchen asked, "Any kayaks in there?"

"No. Checked the garage, too. Nothing but an old beat-up truck."

Josie asked, "What else did you find?"

"In his dirty laundry we found a coat with some blood on the sleeve. Also, two long auburn hairs."

"Shit," said Noah.

"We can type the blood right here on-scene to see if it

matches either Eden's or Amber's blood type, but DNA testing of that and the hair is going to take a lot longer."

Josie felt the flutter of heart palpitations in her chest. Everything about this case, everything about her experience as a police officer told her Amber was dead and yet, the more evidence that came in to potentially confirm that, the more heartbroken she felt. As if sensing her sadness, Noah squeezed her more tightly to his side. Pushing her feelings aside, she thanked Hummel and told him to let them know as soon as he typed the blood on the sleeve of Gabriel Watts' coat. As soon as Noah rolled up the window, Josie said, "We are not telling Mettner that. Not yet."

"I'll call him back anyway, tell him we're still on the case," said Noah, releasing Josie and getting out of the car.

"What do you think, boss?" asked Gretchen. "Is Watts our guy? You want to stay here? Join the search?"

"I don't know if he's the guy," Josie said. "But we still need to find him. Right now, it's about all we can do while we wait for all of our requested information from Amber, Eden, and Lydia's phone records and the property listings the sisters searched online. A few hours ago, I thought Thatcher Toland was our guy, and we definitely need to speak with him, but Gabriel ran when we confronted him."

"Never a good sign," Gretchen agreed.

"Can we get a uniformed officer to track Toland down and ask him to come to the station?"

Gretchen's fingers flew across her phone screen. "Of course."

"Let's join the search for now."

THIRTY-EIGHT

By the time they returned to the stationhouse, they were all hungry, tired, and numb with cold. Gabriel Watts had disappeared into thin air. Chief Chitwood had gone out to the scene to supervise the search into the night while Josie, Noah, and Gretchen took a break. They picked up takeout on the way in and ate it quickly at their desks while filling out reports for the day. Gretchen checked in with the uniformed officer tasked with finding Thatcher Toland. So far, the officer had been to the church and three of Toland's properties within a two-hour radius. He was nowhere to be found. He hadn't seen Vivian either or even Paul. Gretchen told him to sit in his patrol car outside the church and to call them if Thatcher or his wife showed up.

Hummel called to advise that the blood type found on Gabriel Watts' coat sleeve was A positive, and according to records they'd been able to get from Amber's family doctor, it was a match to her blood type. This information sent moods plunging. Josie sent his team to Danville next to gain access to Lydia Norris's home—although the way this case was going, Josie didn't expect them to find anything useful.

Soon after that, the stairwell door banged open and Mettner stepped into the room. He walked up to the desks and stood before them, hands jammed into his hoodie pockets, looking almost sickly. His hair was greasy and uncombed. Stubble covered his jaw, and beneath it his skin was so pale it looked almost translucent. Josie could see the veins making blue ribbons across his temples. There were deep circles beneath his eyes. She sent up a silent prayer that they would find Amber alive. Whatever problems he and Amber had to resolve between the two of them was another story, but they'd only be able to work things out for better or worse if she was still alive.

"What's going on?" he asked. "What's really happening? Did you find her brother yet?"

"Sit down," Noah told him.

"I'm not going to sit down until you tell me the truth. I can't sit anymore. This is driving me crazy."

Josie stood and walked over to him, gently touching his shoulder. "I know, Mett. But just have a seat, and we'll bring you up to speed, okay?"

"What is it?" he asked, voice husky.

Gretchen stood up as well and walked over, standing directly in front of him. Her voice was gentle and patient. "It's nothing, Mett. Nothing yet. We're doing everything we can. Working every angle."

He pointed at Josie. "You think she's dead."

"I don't," she replied.

"What are you guys not telling me? I'm cleared, right?"

Noah joined them standing in a semicircle, "You're cleared, yes, but you can't work the case. You know that."

Again, he pointed at Josie. "She worked her own sister's case! When her fiancé went missing, she worked his case! You can't shut me out. We're talking about the woman I love. My future wife, if she'll have me. You don't get to have a different standard for yourself."

"Calm down," Gretchen said firmly.

He took a menacing step toward her. To her credit, Gretchen didn't move. "No! I won't calm down. I want to know what you're not telling me. I know there's something you're holding back. I've worked with all of you long enough to know."

Both Noah and Gretchen opened their mouths to speak, but Josie held up a hand to silence them. "We found a Beretta M9, loaded, three bullets missing from the magazine. There was a coat in his hamper. On it, Hummel found three auburn hairs and dried blood that matched Amber's blood type."

Mettner's eyes widened. When he started to sway, Gretchen grabbed onto him and tucked herself under his arm to keep him upright. "W-what?"

Josie said, "That's what we were holding back. But that's all we know, Mett. We have to keep operating as if she's alive. We have to keep working the case."

He opened his mouth to speak, but all that came out was a strangled cry. His hands clutched at Gretchen, and she slid her arms around his waist, holding onto him. Josie put her face within inches of his and caught his gaze. "Now listen to me, Mett. You're right. I worked a lot of cases where I had personal ties. It was devastating. I don't recommend it. Right now, only the Chief can reinstate you. None of us has the power to do that. But you can sit with us. No one here is going to make you leave right now. If you happen to have some good suggestions or ideas as to where to direct the investigation, every person here will listen. Do you understand?"

He nodded.

"But those big feelings you're having right now?" Josie continued. "You need to find a way to set them aside and lock them up for later. If you're going to help Amber, we need you focused. Stow them, Mett, or go home and wait for us to call."

He swallowed. "I don't know if I can." He looked down at

Gretchen, then at Josie and finally, Noah. "I'm not like you guys."

Noah raised a brow. "Don't be ridiculous. You're one of us, Mett."

"No. I'm not *like* you. I didn't have some fucked-up childhood. I wasn't kidnapped or stalked by a serial killer. I don't have a bunch of murdered relatives. My parents never tried to hurt me, never tried to leave me. I have a great family. I had a wonderful childhood. I—I'm well-adjusted. I don't have all this deep trauma that makes it easy for me to feel nothing."

"You think we feel nothing?" Gretchen said.

"You act like it."

Noah placed a hand on Mettner's shoulder. "We feel all of it, Finn," he said.

"Everything," Gretchen added. "Every. Single. Thing."

"Finn," Josie said softly. "You should be glad you don't know how to compartmentalize just to survive. I'm happy that you're well-adjusted."

"Yeah," said Gretchen. "It's not a character flaw."

"But you need to focus," Noah said. "Josie's right. If you want to help Amber, we need your skills as a detective. If you think you can stay calm, stay. Take a seat. We were just going to go over everything and talk about what to do next."

Gretchen released him. He took a moment to swipe a hand down his face and straighten his clothes. Then he sat at his desk. Once they were all seated, Josie texted the Chief to find out if there had been any progress locating Gabriel Watts. There was none. Josie, Noah, and Gretchen recapped all the other information they had turned up as well as all the other leads they were following, including Josie's interview with Devon Rafferty and the tenuous "Purdue" connection.

"I'd like to track down all these ex-husbands," said Josie. "I don't think anyone has told us the truth about Amber's family yet. They've been hiding something. I think there was much more than them just being toxic or dysfunctional, and much worse than a divorce."

"Like what?" Mettner asked.

Josie shrugged. "I don't know. But the only Watts we are able to speak with right now is Hugo, and he disputed nearly everything we've already heard from Lydia and both the sisters' best friends. Maybe we need to widen the circle and talk to people on their periphery."

"Plus Lydia's ex-husbands were technically Gabriel Watts' stepfathers. I know Hugo said that the husbands wanted nothing to do with Lydia's kids, but that might not be the case. Maybe Gabriel had a good relationship with one of them and that's where he went to hide."

Gretchen said, "I've got the husband list in my notebook. I can run it down, if you'd like."

Josie said, "We don't know what counties these men lived in, though so that might be an issue."

Gretchen lifted her brow. "Are you implying that I'm not as good an internet stalker as you are, boss?"

Josie grinned. "Maybe I am."

Gretchen nodded as she started moving her computer mouse around. "Challenge accepted."

Mettner said, "This is all fine and good, but how does Thatcher Toland fit into this scenario? What the hell was he doing at Amber's house? She doesn't even—" He broke off and looked at his lap.

Noah said, "Doesn't even what, Mett?"

Mettner shook his head. "She hates him. Passionately. Any time he came on television, she insisted on changing the channel, even if it was just a commercial."

"That must have been awkward," said Noah. "Considering you had a weddings brochure from his new megachurch together with an engagement ring in your underwear drawer."

Mettner dropped his head into his hands. "Of course you

found that. Well, yeah, I hadn't even showed her that yet, especially after I realized how much she hated the guy. I mean, I tried to talk to her about him because I had watched some of his videos online. He's really not that bad. I mean, he's got a good message. Amber caught me watching one of them once and went ballistic. You'd think she caught me watching porn or something. Then when she found the copy of his book—"

"You were reading his book?" Josie said.

"No. My mom read it and then she gave it to me. She gave one to all her kids. She's really into this guy. Anyway, with the grand opening of the new megachurch on Christmas Eve, my mom wanted all of us—the whole family—to go to the Christmas service this year."

"That must have gone over wonderfully," said Gretchen.

"Amber was horrified. She said we could not go. I told her, 'It's just one church service. My mom's not asking us to join the church, just to go to one service with her,' but Amber blew a gasket—again. She said he was a liar and a disgusting human being and that anyone who bought into his bullshit was an idiot."

"Oh boy," said Gretchen.

Mettner nodded. "Yeah. So then I was like, are you calling my mom an idiot? It turned into this whole ugly thing. I said I would go without her, but she didn't want me anywhere near Toland, she said. So I told her, 'This is my family and it's not going to be easy for me to get us both out of this. It's the only thing my mom asked for.' Then Amber basically wanted me to choose between her and my family. I told her she was acting crazy and that he was just some televangelist. Then I said some ugly things I'm not proud of. She cried. I tried to apologize, but it was too late. She picked up the book and read some stupid passage to me, and then she said all this shit, like, 'What do you think he's talking about, Finn? Think about it.' I said I had no idea what he was talking about and then she said, 'We have nothing to say to one another now.' She took the book and left. That was it."

Josie stared at him intently. "The book at her house was yours?"

"My mom's."

Noah said, "What was the passage?"

Mettner shrugged. "I don't know. I never even read the book!"

Josie fished the copy Devon Rafferty had given her from under a stack of files on her desk and tossed it to Mettner. "Find it," she told him.

"Are you serious?"

"Yes," said Josie.

"But I never read the book."

"Then read it now."

He shook his head as he stared at Toland's face on the cover. "Why was this guy at Amber's house? Did they know one another?"

Gretchen leaned back in her chair, steepling her fingers beneath her chin. "It sure sounds like it, doesn't it? You don't have that strong a reaction to a celebrity you've never met. At least, that's my take."

"Shit," said Mettner. "I'm so stupid. I didn't even catch on. What's wrong with me? Plus, you said he talked to her sister, too? Before she died?"

"We believe he did," said Noah. "But we can't prove it."

Mettner tapped his fingers against the book cover. "What did he do? What did he do to Amber?"

"I don't know," said Josie. "But Mettner, he keeps coming up, just like Russell Haven Dam does. There's something there, we just don't know what yet."

"Eden told her best friend that the old guy she met with in the coffee shop was an old neighbor," Gretchen said. "There's a good chance she just said that to get Karishma off her back, but it could be true."

Noah said, "We don't even know all the places the Watts kids lived growing up."

"Unless they were the houses that both Eden and Amber looked up before Eden died and Amber disappeared," Josie said.

"I can search our databases for former addresses of Thatcher Toland, Hugo Watts, and Lydia Norris and then cross-reference to see if any of them match up," Noah suggested. "Maybe Amber and Eden lived in a certain town at the same time as Thatcher Toland did."

"He had a small church," Josie pointed out. "That's where he started. Maybe they went there."

Mettner stood up. "I'm going to go get you guys some coffee, and then I'll see if I can find the passage in his book Amber was talking about."

THIRTY-NINE

They worked until midnight, filing reports, going over the evidence again and again, talking the case out while Mettner read as much of the Toland book as he could without falling asleep. The patrol officer Gretchen had posted outside of Toland's church returned to the station to tell them that Paul had finally arrived at the megachurch at eleven thirty to check that all the doors to the building were locked, and told him that both the Thatchers had gone to New York City for press until the grand opening of the megachurch.

The Chief showed up at midnight to send them all home. The search for Gabriel Watts had been suspended until the morning. Everything was at a standstill. The last thing Josie wanted to do was go home. It felt like defeat, like abandoning Amber. What if she was still alive? What if she was out there somewhere, being held, waiting and hoping they'd find her? On the ride home, the image of the Post-it note Amber had affixed to her childhood diary with Josie's name on it kept flashing through her mind. Had Amber meant for Josie to find that diary with those numbers inside? But what was Josie supposed to make of them? The Chief hadn't even been able to decipher them, and he had decades of experience as an investigator. What had Amber hoped to accomplish by leaving the diary behind? Had she suspected something might happen to her? Was that why she had put it there? Hidden it at work instead of home? Or was she planning on giving it to Josie one day? Were the numbers something she was going to ask for Josie's help with?

"Stop," Noah said from the driver's seat as he pulled into their driveway.

"Stop what?" Josie asked.

"Working in your head. You need rest, Josie. We both do."

She knew he was right. Inside the house, Trout's excitement and wet, doggy kisses were a welcome salve to her soul after the day they'd had. They took him for a quick walk, fed him, and spent some time playing with him before they went to bed. Happily, he tucked himself between them, his back pressed into Josie's side and his feet pushing into Noah's hip. For a small dog, he took up a lot of bed. Josie lay on her back staring at the dark ceiling and listening to Trout and Noah's dueling snores. She was thoroughly exhausted and yet, sleep would not come. Every time she closed her eyes and started to drift off, the sensory memory of Eden Watts' fingers grasping her wrist came rushing back, startling her awake again. After three times, Josie gave up trying to sleep.

Quietly, she opened the drawer of her nightstand and felt around until her fingers touched a set of beads. In the glow of the clock display, she could see the smooth green beads of the rosary bracelet that her Chief had given her when her grandmother lay dying in the hospital. Josie cupped them in her hand and closed her eyes. For months she had carried them around with her until one day she forgot to put them in her pocket. Since then, they lived in her nightstand. Sometimes, when she felt like her insides might break or spill out of her, as though her psyche was a flimsy bit of tissue paper, she reached for them.

She wasn't Catholic. She wasn't even particularly religious, but that wasn't why the Chief had given them to her. They were for comfort. She still remembered with perfect clarity the day he'd given them to her.

"What's this?"

"Rosary bracelet," he said.

"I'm not Catholic, sir," Josie said.

"Neither am I."

She stared at the bracelet. There was a medal with a woman in flowing garb on it. Around her were the words: "Our Lady Untier of Knots."

Josie was too tired to figure out what Chitwood was doing. "I don't understand, sir."

He reached forward and curled her fingers over the bracelet. "Someday, I'll tell you the story of how I got that thing. All you need to know right now is that even if you never prayed a day in your life, when someone you love is dying, you learn to pray pretty damn fast. Someone who believed very deeply in the power of prayer gave that to me, and at the time, it was a great comfort. Maybe it won't mean shit to you. I don't know. Regardless, if this is Lisette's time, nothing's gonna keep her here, but you? You're gonna need all the help you can get. You hang onto that until you're ready to give it back to me, and Quinn, I do want that back."

"How will I know when I'm ready to give it back?" Josie asked.

Chitwood started walking away. Over his shoulder, he said, "Oh, you'll know."

Josie wasn't ready to give it back. She still didn't understand how she would know. Chitwood always made her feel like she was playing a game in which she didn't actually know the rules. She squeezed the beads until the medal dug into her palm.

What comfort had Gabriel Watts found in Thatcher Toland's church? What sins had Eden believed she had to atone for? What had the Watts family been involved in that all three children had more or less stopped having meaningful relationships with their parents? What was the connection to Toland? What about Russell Haven Dam? Where did that fit into all of this? She was certain she wasn't wrong about it being significant. And those damn numbers! What did they mean?

Josie sat up and threw her legs over the side of the bed. Trout moaned in his sleep and promptly flipped over so that his back was flush with Noah's side. After tucking them both under the covers, Josie padded downstairs to the kitchen where her laptop waited on the table. She booted it up and started by looking for any connections between Thatcher Toland and Russell Haven Dam. Why hadn't she thought of it before? But there was nothing. Frustrated, she ran a search just for Thatcher Toland. Hundreds of thousands of results came up. She clicked on one news article whose headline read:

Thatcher Toland Was Never In It For The Money

Now a bona fide televangelist with tens of thousands of congregants and an online following in the millions, Thatcher Toland seems anything but. When he sat down for brunch with me on a sunny Saturday morning in his hometown of Collegeville, he could have been any average guy in his sixties. Dressed casually in jeans and a windbreaker, his hair mussed from the breeze, he couldn't be pretentious if he tried. That's part of his charm, I've learned. Sure, he's got a message that he wants to get out to millions of people. Sure, he hopes to change the world through his ministry. Sure, he wants to find the downtrodden, the sinners among us, and give them hope and purpose and maybe even a new lease on life. But when you have a meal with Thatcher Toland, he's just a man who likes his eggs over easy and his bacon crispy. He asks the waiter his name and inquires as to how his morning has gone—and Toland seems genuinely interested. He hasn't lived in this town for years. He doesn't know anyone here anymore.

When he turns his attention fully to me, he also seems genuinely interested. In fact, he asks so many questions about my life and family, I find it hard to keep redirecting the interview toward him. When I point out for the third time that we're there to discuss him and not me, he laughs and apologizes. "Go ahead," he tells me. "Ask me anything. I'm an open book." Sounds fake, right? Like he's trying to sell me on the Thatcher Toland he wants the world to see. The thing is, though, that when you talk to him, he is entirely sincere. His answers are sometimes brutally honest. When I ask him about the business side of his ministry, he winces and admits, "I wish there was no money. I was never in this for that. You know, I grew up with wealth. My parents owned a freight company, and it was very successful. I never wanted for anything. I could have gone into the family business, but I wanted to do something that would satisfy my soul."

Except that if you've read Toland's new book, Wake Up To Faith, *you know the early days of his career as a pastor at a nondenominational church in Southeastern Pennsylvania were anything but satisfying. "I thought I knew what faith was," he tells me of those early years. "But I was young and stupid and tempted by all the wrong things. I had relationships I regret. Inappropriate relationships. I thought that I was above all of society's rules because I was a man of God. I thought I could just do anything I wanted, but I was wrong. I hurt people and I hurt myself."*

When I ask him what he means by "inappropriate relationships," he gives a pained smile and says that for the privacy of the people involved, he prefers not to say. "That's not really the point, is it?" he tells me. "I know people speculate online. Was I having an affair with a married person? Was it with someone in the church? A colleague? Did I take advantage of someone? It's not that I'm reluctant to admit to the world what I've done. It's simply in the interest of protecting the other people involved. I've already done enough to harm them. Putting them into the public spotlight without their permission would only make my sins more egregious. What I'm trying to do is rectify the mistakes I've made in the past. That's what my work is about. I believe that if we all choose to wake up from our slumber of self-deceit and take responsibility for our sins, we can live freely and in God's love. It's life-changing."

Josie found nothing of use in the rest of the article, so she clicked out of it and kept looking through the results. There were a few articles about how he met his wife. She was a real estate agent who sold him his first house. It was a long courtship and an even longer engagement, but Thatcher believed God had brought her into his life to help grow his congregation so that more people could learn to wake up to faith and rectify their mistakes.

Josie kept going, reading through the results more quickly, eyes burning with fatigue. She clicked on another site that asked, "What is Thatcher Toland's Net Worth?" The author of that article estimated it to be in the neighborhood of twenty-five million dollars.

"Holy shit," she muttered.

Clicking out of that, she logged into a database and pulled up his driver's license. He was required to list a home address on his license, although with a net worth of twenty-five million dollars and a wife who used to be a realtor, he likely had many properties. It turned up a property in Gilbertsville, Pennsylvania in Montgomery County. It was about an hour or so south of Denton. Josie logged into the Montgomery County tax assessor's office and pulled up the property record. Toland and his wife had bought it ten years earlier for over a million dollars. Josie was about to close out the listing when something caught her eye.

"No way," she breathed.

She ran upstairs to get her phone. Neither Noah nor Trout woke or even stirred. She left them there. Downstairs, she pulled up the photos she had taken of Amber's childhood diary. Swiping to the page with the numbers on it, she found what she was looking for. It wasn't a perfect match, but it was a start.

There would be no sleeping tonight.

FORTY

By nine a.m. when she stood in front of the team in the great room at the stationhouse, Chief Chitwood included, Josie was still buzzing with adrenaline. She'd come into work before Noah woke up, leaving him a note asking him to come in as soon as he woke. She needed his help putting this all together, especially after all the research he had done concerning the real estate listings. While he organized stacks of paper on their desks, the ancient printer in the corner of the room was still whirring, but she had what she needed.

"Come on, Quinn," said Chitwood. "The suspense is killing me."

She handed out a sheet of paper with the numbers from Amber's diary printed on it. She had highlighted the twelve-digit numbers. Chitwood said, "You figured these out?"

"I did," Josie said.

Mettner looked up from the sheet. "You're kidding me. How?"

"Insomnia, by the looks of it," Gretchen mumbled.

"Well, yeah," Josie agreed.

"What are we looking at here, Quinn?" asked Chitwood.

"That is a list of parcel ID numbers," Josie announced.

"I don't know what those are," Mettner said tiredly.

Noah said, "The parcel identification number is the number that the county tax office assigns to a parcel of land. That's how they keep track of whether or not property taxes have been paid. But each county is responsible for collecting its own property taxes, and each county does it differently."

"Which means that each county in Pennsylvania has a different number format for their parcel identification numbers," Josie added. "Last night I couldn't sleep, so I got up and started doing some research into Thatcher Toland. On his driver's license, his home address is in Montgomery County. When I looked it up on the property search site, I noticed the parcel ID number was similar to some of the numbers on the list Amber wrote down."

Noah said, "I had researched a few of the property listings that Amber and Eden both looked up on their devices which were located in Montgomery County, but I didn't really take notice of the parcel ID numbers."

"No one notices them, I'm sure," said Josie. "I saw those listings as well when Noah brought them up but I didn't notice the parcel ID numbers either. But since then, I've been going over these damn numbers again and again and again, I've practically got them memorized."

"Does that mean the highlighted ones correspond to properties in Montgomery County?"

"Yes," Josie said excitedly. "But that's not all. It took some digging through the records that Noah had gotten from the various county records offices, but I've matched up not only those numbers but almost all of the other ones. Here."

She began handing out one of the packets. "What you've got in your hands is an agreement of sale and some estate documents."

"A house in Dauphin County," said Gretchen, skimming

the pages. "An expensive house. The parcel number is on the list Amber made. Purchased several years ago by a Lemuel Purdue. That's one of Lydia Norris's husbands. I looked him up."

"I don't get it," Mettner said.

Gretchen said, "She was married to a Lemuel Purdue for eighteen months."

"I still don't get it," said Mettner.

Noah said, "Look at the section that lists the buyer's realtor."

Chief Chitwood gave a low whistle. "Nadine Fiore was his realtor."

"Yes!" Josie said. "Nadine Fiore was his real estate agent when he bought the house."

"Wait a minute," said Gretchen, pulling her notebook across her desk and flipping some pages. "The dates. These dates. Nadine Fiore sold Mr. Purdue this house six months before he married Lydia Norris."

"Yes," said Josie. She pointed to a stack of papers on her desk. "We've got everything here. Nadine Fiore sold houses to each and every one of Lydia Norris's husbands within a year of Lydia marrying them."

"All the husbands were rich, weren't they?" asked Mettner.

Gretchen flipped another page in her notebook. "Not only were they rich but they were very old when Lydia married them. The five husbands that Hugo mentioned? Chasko, Purdue, Kleymann, Vawser, and Norris? They're all dead. In fact, they were elderly when Lydia married them, and when I say elderly, I mean not one of them was younger than eighty years old."

Mettner's face filled with disgust. "Wasn't Lydia..."

"In some cases a full forty years younger than these guys, yes," Gretchen supplied.

"Also, they were all childless, so Lydia inherited everything.

I thought that was going to be the most shocking revelation of the morning. Looks like you're the better internet stalker after all, boss."

"It was a scam," said Noah, reaching over to the stack on Josie's desk and pulling off another set of documents to hand out. "As the realtor, Nadine Fiore would have been privy to her client's financial information. Assets, debts, Everything."

"And she also would have known which clients were elderly, childless, and unmarried," Chitwood added.

Mettner said, "Nadine finds the men when she sells them a house. She puts Lydia on to them. Lydia seduces and marries them. Not long after, he dies. She inherits everything."

"Now look at the estate documents for Lemuel Purdue that Noah just gave you," said Josie. She was so exhilarated, she was bouncing on the balls of her feet.

Everyone began sifting through the new document. "This cannot be right," Mettner said. Josie could tell by his pale expression that he was having the same reaction she had had earlier that morning. Some of the pieces were now falling into place, and the picture was startling.

Chitwood said, "Hugo Watts was the attorney who handled the estate?"

"Yes. In fact, he was the attorney and the executor not just for this estate but for all of Lydia's dead husbands' estates. Because he was both attorney and executor, he practically doubled his fees. Not only that, but Lydia didn't hold onto any of her husbands' million-dollar and sometimes multimillion-dollar homes. She sold them." Noah said.

"And her agent was probably Nadine Fiore," said Chitwood.

"No," said Josie. "This is where it gets really interesting."

They all looked up at her in surprise. Mettner said, "More interesting than this insanity?"

"Yes," Josie said. She reached for a new stack of documents

and quickly handed them out. "Another agreement of sale. We're still using the Purdue marriage as the example. This is after Mr. Purdue died and Lydia sold the home to someone else."

Mettner read off the name of the realtor that Lydia had hired to sell the home. "Vivian Smith. So what?"

"Well," Josie said. "She's not Vivian Smith anymore. She got married since her days at the real estate office. Now she's Vivian Toland."

Again, all eyes were on her. Gretchen let out a long stream of expletives.

"Vivian and Nadine worked together," Noah explained. "They started out at the same real estate agency. Vivian lied to our faces when she told us she'd never heard of or met Nadine Fiore."

"Fiore owned the property in Sullivan County," Josie added. "But she also owned several others all over the state. She lived in Montgomery County, the same as Vivian Toland, for many years while they were running these cons."

Mettner motioned toward the other stacks of paper on Josie's desk. "Are they all like this?"

Josie nodded.

Chitwood looked up from the papers in his hand. "Let me get this straight. We're talking about a con that Nadine Fiore, Hugo Watts, Lydia Norris and Vivian Toland were all in on together?"

"For years," Josie said. "Nadine found well-off men looking to buy expensive homes. She identified the ones who were closer to death than not and who had no children. Lydia seduced them, got them to marry her. They died. Hugo handled the estates, collected exorbitant fees, and then Vivian sold the houses once all was said and done."

"But wait," said Mettner. "Lydia's got all the money. She must have racked up millions in assets over those years."

"I don't know how much," Gretchen interjected. "From my research, these guys were wealthy but not mega-rich."

"Mega-rich would have drawn too much attention," Chitwood said. "If someone is uber-rich there's bound to be some family members coming out of the woodwork to dispute a new, younger wife's inheritance. Distant cousins... someone."

"That makes sense," Mettner said. "But we're talking about five marriages. Surely that netted her a decent amount of money."

"Could be," said Gretchen.

"Four marriages between her two marriages to Hugo," said Noah. "She didn't marry him the second time for the kids, or because they were in love or trying to 'patch things up.' She remarried him so he could get his hands on his share of the assets."

"Holy shit," said Mettner. "Wait, where does Vivian fit into all of this? It looks like she was just getting a standard realtor's fee."

Josie's excitement faded for a moment. "That's what I can't figure out. The only thing I could think of was that perhaps she caught on to what they were doing and threatened to out them somehow, so they cut her in by letting her handle the sales on the back end."

"This explains why they had to move around so much when Amber was growing up," Mettner said. "What a mess. I wish she had told me."

Gretchen waved a document in the air. "If this was your childhood, would you want to tell anyone?"

Mettner grimaced. "Good point."

"What about the kids?" Chitwood said. "We haven't talked about them and how they fit into this whole thing. I mean, if Hugo, Nadine, Lydia, and even Vivian Toland had accumulated so much wealth from all of Lydia's exploits, why was Eden living in a one-bedroom apartment and working as a barista in Philadelphia?"

"And why was Gabriel living in such a dump?" Gretchen added. "We know Amber left, cut all ties. She didn't want anything from them, not even to pay for college. But what about the other two?"

"Neither Hugo nor Lydia seem like model parents," said Josie. "I'm sure once their children were grown, they were no longer interested in providing for them. The better question is, what did these people have these kids doing?"

"They were with the abusive aunt," said Mettner.

"Not always," said Josie.

"Then they were being shuffled around from one place to another every time Lydia got remarried," he suggested.

Chitwood said, "You really think these sociopaths didn't try to use their kids somehow to con people out of money?"

"But how?" said Mettner. "How would they use their kids to get money?"

"Russell Haven Dam," Josie muttered.

"What's that?" Noah said.

"Russell Haven Dam," Josie repeated. "The Chief is right. They did use the kids."

"What are you talking about?" Mettner said.

"When the kids were young, Lydia had to have spent months and sometimes years establishing relationships with these men. Hugo would have had the children on his own for long periods of time between Lydia's husbands' deaths. Periods where he wouldn't have access to the money Lydia had. Yeah, he left them with Aunt Nadine sometimes, but they didn't live with her continuously. From everything we've heard about her, I doubt she would have agreed to raise Hugo's children while he lived his own life and Lydia conned wealthy men out of their estates. Hugo would have had them a pretty fair amount of the time. He told us himself that he moved them every time Lydia got remarried."

"So they could be close to their mother," Gretchen said.

"No way," said Noah. "He did it so he could keep an eye on Lydia and make sure she was doing her part in the con."

"Makes sense," Josie agreed. "He must have used the kids. If he was able to use the kids to run smaller-scale cons, he could have brought in enough money to keep himself and the kids afloat while Lydia was off doing the big jobs."

"He's a lawyer," said Mettner. "Why would he need to use his kids to scam people out of money to stay afloat?"

"I don't think he was practicing much law," said Gretchen. "Not the way he moved from county to county. Maybe his practice wasn't bringing in regular cash, or maybe he blew through whatever money he got too fast. I think the boss is right. He used the kids to run small-time cons for his own benefit while Lydia was running long cons."

Josie nodded. "Yes, exactly! I kept thinking that Ella Purdue was really Lydia using a fake name, becoming a patient of Jeremy Rafferty, and blackmailing him, but what could a grown woman possibly use as blackmail? Rafferty was widowed."

"A sexual assault allegation?" Mettner suggested. "Maybe she threatened to go public and lie and say he had sexually abused her?"

"No," said Josie. "I mean, yeah, that would make sense, but I don't think that Lydia would have had time for all that. Also, she wouldn't want to bring that kind of attention to herself because it might taint her in the minds of future husbands. Plus, like I said, Hugo would have needed the money."

"He made one of the girls become Jeremy Rafferty's patient," Noah said.

FORTY-ONE

The sentence hung in the air. The many cups of coffee Josie had consumed that morning burned the lining of her stomach. She tried to imagine Amber or Eden as teenage girls being made to lie to and manipulate much older men.

Mettner said, "You're saying Hugo made one of his daughters become a fake patient of Dr. Jeremy Rafferty?"

"I think so," Josie said. "And then, at some point, he made them falsely accuse Rafferty of inappropriate behavior. He probably threatened to go public or to the police if Rafferty didn't pay him. Fifty thousand dollars. Jesus."

Gretchen grimaced. "That's beyond evil."

"Rafferty paid," Josie said. "But he still couldn't live with it."

"Unless he really had been inappropriate," Noah said.

Josie thought of Devon Rafferty's passionate mission to clear her father's name. "I'm not so sure about that," she said. "Although I suppose anything is possible. Regardless, the point is that Hugo was using the kids to do his dirty work. To bring in money between the deaths of Lydia's husbands."

"Now Amber wanting absolutely nothing to do with her

family makes a lot more sense," said Gretchen. "And her not wanting to say why also makes sense."

Chitwood walked over to Josie's desk and began riffling through documents. "We know that Rafferty killed himself thirteen years ago. Lydia was married to husband number four by then. The last one before she remarried Hugo, anyway. She married one more older man after that, but she didn't bring Hugo or Nadine in on the score. She was finished after that."

"I'm sure all of them knew what was going on and what happened with Rafferty," said Noah. "It's possible even Vivian Toland knew. They were running these scams together for years. At that point she wasn't even married to Toland yet."

"Unless it was something secret that Hugo was doing on the side," Chitwood said.

"Maybe Vivian didn't know," Josie said. "But I'm sure that Lydia did and possibly Nadine."

"Lydia received a postcard with Russell Haven Dam on it," Gretchen pointed out. "So she knew for certain. Except that she only emailed Amber. Why?"

"Maybe Amber was the one who accused Rafferty," Josie suggested. From the corner of her eye, she saw Mettner wince.

"Detectives," Chitwood said. "We still haven't addressed the larger issue here. Why is someone killing all these people now?"

"Atonement," said Noah. "Gabriel joined Thatcher Toland's church years ago. He's been a devoted follower. It's actually kind of creepy. He's all about atoning for sins. He admitted he tried to help Amber atone, but she wanted no part of it. Eden was getting there. He was seen accosting Amber before she disappeared. His prints are on her surveillance camera. We found blood evidence and hairs linked to her—in all probability, pending final lab confirmation—at his house, and he attacked Josie when confronted by police."

"But killing them," Gretchen said. "How is that atonement?"

"It's not," Mettner said. "It's vengeance."

"Also, where does Thatcher Toland himself fit into all of this?" asked Chitwood. "Does he know his wife is a con artist?"

"I don't think so," Josie said. "He might be one of her cons. She sold him his first house, remember? He came from money. Did you know that? He already had a lot of money before his ministry took off. She would have known that when she became his realtor. Maybe she saw an opportunity to get more for herself than just realtor fees from the long cons that Lydia, Hugo, and Nadine were running."

"Or the whole thing is a con," said Noah. "Thatcher is in on it. He and Vivian are working together. He didn't become Thatcher Toland, famous televangelist, until Vivian came along. The church is the con."

Chitwood said, "I can't see a guy in Toland's position wanting to kill people like this, even indirectly, and besides, what beef does he have with the Watts family? Vivian helped them but she really wasn't instrumental in swindling these elderly men out of their money. Really all she did was sell a few houses."

"Speaking of houses," said Gretchen. "There were eleven parcel ID numbers on Amber's list. Lydia only had five rich old husbands."

"Right," said Noah. "The other parcel ID numbers were for homes that these husbands had as either vacation or rental properties. I think Amber was trying to compile a list of all the houses that changed hands as a result of the scams that Lydia, Hugo, Nadine, and Vivian were running."

"Then Eden was looking around the same time," said Gretchen.

"They must have been in contact somehow," said Chitwood.

"That's why we need the phone records," Josie agreed. "Amber might have deleted calls between her and Eden in her call history, but the records will still show if any took place."

"Okay, okay," said Chitwood, holding his hands up. "It seems clear that the sisters were gearing up to expose the adults in some way. That still doesn't tell us who killed Eden and Lydia or who made Amber disappear."

"I think we need to look at Gabriel," Noah said. "The guy definitely has a few screws loose. He obviously disapproves and holds a grudge against his family for everything they did or he wouldn't have approached Amber at all."

Chitwood said, "All right, let's run with that logic. Gabriel decides he's going to kill his sisters and mother because they lied and cheated a bunch of men out of their money and even drove Dr. Jeremy Rafferty to kill himself. Maybe he was even planning on killing his dad, too, but hadn't gotten that far yet. But was he going to leave Vivian untouched?"

Gretchen said, "Vivian could easily claim ignorance. Like we said, all she did was sell some houses for Lydia."

Chitwood nodded. "Okay, let's keep going then. Gabriel starts with his Aunt Nadine. He travels to Sullivan County and drowns her in her pond. Then he decides to kill Eden. He kidnaps Amber. Then he kills Lydia. He dumps Eden and Lydia at Russell Haven Dam because that's where Dr. Jeremy Rafferty's body was recovered."

Noah said, "Driving a man to suicide is a pretty egregious sin. Much worse than convincing a lonely old wealthy guy to marry you and then keeping his money after he dies."

Mettner said, "But again, what's Thatcher Toland's part in all of this? From what we can tell, he spoke with Eden before she left Philadelphia, and then the other day he went to Amber's house."

"Maybe Gabriel unburdened himself to Thatcher," Josie suggested. "Vivian lied about not knowing Nadine Fiore. It's not a stretch to think she lied about Thatcher not knowing Gabriel personally. Maybe Gabriel went to Thatcher and told him everything. Maybe Thatcher realized that Gabriel had some disturbing ideas as to how his family could atone for their sins, and he was trying to smooth things over—to avoid murder. Maybe he told Gabriel he'd handle it by talking to both Eden and Amber but that wasn't enough for Gabriel."

"That's assuming that Thatcher Toland isn't some slimy, disgusting, scheming TV preacher who is only out for money. He did marry a con woman, after all," Gretchen said. "I'm still not sold on the theory that he knows absolutely nothing about his wife's former activities."

"You don't think he's for real?" asked Mettner.

"I don't think any of those guys are for real," Gretchen said.

Something was fighting its way out of the darkness in the back of Josie's mind, but she couldn't quite make it out yet. Mentally, she tried to pull it into focus, but it wouldn't crystallize. Something about their theory. All the pieces fit, and yet something felt off. Like when you worked on a jigsaw puzzle and you had a piece that almost fit into place, but one of the edges was just a little too large or too narrow; too rounded or too edged. You could force the piece into place and it seemed fine— until you found the puzzle piece that truly went there. Only then could you see how easily and perfectly it fit and how wrong you were about the first one.

"Shit," she said.

"What is it?" Noah asked.

She shook her head. "Nothing. I don't know. Never mind. Right now we need to get to work."

"Where should we start?" asked Gretchen.

"We need to find Gabriel Watts," said Josie. "That's first. We should have Hugo come back in for another chat. Then we need to speak directly to Thatcher Toland. I also want those phone records. Amber, Eden, Gabriel, and Lydia."

The stairwell door opened, sending a whoosh of air through the room. Sergeant Dan Lamay shuffled through, wearing a Santa hat and a necklace made of Christmas lights around his neck. In his hands was a tray of Christmas cookies. Everyone turned to stare at him. He froze.

"Lamay," said Chitwood. "Just what in the hell are you doing?"

Dan looked over his shoulder at the closed door as if wondering whether there was a way to leave without answering the Chief's question. Apparently realizing there wasn't, he turned back and held out the cookie tray. "The holiday party. It's started downstairs. Just wanted to see if any of you wanted to join in."

"Holiday party?" Noah said. "That's today?"

Dan walked over and put the cookies on one of the desks and then backed away as if they were an explosive that might detonate at any second. "Never mind then. I'll just see you all later."

Once he left, Gretchen started digging into the cookies. "At least holiday parties are good for tasty treats."

"That means Christmas Eve is tomorrow," Josie said.

"Don't remind me," Mettner groaned. He stood up. "Listen, I can help. I'll go over to—"

Before he could finish, Chitwood laid a hand on his shoulder. "Sit down, son. You're staying here to follow up on the warrants for the phone records. Also check in with Officer Hummel. I understand he went to Danville last night to process Lydia Norris's house. Find out if he found anything helpful."

Mettner's lips pressed into a thin line. Josie knew he wanted to argue. He wanted to be out in the field, likely hunting Gabriel Watts down, but he also knew that one wrong word to the Chief could have him sent home altogether to wait for news. "Fine," he said, sitting back down.

Chitwood pointed in the direction of Josie and Noah. "You two, you're on Hugo and Toland."

Mettner said, "They'll never get Toland. He's away till tomorrow, unless that was a lie, in which case it sounds like he's already ignoring you."

"But tomorrow Thatcher will be giving his first sermon at the new megachurch," said Josie. "And guess who his wife personally invited to attend?"

Everyone stared at her and Noah.

Chitwood grinned. "All right, Detectives. Let's see how far we get. You two find Hugo and see where you get with Toland. If you can't get him today, we show up at his megachurch tomorrow. Palmer and I will resume the search for Gabriel Watts. Come on, Palmer. Let's call the press."

FORTY-TWO

Hugo Watts had checked into the Eudora Hotel, which was the largest and most lavish hotel in Denton. Standing twelve stories high, it took up half a city block. It was as old as the city itself, and its ornate brickwork had been on the historic register for as long as Josie could remember. Stepping into the lobby was like stepping one hundred years into the past. The emerald carpet was even more lush than Rectify Church's new carpets. Antique furniture filled the lobby. Marble pillars reached high to the coffered ceilings. Crystal chandeliers hung overhead, giving off a soft and inviting light. From somewhere unseen, instrumental music fed into the lobby.

The manager gave them Hugo Watts' room number once they told him that they had to serve a death notification. They had deliberately not called ahead. Josie didn't want to alert Hugo and risk him taking off. They were already expending tens of thousands of dollars in police resources looking for one Watts man. Josie wanted to maintain the element of surprise for the other.

On the ninth floor, the housekeeping carts stood outside of several open rooms, piled high with toiletries, towels, and other linens. Hugo Watts had placed a "Do Not Disturb" sign on his doorknob to indicate that he didn't want housekeeping to turn over his room that morning. Josie banged on his door. There was no answer. They waited a long moment and then Noah pounded, harder this time. Still nothing.

"Mr. Watts," called Josie loudly. "It's the Denton Police. We need to speak with you."

She heard footsteps then and a second later, the door swung open. Hugo stood there in a pair of pressed black slacks and a button-down shirt that hung open, revealing a white tank top beneath it. His shirt cuffs were undone and his feet were bare. His hair was damp and looked freshly combed. Josie caught a whiff of soap and shampoo when he stuck his head out into the hallway, looking from side to side. "You don't have to yell," he said. "I'd prefer if you didn't cause a scene. What is this all about? Why didn't you call?"

Noah said, "What we have to talk about is not the sort of thing you discuss over the phone."

Hugo stepped back into his room, expression frozen. There was definite fear there, Josie thought. "Can we come in?" she asked as she crossed the threshold and edged past him. Noah followed, closing the door behind them. Deeper into the room, Josie saw that his bed was unmade, a small overnight bag on top, its zipper open. A shaving kit peeked out. A suit jacket and tie were laid out across an armchair in the corner. His socks and shoes sat in front of the same chair.

Josie walked over to the window and looked out at the panoramic view of the city. It was always breathtaking from the upper floors of the Eudora. To her left, the television was on, muted. Chief Chitwood and Gretchen appeared on camera. They stood outside of Gabriel Watts' home in Woodling Grove.

Noah took up position near the bathroom door while Josie remained at the window. Hugo stayed near the door. He said,

"Detectives, I'd appreciate it if you got straight to the point. I have to check out in twenty minutes."

"Going somewhere?" Noah asked.

Hugo fastened one of his shirt cuffs. "Home. I have to go home. Lydia is handling Eden's funeral arrangements. I left her a message telling her to let me know when the service will take place. Until then, there's not much I can do here."

"You haven't seen the news in the last twenty-four hours?" asked Josie.

Guiltily, Hugo glanced at the television. "I haven't been paying much attention."

"Your son attacked a police officer," Noah said. "He's on the run and he's wanted in connection with the disappearance of your daughter, Amber."

And her murder, Josie thought as a wave of emotion she'd been holding back for hours threatened to overtake her. No, she told herself. She wasn't going there. She wouldn't believe that Amber was gone until she had cold, hard proof.

"Your ex-wife is dead," Josie added.

Hugo's head snapped in her direction. His mouth hung open. It flapped a few times before he finally said, "What?"

"Lydia was murdered. Someone hit her over the head and then dumped her into the fish lift at Russell Haven Dam, where she drowned," Josie explained.

Hugo said nothing. Eyes still on Josie, he tried to fasten his other shirt cuff but his fingers were trembling too badly. "I'm very sorry to hear that, to hear both of those things, but I have nothing to do with any of this. I can't help you."

Josie said, "That's not true. I think you can help us. More importantly, I think you can help yourself. I would not advise going home right now, Mr. Watts."

Noah added, "If I were you, I'd stay another night or two. The security here is very good."

Hugo looked from Noah to Josie and back. "Security? What are you talking about?"

Josie said, "You haven't figured it out yet? Everyone in your family except your son and Amber, whose whereabouts we don't know, is dead. You're probably next."

His fingers fumbled again unsuccessfully with the shirt cuff. "Why would I be next?"

Noah folded his arms across his chest and shook his head, as if in disappointment. "Come on now, Mr. Watts. We all know you're not that stupid. Why wouldn't you be next?"

"W-who do you think is doing this? Is killing—"

"The members of your family?" Josie filled in. She looked at Noah. "The lieutenant here thinks it's your son. I'm not so sure. I thought if we had a little chat, maybe you could fill in some of the pieces and convince me once and for all."

His hands dropped to his sides. "Pieces? What pieces? I don't understand. You think that my son killed Eden and Lydia—"

"And Aunt Nadine," Noah put in.

"And my sister," Hugo said. "And took Amber? Why would you think that?"

"The evidence," Josie said. "We think that because of the evidence."

"What evidence?" Hugo asked. "Stop being so cryptic and tell me what the hell is going on!"

Josie waited a beat, drawing the moment out until she saw a small tremor in his jaw. Then she said, "What's going on is that we know all about the cons that you, Nadine, Lydia, and Vivian Toland were running when your kids were young."

"I-I don't know what you're talking about."

Noah said, "No problem. We can refresh your memory. Your sister was a real estate agent. When she sold a property to a wealthy, childless, elderly man she would alert your ex-wife, Lydia who would, in turn, strike up a relationship with that man. Eventually she'd marry him; he'd die; she'd inherit all of his wealth; and then you would handle his estate. When everything was all finished and Lydia needed to get rid of his properties, Vivian would step in and make the sale. Lydia did this four times before she married you for the second time, giving you access to the wealth she'd accumulated."

Hugo's jaw was clenched so tightly, Josie could see the small muscles tremor. She said, "We're not sure what your arrangement with Nadine was in terms of cutting her in, but that doesn't matter. It's beside the point. The important thing is that what you four did was morally repugnant."

Hugo swallowed and then he spoke, his voice taut. "Maybe it was morally repugnant, but it was not illegal."

Josie had given this a lot of thought in the last few hours. "No, it wasn't," she agreed. "There's nothing illegal about marrying an older, wealthy man so long as he is of sound mind and enters into the marriage willingly. There's nothing illegal about handling the estates of your ex-wife's late husbands. You were just doing your job as a lawyer. There's also nothing illegal about Vivian Toland selling Lydia's properties as a licensed realtor in Pennsylvania."

Noah said, "But I don't think your son is all that concerned with the legal aspects, so much as the moral and ethical problems. He is, after all, a member of the Rectify Church now. We chatted with him yesterday, you know. He seemed to imply that all of you had a lot to atone for."

Hugo said, "He's crazy. I told you that. So what? He's taken some kind of moral high ground now that he's joined this church, and he wants all of us to pay for our supposed moral failings. That's his issue, not mine."

"It's your issue if he decides to find you and make you atone for your sins," said Josie. "Which is interesting because when we talked with him, he seemed mostly concerned with the sins of his sisters. Why do you think that is, Mr. Watts?"

"I have no idea. Like I said, he's crazy. Fine, I'll stay here if that's what you want, if you think that's safer, but I'd like you to leave now."

Ignoring him, Josie said, "The only reason I could come up with for why Gabriel would think that your daughters had to atone for something is what they did to Dr. Jeremy Rafferty. That didn't end so well, did it?"

At his sides, Hugo's hands shook. He clenched his fists to try to still them. "Get. Out."

"That wasn't just morally repugnant, now, was it?" asked Josie. "That actually was illegal. Sending in one of your daughters to pose as a patient. Forcing them to make up lies about him. Blackmailing him. After he paid you the $50,000 you asked for, he threw himself into the river. He took his own life."

The quivering moved up Hugo's arms into his shoulders. "If I have to ask you again," he said. "I will call security. Get out of my room. Now."

Josie and Noah waited, letting another long minute draw out. Their postures relaxed. Glancing back at the television, Josie saw Thatcher Toland's face. It was a clip from the interview he'd done the other day, the one that had been playing when Josie ran into him at Komorrah's. The chyron read: *Thatcher Toland's New Megachurch Grand Opening Tomorrow*. The segment wrapped up and then Gabriel Watts' driver's license photo appeared above a chyron that now read: *Local Man Wanted in Connection with Missing Woman*. That segment played and then the graphics changed to a snowy Christmas vista. *Heavy Snowfall Expected Over the Holiday* read the next chyron. When Josie looked back at Hugo, he too was staring at the television. His voice was softer when he said, "Please leave now, Detectives."

Josie and Noah slowly walked toward the door. He held it open for them. As they walked past him, first Noah and then Josie, she stopped in the doorway and said, "You know where to find us if you want to talk or if your son shows up to discuss your atonement."

She stepped over the threshold. The door was nearly closed when Hugo called out, "Detectives."

Josie and Noah looked back. Only a sliver of his face was visible through the door. He said, "If you're trying to root out activities that are both morally repugnant and illegal, you're looking at the wrong man. There are worse things that can happen—that did happen back then when my girls were young."

FORTY-THREE

In the car, Josie cranked up the heater. Noah pulled out of the Eudora parking lot and headed for Thatcher Toland's megachurch where Josie had no doubt they'd be stonewalled once more. Although Paul had told the patrol officer that the Tolands were in New York for press, neither she nor Noah believed that to be true. She had a feeling the only way they were going to get access to the preacher was at the Christmas Eve service.

"What the hell was that all about?" asked Noah.

"I'm not sure," said Josie. Again, the shapes in the back of her mind shifted, hiding behind a veil, out of focus and out of reach. "He's deflecting. The only thing we can be absolutely certain about when it comes to Hugo Watts is that he lies."

"That's true," Noah said.

They drove to the Rectify Church in silence. Amber filled every corner of Josie's mind. The confrontation with Hugo had only crystallized her fear. If their working theory about Gabriel was correct, and he was murdering his family as some twisted form of atonement for all the deceitful, immoral, and illegal things they'd done, why would Amber still be alive? What reason would Gabriel have for holding her? Josie thought of Dr. Feist's autopsy findings, which were consistent with Eden having been held and repeatedly beaten for approximately two weeks before her death. Why had Gabriel held Eden for so long before killing her? Had he tried to force her to atone in some way that was ultimately not satisfactory to him? Just how unmoored from reality was Gabriel? Once again, Josie had the sense that they were all forcing mismatched puzzle pieces together.

"Oh look," Noah said, interrupting her thoughts. "Our friend, Paul."

Outside the entrance of Rectify Church, Paul stood with a clipboard. Next to him was a man wearing some kind of uniform and baseball cap. Together, they studied the clipboard. Occasionally, the man pointed to some item on it and spoke while Paul marked something down. They both paused and looked up as Josie and Noah parked and got out of their vehicle. Paul walked over, holding one of his hands up in a stop motion. "As I told the officer last night, they're not here," he told them. "Mr. and Mrs. Toland aren't here. I can have them call you when I speak with them again."

"Sure," said Josie. "Like all the other times we were 'promised' they would call?"

Paul rolled his eyes. "I'm just doing my job here, miss."

"Detective," Noah corrected Paul. "Just mention to Mr. Toland if you speak with him that our questions won't take very long. Then we can get out of his hair so he can focus on his congregation."

This seemed to mollify Paul, whose posture relaxed slightly. "Sure," he said. "Of course."

They got back in the car and drove off. Noah said, "It physically hurt me to be nice to that guy, but seeing as we'll need to come back here tomorrow, I don't want to piss him off too badly."

"I know," said Josie.

Snow flurries bustled through the air as they pulled into the municipal parking lot behind the stationhouse. Josie knew from text messages that the Chief and Gretchen were still out overseeing the search for Gabriel Watts. In the great room, Mettner sat at his desk with the Thatcher Toland book open in his lap. In front of him was an array of food on holiday plates. The holiday party, Josie remembered. Sadness settled in her stomach like a weight as she thought about how Amber had been the one to organize the whole thing. As expected, thanks to her stellar organizational skills, the party had gone off without a hitch even in her absence.

Mettner shot up out of his seat when he saw them. "I got it," he said. "I found it."

Josie and Noah sat at their desks. "The passage?" Josie asked.

"Yes! The one Amber read to me when she was trying to make the point that Toland was a disgusting human being."

"Read it," Noah told him.

Mettner flipped to a page he had marked with a yellow Post-it note, licked his lips, and began to read aloud. "*I preached every Sunday in this small church in a small town to a small congregation. Every week I stood in front of them and talked about the word and will of God. I loved it at first but as the years passed, I came to realize I was mistaking adulation for fulfillment. I wasn't satisfying my soul by doing this work, I was merely enjoying the fruits of being someone others respected, looked up to, and listened to. I began to feel like a fraud. I was a fraud. I had come to the church for all the wrong reasons. I had a crisis of conscience, of faith. Is this really what I was meant to do? Is this what God wanted of me? I entered a dark period where I had to take a good, hard look at my soul and not turn away when I didn't like what I saw. I had made many mistakes, committed many sins: pride, gluttony, envy, greed, and even lust. Perhaps worst of all were the lustful sins I actively and willingly engaged in which stained my soul so deeply I despaired that God would ever look on me with love again.*

"It was at that moment that I woke up. I felt as though God himself was standing beside me saying, 'Thatcher, you will never get the stain out but you can gain my grace if you truly, and with your whole heart, accept responsibility for what you've done and do everything in your power to atone for it.' You see, as a younger pastor, I had entered into a relationship with someone who was not appropriate for me. I had become entangled with someone who was not in a position to make the kinds of decisions that I made easily every day. I took advantage of someone. At the time, I told myself I was in love. It was exciting, and I believed, wrongly, that this person loved me when in fact, I don't think I ever truly saw this person. I merely took what I wanted from them, gratifying only myself and never once considering the moral obligations I had to them or to the world at large and most importantly, to God."

Mettner looked up from the book, first glancing at Noah, then at Josie. "I looked it up, you know. There's been a lot of speculation online about this since the book came out. The prevailing theory is that he had an affair with a married woman."

"That's not it," said Noah.

"You don't think that's it?" asked Mettner.

"Can't be," Noah said. He leaned forward in his chair and plucked a piece of cheese from the meat and cheese tray Lamay had left for them, popping it into his mouth.

"He's right," said Josie. "If he'd committed adultery, I think he would just come out and say that. Why not?"

"Because if you outright say it, people can get pissed at you. The whole 'atonement' thing can backfire," Mettner said. He waved the book in the air. "This is just vague enough that it won't make people so disgusted with him that his career would be ruined."

Noah shook his head. "Think about what he said, Mett. Inappropriate. A stain on his soul. Taking advantage. Gratifying only himself. Moral obligations."

"Could all apply to adultery," Mettner said.

"You're both missing the major tell," Josie said. "Let me see the book."

Mettner handed it to her. She flipped it open to the Post-it note and ran her fingers over the text until she found the line she was looking for. "Here it is: 'I had become entangled with someone who was not in a position to make the kinds of decisions that I made easily every day.' Who would not be in a position to make the kinds of decisions he made easily every day?"

They both stared at her. The puzzle pieces in the back of her mind were shifting at warp speed now. "Really?" she said. "You don't know?"

Neither of them spoke.

She tossed the book onto the desk, knocking over a plate of pigs in blankets. "A minor!" she said. "An underage girl or boy!"

Both of their faces changed as the realization dawned on them. Mettner's features drooped, a pallor creeping into his skin. Noah made a face as though he'd eaten something sour. He said, "That's what Hugo was talking about when he said we were looking at the wrong man."

"What do you mean?" asked Mettner.

Josie told him about their meeting with Hugo Watts.

Noah said, "What could be worse than what Hugo did by forcing one of his daughters to falsely accuse Dr. Rafferty and then blackmailing him?"

"Actually having a sexual relationship with an underage girl," Josie answered. Suddenly, all the food displayed before them made her nauseated.

Mettner's voice was a croak when he said, "Oh my God, it

was Amber, wasn't it? It had to be one of them, right? Her or Eden? I mean, I guess it could be Eden, but Eden talked to him in the coffee shop. She watched all his videos. She wouldn't do that if it was her, right? Amber hated him. She hated him so much, and she wanted me to choose her over my family because they wanted to join his stupid church. It was her, wasn't it? He did things—he—" The words lodged in his throat. "He was going to her house to atone, wasn't he? Except she was already gone."

Josie stood up and guided him back to his chair. "We don't know that for sure," she said. "Mettner, all of this is still speculation. You understand that, right? We could be wrong about some or all of it."

Mettner stared at his lap. A tear fell down his cheek. "But you're not," he whispered. "You never are."

"Sure I am," Josie assured him. "Listen, the most important thing right now is to find Amber. Are you listening to me?"

Noah stood and walked over, putting a palm on the back of Mettner's neck. "Finn," he said. "I know this is upsetting. I want to throttle this guy just as much as you do, but Josie's right. We have a job to do. Right now, we have one focus and that's finding Amber. The best thing you can do for her at this point is to keep it together, okay? You've been a huge help to us so far just by sitting here at your desk. We still need you. Are you with us?"

Mettner's head shook slowly from side to side. He shrugged off Noah's hand and stood up. Without looking at either of them, he rasped, "I have to get some air."

FORTY-FOUR

Mettner didn't come back. Josie and Noah wrote up a few more reports and then they drove past his house to make sure he was accounted for and not off on some vigilante mission to destroy Thatcher Toland. His truck sat in the driveway. The lights glowed from his first-floor windows. Josie walked up and took a peek through one of the windows where the curtains parted just enough for her to see inside. Mettner sat on his couch, head in hands. She wanted to knock on his door and try to console him, but she knew there was nothing that any of them could say or do for him now. Except bring Amber back, and with every hour, that possibility seemed more and more remote.

Back in the car, Noah held up his phone. "Talked to the Chief. He and Gretchen are still out there overseeing the search for Gabriel. No luck. They're talking about calling it off altogether. Called the Eudora. Hugo Watts is still there. Hasn't left his room all day. Spoke with Hummel. His team processed Lydia Norris's house and found nothing. The Russell Haven postcard was still there. They took it into evidence, got some prints from it but none of the prints are in AFIS."

Josie groaned, resting her head against her seat back and closing her eyes. "Where is Amber, Noah?"

He didn't answer. There was nothing he could say. Nothing he wanted to say out loud, she realized. If Gabriel had taken Amber, and it looked as though he had, then where would he keep her? She wasn't at his house. He didn't own any other property. The only alternative, it seemed, was that Amber was dead and he'd dumped her body somewhere. The thought of it made the lump in Josie's throat grow so thick so fast, she felt like she might choke.

The snow flurries had become full-blown flakes. They fluttered down from the sky at a steady pace, unexpected beauty in a world of horror. Noah said, "The Chief wants to meet tomorrow morning at eight a.m. to go over a plan for approaching Thatcher Toland at his church tomorrow. The Christmas Eve service begins at ten a.m."

Josie opened her eyes and waved a hand dismissively. "Fine," she said. "We confront Toland. Tell him that we know he had an inappropriate and illegal relationship with Amber or Eden when they were underage. Even if he admits it, which he won't, that doesn't help us find Amber."

"You don't think he's a part of this?" asked Noah. "He was seen with Eden before she died. He went to Amber's house. He was the last person to see Lydia Norris alive."

"You think he's out there murdering members of the Watts family?" Josie said. "To what end? To shut them up? Keep them from exposing him? He's already publicly admitted that he had some kind of inappropriate relationship."

Noah said, "The statute of limitations for sexual crimes against a minor in Pennsylvania is extremely long. He's still well within the possibility of facing criminal charges if his victim were willing to testify."

"Eden is dead. Amber is missing. No matter which one of

them it was, neither is here to testify against him. Still, I can't see him doing the actual dirty work."

"Then we're back to Gabriel," Noah said with a frustrated sigh. "As Toland's proxy."

"This just keeps going round and round."

"We need clarification from Toland," Noah said. "Tomorrow. One way or another, he's going to talk with us."

"Or his lawyer will talk with us," Josie said.

Noah laughed, breaking some of the tension in the car. "True. Where to now? Home?"

"No," Josie said. "There's one stop I need to make."

She gave him the address to Devon Rafferty's house. The Land Rover sat in the driveway, now covered with a coating of snow. Christmas lights hung from the eaves of the house. The lights in what Josie remembered was Devon's home office were on. She knocked on the door, feeling nothing but dread deep in her stomach. Noah's hand slipped under her oversized coat and found the small of her back. "You're doing the right thing," he said. "She deserves to know."

The door swung open. Josie expected Lilly, but instead found Devon staring at her. Josie said, "Can we talk?"

FORTY-FIVE

Josie tried to sleep after they left Devon Rafferty's house, but it simply would not come. She kept replaying the conversation over and over in her head. Mostly, though, she couldn't get the image of Devon's changing facial expressions out of her mind. As Josie and Noah laid out what they knew and what they suspected about the Watts family's involvement in setting up and blackmailing her father, Devon went from looking almost excited and relieved at finally having some answers, to looking devastated and angry. She'd thanked them when they left but she'd still been crying. Trinity and Josie's parents were due to stay with Josie and Noah until after Christmas. Josie's family was excited to have them home in time for dinner, and they had all shared a meal. As everyone laughed and chatted around her, Josie had to bite her tongue to keep from bringing up the Jeremy Rafferty case at dinner and asking Trinity to do a show on him. Even though Devon finally had some answers, the truth of her father's demise was a long way from being made public, if it ever could be.

In bed, Josie held onto the Chief's rosary beads until she fell into a fitful sleep. Noah woke her in the morning with a hand across her stomach. She turned and fit herself against his body. Trout had already abandoned them after hearing Christian and Shannon in the kitchen. If there was potential food to be had, he wasn't above leaving his owners behind. Josie loved the feel of her husband's body next to hers, his hands exploring her, and yet, she felt guilty for enjoying this small, stolen moment knowing that Amber's fate was still unknown.

As if sensing her thoughts, Noah kissed her neck and said, "Stop doing that."

"Doing what?" she mumbled.

He shifted so that he could capture her mouth in a slow kiss. Then he said, "Thinking about the case. Right now, be here with me. It's okay. You're allowed to enjoy this."

She wanted to enjoy this moment very much. His hazel eyes twinkled as he stared down at her. Josie turned onto her back and reached for his shoulders, pulling him down to her. "Clear my head," she told him.

An hour later they were showered, dressed, fed, partially caffeinated, and standing in the great room on the second floor of the stationhouse. In spite of the lack of sleep the week had brought, and her high anxiety over Amber, Josie felt more alert and clear-headed than she had in days. She sipped a large coffee while the Chief spoke to all of them. Mettner and Gretchen were seated at their desks, looking even more haggard than the day before. Outside, there were already three inches of snow on the ground, and the forecast called for a lot more.

"First," said the Chief. "We can't find this little shit, Gabriel, for anything. It's like he disappeared into thin air. The K-9s didn't even have any luck. They lost his scent somewhere in the damn woods, too, so it's not like he got into a vehicle. I've got a small crew out there looking now, and we've got his photo out to every department in the state. At this point, we just have to wait for him to make a mistake and show his face somewhere. That said, I'm not so much interested in him right now."

The Chief had everyone's attention now.

"I took a look through the phone records you all were able to get—they came in early this morning. Guess who Gabriel Watts was having regular calls with the last six weeks?"

"Thatcher Toland," Noah guessed.

The Chief made a sound like a buzzer. "Wrong. Vivian Toland."

"What?" blurted Gretchen.

"Are you sure?" asked Mettner.

Chitwood rolled his eyes. "No, I'm not sure. Maybe it was Santa Claus or Rudolf the damn Red-nosed Reindeer. Of course I'm sure. Gabriel Watts and Vivian Toland have been talking on the phone several times a day for the last six weeks. The last call between them was two days before you three—" he pointed to Noah, Josie, and Gretchen. "Went to his house and he ran off."

More of the puzzle in the back of Josie's mind slipped into place. "Vivian is orchestrating this," she said. "To keep Thatcher's reputation, and more importantly, his financial status, intact. She knows. She knows what Thatcher did with one of the Watts sisters, and she's using Gabriel to silence them."

"Then why kill Lydia?" asked Mettner.

"She probably knew about it," Josie said. "Clearly, Hugo did. They probably all knew about it. She'll keep Gabriel around because he's insanely loyal to Toland Ministries."

"You think that Gabriel would choose Thatcher Toland, a pedophile, over his own sisters? His own family?" asked Noah.

Gretchen piped up. "You said yourself he's got some screws loose. Maybe Vivian manipulated him into thinking that what happened between Thatcher and one of his sisters was somehow his sister's fault."

"But why now?" Mettner asked. "Why is all this happening now? The Watts family has been out there for years with this knowledge. Why did it only become an issue now?"

Chitwood held up a stack of papers. "Phone records," he said. "I've got Lydia Norris's records. Not much here except that a few hours after Quinn and Palmer were with her at Amber's house, she got a call from what appears to be a burner phone. Spoke for nine minutes and thirty-seven seconds."

"The next thing we know she's in the fish lift," said Gretchen. "So whoever called her from that number is probably our killer."

"Except we can't track the phone," said Noah. "Dead end. Did you get Eden Watts' phone records?"

One of Chitwood's bushy brows kinked. "As a matter of fact, I did. She was in touch with Thatcher Toland for about two months before her best friend saw her in a coffee shop with him."

Josie got up and took the pages from Chitwood, taking them back to her desk to page through them. She studied the dates and then turned to her computer, clicking on her internet browser. The search only took a few seconds. "Thatcher Toland's book was released days before his contact with Eden started."

"So?" said Mettner.

"So maybe when his book came out and started shooting to the top of every bestseller list in the world, he got worried that Eden might come forward and go public with what he did to her. It must have been her, not Amber. Amber just hated him for what he did to her little sister. Otherwise, why would he spend so much time in contact with Eden and only visit Amber this week?"

Josie looked around at her colleagues, each of them staring as if waiting for her to say more. When she didn't, Noah said, "He establishes contact with Eden in an attempt to make sure that she plans to stay silent about what he did to her, but then what? She decides not to? Then why did she leave town without even telling her best friend the truth?"

Josie asked the Chief, "Do you have Amber's phone records?"

"Yes," he said. He turned and went back into his office, emerging seconds later with another stack of pages which he handed to Josie. "I already looked at them. Shortly after Toland started contacting Eden, Eden reached out to Amber by phone on three occasions. Amber deleted those calls from the call history on her physical phone, but the calls are still in the records that the phone company maintains."

Gretchen said, "Toland's book comes out. He's now even more famous than ever. He decides to contact Eden to make sure she's not going to tell on him. They start talking. Eden contacts Amber. They both start looking up real estate listings of houses their mother conned men out of, basically. Then what? What are we saying? Vivian somehow gets wind of the fact that Thatcher has contacted Eden, decides Eden is too big a threat to their church to leave hanging out there and that she'll get Gabriel to kill her? Then what? Kill them all?"

"It doesn't quite fit, does it?" Josie said. "It's like we're still missing something."

Chitwood clapped his hands together. "Well let's go over to Rectify and see if Vivian Toland can fill in some of the blanks for us. The service starts in ten minutes."

FORTY-SIX

With almost five inches of snow on the ground and more falling steadily from the sky, it took their little caravan almost a half hour to get to Rectify Church. As they pulled down the long road to the building, cars streamed in the other direction, each person driving slowly and cautiously, hands at ten and two on their steering wheels, knuckles white.

"What's going on here?" said Noah.

"I bet it's the snow," Josie replied. "We're supposed to get a foot, maybe a foot and a half. Toland probably did the responsible thing and sent everyone home before the road conditions got any worse."

"He's pretty thoughtful for a pervert, isn't he?" Noah said.

They parked their cars right out in front of the entrance. No one even noticed or cared. Everyone was too busy making their way to the parking lot. Josie, Noah, Gretchen, Mettner, and Chitwood fought their way through the crowds and into the building. They followed the booming sound of Thatcher's voice from the inner sanctum of the former arena. Entering on the lower level just as they had when Josie and Noah met Vivian

Toland, they struggled against even more people trying hurriedly to exit.

On stage, Thatcher Toland stood in a dark green suit, microphone in hand. "No need to rush," he was saying. "Let's all keep it orderly so everyone gets home safely. Vivian and I don't want anyone to be harmed during this most holy holiday. There will be plenty of time in the future for all of us to be here together in the presence of God."

The floor section near the stage had cleared out completely. The lower-level seats were nearly empty, but the second- and third-level seats were still full of people trying to find their way to the concourse. Josie looked around but didn't see Paul anywhere. Vivian sat in a chair on the stage a few feet from Thatcher. She wore a bright red dress and bright red heels. Her hair had been teased and pulled away from her face by two bright red barrettes. She smiled primly as she kept her eyes on her husband.

The lower and floor sections of the church were deserted by the time Vivian spotted them all walking toward the stage. Thatcher didn't see them at first. His eyes were fixed upward on the congregants still trying to make their way into the second- and third-floor concourses. "Mrs. Toland," said Chief Chitwood. "Bob Chitwood, Chief of Police. May we have a word?"

Thatcher's head swiveled in their direction. Vivian stood up and smoothed her skirt over her thighs. Her smile remained plastered across her face. Their group split when they came to the font, Josie, Noah, and Mettner on one side and Gretchen and the Chief on the other. Noah said, "Mrs. Toland, we'd like to speak with you, please."

Thatcher looked from them to his wife. The microphone caught the end of his sentence. "...what's this about?"

People on the second and third levels stopped to peer down at what was happening. Vivian, still smiling, took three strides toward her husband and then pushed hard against his chest with both hands. Thatcher went stumbling backward and fell into the large baptismal font. Josie heard several gasps from above them and a few shouts. Vivian slipped off her heels and began running.

Thatcher had landed closer to Chitwood and Gretchen. As they climbed over the wall and into the pool to get him, Chitwood looked at the rest of them and said, "Go, go! Find her!"

Josie, Noah, and Mettner took off, sprinting after Vivian. She had disappeared behind the stage. Mettner was looking under the stage when Josie caught sight of her slipping out of one of the lower-level doors and into the lobby concourse. "Over here!" she called. Noah followed.

Within moments, she was back in the lobby, dodging people in the crowd to get to Vivian. The red dress worked in Josie's favor. Josie kept catching glances of it as she pushed past congregants emptying into the parking lot. Some of them stopped to watch as Josie sprinted after Vivian. Behind her, Josie heard the low buzz of murmurs as people wondered out loud what was happening.

"Is that Mrs. Toland running?" someone said.

"Is she... is she running from the police?" another person said.

Josie followed Vivian halfway around the long concourse and then through a set of metal doors with a sign above that said "STEPS." Banging through the doors, Josie stopped to listen for Vivian's footsteps. They sounded as though they were coming from beneath her. Josie leaned over the railing and saw a flash of red pass one of the landings on the stairs leading down to the basement. She took the steps two at a time until she reached the lowest level. Bursting through those stairwell doors, she blinked to adjust to the dull light. The concourse in the basement was dank, gray, and unpainted concrete. They hadn't bothered to do any renovations in this area. Clearly it wasn't open to the public.

Josie turned from side to side, trying to figure out where Vivian had gone. In each direction was a series of closed doors. It was as though she had simply vanished, which meant that she had likely taken refuge behind one of the doors. Josie chose a direction and went that way, jogging from one door to the next. She threw each door open and used the flashlight on her cell phone to pan the rooms while her fingers searched the wall for light switches. Most of the rooms were empty. Some were closet-sized, and others were large. One was an empty team locker room with smaller rooms inside of it and cubby holes where the players had kept their equipment. There were a couple of old hockey sticks and pairs of ice skates still left in the cubbies. Josie felt the seconds ticking away as she checked every inch of it. There was nothing but dust and the faintly fetid smell of old sports equipment.

Back in the long concourse hallway, Josie kept checking rooms. It was clear that no one used this level of the building. Was this where Gabriel and Vivian had been holding Amber? Had they held Eden here before her death? As Josie pushed open another door to a room that held only cobwebs, she realized it was the perfect place to keep someone. As long as the Tolands kept this level mostly off-limits to the construction crews, a person could easily be held in one of the many rooms with no one the wiser. Even if someone screamed from behind one of the doors, it was unlikely anyone would hear them—certainly not from any other part of the building.

The next set of doors led to another stairwell. Had Vivian simply escaped upstairs? "Shit," Josie muttered. In spite of the cooler temperature down here—at least ten to fifteen degrees colder than the first floor—sweat beaded along Josie's brow. She had to make a decision. Go back upstairs to see if Vivian had moved to one of the upper levels, or continue checking the doors here? Vivian could still be on this level, hiding. Amber might even be here. The rest of Josie's team was upstairs, and she was certain the chief would have called for backup by now. If Vivian had made it back to the first floor, there was a chance someone on Denton PD would catch her in the chaos. Even if they didn't, how far would she get in a blizzard in her stockinged feet?

Josie thought about the injuries that Eden had sustained before her death. How she had still been alive when she was marched out to the dam. What if Amber was down here right now? What if she was still alive? Injured but clinging to life?

Josie kept moving, checking each room methodically but as quickly as she could with her phone's flashlight on, hoping she didn't drain her battery too quickly. She came to the second locker room. It was identical to the first one. There was the large team room with all the cubby holes for players to keep their stuff. Here, too, some ice skates were left behind and one goal-tender's stick, as well as a helmet. All of them were draped in cobwebs. Beyond that was a small room with a window that looked out into the team area. This had probably been the coach's office. On the other side of that was a larger room. Over the door, a sign said "PHYSICAL THERAPY." The inside of it held nothing. Then there was the supply closet.

It was locked.

In fact, someone had installed a shiny new heavy-duty stainless-steel hasp to the metal door that joined the doorframe to the door. From it hung a heavy metal padlock.

"Amber," Josie said.

She used her phone's flashlight to find the locker room light switches. One by one, she flipped them on. Only about half of them worked, but it was enough. Josie pounded against the locked door.

"Amber!" she called. "Amber! Are you in there? Answer if you can hear me! Amber!"

She froze and listened. It was difficult to tell because the sound was so muffled, but she was positive she had heard something behind the door. She pressed her ear against the door, but the sound wasn't much clearer. Still, it was something. It had to be Amber. *Please*, she prayed silently. *Let it be Amber.* She pounded against the door again, using both fists, screaming at the top of her lungs.

"Amber! It's Josie. Please answer me! Please!"

From behind the door came a howl that was most definitely human. And desperate.

Josie dropped to her knees and put her mouth as close to the slit where the door met the floor as she possibly could. "Amber?" she called.

Rustling came from the other side. Then Amber's voice responded, hoarse and filled with terror. "Help me! Help me! Get me out. He's holding me here. Please, let me out. You have to let me out before he comes back. Please!"

Josie's heart stopped so long, she could count the seconds where the beats should be. For a moment, her voice was stuck in her throat.

"Josie?" Amber screeched. "Can you hear me?"

Her heart thundered to life, pulse kicking up so hard, her entire body felt like a heartbeat. "Yes!" Josie choked out. "I hear you! I'm here!"

"Josie! Josie! Help me! Get me out! Get me out!"

Josie stood up and looked around for anything she could use to get the door open. She ran back out to the team room and grabbed the old goalie stick. As she returned, the door rattled again. Amber screamed, "Please! It's pitch-black in here. I'm freezing. I'm hurt. I just need—please, get me out." She dissolved into tears, sobbing loudly, shredding Josie's heart. A thousand images from her own childhood flashed through Josie's head. The abuse, the neglect, all the times she'd been locked in the dark closet. Shuddering, Josie took a deep breath to calm herself. "Amber," she said clearly and firmly. "I will get you out. Just hang on."

Josie hacked at the padlock with the goalie stick again and again until her arms and shoulders ached. Sweat poured down her face. Finally, the stick splintered.

"Josie?" Amber squeaked from the other side of the door.

Josie tossed the stick aside and wiped her brow with the back of her hand. "I'm still here. Just give me a second."

She ran back to the team room and searched through the cubbies until she found the pair of skates. Back in front of the closet door, Josie grimaced as she slid her hand into the skate, hoping there were no spiders or other critters inside. With one hand on the inside and one on the outside to steady the skate, Josie brought the blade down on the curved part of the padlock. It took several tries before the padlock cracked open. Josie threw the skate aside and wrestled the padlock out of the hasp.

Tossing the lock to the floor, Josie yanked the door open and saw nothing but blackness. She stepped into the closet. The light from the hall surged in behind her, illuminating the small space. "Amber?" she called.

A body slammed into Josie. Shaking arms wrapped around her. A number of unpleasant smells assaulted her nose. Amber's cheek was clammy against Josie's neck. Her thin body vibrated against Josie's as she sobbed. Getting her bearings, Josie returned the hug. She held Amber close to her with one arm while her other hand stroked her matted hair. In her head, a voice repeated the same relieved phrase: *she's alive. She's alive. She's alive.*

"It's okay," Josie finally managed. "Let's get you out of here."

A shadow crossed the doorway, plunging them back into semi-darkness. Amber lifted her head from Josie's shoulder and gasped. Raising one of her thin arms, she pointed and said, "He took me! He took me!"

Josie turned her head to see Mettner standing there in

shadow. The whites of his eyes suddenly grew large. "What?" he said. "I—"

Behind him another shadow moved and over his shoulder, Gabriel's dark eyes blazed with hatred. The gleam of a pistol flashed. Josie pushed Amber aside, reaching for her weapon. With practiced ease, she unsnapped her holster and drew her firearm. She opened her mouth to form the word, "Mett!" just as the pistol in Gabriel's hand lifted to the back of Mettner's head. Josie had only a split second to register the shock and confusion on Mett's face as she raised her own weapon and took one step to the side to get a better draw on Gabriel. She yelled, "Drop your weapon!" and then another voice yelled it, but Josie wasn't sure if she had actually heard someone else, or if her own command had echoed in the small room. Gabriel's index finger inched toward the trigger. Then the sound of a gunshot boomed all around them. The whole world seemed as though it was in suspended motion as Josie stood there, finger on the trigger of her pistol which she had not yet fired.

She was vaguely aware of Amber screaming. Then Gabriel crumpled to the ground. Behind him stood Noah, smoke spiraling up from the barrel of his gun which was now pointed at the floor. Expertly, he circled Gabriel's prone form until he found his pistol, and then he kicked it away. Blood bloomed from a wound just under Gabriel's right collarbone. He stared up at Noah, mouth gulping for air. Noah muttered, "That is the last time you get near my wife."

Mettner turned slowly, taking in the scene, and then falling to his knees when he realized how close he had come to death. From behind Josie, Amber crawled. "Finn!" she cried. "Finn!"

His head turned toward her voice and his body followed. Soon, they were in each other's arms, and Mettner was rocking her and whispering in her ear, "I'll never let you go again. Never."

FORTY-SEVEN

While Josie and Noah used her coat to put pressure on Gabriel Watts' wound, Finn led Amber out of the darkened room. He pressed her face into his chest as they passed by Gabriel's prone form and guided her out to the team room. From across Gabriel's body, Josie stared at Noah. "Thank you," she said softly. Noah nodded. "Keep pressure. I'll call for backup." Josie pressed her coat down into Gabriel's wound while Noah used his cell phone to call dispatch and the Chief. When he hung up, he took over for her. "Vivian is still on the run, but she's here in the building somewhere. Someone in the crowd said they saw her on one of the upper concourses. People are still trying to get out." He lifted a chin toward the doorway to the team room where Josie could see Mettner and Amber huddled together on a bench. "Take them and go. I'll stay here with him until help arrives."

Josie nodded and got up, herding Mettner and Amber down the long hall to the first set of steps she could find. She left them in the lobby where patrol units had just arrived and begun to seal off every exit so that Vivian Toland could not escape. She went back into the stairwell, climbing to the second-floor concourse. As she raced around it, people still milled, staring at some spectacle ahead. She stopped when she saw that what they were all staring at was a soaking wet Thatcher Toland sitting on a plush tufted bench and blotting his face and hair with a paper towel. Gretchen stood beside him. As if sensing Josie's question, Gretchen explained, "He wants to help find Vivian. He came running up here. We couldn't stop him. Then he fell, and here we are."

Thatcher looked up at Josie. "This is my fault," he moaned. "But you must know that I had no idea things would turn out like this."

"Like what?" Josie said.

Thatcher motioned all around him as if the explanation was obvious. "Like this. With people dead, and my wife... I didn't know! She promised me that after the opening of this church, I could come clean. That's what I wanted to do in the first place. She promised me that I could tell the whole world, for better or worse, and that we could try to become a family, and that she would support me, stand next to me and bear the stain of my horrible sin. Even if there were criminal charges, she said. I told her that Eden would never press charges against me. I thought that she should, even though her father had blackmailed me over the entire thing at the time. I told Eden that when I saw her. I went to unburden myself to her and make amends. I told her that it didn't matter what she thought had happened between us, or whether or not she had ever had feelings for me or thought that she had—I was wrong. Full stop. She was a child. I was the adult. It was my job to protect her, not to exploit her schoolgirl crush on me, or whatever flirtation we had. It took me years to understand that."

Josie held up a hand. "You went to Eden. You approached her."

"Yes!" he said. "How could I go on TV to promote my book,

acting like I'm somehow an expert on rectifying your mistakes when I never apologized to the one person I harmed the most?"

"Why were you at Amber's house the other day?" Josie asked.

"I wanted to talk to her, too. Eden told me how Amber had helped her, how Amber helped save my child! I just wanted to talk, but she wasn't home. Her mother was there instead. I tried to talk to her. Eden had told me everything. She told me about all of her mother's marriages and how her father and aunt were in on them."

"Did she tell you that Vivian was in on it as well?"

Thatcher shook his head. "She said that, but she was wrong. At least, I thought she was wrong. I confronted Vivian after I spoke with Eden. She told me that she knew that Lydia married older men for their money but that all she did was sell their houses after they passed away. She wasn't really 'in' on it. Anyway, I told Lydia I knew everything. Not just about the marriages but about Dr. Rafferty."

"Eden told you about that?" Josie said.

"Yes. She was trying to explain to me that when her father blackmailed me, it wasn't the first time he'd done it. She told me how her sister had made accusations against Dr. Rafferty. Their father made Amber do it so that he could blackmail him. She told me how heavily it weighed on Amber. How it was a regret and a burden to Amber. In fact, when I met Lydia at Amber's house, she was tearing the place apart. She was sure that Amber had left some evidence behind about Rafferty and she wanted to find it and destroy it. I tried to tell her not to bother. That was Amber's cross to bear, and it was up to Amber to decide what to do with any information or evidence she might have kept. That's when Lydia kicked me out."

"Do you know if she found anything?"

"I don't think so. She was very frustrated."

Gretchen said, "Mr. Toland, do you have any idea where

Vivian might have gone? Why she would come up here to the second-floor concourse instead of just exiting the building?"

He shook his head.

"She's trapped," Josie said. "We need to get the rest of these people out of here and then we can find her. She can't hide in here forever."

Gretchen said, "I'm going to escort these people downstairs."

While Gretchen walked away, Josie stared at Thatcher, more of the puzzle clicking into place in her head. "What did you mean when you said that 'we could try to become a family'? Did you mean you, Vivian, and Eden?"

He shook his head again, now using the paper towel to dab at the tears spilling from his eyes. "No. I mean me, Vivian, and my child."

"Your child? Your child with..." Josie prompted.

"Eden. Eden bore my child," Thatcher said. "But I never knew it. I never knew until I went to her to tell her how sorry I was for how badly I had mistreated her and how horribly I had behaved toward her. I wasn't even sure she would listen to me but God bless her, she did. She accepted my apology. We talked for hours on many occasions. Then she told me that she had had my child all those years ago. It was like God himself had come down from the heavens and squeezed my heart right out of my chest. A child! Born of my greatest sin! Eden wasn't even angry with me. She had forgiven me long ago, she said."

Josie could see the flaws in his logic—thinking that his wife would be just fine with taking in a child he'd had with an underage girl while he was the pastor of his first church. Josie tried to look at things from Vivian's perspective. Admitting to having a sexual relationship with a minor was not only a criminal offense but a public relations nightmare for their church, but to have a child? Living, tangible proof of Thatcher's crime? If you were Vivian, and you were ruthless, it would make sense to have Eden killed. Without her, who could testify as to what had truly happened between them? Who better to do it than Gabriel? He would be able to get close to her. Even if they were estranged, he was still her brother. But what about Lydia? Amber? Nadine? They likely all knew about the baby, Josie realized. They must have known. But why hadn't Vivian had Amber killed? Why hold her in the bottom of the new megachurch? Why had they held Eden for so long? It seemed extremely risky.

"Where is the child?" Josie asked.

"I don't know," Thatcher cried. "Only Amber knew. When the baby was born, the family wouldn't let Eden keep it, so Amber took it and found it a home. That's what Eden said."

"Amber would have been what? Sixteen? Seventeen? All those adults in her family knew about this baby and they left it up to a teenage girl to decide what to do with it?"

Thatcher looked up at her, eyes bloodshot from crying and his dip in the chlorinated pool. "They thought that their Aunt Nadine was going to kill it. Amber did it out of desperation. She told Eden that she had taken the baby somewhere safe where it could be placed into foster care and eventually get a good home."

That was why Vivian held Amber. She was trying to get the location of the child from her. Josie shuddered to think what would have happened if Vivian had got her hands on Thatcher and Eden's child.

A commotion from the second-floor seating area drew Josie's attention. Leaving Thatcher on the bench, she went to the nearest set of doors and jogged down the hall to the seating deck. A man stood there, pointing across the arena and shouting, "They're fighting! They're fighting! Someone is going to get hurt."

Josie followed the direction of his finger to see two women

across the arena locked in a tussle. One of them was wearing a red dress. The man took out his phone. "I'll call the police!"

Josie said, "I am the police," and took off running.

She weaved her way through the rows of seats until she reached the other side of the arena. She had to force herself not to look down the entire time or else she'd get vertigo. As she got closer, she could hear the two women grunting as they rolled along the aisle that split two of of the seating sections. Their bodies were locked close together but each one of them tried to punch the other, all the while staying as close as possible to avoid the blows. Vivian bear-hugged the other woman and lifted her slightly, slamming her back against the first row of chairs. Their fused bodies fell into the narrow space between the seats and the railing. Josie moved closer. "Vivian Toland," she shouted. "Stop right there. Stop what you're doing and put your hands up."

The woman beneath her screamed, "She's going to kill me!"

The voice was familiar but Josie couldn't place it immediately, and with Vivian straddling her, Josie couldn't see her face. Taking hold of the metal railing, Josie again averted her eyes from the drop-off and stepped closer to the two women. "Vivian," she said again. "Stop! Put your hands in the air."

Vivian rose up, her back to Josie, and then started raining down blows on the woman beneath her. Josie dove forward and grabbed Vivian under her armpits, dragging her flailing form away from the other woman. "Let go of me!" Vivian snarled. "Both of you, get out of my way."

Vivian pushed her upper body back against Josie. Her feet kicked against one of the chairs, knocking both of them off-balance. Josie's body twisted. Her back slammed into the railing. She felt herself going over the top as Vivian pushed off and away from her. On the brink of plunging head first into the seats many feet below, Josie had time for one thought: *this is how I die.*

Fingers gripped her wrist. Her shock-addled mind immediately recalled the cold grasp of Eden Watts' fingers as Josie struggled to save her from the dam. Josie waited for the inevitable slipping away, but instead the grip tightened and she found herself being pulled back from the abyss and onto solid ground. She fell onto her hands and knees, so grateful to be off the ledge that she could barely breathe. She looked up into the smiling face of Devon Rafferty.

Then she felt a swift and savage kick to her abdomen. Vivian was still there, still on the attack. As she drew back to kick Josie again, Devon leaped across Josie's body and grabbed for Vivian's throat. They struggled for what seemed like an endless moment while Josie heaved herself to her feet. Then their fused bodies lurched to the side, toward the railing. They both made contact just below their hips and the momentum sent them flying over the edge.

"No!" Josie screamed, lurching forward, hands outstretched. She managed to grab Devon's left elbow and a handful of Vivian's dress. The railing was tucked under her arms as she fought to hold onto both women. Devon immediately reached up with her right hand and grabbed onto Josie's upper arm. When Josie was certain Devon had a firm grip, she let go of Devon's left elbow and Devon lifted her arm, wrapping her left hand around Josie's bicep as well. Vivian, in the meantime, flailed, testing every bit of finger strength Josie had. The fabric of her dress stretched and began to tear.

"Stop moving," Josie ground out. The pressure on her arms and shoulders was so great she thought she might pass out. Vivian finally looked up at her as a large portion of her dress ripped, causing her body to plunge abruptly. Quickly, she lifted one arm and grabbed onto Josie's forearm. They hung there, suspended for what felt like hours but was only seconds. Josie was vaguely aware of shouting all around them. With no one to help, using only the railing beneath her armpits to keep her in place, and both arms in use, Josie couldn't pull either one of them to safety. Soon, both of them began to slip lower and lower. Sweat poured from Josie's scalp. Pain seared from her forearms through her elbows and up into her shoulders. "I can't... hold on... much longer..." she gasped.

First Vivian and then Devon slid even further down until each of them was held in the air by only one of Josie's hands. Her muscles were stretched beyond the point of pain now. Her eyes took one last panic-inducing look below them, and she realized she could not save them both. She would have to let go of one of them. She would have to choose which one of them lived.

It was not a decision Josie wanted to make.

She looked at the top of each woman's head. She thought of all the dead bodies that Vivian Toland and Gabriel Watts had left in their wake in the last two weeks, all in the service of keeping a terrible secret; in the service of money, of greed, of staying on top. Then she thought of Devon's daughter, Lilly, and her curious soul.

Josie let go of Vivian Toland.

FORTY-EIGHT

For the second time in only a few days, Josie found herself in the back of an ambulance with Sawyer Hayes. This time, Amber was with her. Amber lay on the gurney while Sawyer checked her over, taking her vital signs, covering her with blankets, and starting an IV. Josie sat on the bench opposite, slumped, her arms like jelly. She still couldn't feel them, not properly, but she knew the next morning she'd be in a world of pain.

Sawyer tapped away at the computer terminal, entering in Amber's vitals. "I think you're going to be just fine," he said. "You're a little dehydrated. Some cuts and bruises. I'll have to clean out that big gash on your hand, but other than that, you're very lucky."

Amber gave him a weak smile. "Thank you," she said.

He rummaged through the drawers to find some bandages and alcohol.

Amber turned to Josie. "You saved me."

Josie shook her head. "I got lucky. We all got lucky today."

Sawyer took Amber's hand in his. He smiled. "Josie Quinn

doesn't get lucky. She overworks herself until she solves the case."

Amber laughed and then winced as he doused her wound with rubbing alcohol. "Sorry," he told her. "I know this stings."

Josie regarded him with a raised brow. "That's the nicest thing you've ever said about me."

Sawyer dabbed at the cut on Amber's hand. "Yeah, well, don't get used to it."

Someone knocked on the ambulance doors. Josie stood unsteadily and used one jellylike arm to open them. Noah stood outside in a half-foot of snow with Devon Rafferty beside him. She was wrapped in a blanket, grinning at Josie.

Josie stepped down onto the snowy ground. "Devon," she said.

"You saved my life," Devon said. "I just wanted to thank you."

Josie opened her mouth to say something about how she didn't really feel like a life-saver. Vivian Toland had left the church in a body bag. But Devon didn't have to live with the choice that Josie had made; Josie did, so she said, "Why were you in the seats?"

Devon's brow furrowed. "What do you mean?"

"Everyone was leaving. You were still there."

Devon laughed. "I was waiting for the crowds to thin out a bit before I left. I knew that it was going to be a mad rush to get out to the parking lot, kind of like how when everyone leaves a concert at the same time? You're stuck in traffic for hours? So I just sat there, scrolling on my phone, waiting for the place to clear out, and here comes Vivian Toland running past me. I saw her push her husband, you know. Saw you all chasing after her. I didn't know what she did but it couldn't be good if the police were after her. Anyway, when she ran past me, I tripped her. Then she got up and punched me and, well, you know the rest. So what happened? Was she trying to kill Mr. Toland?"

Josie looked at Noah. He said, "We can't really say. The investigation is still ongoing."

Devon nodded and pulled the blanket tighter over her shoulders. "Right, right. I'm sorry. It's fine. I shouldn't have asked. Look, I just wanted to thank you for saving me and for being honest with me about what happened to my dad. I know now isn't the time, but could you tell Amber that I would really like to talk to her about it one day?"

"Of course," said Josie. She couldn't even imagine how awkward that conversation would be. Noah stood beside her as they watched Devon tromp off through the snow. Josie glanced at his face. Even through the fat snowflakes falling all around them, she could tell by his expression that something was bothering him. "What is it?" she said, wondering if he was upset about her hanging off a balcony with a grown woman on each hand.

"Gabriel Watts didn't make it."

"I'm sorry," Josie said. One of her rubbery arms reached up and touched his face. "It's tough, isn't it?"

He shook his head, snow dancing everywhere. "Nope. That's not it. It's not tough and that's what bothers me. He would definitely have killed Mett, maybe you, maybe Amber. He killed Eden and Lydia and probably his aunt. I would make the same decision a thousand times over with no regrets. What does that say about me?"

"It says that you're human. We shouldn't have to make these decisions in this job. Those choices should be left up to juries and judges, not us."

He stood for a long moment while snow gathered on both their shoulders. Then he sighed. "I'm going to check on Mettner."

She watched him go until the squalls of snow swallowed him. Hopping back into the ambulance, she stomped the snow off her feet and sat down again. Sawyer was on his computer and Amber's eyes were closed. She opened them when she heard Josie. "I'm sorry," she said. "It's a mess."

"Why didn't you come to me?" Josie said. "Or one of us? We could have helped you."

Amber shook her head. "What we did was wrong. Illegal."

"You were kids," Josie said. "Your father made you do it. He was the one who did the blackmailing."

A tear rolled down Amber's face. "Dr. Rafferty is dead because of me, because of what my father made me do. He was a good man. He didn't deserve that. I've lived with that shame my entire life. I never wanted to tell anyone."

Josie was silent for a long moment. Then she said, "What about the baby?"

With a heavy sigh, Amber said, "When Eden got pregnant, she wanted to keep the baby. My parents said absolutely not. That was supposed to be a short con, just like mine was with Dr. Rafferty. Eden would go to Thatcher Toland's church for a while, arrange to be alone with him a few times, make up some terrible accusations, and Dad would blackmail him. End of story. And that's what happened. The cons my dad ran were always small. The trick was, he said, to only blackmail these guys for enough that they would be able to pay it, but not so much that they would rather go to the police than pay. It worked. It worked on Dr. Rafferty and on Toland. Except that a few months after Toland paid, Eden couldn't hide the pregnancy anymore. It turns out her 'accusations' weren't actually false."

"Was Thatcher already married to Vivian at that point?" Josie asked.

Amber shook her head. "Not yet, but Vivian was running the long con on Thatcher by then. She had watched my aunt, mom, and dad run these marriage scams on unsuspecting men

year after year, accumulating wealth. When Thatcher came to
the real estate agency looking for a new place, she saw an opportunity. She took a page out of my mom's book. Thatcher wasn't
that old, but he was wealthy. Marrying him would be more
lucrative than real estate. That's what I heard her tell my dad,
anyway. She was all set to marry Thatcher. They had a date set
and everything. The baby would have ruined that completely.
Eden hadn't even gotten pregnant when Vivian found out what
was going on. She had seen Thatcher and Eden together at the
church. Instead of saying something to Thatcher or Eden,
Vivian confronted my dad about it privately. I was pretty sick
during that time, home with mononucleosis, so I was home for a
long time. I overheard the entire thing. She showed up at our
house one morning after Eden and Gabe had left for school.
She was furious with him for trying to run some small-time
scam on her 'mark.' She told him to stop immediately, but he
convinced her that getting fifty thousand dollars out of Toland
wouldn't put her con in jeopardy at all."

"So your dad went through with it? Eden made accusations
against Thatcher, your dad blackmailed him, and he paid?"

"Yes."

"Did you tell Eden about Vivian confronting your dad?"

"No," said Amber. "She was already stressed out about
things with Thatcher. I didn't want to put more stress on her."

"Eden got pregnant. You said she started to show? That's
when people found out?"

"Yes," Amber said. "Eden kept going back to the church. I
think she wanted to tell Thatcher. She never went inside, but
she'd ride her bike past it and hang out in the courtyard outside
or the park across the street. That's where Vivian saw her. The
next day, she came to the house. Eden and Gabe were at school.
I was still home sick. Eavesdropping. Vivian asked dad if Eden
was pregnant with Thatcher's child. Dad didn't deny it. At that

point, my parents hadn't decided what they were going to do about the pregnancy. Dad called Mom and she had to come home from playing 'wife' with her latest elderly rich husband. Vivian threatened to go to the police with everything she knew about my parents and Aunt Nadine unless my parents got rid of the baby. When Eden came home, they told her that they had finally decided that she could not keep the baby and that she had to go to Aunt Nadine's house until the baby was born, and that Aunt Nadine would 'handle things' from there. Aunt Nadine made it very clear that she would 'dispose' of the baby when it was born. I went with Eden so she wouldn't be alone."

"She was every bit as cruel as everyone said," Josie remarked.

"And then some. Eden and I were terrified. She made me promise I'd help the baby when it came. I had no idea how I was going to do that. Then I read about Pennsylvania's Safe Haven law where you could leave a baby at a hospital or police station and face no charges. When Eden's daughter arrived, I snuck her out of the house before Nadine even knew, and I left her at a hospital. Towanda Hospital."

"What did you tell Nadine?" Josie asked.

Amber glanced at Sawyer, but if he was paying attention, he didn't show it. "That Eden and I had 'taken care of it' and that the baby was no longer an issue. She believed us and that was that. No one was the wiser until Thatcher released his book and went on his apology tour to Eden. She was so taken with him and his desire to atone that she told him about the baby. I know that because she called me right after to tell me. She was really sorry, she said, but she had to tell him."

Josie said, "And that set off the entire chain of events."

"Gabriel took me because Eden had told Thatcher who told Vivian that I was the only one who knew where the baby was— well, a child now. The trouble was that I don't know what happened to that child. I only know she was safe when I left her at the hospital."

Josie patted Amber's leg. "Okay," she said. "It's okay."

"Do you know what Thatcher is going to do?"

Josie shook her head. "No. But for tonight, you and I only need to worry about staying warm and getting home, okay?"

FORTY-NINE

TWO WEEKS LATER

It was snowing again. They still hadn't gotten out from the two feet of snow that the Christmas Eve blizzard had dumped on them, and now more snow fell from the bruised clouds over-head. Josie navigated her vehicle through the hills north of the university toward Devon Rafferty's house. In the passenger seat, Amber fidgeted with the strap of her purse. Josie kept glancing at her. She was still bruised in many places, and something about her seemed diminished from her experience, but she certainly looked healthier, and Josie was hopeful that one day she would be back to her old self, or at least as close as she could get after the trauma she had endured.

"You don't have to do this," Josie said. "I'll turn the car around. Call Devon. Tell her we couldn't make it because of the snow."

Amber laughed nervously. "No, no. I just want to get it over with. It's been eating away at me. What do you say to someone whose father you basically killed?"

"You didn't kill Jeremy Rafferty," Josie said softly.

Amber stared out the window. Her ordeal with Gabriel had left a long scar on her palm. The fingers of her other hand caressed it. "If I hadn't lied," she said. "If I had stood up to my father. If I had just said something, anything, and not gone along with it, he would be alive today."

"You were a fifteen-year-old kid," Josie said. "Raised by people who lied as easily as they breathed. It was an impossible situation, Amber."

Still, her eyes tracked the snow-covered houses creeping past as Josie drew closer to Devon Rafferty's home. "When you are raised to lie, you don't know any other way. I was going to give you that list eventually, though. The one in my diary. After what happened with Dr. Rafferty, I used that diary to keep track of all the horrible things that my mom and dad and Aunt Nadine did, all the people they lied to and cheated. I thought that no one would even notice the diary. It was so childish for a fifteen-year-old. But Aunt Nadine sniffed it out. Nothing ever got past her. It's a miracle that she bought mine and Eden's story about 'getting rid' of the baby. Or maybe she didn't. I don't know. But she found the diary and read it, and she was absolutely livid. She tore all the pages out and burned them and told me that if I ever tried to expose the family, she'd kill me. Just like she killed Dr. Rafferty."

Josie's foot hit the brake and the car slid, fishtailing slightly on the snowy road. Both their bodies jerked forward and back. Turning to Amber, she said, "What?"

Tears filled Amber's eyes. "I'm so sorry," she whispered. "She only ever said it that one time, only to me. I had no idea if she was telling the truth or if she just said that to freak me out. At that time, the news was saying it was a suicide. The police investigation confirmed that. I never knew whether to believe her or not. I didn't know if she really somehow got him into that river, or if she just said that to me to put doubt in my mind, to scare me, but it worked. I was terrified after that."

Behind them, headlights appeared. A truck lumbered toward them. Josie put her blinkers on and pulled toward the side of the road, giving the other vehicle enough room to go around them. "Maybe Dr. Rafferty threatened to expose your family," Josie said. "And she was telling the truth—they killed him to keep him quiet. Too bad we can't ask your father."

One of the things that still kept Josie awake at night about the case was that Hugo Watts had left the Eudora hotel after the debacle at Rectify Megachurch on Christmas Eve and disappeared into thin air. Amber had told them that no one would ever see him again. He had socked away at least half of all the wealth that Lydia had accumulated during her marriages, and likely had always had a plan to disappear if the police ever caught on to anything he had done. Although at this point, the statute of limitations on just about everything he'd done was long past. He couldn't be prosecuted for fraud or theft by extortion. But if he had had a hand in Jeremy Rafferty's murder and it could be proven somehow, he could still go to prison for that.

Amber said, "The fact that my dad ran makes me think that Aunt Nadine was telling the truth about killing Dr. Rafferty."

Josie said, "You need to tell Devon all of this. She never believed her father killed himself. She needs to hear it. I know you don't want to do this, but it might be more beneficial to both of you than you can imagine right now. What happened after Nadine destroyed the diary? Is that when you made the list of numbers, or did you make them right before you went missing?"

Amber wiped away her tears. Josie pulled the car back onto the road. "Back then," Amber said, "Eden and I were living with Aunt Nadine during the pregnancy. Her real estate paperwork was easily available. I started by going through it and writing down all the addresses, but then Eden was afraid that she'd find those, too, and go off the deep end. So then we came up with this plan to write the parcel ID numbers down so we'd always have them in case we needed them. We always talked about exposing them when we became adults, but then Dr. Rafferty died and Eden got pregnant with Thatcher Toland's baby and by the time we were on our own, all either of us wanted to do was forget the past and start over. Plus, exposing them meant exposing ourselves. We had had a baby and we'd given it away. That felt so wrong. We were both afraid. Even after Eden called me, a couple of weeks before all hell broke loose, we were afraid."

Josie said, "It seems like you two were close, but you hadn't spoken to Eden in almost ten years before she called you."

Amber sighed. "We were close when we were kids because we had to be. When I first left for college, we tried to see one another. She met me a few times for lunch and dinner but it wasn't the same. It was like... being with each other just brought back every horrible thing we'd done and every horrible thing we'd witnessed. It wasn't enjoyable. It was depressing. We were reminders to one another of the worst things we'd ever done. We mutually agreed that it would be best to go our separate ways. The next time I heard from her was when she called me to say that Thatcher had contacted her and that she had told him about the baby."

"Why did she call you?" Josie asked. "Because Thatcher had approached her?"

"Yes. She wanted me to know that he had 'made amends,'" Amber said, a note of disgust in her tone. "I can't believe Eden bought his crap, but she went in for it hook, line, and sinker. She even told him about the baby, and we swore that neither of us would ever, ever talk about that. To anyone. I was so upset. At first she said it wasn't a big deal; that we shouldn't worry about it. You know, Thatcher was the one with everything to lose. She had unburdened herself to him about the baby and our family and everything they did to other people, and she felt like a new person. She was so sure that the secret would be safe with him."

"But it wasn't," said Josie.

"The first time I realized that Thatcher wasn't going to keep the secret was when Gabriel came to see me. He told me that I had to tell him where the child was or that there would be some serious repercussions. I knew then that Thatcher had no intention of keeping quiet about the baby. In fact, he wanted to find his child; that much was obvious. Nothing good could come from him finding that child. I was afraid..."

She trailed off and finally looked over at Josie.

Josie said, "You were afraid he'd kill the child. Eliminate the threat to his reputation."

"His wealth," Amber said. "My parents, Aunt Nadine, Vivian Toland? All they ever cared about was wealth."

The snow fell harder. Josie had second thoughts about visiting Devon that day. At least the storm would give them an excuse to leave quickly if things were too awkward.

Amber said, "Then Eden sent me that article about Aunt Nadine being murdered. It was too coincidental. That was when we talked about trying to come up with a file, or something. A list of misdeeds. Something that we could present to the police if things went sideways."

"You both started working on the real estate listings," Josie said. "Trying to match up the addresses with your list of parcel ID numbers."

"Right. I was going to come to you with my list when it was finished. In the meantime, I put the Post-it note on my diary with your name on it because I figured if I died and all that was left were these mysterious numbers, you'd eventually figure them out."

Josie smiled. "Why me?"

Amber smiled. "Because I've seen what you can do with a whole lot of nothing."

Josie laughed. "Okay, I'll take that as a compliment. Well, you were right about the danger to Eden and Thatcher's child. But not from Thatcher. From Vivian."

"I hadn't even considered her," Amber said. "She was just someone who tied things up at the end of my parents' jobs. I mean obviously, I knew she had only married Thatcher for his money, but she always knew about the baby and she hadn't tried to have any of us killed before."

"She knew that Eden had had a baby," Josie said. "But she thought that Nadine had 'disposed of' it.'"

"True," said Amber.

"The DNA under your Aunt Nadine's fingernails was a match for your brother. It looks like he killed her. Perhaps when Thatcher came home from 'making amends' with Eden and told Vivian that the child was still alive and that he wanted to find her, Vivian decided to get Gabriel involved and target Nadine first."

"That makes sense," Amber said. "Aunt Nadine was pretty much in charge of everything. Vivian probably thought she had lied when she said the baby was 'disposed of', and so she sent Gabriel to find out the child's location. He thought I knew it, that's why he took me."

"But you said that Eden told Thatcher that you were the only one who knew what happened to the baby," Josie pointed out.

Amber shrugged. "Yeah, but I think that Vivian meant to kill everyone who knew about the baby regardless of whether or not they knew the child's present location. I just assumed it was Thatcher who had sent Gabriel to do the dirty work. That he planned to eliminate everyone connected to the secret: Aunt Nadine, Eden, my mother, my father, and me and that poor child, once I had given up the information. Before Gabriel took me from my house, he had come to see me a couple of times. He threatened me. I called Eden in a panic and told her she'd been wrong about Thatcher. I told her he was after the child. She didn't believe me. She thought that Mom or Dad or Aunt Nadine put Gabriel up to it; that they convinced him to try to find the child so they could use her to blackmail Thatcher now that he had so much more money than before. We disagreed on where the threat was coming from or who was behind it, but we did agree on one thing."

"Protecting Eden's daughter," said Josie.

"Yes," Amber agreed.

The tires of the car slid on the snow-packed road. Josie struggled with the wheel until it righted itself and gained purchase again, climbing the hill the rest of the way.

"Then Gabriel took you," she said.

"Yes," she said softly. "He tried to kill me, you know. Three times. He came into the room and put a gun to my head and pulled the trigger. The first time he did it, I tried to stop him by telling him that Finn would be looking for me and that Finn was a police officer, but he never even let me get the words out. After that he apologized to me. At that point I thought he wasn't going to kill me because he thought I had information he needed. Then he fired the gun three times inside that little closet. I guess he was proving a point. My ears rang for hours after that."

Josie felt a chill spread through her body. She thought about the loaded Beretta and its missing bullets. Amber had been lucky none of them ricocheted in that small space, although the ERT had pulled the three rounds from the concrete walls.

They fell silent. Again, Amber's fingers fluttered over the scar on her palm. With a heavy sigh, she looked out the window again. A moment later, she said, "What's Thatcher going to do about the child?"

"He claims all he ever wanted to do was what was right. He says he thought about finding the child and establishing a relationship with her, but now he is wondering if he shouldn't just leave well enough alone. The girl would be what? Ten, now? He's not sure it's worth disrupting her life. He says he tried doing what he thought was the right thing and people ended up dead."

Amber grunted. "That's because of his murderous wife."

Finally, Devon Rafferty's driveway appeared. It hadn't been plowed, but Devon's Land Rover had tamped down ruts in the snow. Josie followed them and parked in front of one of the garage bays.

Neither of them moved. Amber took several deep breaths. Josie turned her head to see Devon's front door open. Lilly grinned and waved.

"Okay," said Amber. "Let's get this over with."

FIFTY

The meeting was every bit as awkward as both Josie and Amber had feared. Devon and Amber stood on opposite sides of the foyer, staring at one another. After Josie made the introductions, she watched as each one of them attempted a smile and then thought better of it. No pleasantries were exchanged. The only thing that made the moment even remotely bearable was Lilly prattling on beside Josie with questions about police work and what it was like to be on television.

Finally, Devon turned her head toward Lilly. "I'm sorry, Detective. Bob was supposed to come get her—it's his week— but he got stuck in Colorado because of the weather. Lilly, please go to your room. You may have an additional hour on your tablet."

Lilly pouted. "Mo-om, I want to talk to Detective Quinn. I can play on my tablet anytime."

Devon opened her mouth to speak but Josie held up a hand to stop her. "It's fine, Devon. I'm happy to chat with Lilly while you and Amber... talk."

Lilly's hand slid into Josie's and she tugged her toward the end of the hall. "I'll make hot chocolate and we can watch the snow."

"Lilly," said Devon in a warning tone.

The girl rolled her eyes. "I won't spill, Mom. Promise."

Smiling tightly, Devon turned her attention to Amber and gestured toward her home office. "Why don't we sit in here? I promise not to take up too much of your time, especially with this storm coming in."

Silently, Amber nodded and walked toward the office, looking like a woman who was marching to her death.

"Detective Quinn!" Lilly said, pulling Josie into the kitchen. "Do you like marshmallows in your hot chocolate? Milk? Whipped cream? We've got everything. Sit."

Josie smiled and sat at the island counter in the center of the kitchen. Like the rest of the house, it was colorful and filled with bright, eclectic items. "Marshmallows, please," she mumbled.

"Those are my favorite, too!" Lilly busied herself making them hot chocolate. Josie's gaze was still on the foyer down the hall, her mind on the look on Amber's face as she went to talk with Devon. Josie couldn't help but think of Eden being marched to her actual death at Russell Haven Dam. Had she worn the same expression as Amber, or had she been too out of it from her head injury to be scared at all about what was to come? The whole case still had Josie rattled. The details gnawed at her when she tried to sleep at night. Loose ends and unanswered questions. Why had Gabriel chosen Russell Haven Dam? He'd killed Nadine in her own pond and left her body there, but he'd made a point of making sure that both Eden and Lydia's bodies were found at Russell Haven Dam. Where had he kept Eden for all those days before he took her to the dam? The ERT had searched the basement of the megachurch but hadn't found any evidence that Eden had ever been there—or in Gabriel's house. Eden's Mini Cooper had never been recovered. Who had sent the Russell Haven Dam postcard to Lydia?

Everyone assumed that it was either Vivian or Gabriel, but the truth was that they didn't actually know.

On more than one occasion, she'd brought these things up to Chief Chitwood. The first two times he'd entertained her questions, throwing out theories to pacify her. Maybe Gabriel chose Russell Haven Dam to make it clear to his living family members about atoning for their sins against Dr. Rafferty. Maybe Gabriel had had enough time to clean up after holding Eden prisoner, and that's why they couldn't find her DNA in his house or at the church. Maybe there was some other location none of them even knew about. Maybe he'd sunk Eden's Mini Cooper into the river and they'd find it in the summer when the water levels dropped. Maybe Gabriel or Vivian sent the postcard to taunt Lydia.

"But none of that matters, Quinn," he told her. "What matters is that we found the killer and his accomplice. Both of them are dead, which means no more bodies, and we got Amber back."

When she went back to him a third, fourth, and fifth time with her concerns, he told her, "Drop it, Quinn. The case is closed. You know damn well that not every case wraps up into a tidy little bow. Life is messy, and so is murder and kidnapping. The pieces don't always fit together to make a perfect picture in the end. You just have to live with it."

"Are you listening to me?" Lilly said.

Josie blinked and Lilly came into focus. "I'm sorry," she said. "What were you saying?"

"I was saying, let's get down to brass tacks."

Josie turned her head toward the girl, who now sat on the other side of the island, stirring powdered cocoa into a steaming hot mug. A bag of small marshmallows lay open beside it. Behind her, a large window looked out over their backyard where patio furniture and a swing-set were covered in snow. Josie laughed. "Did you just say, 'let's get down to brass tacks?'"

Lilly reached into the bag of marshmallows and grabbed a handful, depositing them into the mug. Cocoa sloshed over the sides of the cup. "That isn't a real spill," she said to Josie. "And yes, that's what I said. My dad says it all the time. It's like, let's talk about the actual important stuff and not all the dumb stuff that doesn't mean anything that people talk about all the time. It's a nineteenth-century saying. I looked it up, 'cause I thought my dad was always talking about brass thumbtacks."

She walked over to the counter and ripped three paper towels from the dispenser, returning to the table to sop up her "not real" spill.

Josie said, "Okay, what's the really important stuff?"

Lilly pushed the mug across the countertop to Josie. "Have you ever been in a car chase?"

Relieved that she wasn't going to ask again whether or not she had ever shot anyone, Josie said, "A high-speed chase? I don't think so."

"Not gonna lie," said Lilly. "That's disappointing."

Josie laughed and sipped her cocoa which was so sweet, she'd probably have diabetes if she tried to finish the entire thing.

"Okay, if you were going to be in a high-speed chase, what kind of car would you want to drive?"

Josie plucked a marshmallow from the mountain of them melting into the chocolate of her cup and ate it. "Something small and sporty, easy to maneuver."

"What color?"

"Black," said Josie.

Lilly wrinkled her nose as she stirred cocoa into her own mug. "That's boring."

"Okay, red then?" Josie suggested.

"Yeah, like Mom's new car."

"Sure," said Josie slowly, the buzz of whirling thoughts about the Watts case suddenly coming to a complete standstill in her mind. Then they kicked into high gear again. Puzzle pieces shifted at breakneck speed, trying out new configurations. "Your mom has a new red car?" she asked.

Lilly stopped stirring and smiled at Josie, her eyes bright with mischief. She put her index finger over her lips. She looked down the hall to the foyer, but Amber and Devon were still inside the office. The door was closed. Lilly walked over to a door in the corner of the kitchen and beckoned for Josie to follow.

The door opened into a small hallway with a washer and dryer inside. At the other end was another door. Lilly opened it and cold air slipped past their legs. Josie knew it was the garage, but all she could see were vague shapes. Lilly jumped down the two steps onto the concrete floor. Josie followed, closing the door behind her. She heard her shuffling around and then an overhead light snapped on. There were three bays, separated only by metal poles that stretched from floor to ceiling. Most of the space was filled with things like lawn equipment, tools, firewood, a log-splitter, a tractor, a snowblower, a detachable roof rack, and three kayaks. At far end was a small vehicle covered entirely by blue vinyl tarps. They were held in place by sandbags, which had been placed on the hood and roof. Lilly walked over and lifted the edge of one of the tarps, revealing a flash of red beneath.

Josie's heart tapped out a frantic rhythm. She barely felt her legs as they carried her across the space. When Lilly spoke, the words seemed to come from far away. "You can't tell my mom, okay? I'm not even allowed in the garage. 'Cause one time I was in here and had an accident with the garden shears."

Josie walked around to the back of the vehicle and knelt down, picking up the edge of the tarp until she could see the license plate on the back. Every fine hair on the back of her neck stood up. The pounding of her heart reached an alarming crescendo. She knew the tag number because she was the one who had issued the BOLO.

Eden Watts' Mini Cooper was sitting in Devon Rafferty's garage.

All the jagged pieces of the puzzle that Josie had been trying to force together for two weeks tumbled into place. "Son of a bitch," she murmured.

"Are you okay?" Lilly asked.

Josie looked up. Lilly stood right beside her. Josie's brain started making calculations. Lilly. Amber. The storm. Josie didn't have a gun. It was her day off. She'd been making a social visit with Amber. Her phone was in her hand, fingers flying across the screen in a text to Noah. A red exclamation point appeared next to the text box. *MESSAGE FAILED.*

Josie took a deep breath, willing her heartbeat to slow. She stood up. "Lilly," she said. "If your mom doesn't want you in here, then I don't think we should be in here. Why don't we go back into the house?"

Looking disappointed, Lilly shrugged. "Sure, I guess."

Josie placed a hand on her shoulder and steered her away from the car. "Also, I don't think we should tell your mom that we broke the rules, at least not today. What do you say?"

"A police officer teaching my daughter to lie to her own mother?" Devon's voice sent an invisible shudder the length of Josie's body. Beneath her fingers, Lilly's muscles tensed. They both looked up to see Devon in the doorway to the garage. A chilling smile curved her lips. "Lilly," she said. "Please go into my office and ask our other guest to come out here. Then I'd like you to go to your room. Don't come out until I come get you, do you understand?"

Josie expected Lilly to protest or ask questions but instead she said, "Okay Mom," in a defeated tone. As she slipped out of Josie's grasp and scurried toward the door, Devon stepped aside and let her through to the house. Then she closed the door.

Instinctively, Josie's hand reached for her gun even though it wasn't there. It was muscle memory. Devon walked toward her. Josie wanted to back up, to flee, but she stood her ground.

Devon stopped a few feet away. Without taking her eyes off Josie, she reached behind a flower pot on a nearby shelf and pulled out a Glock 19. Before Josie could react, she racked the slide, pushing a bullet into the chamber. Now all she had to do was point and shoot. But instead, she held the gun at her side. "I trust you'll believe me when I tell you that I hoped it wouldn't come to this. I truly like and respect you. If Thatcher Toland hadn't shown up here three weeks ago to tell me all about how Eden Watts confessed to him that her family lied to, manipulated, and blackmailed my father, you would have unearthed it yourself."

Josie's phone was still in her hand, but she couldn't very well call for backup with Devon looking right at her, assuming she could even get service. Until she thought of a way out of this that was safe for all of them, she had to keep Devon talking. "Thatcher Toland came to you?"

"Dr. Rafferty?" Amber called as she stepped through the door from the house.

Devon didn't take her eyes off Josie, instead calling, "We're in here. Come on over."

Josie met Amber's eyes as she walked slowly toward them, weaving her way around the items scattered all over the garage. With her gaze, Josie tried to communicate a warning to Amber. But Devon was still holding the gun down by her side. Josie was sure Amber hadn't seen it when she passed her. Even so, as she walked over to stand beside Josie, Amber again had the look of being marched to her doom. "What's going on?" she asked, voice small.

With her free hand, Devon reached out, gripping Amber's upper arm and yanking her off balance. Then she shoved her into Josie. Both of them went tumbling to the concrete. Immediately, Josie scrambled to her feet, putting her body between Devon and Amber's prone form. Devon used both hands to hold the barrel of the gun to Josie's chest. Josie wondered if Devon could feel the vibration of her thunderous heartbeat through the metal of the gun.

"What are you doing?" Amber asked.

Without taking her eyes off Devon, Josie said, "She killed Eden and your mother."

Stumbling to her feet, Amber looked from Josie to Devon and back. "What are you talking about?"

Josie said, "She just told me that Thatcher Toland came to see her after he talked with Eden."

The gun pushed into Josie's sternum. "Your stupid sister told him everything, about how your family ruined my father's life and drove him to suicide. He thought that either she or you should come to me and 'unburden' yourselves. He thought one of you should admit to what you had done. Eden told him that was never going to happen, so he took it upon himself to do it for her. He thought I deserved the truth."

From the corner of her eye, Josie saw Amber's lower lip tremble. "Why would he—?"

"Because unlike you and your horrible family, Thatcher Toland is not a liar. He's genuine. Did you know that? This televangelist stuff? It's not an act. That's him. Eden told him what you and your father had done to my dad—setting you up as a patient, making you lie and say my father did terrible things to you, and then blackmailing him. Thatcher wanted me to know the truth. I waited thirteen long years to find out who killed my father and why. Thirteen years to find out why my life was destroyed. Did you think I would just let that go?"

Josie said, "When I came to see you, you asked me to talk to my sister about featuring your dad's case on her show. You showed me your binder. You... but you already knew exactly what had happened by then. You lied to me. That was all for show."

"Of course it was," said Devon. "I had to keep up the appearance of being obsessed with my dad's death. Everyone who knows me knows that it's the only thing I care about. Imagine if one day, Denton's most famous detective shows up at my house and I don't even mention it? How would that look?"

"But it was just the two of us," Josie said, still hyper-aware of the gun's barrel over her heart. "You could have told me nothing and sent me on my way. Why the act?"

"It worked, that's why," said Devon. "You didn't suspect me."

That was true, Josie had to admit. Painful, but true. But there was another reason Devon had needed to put on an act and make sure suspicion didn't fall on her. She had already killed Eden by then. She had already kept Eden for ten days by that point, and tortured her.

"You were going to kill all of them," Josie said.

Devon smiled. "You're damn right. Except Nadine had already been murdered by the time I found out where she lived. But her death did give me an idea. What could be more poetic than making each and every one of these monsters drown in the very place where my father's lifeless body was found?"

It didn't seem like Devon's arms were getting tired of holding the gun aloft at all. Josie said, "Eden came to see you."

"Because Thatcher told her that he'd talked to me. She panicked. She was afraid I would go after Amber! She was the one who told the lies that got my father killed. Eden was worried about her horrible sister so she showed up on my doorstep one day. Bob had Lilly so I was here alone. I let her in. She started talking. I got so mad. I don't remember much of what happened except that I beat her so badly she couldn't stand up for a long time. I kept her out here. No one comes out here except me. Lilly is forbidden. I was trying to figure out what to do with her. I couldn't let her go, right? I had to kill her, and if I was going to kill her, then why shouldn't I wipe out the whole clan? They're an abomination. Eden was the one who told me Nadine had been murdered. I looked up the article and that was it. My idea was born."

Amber's voice shook. "You killed my baby sister? Finn told me she was—she was tortured. How could you?"

Devon turned the gun on Amber who shrieked and jumped backward, nearly falling. Josie caught her by the elbow and kept her upright, but Devon kept the gun loosely trained on Amber's head. "How could you kill my father? How could any of you live with yourselves at all? Your sister and your mother and your aunt all got what they deserved. You were going to be next, and your brother and father, but then you disappeared, and everything went to hell. In fact, you were supposed to die with your sister. I left you that message about Russell Haven on your windshield. I knew you'd know what it meant immediately. I figured you would come, and you could watch someone you love die and know what that feels like. Then I'd kill you, too. I watched my father decline for months before his death. With each day he got more depressed. I wonder now, if your aunt hadn't killed him, maybe he would have killed himself after all. I wanted you to know what that felt like, but you didn't come to the dam."

"She had already been taken by Gabriel by that point," said Josie.

The windshield message had been one of the other confounding things Josie had been turning over in her head the last two weeks. The team had assumed that Gabriel had left it, but Josie had always been bothered by the time: five a.m. If Amber left her house at seven a.m. each morning, then she'd never see the message in time. They knew that Gabriel had been in town for two weeks, lurking around and accosting Amber. He could have figured out her routine and then made sure to leave the message at a time when she would definitely see it. However, if he had simply taken her, then why had he left the message at all? Of course, now Josie knew all those questions were moot because Gabriel had not left it. Devon had, and Devon had clearly not taken the time to do reconnaissance and make sure that Amber would see the message in time to get to the dam.

"It worked out pretty well though, didn't it?" Devon said. "After today, only your father will be left."

She took another step toward Amber, the gun nearly touching her forehead. Josie tried to distract her, "You sent the Russell Haven postcard to Lydia Norris."

Devon nodded. "She was on my list. I wanted her to know that someone out there knew what they had done. That it wasn't over."

"How did you get to Lydia?"

"I got her cell phone number from Eden's phone. I had to buy a prepaid cell phone, one that you don't have to register with your real name, and I called her. As it turned out, she was already right here in town. It didn't take much to convince her to meet me at the dam. She was a tiny thing. One good knock on her head and she was out of it. All I had to do was bring her back here, wait until the middle of the night, and take her back over to the dam. Had to crack her a few more times by then to make sure she wasn't going to fight back. She never did wake up. I towed her behind me in a second kayak. Easy-peasy."

Josie worked through the case in her head as quickly as she could now with a new perspective. Thatcher Toland released his book, which became an instant bestseller. He tracked down Eden to make amends. She accepted his apology and told him every foul thing the Watts family had ever done, including blackmailing Dr. Rafferty which ultimately led to his suicide—since Amber was the only one who knew he'd actually been murdered. Then she told him about their baby. Eden claimed that only Amber knew what had happened to the baby. Thatcher went home to his wife and told her everything, insisting that he wanted to find the child. Vivian told him to wait until after the megachurch opened. Thatcher had then shown up at Devon's house to tell her the truth about her father, since neither Eden nor Amber were ever going to do it. Vivian sent Gabriel to either talk to or kill Nadine. Either way, Nadine had ended up dead. In the meantime, Eden had traveled to Denton to talk to Devon who took her prisoner, tortured her, and then took her to Russell Haven Dam to die. Devon had also tried to lure Amber to the dam but by that time, Gabriel had taken Amber and held her at the church, trying to get her to tell him the location of the child. Devon had then murdered Lydia.

There was still something that didn't make sense.

"Why would Thatcher Toland come to you to unburden himself on behalf of Eden?" she blurted. "Did he go to every person that the Wattses ever screwed over and do the same? What are you not telling me?"

With lightning speed, Devon lifted the gun and brought the pistol grip down hard on Amber's nose. Josie heard the crunch from where she stood. Amber crumpled to the ground. Josie stepped in front of Amber and put both hands up, trying to calm Devon, but she could not be swayed. She held the gun in her right hand now and shook it in Amber's direction. Spittle flew from her lips as she shouted, "You think everyone else in her family is a con artist? She's the most conniving and deceitful and cruel of all."

Amber looked up, tears pouring from her eyes, blood dribbling from her nose. "Eden and I were kids," she spluttered. "We didn't know what to do. We had no resources. All we wanted was to protect the baby. That's it. I didn't even know about the Safe Haven law until I was in my twenties. Do you think I wanted to come to you? No one was ever supposed to know. Not even you!"

"Lilly," Josie said. "Oh God. Lilly." She looked down at Amber. "She's Eden and Thatcher's daughter."

No one spoke.

For the first time since she'd come out to the garage, Josie really felt the cold. It was like a living thing creeping all over her body. She thought of what Amber had said in the car. *When you are raised to lie, you don't know any other way*. Josie put a palm to her forehead, again trying to shift all the puzzle pieces in her mind.

Devon kept the gun pointed downward, at the top of Amber's head. "My father was dead. I had had five miscarriages. My husband had left me. One day, this pitiful little girl shows up on my doorstep with a little tiny baby. She told me that she worked at the coffee shop my dad stopped at every day and that she had gotten to know him well. She said he was always so upset that I kept losing baby after baby, and he said he didn't know how much more I could take. Then she told me her sister had been raped. She said they'd hidden the pregnancy from their parents by running away. They were so stupid, she told me. They hadn't thought anything through, but they couldn't go back home with a baby and they didn't want to go to the police. She said she remembered my father talking about me and wondered if I still wanted a baby. She was very convincing."

Josie said, "You took a baby from a seventeen-year-old stranger?"

Devon's head snapped toward Josie. She glared. "Lilly would have gone into foster care. Who knows where she would have ended up? I gave her a stable and loving home. She was my miracle. She even got me my husband back for a short time. Lucky for me, we'd slept together a few times nine or ten months before Lilly arrived. Then he went away to the Middle East to do some kind of independent contracting work for almost a year. It wasn't easy to contact him while he was there, so I had that going for me. By the time he returned, Lilly was already two months old. He was furious that I never even told him I was pregnant, but he got over it pretty fast the first time he held her. We had five great years as a family before things fell apart again. And she arrived in my life on my father's birthday." Devon nudged Amber with a sneakered foot. "Did you know that? Did you do that on purpose?"

Amber shook her head, wiping at her face with the back of her sleeve. "All I knew was that you wanted a baby, that your father was a great man, and I thought you must be great, too because he raised you. I thought she would be safe with you."

"She was!" Devon shouted. "She was, until your sister opened her big, stupid mouth."

Amber pointed to her own chest. "I was supposed to be the only person who knew where Lilly went! I never even told Eden. That was our deal. No one could know, not even her."

"Then how did she know?" asked Devon, nudging Amber with the barrel of the gun again. Josie tried to calculate whether or not she could successfully tackle Devon without the pistol going off, but her finger was on the trigger and they were in extremely close quarters. Too dangerous.

"I didn't tell her," Amber said. "I swear. After I brought Lilly to you, I told Eden that I had found her a very good home. She never questioned it. Not until after she came clean with Thatcher. After she told him the truth, she called asking me all kinds of questions about the baby, like how I knew she was safe. All I told her was that I knew her daughter was safe because the person I gave her to had wanted a baby for a long, long time, and I knew she would be a good parent. That's all I said."

"Then how did she figure it out?" Devon shouted.

Amber stared up at Devon with wide, teary eyes. More blood trickled from her nostrils. "I don't know! Maybe because when we were teenagers there was a limited number of people we knew who might just accept a baby with no questions asked?

She knew how much guilt I carried over what we did to your father. I've never gotten over it. I knew about your miscarriages. That was true. Your dad did tell me all those things, just not in a coffee shop. He told me when I came in for sessions. He was usually on the phone with you when I got there. He was so distraught over everything you went through. Back then, I always cried to Eden about how horrible it was that you had lost all those babies and your father. I think Eden just figured it out and told Thatcher her theory. But I promise I did not tell her. She shouldn't have told anyone either."

Devon pressed the gun into her forehead. "Thatcher Toland came here looking for a little girl. He said he knew all about what the Watts family had done to my father. He said he believed that one of them had brought me a baby and then he said that baby was his. I lied and said it wasn't true, of course. Do you think I'd let him get his hands on my Lilly? Do you think I'd let any of you get your lying, filthy hands on my angel?"

"Why not kill him?" Josie asked. "After Eden, he had the biggest claim to Lilly."

Devon kept the gun trained on Amber's head but glanced at Josie. "I would have, eventually, but killing someone as famous as Thatcher Toland? That was going to take some research."

Josie thought about the book Devon had given her. "You weren't really a member of his church, were you?"

"Of course not," Devon spat. "I only read his book to find out more about him. I went to the church to see what kind of security he had around him."

Josie looked down at Amber. She was shivering. "You found that empty patient file on your father's desk after his death marked 'Ella Purdue.' You had no idea that Amber was Ella Purdue all this time?"

Devon shook her head. "No, of course not. I just thought she was some scared, stupid teenage girl. When she started working as the press liaison here, I recognized her but I never dared approach her. We made a deal."

Josie tried to put herself in Devon's shoes. A young married woman desperate for a child. Miscarriage after miscarriage. A failed marriage. Her father's mysterious and sudden death. It must have seemed like a miracle when a young girl showed up on her doorstep with a baby on her father's birthday. Josie could see how in Devon's warped mind, it must have seemed like her father had somehow given his blessing to the arrangement. And it had gone off perfectly for ten years until one day Thatcher Toland showed up at her doorstep and told her everything. He put names to the faces behind Jeremy Rafferty's demise. Josie tried to imagine Devon's shock when she realized one of those faces was the very girl who had given her a child.

Even though Thatcher hadn't seen Lilly that day, it would only have been a matter of time before he figured it out for certain. A simple DNA test would have blown all of their lives apart. Devon's plot to annihilate the entire Watts family served both her need for revenge and her need to protect her daughter. Vivian Toland and Gabriel had likely been on the same path, but their goal had been to eliminate the Wattses in order to protect Thatcher.

"Now," said Devon, pressing the barrel of the gun so hard into Amber's skin that she winced and shrank away from it. "I don't want to do this here. Not with Lilly in the house. I also don't want her asking too many questions, so the three of us are going to go for a walk."

Josie thought about the fact that both Finn and Noah knew they were coming to see Devon. Even if Devon hid Josie's car, as she had with Eden's, that wouldn't buy her much time. Noah would come at her hard and not let up until he found the truth. Great, thought Josie, our murders will be solved.

Devon herded them to the back of the garage where another door led to the backyard. They stepped out into the snow, which was now up above Josie's ankles. She kept waiting for a chance to use her phone or catch Devon off guard so that she could attack, but no opportunities came. Devon stayed behind them, her gun wavering back and forth between their heads as they walked side by side to the edge of the yard and the woods beyond.

Everything was covered in snow and flakes were coming down at a furious pace now, making it difficult to see a few feet in front of them.

"Where are you taking us?" Amber asked. Her teeth had already begun to chatter.

"Somewhere you won't be found until the spring, and by that time, I will have figured out how to fix all this."

Josie tried to bring up a satellite image of this area of Denton in her mind. It was more remote than most places in the city, but there were still neighbors to consider. She racked her brain trying to think of what was behind Devon's house. Before she could figure it out, they emerged from a line of trees into a clearing. Ahead, just a vague shape in the distance, was a barn and corn silo. A farm. Her eyes searched for a house or a vehicle. Any sign of life. Anyone who could help them.

"They're not home," Devon said, as if reading Josie's mind. "They're in Costa Rica for two weeks. It's not a working farm. A couple of artists bought it. They use the barn and silo as a studio."

Josie blinked away the snowflakes gathering on her eyelashes. Her teeth started to chatter as well. Amber's frigid palm slid into hers and squeezed. She had to do something. Glancing back, she saw that Devon's finger was still on the trigger. The Glock 19's safety was on the trigger. Devon need only apply a little extra pressure to shoot and kill one of them instantly. Josie couldn't risk rushing her or trying to trip her. She just had to wait for the right opportunity.

"Over there," Devon said, waving the gun to their left.

Beside the barn was a slight incline and then what looked like two wooden pillars jutting up from the piles of snow. Beyond them was a rope bridge. It was hard to make out in the white-wash but as they got closer, Josie could see where the snow had fallen through the planks of the bridge. Amber hesitated when they reached it. Turning to Devon, she said, "What is this?"

Josie already knew what it was, and she was trying to figure out how Devon intended to drown them in a pond when it was likely frozen.

Devon pressed the barrel of the gun to Amber's temple and said, "Shut up and walk."

The pond was huge. The rope bridge stretched so far away that Josie lost sight of the other shore in the snowfall. When they reached the middle, Devon made them stop. Josie tracked their positions. Both Devon and Amber were now closest to the rope, their waists actually touching it. Josie was on the other side from Amber. Together they formed a strange triangle, Josie being the point and furthest from the side where Devon had chosen to stop. Devon turned her body and looked down. Turning just slightly, Josie followed her gaze. About three feet below them Josie saw what she assumed was the surface of the pond, covered in snow. Devon pointed the pistol down and fired off three shots in quick succession. Amber flinched, her hands flying up to cover her ears. Josie pivoted her body. Using her forearms like a bar, she rammed into Devon's back, just below the shoulder blades. Devon pitched forward. The gun bobbled in her hands and dropped into the snow below. Josie fell to her knees and wrapped her arms around Devon's legs, lifting with all her might until Devon's entire body toppled off the bridge and into the ice below.

The ice didn't shatter when Devon landed. But when Amber landed on top of her; that did the trick. Josie tried to catch Amber before she went over but she was too late. As Devon tumbled, she snagged one of Amber's arms and took her along. In horror, Josie watched as the two women sank into the jagged hole in the broken ice. Their heads bobbed once, twice. Devon lurched upward and used her hands to push Amber's shoulders down. Amber didn't come back up. Josie knew that once she was under the ice, she'd be disoriented, moments away from hypothermia, and it would be dark. She would not be able to find her way back to the opening.

Josie took a few steps away from where Devon and Amber had fallen and jumped onto the pond. The half-foot of snow padded her landing but under her feet she heard a crack. Devon's bullets had weakened the integrity of the ice. The closer Josie got to them, the more the ice would crack, and she might be next. Ignoring the cold and the panic sending her heart into overdrive, Josie dropped to her stomach and spread her hands and legs as much as she could, trying to evenly distribute her weight across the ice. The muscles in her arms hadn't fully recovered from the experience at the church and putting any pressure on them sent pain streaking from her wrists to her shoulders. She ignored it and kept going. As she clawed her way to the opening, listening for the splashes, she heard more tiny cracks. Snow gathered in her mouth, and she spat it out. It clung to her face and ears and the back of her neck. It was so cold it felt hot.

One of her hands touched water, then a fragment of ice. Devon's head rose up, water sliding off her as if she was some sea creature. She howled and reached out toward Josie, trying to grab on. Josie quickly rolled to her side and kept feeling along the edges of the fragmented ice. Devon sank again. More splashing sounded. A hand shot out of the water. Josie blinked snow away, and with perfect clarity, saw the scar on Amber's palm. She lunged for Amber, both hands reaching out and clasping Amber's wrist. Beneath her, the tiny cracks in the ice sounded almost like a symphony. As she struggled to her knees, pulling Amber's body from the freezing water, Josie felt the ice giving way. Amber's upper body came out of the opening. She used her free hand to grab at ice that crumbled in her grip.

"Take my other hand!" Josie screamed but Amber was too disoriented. Her palm flailed but couldn't seem to find Josie's other hand. Josie felt the area beneath her shift again. She scrambled backward on her knees, still pulling Amber with her, trying to find some solidity.

The discordant notes of ice cracking continued. Another hand punched through the broken ice near Josie's knees. Devon's face appeared, mouth turned toward the sky, sucking for air. "He-he-help me!" Her hand flailed in the air. "M-m-y h-hand. T-t-take it."

She reached for Josie's free hand. Everything seemed to stop in that second. The snow. The blood in Josie's veins. The air in her lungs. Two hands. Amber and Devon. Her mind flashed back to Christmas Eve at the megachurch. The upper seating level. Two hands. Devon and Vivian. Josie thought then that she had made the right choice. What she hadn't known was that there weren't any good choices in that scenario. But now, today, there was a good choice.

She already had a grip on Amber. If she took her other hand, she could pull both herself and Amber to safety. If she took Devon's hand, she would either have to let go of Amber completely or let them all die. She couldn't save them both. She couldn't hold onto both women at the same time and get enough purchase on the fracturing ice with her legs to pull all three of them to safety. As soon as she pulled one of them out, the already cracking ice would shatter beneath their weight, and it would be a race to get to shore without becoming submerged. Josie was confident she could lift and then tow one woman across the fragile ice, but not two.

Just as she had in the church, Josie thought of Lilly. Then she took Amber's other hand and pulled.

FIFTY-ONE

ONE MONTH LATER

The cheering coming from Josie's living room could only mean one thing: someone had scored a touchdown in the Super Bowl. Shaking her head, Josie turned back to her kitchen table and resumed pouring salsa into the center of a large tray of nachos. At her feet, Trout watched every small movement as if she were performing some kind of surgery. Misty breezed past with a tray of bacon-wrapped scallops and bumped Josie's hip with her own. Smiling, Misty looked at the nacho tray and said, "Well done."

Josie was just thrilled to have a food-related duty that didn't involve anything that could potentially start a fire. Satisfied with Misty's stamp of approval, she lifted the tray and went to the living room. She had to pick her way around several people seated on her floor in front of the television to get to the coffee table. She set the nachos down next to her grandmother's urn. Again, Harris had insisted that Lisette have a front row seat to the festivities.

More cheers went up. Josie gave the television a passing glance and then weaved her way back toward the foyer where

Sawyer Hayes stood leaning against the doorway. He gave her a half-smile. "You don't like football?"

"I have no feelings about football one way or the other," Josie told him. "But I don't usually celebrate the Super Bowl."

Sawyer laughed and Josie realized it was the first time, maybe ever, that she had heard a genuine laugh pass his lips. It reminded her of her one-time father, Eli. There it was, Josie thought. The blink of sadness that accompanied every moment of joy after loss. You could no longer have one without the other. That was what Lisette had tried to tell her on her deathbed. *"You have to learn to live with them both, my dear. The grief and the joy."* Once you lost someone, the grief was a permanent part of your life, of who you were. Josie thought about sweet, funny, curious Lilly Rafferty. In spite of everything Amber had done to try to protect the girl, she'd lost the only mother she'd ever known. A mother who was also a killer. Lilly wouldn't remember that. She would only remember Devon as loving and kind. Josie knew she'd struggle with this for the rest of her life, and she felt sad that the girl would be saddled with the ever-present blink of grief in all her moments of joy, from such a young age. At least, Josie thought, Lilly would get to stay with Devon's ex-husband, Bob. After Devon's death, Josie had told Thatcher Toland about Lilly's true identity. All he'd asked for was a meeting with Lilly and Bob—not as her biological father, just as the preacher from her mom's church. After seeing Bob and Lilly together, Thatcher decided it would be best for everyone if Lilly stayed with the only father she had ever known. He stepped aside, telling Josie in private that he would never interfere in Lilly's life but that she would be heir to his estate.

"Flag on the play!" someone yelled.

Josie turned away from Sawyer and surveyed the living room. Noah was there, snug on the couch with Harris on his lap. Gretchen's daughter, Paula, sat beside them. Gretchen was on duty, but Josie had promised to send food home with Paula. Josie's brother Patrick and his girlfriend were also crammed onto the couch. In folding chairs around the perimeter of the room sat Shannon and Christian. Even Drake had made it, and he now sat on the floor with Trinity. Dan Lamay and his wife and daughter had come, as had Josie's former mother-in-law, Cindy Quinn. All of them also sat in folding chairs. Mettner and Amber were also there, squished together in the recliner. Amber's head rested in the hollow of Mettner's shoulder. While everyone else watched the game with rapt attention, she dozed, safe in the cocoon of his arms. The plan was for everyone to eat lots of food, have some drinks, watch the big game and then, most important of all, the premiere of Trinity's new show. Josie thought of it as Trinity's Watch Party, Take Two. Hopefully at the end of the evening everyone would still be accounted for.

Misty appeared with an armful of beer bottles. Standing between Josie and Sawyer, she called, "Who needs a drink?"

Hands reached out, relieving her of her burden. Mettner extricated himself from Amber, planting a kiss on her lips before walking across the room for the last bottle. Amber tucked her feet under her and watched the television. Soon, her eyelids drooped again.

Quietly, Josie said, "She still having trouble sleeping at night?"

Mettner sighed. "Yeah. We're working on it, though. She's seeing a therapist now, so we're hoping that will help. But I feel so... helpless. It feels like all I do is watch her suffer. I can't fix it."

Josie looked over toward Amber, but her eyes were fully closed. Even if she was awake, there was too much chatter in the room and too much noise coming from the TV speakers for her to hear their low voices. "It takes time, Mett. Lots and lots of time." She glanced at Noah. "And support. Believe me, being there to witness her pain and listen to her, it goes a long way.

Being there no matter what—even if you can't fix anything—that's the best thing you can do for her right now."

He, too, looked at Noah and then back to her. "I'm not going anywhere," he told her.

A moment slipped by. Josie was aware of Sawyer on the other side of her, eavesdropping. Mettner downed more of his beer and used his knuckles to wipe at his lips.

Josie said, "Does she know that?"

"Well yeah, I—I mean, I guess she does. You think I should propose?"

Josie laughed. "Let's not get carried away. I'd wait on the proposal till she's in a better place in her own head."

A round of angry "come ons!" rose up from the room. Someone hollered, "Stupid ref!"

Mettner's face paled. "You think she'll say no?"

"I think you need to spend some time building trust with her before you propose."

"You think she doesn't trust me?"

"I don't think she's ever trusted anyone," Josie said. "Not really. Amber grew up in a house full of liars. All she has ever known is deceit. People who say one thing and act one way and then do something completely different. I think that makes it hard for her to trust. The best thing you can do for her is to be consistent. Every day you need to show her that you're not going anywhere."

He looked across the room at Amber. Her eyes fluttered open and for a split second, Josie saw blind panic. Then she blinked the room into focus. Her chest heaved with what looked like relief. She noticed them watching her and gave a weak smile.

Mettner said, "Right. The proposal can wait until things are better. And boss, I'll do whatever it takes to show her that I'm in this for the long haul."

"Don't tell *me* that," Josie said, nudging him with her elbow.

He looked down at her and gave her a quick grin. In three easy strides, he crossed the room and snuggled back into the chair with Amber. Josie watched them gaze at one another like there was no other human being in existence. A little bit of peace settled into her heart.

The doorbell rang. Trout's nails clicked on the hardwood floor as he ran to see who it might be. Josie answered to see Chief Chitwood standing on her front stoop, a casserole dish covered in foil in his hands. "Am I too late?" he asked. "Can I join you?"

Josie gave a bewildered smile. "Sure," she said, standing aside so he could enter. "Take that to the kitchen. Misty will tell you what to do. She's in charge of food."

Chitwood walked past her, giving Sawyer a mock salute as he went by. Josie rejoined Sawyer in the doorway. She said, "I'm glad you came."

She looked up to see him nod. That was about the best she could hope for from him, she thought. Then he turned his head and met her eyes. For a split second, she saw the same blue sparkle that Lisette's eyes had always held and her breath left her body.

"You know what Lisette said to me before she died?" he asked.

"No," Josie mumbled. They'd both been with their grandmother when she took her last breaths. Before she passed, she had said something to each one of them, privately, into their ears.

"She said, 'Dear, you have to find your family.'"

A LETTER FROM LISA

Thank you so much for choosing to read *The Drowning Girls*. If you enjoyed the book and want to keep up to date with all my latest releases, just sign up at the following link. Your email address will never be shared, and you can unsubscribe at any time.

www.bookouture.com/lisa-regan

It is one of the greatest pleasures of my life to continue bringing you Josie Quinn books. You should note that the dam in this book is completely fictional. I took a number of different aspects from dams I had researched and made up my own. Usually, I like to get out into the field whenever possible for research, but because of COVID, I wasn't able to physically tour any of the dams I researched. I had to rely on my dam expert, several people who had been to said dams, the internet, and my own imagination. As always, I do my best to make the police procedural elements as authentic as possible. Some things simply must be modified for the sake of pacing and entertainment value. All of this is my long way of saying any errors or inaccuracies in the book are my own.

I adore my readers. You are the best readers in the entire world, and I love hearing from you. You can get in touch with me through my website or any of the social media outlets below, including my website and Goodreads page. Also, if you are so inclined, I'd really appreciate it if you'd leave a review and perhaps recommend *The Drowning Girls* to other readers. Reviews and word-of-mouth recommendations go a long way in helping readers discover my books for the first time. As always, thank you so much for the relentless passion you've shown for this series. I am astounded and deeply moved by your enthusiasm! I hope to see you next time!

Thanks,

Lisa Regan

www.lisaregan.com

 facebook.com/LisaReganCrimeAuthor
twitter.com/LisalRegan

ACKNOWLEDGMENTS

Amazing, wonderful readers: thank you for coming back to join Josie on a new adventure. Many of you incredibly lovely people have been following my personal journey along with Josie's fictional journey. You know that my dad died unexpectedly and quite suddenly in April 2021 while I was almost done with Book 12. At the time, I thought one of the hardest things to do after his death was finish that book. I could not have been more wrong. When I began writing Book 13, some of the shock of his death had worn off and I was left alone on the rocky shoal of grief, floundering emotionally and creatively. Dear readers, there are many things my dad always said to me—motivational taglines for life, if you will—and one of them was simply: "Go to work." So I did. I jumped right into the treacherous waters surrounding my shoal of grief and tried like hell to swim to shore. I've tried like hell to bring you a good book. I hope that I did.

Thank you, as always, to my husband, Fred, and my daughter, Morgan, for not letting me panic. Thank you to my first readers: Dana Mason, Katie Mettner, Nancy S. Thompson, and Torese Hummel. Thank you to Matty Dalrymple and Jane

Kelly—my critical book-saving first responders who came to my rescue yet again! Thank you to my lovely friend and kick-ass assistant, Maureen Downey, for holding me up during the writing of this book. I'm not sure this book would exist without your unwavering support and your unflappable belief in me. Thank you to my grandmothers: Helen Conlen and Marilyn House; my parents: the late Billy Regan, Joyce Regan, Rusty House, and Julie House; my brothers and sisters-in-law: Sean and Cassie House, Kevin and Christine Brock and Andy Brock; as well as my lovely sisters: Ava McKittrick and Melissia McKittrick. Thank you as well to all of the usual suspects for your spreading the word—Debbie Tralies, Jean and Dennis Regan, Tracy Dauphin, Claire Pacell, Jeanne Cassidy, Susan Sole, the Regans, the Conlens, the Houses, the McDowells, the Kays, the Funks, the Bowmans, and the Bottingers! As always, thank you to all the amazing bloggers and reviewers who continue to stick with Josie or who met her somewhere in the middle of the series and have been so vociferous with their support! It means the world!

Thank you to Rusty House, Van Wagner, and Miranda Kessel for all your help with all things dam-related, including fish lifts and ladders! Thank you to Michelle Mordan and Ken Fritz for answering all my paramedic/EMS-related questions. Thank you to Karmen Harris, BSN, RN, SANE-A, D-ABDMI for all of your help nailing down the medical/autopsy aspects of this book. Thank you, as always, to Sgt. Jason Jay for answering all of my questions all the time, constantly, at all hours of the day and night. Thank you to Lee Lofland for always putting me in touch with the best resources!

Thank you to Jenny Geras, Kathryn Taussig, Noelle Holten, Kim Nash, and the entire team at Bookouture including my lovely copy editor, Jennie, who is a saint and a genius, as well as my proofreader, Jenny Page. Last but never least, my amazing editor, Jessie Botterill. You never lost faith in me, and that means the world. Thank you for talking me off the figurative ledge so many times. Thank you for being so patient and steadfast. Thank you for guiding me through this treacherous time with grace, warmth, kindness, and empathy. Every encouraging email was a life preserver I clung to in order to keep going. You are an exceptional human being. I'm so grateful for you.

Made in the USA
Middletown, DE
16 March 2023